D0907157

PAGE 214. **Berkeley Barb**, San Francisco Bay, March 1973.
Freud and cocaine.
Look up Freud on the Internet and have a laugh at his cocaine use, his paranoia, and his Oedipus complex. Then think about what Sartre's *Being and Nothingness* owes to amphetamines – they certainly make you a sparkling conversationalist.

PAGE 215. **Berkeley Barb**, San Francisco Bay, February 1976.
Conspiracy theories.
In India, Charles Sobhraj drugged hippie travellers, murdered them and burned their bodies. In Arizona, people were mystified by the mutilated corpses of cows. And kudos to Spain Rodriguez, whose masterly art almost makes you believe in such things.

PAGE 216. **New York Rocker**, New York, February 1976.
Rock is reborn.
In the wake of the New York Dolls came the unjustly forgotten transvestite Wayne (later Jayne) County, Television, the Ramones, Blondie and Talking Heads – the clean-cut face of punk.

PAGE 217. **Search and Destroy**, San Francisco, 1977.
Eyes to the sky.
A punk paper named after an Iggy Pop song, which prefigured punk disgust in the violence of its anti-Vietnam lyrics. **Search and Destroy** was the intellectual of the punk press, mixing William S. Burroughs and J. G. Ballard with graffiti, the Sex Pistols and the Dead Kennedys.

PAGE 218. **Actuel**, Paris, 1974.
Mental straitjacket.
Actuel practised satire, the art that flourishes in times without ideals. As in this drawing by Roland Topor, tighten your belts.

PAGE 219. **New York Rocker**, New York, 1976.
Blank Generation.
From 1974 to 1976, punk was invented in New York, and at its centre was Patti Smith, who was much more than just the main squeeze of Robert Mapplethorpe and Tom Verlaine, who himself was the childhood buddy of Richard Hell. A season of hell – enough said. *Blank Generation*, Richard Hell's hymn, ripped T-shirts, and we mustn't forget that a certain Malcolm McLaren was buzzing around, after gorging himself on Situationism in Paris. His Sex Pistols would soon beat them all.

PAGE 220. **Libération**, Paris, 1977–78.
Graphics go punk.
The design collective Bazooka squats in the pages of **Libération**, and shows us its modern gaze through dilated pupils. Jean Rouzaud's page design serves as an ad for the Bazooka monthly **Un Regard Moderne**. Since then, the underground press has seen many ups and downs: it's been manipulated, honoured, excreted, exploded, censored, euthanized and resurrected by the rise and fall of tolerance and political correctness.

PAGE 221. **East Village Eye**, New York, September 1980.
Art or fashion? A sideways glance.
For four years, the **East Village Eye** took over from the **East Village Other**, until the new wave came to an end and the great slumber returned.

PAGES 222–223.
National Lampoon, New York, 1981 – **East Village Eye**, New York, 1980.
Punk: the big wash-out.
In 1967, the Diggers buried the hippies before they could be parodied. In 1981, we find a similar scenario: **National Lampoon** mocks the great-crested punks, while the **East Village Eye** wipes them up with a swift, Kleenex-clean operation. The page was turned on the last great rock'n'roll rebellion, which lasted up to grunge, ten years later. Nothing beside remains, not even Kurt Cobain.

Where They Bury You

Where They Bury You

A Novel

Steven W. Kohlhagen

SUNSTONE
PRESS

SANTA FE

Sunstone books may be purchased for educational, business, or sales promotional use.
For information please write: Special Markets Department Sunstone Press,
P.O. Box 2321, Santa Fe, New Mexico 87504-2321.

Book design › Vicki Ahl
Cover design › Veronica Zhu
Map › Lori Johnson
Body typeface › Perpetua
Printed on acid-free paper

Library of Congress Cataloging-in-Publication Data

Kohlhagen, Steven W.
 Where they bury you : a novel / by Steven W. Kohlhagen.
   pages cm
 ISBN 978-0-86534-936-0 (softcover : alk. paper)
 ISBN 978-0-86534-939-1 (hardcover : alk paper)
 1. Murder--Investigation--New Mexico--Santa Fe--Fiction. 2. New Mexico--History
--Civil War, 1861-1865--Fiction. 3. Arizona--History--Civil War, 1861-1865--Fiction.
4. Historical fiction. 5. Western stories. 6. Mystery fiction. I. Title.
 PS3611.O3676W48 2013
 813'.6--dc23
                        2013000183

WWW.SUNSTONEPRESS.COM
SUNSTONE PRESS / POST OFFICE BOX 2321 / SANTA FE, NM 87504-2321 /USA
(505) 988-4418 / ORDERS ONLY (800) 243-5644 / FAX (505) 988-1025

To Gale

And to Tassie, Cheyenne, and Whiskey

PREFACE

Cowboys and Indians and the West have long captured people's imaginations and formed an important part of their impressions of America. In July 1861, the Civil War interjected itself into that Cowboy and Indian dynamic for nine long months in the New Mexico and Arizona Territories.

Hampton Sides has written by far the best, and most entertaining, non-fiction narrative of this period of history in his excellent book, *Blood and Thunder*. While reading Sides' book, a curious incident jumped out at me that inspired my own research. My search through the National Archives led me to find letters from Kit Carson that confirmed that on August 18, 1863, during the Navajo campaign "…(I heard of) the death of the brave and lamented Major Joseph Cummings who fell shot thro' the abdomen by a concealed Indian."

Cummings' Military Records report that, on his death, he had $4,205.78 in cash and $826 worth of other items that the Army auctioned off. Depending on how you calculate it, $5,032 in 1863 is the equivalent of $700,000 to $1,000,000 today. In the belongings of a just-murdered U.S. Army Major? Who was this fellow?

My research through the National Archives and, ultimately, through dozens of published histories about the times, including an important book by Jacqueline Dorgan Meketa, *Legacy of Honor: The Life of Rafael Chacon, A Nineteenth-Century New Mexican*, drawn from Chacon's memoirs, led me to learn a great deal about Cummings. And, of equal importance, led me to learn of Augustyn P. Damours and Rafael Chacon.

I came to the conclusion that Kit Carson must have been mistaken. Carson, the U.S. Army, the Franciscan Church, and the Department of New Mexico were all duped by both Damours and Cummings. Cummings, who I believe was not killed by "a concealed Indian," among other activities, was actually sent by the Army to track down Damours and find the missing funds.

And therein lies a tale.

This book is a novel. It is a fictionalized version of factual, historical events. To the extent possible, I have kept true to the history of the actual Apaches, Navajos, Civil War soldiers, and New Mexicans living in the Territories from early 1861 to Cummings death on August 18, 1863. Many of those historical characters lived on after Cummings' murder, and I have added their brief biographies in the additional Author's Notes at the end of this book. The Civil War battles, the wars with the Apaches and the Navajo, the heinous crimes committed by many of these historical figures are as true to life as I could make them within the bounds of a novel.

I do not believe for a minute that Joseph Cummings was killed by a concealed Indian in an arroyo near what is now the Hubbell Trading Post in Ganado, Arizona. The activities and motives of the characters leading up to Cummings' death in this novel are, necessarily, speculative and fictionalized. But they are written in the context of what was actually happening to the people in that place and at that time. Any errors on my part, changes to scenes and characters' names to make the narrative more efficient, and interactions between fictionalized and historical figures, should be viewed by Civil War buffs and scholars of "Cowboys and Indians" as part of the fiction. As an example, the July 15–16 battle in Apache Pass between Cochise and the California Volunteers is compressed into one battle in one day.

I would like to thank my two editors, Jennifer Fisher and Marjorie Braman, for their welcome editorial contributions that have made, despite my innate stubbornness, this work, happily, much better, and, sadly, much shorter. I would also like to thank Barry Goldman for his base ball suggestion and Ron Star for keeping me out of the dark grey area. My wife Gale's patience, "sightseeing" research in New Mexico and Arizona, and helpful comments made this book possible.

"You can fool all the people some of the time
and some of the people all the time, but you
cannot fool all the people all the time."
—Abraham Lincoln, Augustyn P. Damours,
P.T. Barnum, et. al.

CAST OF CHARACTERS
(In Order of Appearance)

HISTORICAL

Cochise: Chief of the Chiricahua Apaches.

Dos-teh-seh: Cochise's wife.

Naiche: Cochise and Dos-teh-seh's 4-year old son.

Mangas Coloradas: Chief of the Mimbres clan of the Chiricaqua Apaches. Dos-teh-seh's father, and, thus, Cochise's father-in-law.

Augustyn P. Damours: Gambler, con artist in the New Mexico Territory.

Joseph Cummings: Gambler, womanizer throughout the West.

George Bascom: U.S. Army Lieutenant serving in Arizona Territory for first tour of duty after graduation from West Point.

John Ward: Arizona rancher.

Coyuntura: Chiricahua Apache, Cochise's brother.

Geronimo: Chiricahua Apache, Bedonkohe clan.

Sylvester Mowry: Arizona businessman, mine owner in the Tucson, Patagonia, Tupac area.

Nahilzay: Chiricahua Apache.

Loco: Chiricahua Apache.

Kit Carson: Mountain man, explorer, trapper, adventurer, Indian fighter, U.S. Army officer and scout, Indian Agent. One of the American frontier's greatest legends.

Josefa Carson: Kit Carson's wife in Taos, New Mexico.

Kaniache: Chief of the Mouhache, Muache, Utes.

Tom Jeffords: Mail runner, Butterfield mail; scout.

Edward S. Canby: Major, U.S. Army, New Mexico Territory.

Rafael Chacon: Captain, New Mexico Volunteers.

John Baylor: Colonel, Confederate Army; head of the advanced force of Texas Volunteers.

Father Ussel: Catholic Priest in Taos, New Mexico.

Moses Carson: Scout, half brother of Kit Carson.

Felix Ake: Arizona rancher.

Henry H. Sibley: General, Confederate Army; head of the Texas Volunteers, Confederate Army of New Mexico.

Thomas Green: Colonel, Confederate Army; second in command of the Texas Volunteers.

John Chivington: Major, Colorado Volunteers.

Ferdinand "Lon" Ickis: Private, Second Colorado Volunteers.

James H. Carleton: Colonel, Commander of California Volunteers.

Joseph West: Colonel, second in command of the California Volunteers.

Jack Swilling: Arizona businessman, officer in the Arizona Guard.

John Slough: Major, Colorado Volunteers.

Ben Wingate: Captain, U.S. Army.
Charles Pyron: Major, Texas Volunteers.
William Scurry: Colonel, Texas Volunteers.
Tom Roberts: Captain, California Volunteers.
John Cremony: Captain, California Volunteers.
Victorio: Chiricahua Apache.
Padre Guerrero: Catholic Priest at San Miguel.
Albert Pfeiffer: Captain, New Mexican Volunteers; sub-agent for Utes.
Cadete: Chief, Mescalero Apaches.
Delgadito: Navajo Chief.
Barboncito: Navajo Chief.

FICTIONAL

John Arnold: U.S. Army Captain serving in the Territories
Lily Smoot: Santa Fe Poker dealer, among other things.
Jim Danson: Gambler, con man, ex-California gold miner.
Sergeant Wilson: Sergeant, U.S. Army in Arizona Territory.
Yellow Horse: Chief of the Jicarilla Apaches
Red Cloud: A Chief of the Mouhache, Muache, Utes.
David Zapico: Santa Fe store owner, businessman.
Pepper: Prostitute, bank robber in Santa Fe.
Angela: Bank robber in Santa Fe.
Sarah Zapico: Wife of David Zapico.

New Mexico/Arizona Territories 1861-1863

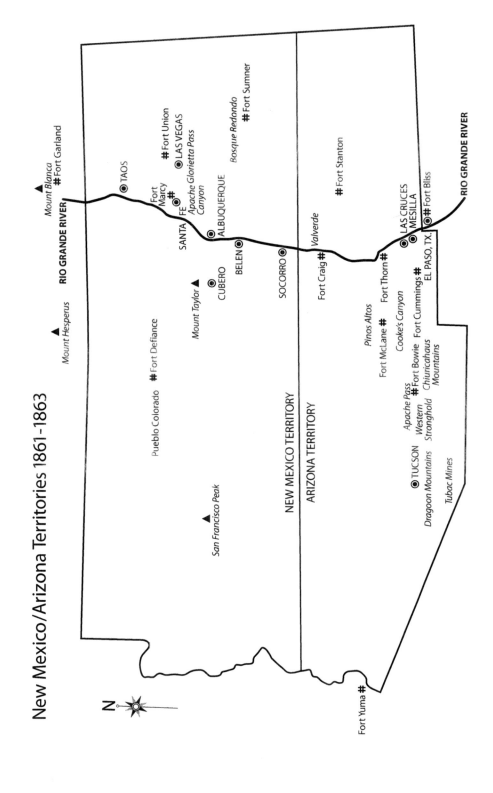

Mount Blanca
Fort Garland

TAOS

RIO GRANDE RIVER

Fort Union
LAS VEGAS
Apache Glorietta Pass
Canyon

Fort
Marcy
#
SANTA FE

ALBUQUERQUE

Bosque Redondo
Fort Sumner

Mount Hesperus

CUBERO
Mount Taylor

BELEN

Pueblo Colorado # Fort Defiance

SOCORRO

Valverde

Fort Stanton

LAS CRUCES
MESILLA
Fort Bliss
EL PASO, TX.

RIO GRANDE RIVER

Fort Craig #

Fort Thorn
Fort McLane #
Cooke's Canyon
Fort Cummings

Pinos Altos

San Francisco Peak

NEW MEXICO TERRITORY

ARIZONA TERRITORY

Apache Pass
Fort Bowie
Chiuricahaus
Mountains

TUCSON
Western
Stronghold

Dragoon Mountains

Tubac Mines

Fort Yuma #

PART I
THE TERRITORIES

1

"I'll be damned. She's on time," Captain John Arnold said, looking at his watch.

He and everybody else watched the Butterfield Stage Coach race into Apache Pass from the west and pull up at the station. The dust from the drought that had been hanging over the Arizona and New Mexico Territories for a decade covered the coach, the horses, and the passengers, and also swirled behind and above them. The Butterfield Overland Mail Coach, run by Wells Fargo, carried passengers and mail between San Francisco and St. Louis. Apache Pass and Apache Springs was a standard stopping point between Tucson and El Paso.

It was customary for anybody in the Pass to offer help to the drivers and passengers, mostly to catch up on any news and gossip. And, in this particular case, to look at the beautiful young woman who stepped out of the coach.

She was petite, but attractive. Jet black hair up in a bun under her blue bonnet, full figured. In her mid-twenties. Nobody around the station took any notice of the three men who got out after Arnold lifted her to the ground.

She looked around. Noticed the six Indians standing by the wood pile, including a woman and a little boy, and turned to Arnold.

"Captain, do you know how long we stay here? And, I guess, can you tell me where exactly we are?"

She put her hands on her hips and looked up at him more carefully. He was six feet, maybe a little bigger, army fit, a veteran, grey beard and grey hair sticking out from his cap.

"Well, Miss. I'm not exactly in charge around here, but I think the stage from Tucson usually sits for a half hour or so. And this is Apache Pass."

She took in the scene. A large meadow leading over to some Willows and a stand of trees to the east. Horses grazing and drinking by the trees. Probably a spring over there, since there was no evidence of any vegetation away from that spot. High mountains in the distance to the south, forbidding cactus cluttered hills to both the left and right, with the road meandering off to the left around that hill. Everybody staring at her except the Indians, who had resumed chopping wood. Two of the men teaching the little boy something.

"What are you in charge of then, Captain?" She said, deciding to at least have a little fun in this godforsaken place.

He smiled. "Name's Arnold, Miss. Captain John Arnold, U.S. Army. I'm in charge of these soldiers. Normal reconnaissance from Fort Buchanan. About a week's ride over that way," he said, pointing over the hill to the right of the big mountain. To the south and west.

She looked in that direction, to a spot directly over the Indians.

"And who are they?" Nodding her head at the Indians. "They don't seem very alarmed by you, Captain."

He laughed. "C'mon, I'll introduce you. They're Chiricahua Apaches. The big one is Cochise, their chief. The woman is his wife and that's his little boy there. Playing with the hatchet."

She looked thoughtful. She was used to seeing essentially naked Indians, but this big Apache was, well he was *big*. She hadn't thought Indians came in that size. He was bigger even than Arnold.

Then she noticed that Arnold had stopped and was facing her. "Pardon me, Miss."

"Yes, Captain."

"I can't introduce you to Cochise and his wife until you tell me your name."

"Good point, Captain. Let's go."

She walked straight up to Cochise, and, without hesitation, held her hand out to the impassive Chiricahua chief.

"My name's Lily Smoot. What's a famous, treacherous, blood thirsty Apache doing chopping wood for the stage line?"

Cochise cocked his head to the side and bowed as his wife laughed good naturedly. "Do you believe things men say about me?" he said.

"Actually," she said, "I don't believe *anything* men say to me."

This brought a laugh from the soldiers as Arnold looked on with amusement.

Lily then walked over to Cochise's wife. "I'm Lily Smoot. How old is your little boy?"

"His name is Naiche and he is four." She took Lily's proffered hand. "My name is Dos-teh-seh. My husband chops wood for the stage station both as a gesture of our peaceful intentions and in exchange for food for our people."

"Is he too shy to tell me this himself?"

"No, I am not," Cochise said. "But I do not have much experience with white women coming directly to me with questions."

"Do I have your permission, Cochise, to walk over to the Springs with Dos-teh-seh and Naiche?"

"They do not need my permission. I'm sure they will be happy to show you Apache Springs."

Lily took Naiche's hand and walked him over to the stage coach. She had him climb up into the coach with her. When they came down, the little boy was carrying a small replica of a wooden dog in both hands. He carried it with him as he walked between the two talking women all the way to the Springs and back again.

When they arrived back at the station, Lily walked over to Cochise.

"Thank you for allowing that to happen Cochise. You have a wonderful family."

He shrugged and said, "I did nothing Miss Smoot. It was you who made the gesture. I should thank you for making Dos-teh-seh feel so welcome."

"How long have you and your people been at peace here?"

"Three winters."

She shook his hand, nodded to the other Apaches, and walked over to Arnold.

"I don't think my friends in Virginia City or Tucson would believe me if I told them what just happened."

"I watched and I don't believe it. You just might be the first white woman he ever talked to. What were you doing in Virginia City, if I may ask, Miss Smoot?"

She immediately realized her mistake and decided there was no point in befriending this soldier. "Nothing special, Captain. I worked in some of the saloons. Dealt some poker. Mostly I was just passing through."

"To where?"

"You ask a lot of questions of a lady, Captain. Didn't they teach you manners at West Point?"

"I'm not a West Pointer Miss Smoot, and I'm sorry if I've offended you. The Territories aren't a good place for a lady to be wandering through. But I'm impressed how you handle yourself. Dealing cards and serving drinks to gunslingers must be good training."

She laughed as he tipped his cap to her. "You haven't offended me, Captain Arnold. And I'm not exactly wandering. It was a pleasure meeting you. But you're going that way." And she pointed to where he had indicated Fort Buchanan was, to the southwest. "And, in about five minutes, I'm going that way," pointing in precisely the opposite direction. "It was a pleasure meeting you."

As she turned to return to the coach, she had second thoughts about her treatment of this old officer. He had meant her no harm.

"Tell me, Captain, is Cochise really at peace with us?"

"It's complicated. Cochise is the chief of the Chiricahua Apaches. His people live over there," pointing at the mountain to the south. "In the Chiricahua mountains. And in the Dragoon Stronghold due west about forty miles."

He paused to make sure the Apaches weren't listening.

"They generally have made a living, as they call it, raiding in Mexico and trading what they steal down there for supplies up here. The guns and ammunition they keep and then trade for more from the gun runners in both Mexico and here. They used to raid up here, too, but the Army made it too costly. The Apaches hate all Mexicans with an irrational passion. Fifteen years ago an American bounty hunter killed Cochise's father in Mexico, but he seems to have let that go for reasons of practicality."

"Then why do people think the Apaches are still at war with us?"

"These are just the Chiricahua Apaches. The Mescaleros east of here and the Mimbres, the Gilas, to the north are different clans of Apaches. In fact, Dos-teh-seh's father, Cochise's father-in-law, is Mangas Coloradas, the chief of the Mimbres. He is still warring with the miners at Tucson and Pinos Altos north of here."

Lily looked thoughtfully back over at the Apaches, still chopping wood. "You're right, it sounds complicated. In answer to your earlier question, Captain Arnold, I have a job waiting for me in Santa Fe."

"Dealing cards," he said. But his smile seemed skeptical to her.

"Yes, dealing cards, Captain."

"Well, as luck would have it Miss Smoot, I'm being reassigned to Fort Marcy, a twenty minute walk from Santa Fe. How would I be able to find you when I get there?"

The driver pulled himself back onto the stage coach and whistled at the horses.

"I'll tell you what Captain," she said as she pulled herself up into the coach and waved good bye to Naiche. "I'll stroll over to the fort on my day off and look for you. How's that?"

And she pulled the door closed as the driver whipped the horses east and around the hill to the north of the meadow.

2

January 24, 1861

"Name," the girl behind the Exchange Hotel counter said.

"Damours. Augustyn P. Damours."

"How long you plannin' on stayin' here in Santa Fe?"

The young Mexican-looking girl glanced down at the ledger, then back up at the much taller man.

He'd seen that look a thousand times before. They all thought he looked so boyish. She probably thought he was a teenager instead of pushing twenty-five.

"Longer in Santa Fe than here at the Exchange. I'm meeting my partner here in a few days. Let's say a week and see how it goes, okay?"

"Sure. Is that French? Damours, I mean."

"It was. My Dad had a French accent and an apostrophe. I didn't have the accent, so I didn't want the foreign spelling neither." He appraised the girl good naturedly. "It's American now, I guess," he said.

She laughed. "We're all Americans now, huh?"

She glanced from the young man to the soldiers sitting across the lobby watching them.

"What's your name," he said.

"Hattie."

"Hattie? Really?"

"It's a long story."

"Okay. My friends call me Auggy."

He turned and nodded toward the soldiers, then carried his bags up the two flights of stairs and walked toward the door of his room. The hall was standard for a western hotel. Long, dark, narrow with doors on both sides. No rugs, no windows, no pictures on the walls. Just wood planking all the way down to the staircase at the other end.

He opened his door. As if he needed another reminder he was no longer in San Francisco, he looked in at the stark plainness of his room. Bed, commode, dresser. That was it. A cheap desert landscape over the empty wall across from the window and a faded painting of the New Mexican mountains over the bed.

He dropped his bags on the bare floor and walked over to the window. The view out over the Plaza was the only thing pleasing about the room.

He walked out the door of the hotel, stood on the porch, looked to his right at the Plaza, and tamped tobacco into his cigarette paper. Striking a match against the log post, he took the first deep drag. It was a beautiful winter's evening. Definitely a change from the cold and damp of San Francisco. People had told him he'd like the dryness, but they hadn't alerted him to the beauty. The mountains, the adobe buildings, the green of the Piñon and Fir trees.

As he walked around the town, he was struck, as he always was in desert towns, by the contrast between the huge, dominant churches and the low, one or two story buildings of the homes and shops. Here the contrast was heightened by the Palace of the Governors with its long porch facing the Plaza and the amount of space occupied by the relatively small number of other buildings.

He could see Fort Marcy looming over the buildings to the northeast of town. Looked to be less than a mile from the Plaza. Not a distance that was likely to keep the soldiers away.

That would be good for business.

Coming directly from San Francisco, he was used to a constant bustle of whites, interspersed with Chinese and Mexicans. Here there were far fewer whites, and the Chinks had been replaced by all manner of Indians and New Mexicans. And it was clear that the New Mexicans, as he had been warned they called themselves, not Greasers as many of the whites called them, were a mix of Indians and Spaniards.

The apparent poverty of the Indians hanging around the Plaza was also a surprise. No, not poverty, just, well, less prosperity somehow. Apaches? Navajos? Something else? He couldn't tell. There had been more Indians around when he had arrived than there were now, as evening and the smell of piñon fires slowly began to descend upon the brown adobes.

The soldiers here weren't the U.S. Army he'd seen back East, or even the quality of the Volunteers in California a few months ago. These were New Mexican Volunteers. Rugged, yes, but green and undisciplined. You could see it in the cafes, in the Plaza, in the bars, and outside the many bordellos.

In California the discussions of the impending Civil War were distracting the soldiers. Most discussions there were about who was staying and who was thinking about joining the rebels. Was that also true here, and would it matter?

He'd have to find out and report all this to Danson. At first glance, it did look as if he'd had been right. This was going to be the place to be for the next couple of years.

California was the past. The easy pickings they'd failed to earn during the Gold Rush were now over. New Mexico was going to be the future. Gold and all its riches had eluded them in the California madness. Unfairly.

He wasn't going to let this opportunity slip though his fingers.

3

February 2, 1861

Jim Danson looked at the bearded Mexican across from him and winked as he tossed the money into the pot. "I'll raise you a quarter," he said.

"Fold," said Damours as he glanced at his partner, got up, and headed to the bar.

The three other men, including the Mexican, called the raise. Danson watched carefully as Lily Smoot dealt each of the men their three new cards.

"I'll take only one," Danson said.

He flicked the discard on top of the money in the center of the table, picked up his new card, and watched the other men without glancing at his hand.

"Your bet," Lily said, nodding toward Danson.

"Fifty cents."

"You never even looked," said the blond cowboy to Danson's left, the one with the odd straw hat.

"Don't need to 'less somebody raises me kid."

"I'll fold then."

The kid curious to see what Danson had, but not willing to pay.

"Me too," said the Mexican.

The Sergeant on Danson's right looked thoughtful.

"Okay. I'll raise you and make you look," the Sergeant said, tossing a silver dollar into the pot. "I doubt you got it. I'd get some satisfaction makin' you look and then watching you fold."

Damours walked back to the table with a fresh whiskey. He didn't sit. He looked amused at the Sergeant and then at Danson. Sipped his whiskey.

"Show the Sergeant what you got, Jim. If he caught anything at all on the draw, it'd be his first hand of the night."

The Sergeant didn't look up. Just looked at Danson. Waiting for him to look at his hand.

"Fold," Danson said without even looking at his fifth card, tossing all five into the pile, and standing up.

"C'mon Auggy let's go get some dinner."

"You didn't even look," the cowboy said.

"Hell," Danson said. "I couldn'a had anything that would beat what Sarge was willin' to bet a day's pay on."

The Sergeant grimaced at Danson's implied insult at his pay grade.

"What's your name again darlin'?" Danson said to Lily as he stood and gathered his money.

"Lily. Lily Smoot. And I ain't yours or nobody else's 'darlin'," she said as she winked over at Damours.

But she now looked more closely at Damours' friend as she shuffled the cards for the next hand. Jim Danson he'd said. Looked to be in his mid-thirties, but more'n likely pushing forty. Like a big brother to that sweetheart Damours, but maybe fifteen years older. Trying too hard to be a cowboy. Worn out old black cowboy boots, spurs, leather jacket over an old blue cotton shirt. Red kerchief around the neck. Beaten up old tan cowboy hat. Soft eyes never sittin' still, always moving around the room.

An operator, definitely an operator. Not somebody anybody would probably feel comfortable getting close to. Nobody, except maybe Damours. Damours looked up to him. For the life of her, she couldn't see why. At least not so far.

Danson caught her look of appraisal, smiled down at her, and tossed her a nickel tip.

She snatched the nickel out of the air and watched thoughtfully as the two friends headed to the bar. Auggy definitely needs somebody to watch over him, she thought to herself.

Maybe Danson's already got that job. She shrugged and turned back to dealing five card draw.

"Did you see him?" Damours said. "Over there," he pointed with his head. "The guy who busted us both at that high stakes game in San Francisco when we first got there? John Cummings. Something like that."

Danson looked up at Damours over his steak.

"C'mon, Auggy. His name's Joseph, not John, and you know it. Save your cons for our marks. Don't practice on me. Everybody else may think you look like some guileless, teenage version of that actor John Wilkes Booth, but I know who and what you are."

Damours frowned. "He's supposed to have been in Arizona for the past couple of years. Or so we were told."

Damours knew he and Danson weren't here just for the gambling. And staying away from Cummings at the card table would be easy enough. Having Cummings show up here after he had spent time in Arizona wasn't too much to worry about. Plenty of people were looking back to New Mexico as a frontier to make a play for.

"And, yes, I saw him," Danson said. "So what? New Mexico's big enough for both of us."

Damours was thinking to himself, damn bad luck, though, Cummings showing up here. Even before Cummings had cleaned them out, he'd treated Damours like a kid. Even called him 'kid' most of the time. Kept teasing him about how Damours was the only guy he knew came out of the hills with less gold than he'd gone in with.

"Wasn't it Cummings blew the whistle on our deal with the Chinaman that day?" Damours said.

Danson looked up from his plate. "Oh yeah, I forgot about that. He apologized, though. Said it was an accident. He told me that the Chinaman was playing us and that he was just saving us."

Danson looked again over at the pretty little dealer "You think I could get Lily?"

"Lily? Doubt it. She's younger than me, for Pete's sake."

Thinking to himself how do I let him know about me 'n Lily before he gets his feelings hurt? He decided to just jump in with it. "In case you hadn't noticed, Danson, she was feeding me cards all night. She and I have been going out mornings after her shift since before you got here."

Danson looked startled, then angry. "Dammit, Auggy. Oh well, people like and trust you. Women especially, I guess. Hell, you're easy to like. Easy to trust. After all, it's your job."

Damours just grinned over at him.

"I guess," Danson said. "I was too busy setting up the Sergeant for what we gotta do to notice you hadda girlfriend. Do you think you can get your head out of the girl long enough to work with me on our current job?"

"You brought her up's all. I just didn't want you angry at me when you found out."

Then he brightened. Looked up from his plate. "She's got a friend. They asked me if you wanted to meet her some mornin'."

"Auggy," Danson said. He looked across the room at Cummings now talking to Lily during her break. "Auggy." Making sure he had his attention. "We came here to make a fortune bigger'n if we'd scored gold in the California hills. We need to be concentrating on that. Not on a pair of floozies looking for their marks. Not on some nitwit that happens into town at the wrong time. Right now, let's work on the Sergeant and try to stay out of everybody else's crosshairs. Okay?"

"Sure Jim. You go ahead and set it up. Just like always."

Damours looked earnestly at his friend, wanting to make sure he understood. "But I don't think Lily's a floozy. And neither's Pepper. Least not so far's I can tell."

"Okay. Okay," Danson said. "I don't want an accounting or a progress report. I ain't your Pop. But I'll tell you from this end of the experience scale kid, women will sleep with you for one reason and one reason only. They'll claim it's for any of three reasons: love, fun, or money. But I ain't ever met a girl, lady, or woman; white, Mexican, or Chink; who'd do it for long for love or fun without knowin' the money would be coming eventually. They're gone in a heartbeat if they realize the money's not ever comin'. Even if they convince themselves at first that it was for fun or love, in the end it's only about the money."

He looked to make sure Damours was listening.

"Common thieves'll have the good grace to ask you for your money or your life, Auggy. But women? They'll always want both."

"Sure, Jim. Thanks."

"And hell, kid. Santa Fe is nothing but gambling and whores. You knew that when we headed here, and you had a week ahead of me to see for yourself."

They both looked up, startled, as Joseph Cummings arrived at their table and pulled up a chair.

"Well, well, well, if it's not the Chink gold dust twins."

4

February 3, 1861

Lieutenant George Bascom, less than three years out of West Point, arrived at Apache Pass at the head of his very first military command.

He was accompanied by fifty-four soldiers and John Ward, the step-father of a boy who had been kidnapped from his Arizona ranch by raiding Indians. Ward had convinced the Army that Cochise were now holding his step-son captive.

They were met upon their arrival in Apache Pass by Captain Arnold at his temporary camp in the meadow near the stage station.

Arnold looked up at Bascom on his jet black horse. The horse was much more impressive than the man. Bascom's short, yellowish brown hair and beard made him look even younger than he really was. Arnold knew this was Bascom's first command.

"Captain Arnold," Bascom said. "We've been sent from Fort Buchanan to retrieve some cattle and a small boy captured from the Ward ranch at Sonoita Creek about a week ago."

"Well Bascom, with respect, I doubt any of the bands around here were involved."

"The boy's father has reason to believe that it was the Chiricahuas, Arnold." He gestured back toward Ward. "Cochise's Chiricahuas to be specific."

Ward edged his horse closer to the conversation.

"Again, with respect Lieutenant, that's very unlikely. Cochise has been at peace with us for over two years. The Indian agent, the Butterfield Stage line, and I have found him to be extremely helpful. For God's sake, Cochise has even been trying to get us to go with him against the Mexicans. Says we can have their land if he can have their livestock."

"That's just the point, Captain," Ward said. "He took our cattle and then took my boy."

Bascom put his hand up in front of the rancher for silence. "Let me handle this Ward." He looked back at Arnold.

"As you well know, Captain, Cochise raided near Tubac twice last May, and even agreed to return the livestock after he did it. After a week on the trail, we've found no trace of these thieves anywhere else Ward tracked the cattle from his ranch straight to the San Pedro and then here toward the Chiricahuas before he lost the trail."

"There's been no evidence of any such Apache activity from these parts for months," Arnold said. "We'da seen some sign of those cattle if they brought them here. I think whoever took the boy veered off somewhere else after the trail went cold. Cochise would never jeopardize his peace by taking an American boy."

Ward started to say something, but Bascom put his hand up. "Captain, I have my orders. We need you to arrange a meeting between us and Cochise. Under a white flag."

He looked hard at Arnold.

"Yes, Lieutenant," Arnold said.

5

Cochise arrived on foot late the next afternoon, accompanied by Dos-teh-seh, his brother Coyuntura, his two grown nephews, and Naiche, all of whom were curious to see the new chief from the soldiers' fort.

Cochise and the other three Apache men were dressed only in breechclouts and moccasins with deerskin leggings up above their calves.

He hesitated when he saw so many soldiers, but he trusted Arnold.

"See the white flag over the tent," Arnold said in passable Apache. "The new Lieutenant just wants to meet the famous Cochise. He has a question and comes in friendship."

"My family is not comfortable in the soldiers' tent with so many soldiers."

"The Lieutenant is in the tent and has already set up food for the meeting. He will be offended if you refuse to join him."

Cochise looked at Arnold without expression. He'd expected more presents and fewer soldiers and was suddenly uncomfortable. He'd become accustomed to being at ease with white men. He sensed all was not as he had been told. But he felt had no choice and reluctantly led his family into the tent.

Lieutenant Bascom had a Mexican interpreter with him. Three white soldiers and a red bearded white man Cochise had never seen stood behind him as well.

Cochise read Bascom's barely concealed surprise in his eyes. He had seen this reaction from inexperienced white men before. They came expecting to see a chief and were startled to see, instead, a simple, nearly naked man. It had long stopped bothering him.

He stood impassively before the young officer.

"Cochise," Bascom said. "Let me get straight to the point." There was no pretense of friendship . "Mr. Ward's ranch here," he gestured behind him to the red bearded stranger while the Mexican interpreted, "Was raided by Indians last week and his young son was captured, along with some horses and cattle. We've come to get them back."

Chiricahuas were always uncomfortable with the white man's use of direct names, but whether this boy soldier's rudeness was intentional or just out of ignorance he couldn't tell. Cochise looked from Arnold to red beard to the Lieutenant. "Why are you here, Lieutenant?" Cochise said.

"You can turn over Mr. Ward's son and the livestock you stole. And we will return to the fort in peace."

Cochise didn't move a muscle. He looked down at Naiche, who was playing with the toy dog the white woman had given him at this very spot a month before. The young boy oblivious to the rising tensions in the tent.

After a long moment Cochise said, "We have no knowledge of this. We will be happy to join you and your soldiers as scouts in looking for the boy."

"We have reason to believe that your Chiricahuas attacked the Ward ranch."

Cochise began to feel a long-dormant fear and anger well up. He had been at peace with the white man long enough now to have started to take it for granted.

When Geronimo had approached him to join Mangas Coloradas last summer to avenge the humiliating bullwhipping of the great chief at the hands of the miners at Pinos Altos, he had refused. Cochise felt it was simply best not to bother the whites.

Why was this boy soldier and red beard rancher risking that peace? He sat quietly, calculating his options. "We are at peace with the whites. Yes, we still kill the Mexicans," here he stared at the interpreter. "But none of my Chiricahuas would risk our peace. As your soldiers know, last summer I declined to join the other Apaches."

He looked directly at Ward.

"I am sorry to hear about your son. We did not do this. But we will go with the Lieutenant and find those who did." He now gestured toward the other Apache men with him. "We will gather the Chiricahuas and join you to find who did this. Maybe the Mescalero, the White Mountain Apaches, or the Navajo."

Cochise moved as if to stand, and the soldiers drew their pistols and held them at their sides.

Bascom spoke first in the unsettling tension. "Ward tracked the war party to the base of your band's territory."

Cochise looked at his wife and son and now chose his words very carefully. "My family and I came here today at your invitation to meet and talk in peace under your white flag. We did not do this thing, and we offer our help. What more can we do, Lieutenant?"

"You can turn over the Ward boy."

"Lieutenant Bascom," Arnold said. "Can we step outside to discuss an alternative?"

"No Captain Arnold. Cochise has the boy and will turn him over to his father as I have directed."

Bascom looked down at the assembled Apaches, while Cochise said, "We would like to help you find the boy."

"Tell him slowly and clearly," Bascom said, looking directly at the interpreter, "No. You won't. You are my prisoner until your people bring the boy in."

As the Mexican nervously repeated the message in Apache, he could not bring himself to look at the Chiricahua chief.

Bascom signaled to his soldiers. They immediately surrounded the small band. The soldiers outside the tent could be heard moving into place.

The Chiricahuas, the Mexican interpreter, and Arnold were all equally astonished. Only Cochise remained outwardly calm.

He forced himself to contain the fury he felt. It would be no trouble to find who had attacked the ranch and taken the boy. He stared at the Mexican. If this was what the boy Lieutenant came here to do, even if his inexperience was the cause, Cochise knew what he had to do.

But he wanted to take one more try at avoiding tragedy.

"Lieutenant Bascom. My men and I will go with you to find the boy and bring the captors in. You and your soldiers can take me, unarmed, to my camp to organize a search. But as your prisoners we cannot help."

Cochise prepared himself mentally, never taking his eyes off the Mexican. Knowing the answer would be in the interpreter's expression long before the words came out of his treacherous mouth.

Lieutenant Bascom responded. As Cochise saw the amusement on the Mexican's face and the horror in Captain Arnold's eyes, and before the Mexican could speak the first Apache word, Cochise leapt forward. He was up and his knife was out of his leggings with blinding speed. In one stride and one sweep of his right arm, an astonished soldier lay on his back, the tent was rent, and Cochise was out, leaping through the soldiers outside with their rifles at the ready.

As he ran at full speed, bent over and zig zagging his way through the Cottonwoods and across the creek toward Apache Springs and the boulders, the soldiers opened fire. He purposefully ran away from his Rancheria and toward the Chiricahua Mountains directly to the south. He was hit on the leg, but didn't slow down. He could do nothing for his family or his people as a prisoner of the boy soldier. Or as furious as he felt.

He had to get to the safety of his band. Certainly even someone as foolish as the Lieutenant wouldn't harm Apache women and children. And certainly not Cochise's children.

Arnold led the search parties for Cochise all afternoon. But, as he knew, once the blood trail stopped where Cochise had broken off the Cholla stalk and caulked the wound, no further trace of him could be found. He was somewhere in the Chiricahuas. There was no point in continuing the search.

Arnold couldn't help but feel frustrated that the inexperience and stubbornness of one officer had almost certainly started an inevitable chain of blood and violence. It could lead to the deaths of hundreds, if not thousands, of innocent people. Precisely what Bascom had been sent here to prevent.

6

February 5, 1861

Damours just listened as Cummings and Danson talked.

"Look," Cummings said. "As soon as I got here from Tucson I heard you two were here. It's a nice coincidence. I have a proposal for you." He looked at each in turn. "War's coming," he said as if he knew some vital secret. "Once Lincoln is inaugurated next month, South Carolina is going to join the Confederacy and all the slave states are going to follow. We can make a fortune together stealing from the Army payrolls. The military forces are going to be primarily New Mexico

Volunteers, and nobody in these parts has any idea how to run the finances of a volunteer army. How to keep it going."

"But why us?" Danson said. "Why are we the lucky ones?"

"Because between the two of you, you haven't worked an honest day in your lives." Cummings grinned at them. "Call it a wild hunch, but I'm guessing that you two didn't come here to join the U.S. Army or the New Mexico Volunteers and fight the Texans and Arizona southern sympathizers."

Neither man responded.

"C'mon, you're here looking for small time scams. Just like you were doing in California. Honest people worked the gold mines and the streams, or provided food, clothes, or equipment for the miners. And the suppliers got richer than the miners. But try as hard as you two did, you couldn't even make your little confidence games work there. In the middle of all that loose money."

"Okay, let's say you're right," Danson said. "But I still don't think our experiences in San Francisco make the three of us an obvious partnership. Why would you trust us?"

"It doesn't matter if *I* trust you. I've never met anyone who people instantly trust as much as people trust him." Cummings pointed at Damours. "He reminds everybody of that actor back East. From Baltimore. Booth something?"

"John Wilkes Booth," Danson said. "Especially now that Auggy's grown that silly drooping moustache."

"Right," Cummings said. "John Wilkes Booth. Of the Booth family. Auggy doesn't trust me as far as you can throw that Sergeant you failed to scam last week. But he trusts *you*, Danson. He'll trust you to work with me. I've got plans and I've got backing. Damours is the perfect confidence man. And you? Well you've got the kid's trust. And we'll need that all the way to the end."

"What's the con?" Danson said.

"Unh, uh. No way. Not until we've worked more together. I'll tell you the part we want known for now, though. Since I left California, I've been working with Sylvester Mowry of the Mowry Mines, in Patagonia. Near Tucson. Near the Mexican border. He's a former army officer and he plans on providing both sides with munitions. I've agreed to be his New Mexico operation. For both sides."

Danson looked thoughtful, then looked over at Damours.

"What do you think, Auggy? Are you willing to work with this guy?"

"I need to think about it. It sounds likely to be worth more money than our idea. More complicated, too. Probably riskier too I'd bet."

"Correct on all counts, kid," Cummings said.

"I ain't doin' it without Danson," Damours said. "I'm telling you that up front."

"You guys let me know," Cummings said. "You're not the only prairie dogs in the Territory."

"Tell me one thing, Joe—"

"—Joseph, Danson. It's Joseph, not Joe."

"Okay. Joseph," Danson said. "How exactly do we expect to get inside the military network?"

"Simple. Patriots that we are, the kid here and I are joining the Army. With Mowry's supplies and capital, my inside Santa Fe connection, us in the Army, and you free to work the outside, you'll have more money than if you'd hit the mother lode in those California hills."

"And just who's your inside connection?" Danson said.

"Lily Smoot. She and I have been friendly since I met her in Virginia City. She was the best whore in 'The Brickhouse' the last coupla times I stopped there." He looked puzzled in response to the look on Damours' face and the stunned silence. "You know? Cad Thompson's place? In Virginia City? Cad runs the best whore house in the West. Bar none. And kid," he looked over at Damours. "Lily thinks you're the best con man she's ever seen for a job like this."

Cochise and his Chiricahuas, now fully armed and in battle dress, approached Apache Pass on horseback, coming out of the Chiricahua Mountains from the south. The Apaches wore war paint, were armed with rifles, spears, war clubs, and bows and arrows, and were, with one lone exception, excited at the prospect of being back at war with the whites.

Cochise, his fury now abated, was focused on taking one more try at preventing a war. But it would require that the boy soldier Bascom also be looking for a way out.

He sent two of his best warriors, Nahilzay and Loco, out under a white flag. They stopped above and close enough to the camp to be seen, but not close enough to be shot.

Nahilzay called out for Captain Arnold, waving the white flag. The startled soldiers trained their field glasses on the pair of Apaches.

"Well Lieutenant, it looks like you get to see Apaches dressed more like you expected," Arnold said, handing the glasses over to Bascom.

"Captain Arnold," Bascom said. "Take the Mexican up there and find out if they've brought the Ward boy."

Arnold mounted up.

The Mexican looked stricken and said, "I think Captain Arnold's Apache is good enough, Lieutenant."

"Get up there and find out what those savages want," Bascom said. "Now."

Everyone except the inexperienced Bascom knew that the Chiricahuas thought nothing of killing Mexicans for sport.

"Cochise has sent us a message," Arnold said to calm the terrified Mexican as they rode up the hill. "If he wanted to kill us, he would have already tried at dawn. We'll be okay here."

The two stopped a hundred yards from the two Apaches. They could see more plainly now that the two warriors had prepared themselves for war. They had painted white war stripes horizontally across their noses, under their eyes. Both had their hair bound back with a red cloth covering their foreheads. The white flag was in direct contrast to their preparation for war.

Out of deference for the white flag and the fact that the Apaches had requested this meeting, Arnold sat quietly on his horse. Politely waiting for the Indians to speak.

Nahilzay abandoned normal Apache manners and blurted out a clear threat. "I think this will all end badly for you. Especially for you," he said, pointing his lance at the nervous Mexican. The black handle of the lance was newly decorated with the red zig zag pattern that indicated preparation for a war blessing ceremony. "Tell the boy soldier from me, that our shamans tell us that they know he is a witch. Child of the Water came to two of our shamans to tell us that the Lieutenant will experience an early and terrible death. But an owl warned us that he is also a ghost and that we cannot kill him. Tell him that he will die horribly at the hands of his fellow White Eyes."

"Is that what Cochise sent you to tell me, Nahilzay?" Arnold said, intentionally insulting him by using his name.

"No. Also tell the boy nantan," insulting the Lieutenant down below with the derisive Apache term for boy white soldier, "And this is from Cochise. Tell him that the Chiricahuas are armed and here to help him find the boy. If he will release our people, we will join with the soldiers to find those who stole the boy from the ranch."

"Does Cochise know where he is now?"

"No. But we will look for him with you when you release the hostages."

"I will ride down with the message and come back with Lieutenant Bascom's response."

Arnold and the Mexican turned their horses to head back down to the camp.

"No."

When Arnold turned, he saw that Loco had wheeled his horse to block the Mexican's path.

"The Mexican stays so that you will come back."

Arnold looked at the terrified interpreter. "We are here under your white flag. You have my word that we will come back with your answer."

"No. The boy nantan," again deriding Bascom, "Holds our people hostage. We will hold the Mexican until you ride back up."

"And then?"

"And then, we will see. It depends on your nantan. What will he do, Captain Arnold?"

Arnold looked at the interpreter's wild eyes, nodded at him with as much assurance as he could muster, and then glanced at Nahilzay. Only then did he see Cochise in his full war regalia up above them in the Mesquite on his famous war pony, looking down at them like some god of doom.

Arnold wheeled his horse around and sped down the hill without a word.

When he arrived, nobody knew where Bascom was.

"Damned greenhorn," Arnold said to Sergeant Wilson. "What on earth do they teach at West Point? All our lives at risk here, and the damn Lieutenant can't even stay in sight."

He rode through the camp until he found him in a back tent, talking to Ward.

"Lieutenant," barely concealing his displeasure, "Cochise has returned with all his Indians to help us find the boy."

"He already has the boy," Bascom said. "Tell him to return him and we will return his family to him."

"Sir, with all due respect, I have worked with Cochise for years. He has never lied to us. He's offering to help you find the boy."

"Go back up that hill and tell him I know he has the boy. That he's a liar."

Arnold audibly sucked in his breath. "Lieutenant, whoever goes back up that hill under those orders will never return. No matter how many you send up there, they will die on the spot, along with your interpreter they are holding."

"You have your orders, Captain."

"Lieutenant Bascom, with all due respect, this whole thing can go away. We are at peace with the Chiricahuas. Release the Apaches and Cochise will honor his commitment. I guarantee it. Need I remind you that I outrank you here?"

"Captain Arnold, these are my orders directly from your Commanding Officer at Fort Buchanan."

"You cannot call Cochise a liar and expect him to stay at peace with us," Arnold said. "You cannot do this, Lieutenant."

"Either go up that hill or I will have you arrested Captain."

Arnold tried a different approach. "Lieutenant, the Apaches told me that their priests have said that you cannot die at the hands of Apaches, but that you will be killed by whites."

Bascom looked amused.

"Since they believe this," Arnold said. "If you go up to Cochise with your message, he will respect the prophecy. And he will admire your courage for delivering the message yourself. If you send anyone else, he will kill him. And it won't be fast and it won't be pretty. You haven't seen what the Apaches do to captives. I have."

"Captain, are you disobeying a direct order?"

"No sir. If you order me to go, I am prepared to die following your orders. I'm telling you that it is a mistake and will be fatal, not only to whoever you send up that hill, but to many of the soldiers in your command. And possibly for hundreds or thousands of innocent settlers. The only hope for a way out is for you, personally, to take the message. To earn Cochise's respect. You are untouchable in his eyes."

Bascom looked up the hill where Arnold was pointing.

"Captain Arnold. I understand you don't think they have the boy. But do you think they know where he is?"

"No, sir."

"How do you think the savages' behavior would be different if they did?"

It was a good question. Arnold begrudged him that. He thought about it while he looked up sympathetically at the Mexican.

"I think that if Cochise had the boy, he would never have brought his family to meet you. As you've seen, he's confident in his ability to escape you. But subjecting his wife and young son? I don't think so. And if he knew where the boy was now, he would tell us. He has no reason to withhold the information from you if he knows that the Mescalero or Navajo have him. It's not worth his family. Not worth ending his peace."

He looked back at Bascom.

Now it was Bascom's turn to look up the hill. "Do you know what I think, Arnold? I think once you all have been out here a while, I think you get too close to these savages. But you're right about one thing. It's my job to go up there and tell him."

"Lieutenant Bascom, sir," Sergeant Wilson said. "I don't think that's such a good idea."

"No, Wilson, he's right. It's the right way to do this."

Bascom walked over to his horse, all but leapt into the saddle, and galloped confidently to the other side of the camp and up the hill with his eyes on the two Apaches and the Mexican.

When he reached them, he said, "I want to talk to Cochise."

"I speak for Cochise," Nahilzay said, looking closely at the boy soldier for the first time. "Are you Lieutenant Bascom?"

"Yes. I want to speak to Cochise. I have received his offer and I now bring my response. "

"I will personally carry your response to Cochise."

"And I will personally await his arrival."

Cochise suddenly appeared behind his two warriors. Nahilzay and Loco moved their horses aside so that their chief could approach Bascom.

"Lieutenant Bascom," Cochise said. "What is your response?"

Bascom looked up at the Apache, reigning in his horse as it twisted and turned from side to side.

He was now a totally different adversary. It was an amazing transformation. Where he'd been a naked savage sitting in the tent before, he was now a ferocious presence in his ceremonial leather. His clothing and his exposed arms and hands were decorated in a fierce array of colorful hieroglyphs. His horizontal band of face paint was red, to match his headband.

"I believe you have the Ward boy," Bascom said. "When you hand him over to me, I will release my prisoners. If you do not hand him over to me, we will take your family to the fort."

Cochise stared at him, waiting for the Mexican to translate.

"You are either the bravest or the most foolish man in the American Army," Cochise said. "We are at peace, you and I. You invite me to meet you under a white flag. You accuse me of things I have not done. You call me a liar and then arrest me and my family. You then come up this hill alone to call me a liar again in front of my men."

Bascom did not respond.

"I spent six weeks chained in a Mexican prison, Lieutenant Bascom. For which the Mexicans have paid dearly for many years." Cochise looked for the first time at the interpreter. "And will continue to pay. A new war is not something I wish for my family. Nor do I wish to have to make war on the White Eyes to avenge my family. We do not have the Ward boy. But we will help you find him."

"One last time, will you release the boy?" Bascom said.

Before anyone could respond, the three Apaches turned their horses in concert as gunshots rang out. Both Bascom's and the Mexican's horses went down, dead on the spot.

Gunfire now sounded both from above and below. Bascom hit the ground, reached for his pistol, and aimed up the hill where he heard rapidly receding hoof beats. But the Indians were gone. The interpreter were nowhere to be seen.

When the Apaches reached their camp, Cochise turned the unconscious Mexican over to the women and children.

It was the duty of all Chiricahua boys to learn the art of torture before they could become real warriors. It was a natural part of their life. And Cochise had no need for Mexican hostages here. The interpreter's screams would be heard coming from the Chiricahua camp for the next two days.

A furious Cochise then ordered Nahilzay and Geronimo to take seven warriors and bring back at least three White Eyes from one of the approaching stage coaches by the next morning.

"And Nahilzay."

Nahilzay rode back as his pony pranced nervously back and forth in front of the chief.

"Remember, we have had no war dance. You are not yet blessed by the enemies-against-power. Do not kill any White Eyes, not even by mistake."

"Yes. I understand."

And Nahilzay and Geronimo rode excitedly back into the center of their camp.

Cochise then turned, oblivious to the encroaching night air, and rode far from his camp, alone up toward the higher mountain passes deep into the Chiricahua Mountains that he considered his home.

He had settled into earning his living off the Mexicans, not white men. It had become their way of life. It was hard work, but it was a living.

He had pursued this path in his desire for a better life than his forefathers who had spent their lives killing and fighting everybody.

He had wanted something better for the People. Even though a white mercenary had worked with the Mexicans to kill his own father, he had chosen to treat them, and their soldiers, with the respect he wanted for his own people. Even though Mangas Coloradas and Geronimo and Juh had asked him last year to join them in their fight against the white man.

Now all he had worked for might be lost. He would soon be at war with the White Eye soldiers and all the Americans. And everybody else. Simply because some boy soldier could not respond honorably to being treated honorably. Small consolation that this Lieutenant, this witch, would die at the hands of his own people.

Maybe Mangas Coloradas had been right all along. Join with the Mimbres. Together they could fight the Americans to regain the glory of their fathers. Drive the White Eyes back where they had come from. Or maybe make them go to this place they called California and leave this country to the Apaches and the Mexicans.

Cochise raised his head to the darkening skies and let out a long, wailing Apache war cry. It was heard down below at the Chiricahua camp with increasing excitement in anticipation of the days to come.

Nahilzay and Geronimo had left for the raid.

Cochise was now in his own solitary war council.

Damours had heard so much about Santa Fe's dance parties, fandangos, that he decided tonight was the night to see for himself.

Having been given no specific recommendations from the whores at either Jose's Crib or Maria's, he figured he'd just walk around and see what he could find by himself on this cold, crisp New Mexico evening.

It took him ten minutes of exploring to find three fandangos. Each was identifiable by the bright lights above the door, the sound of the celebrants and music coming through the windows and doors, and the people mingling outside, all smoking little hand rolled cigarritos. With nothing else to guide him, Damours chose the one with the prettiest girl standing outside, Val Verde Hall.

There were two rooms. The first was dominated by a large table covered with food, wine, and champagne. He had not seen this much food since he'd left San Francisco.

There were platters of roasted pork and shelled oysters. Mounds of oysters. How did they get oysters in New Mexico? He helped himself to a plate of pork, red chilies, and onions, cebolla, on a tortilla, and a glass of champagne.

The pretty little girl who had followed him in promptly asked him for a dollar, and Damours happily complied, then entered the second room.

It was slightly larger than the first. There were benches along the walls and a band at the front of the room. The benches were filled with all manner of people. Wealthy ranchers, little girls, old men, New Mexicans, two girls he recognized from Maria's, impoverished farmers in sandals, Mexicans, even a couple of whites, maybe soldiers. At least a dozen blazing candles and pictures of the Christ and some Saints adorned the cloth-covered walls. Everybody, man, woman, and child, was smoking cigarritos.

The center of the room was filled with dancers. Couples of all shapes and sizes, dancing a giddy waltz together. Three old men, comprising the surprisingly excellent band, played a guitar, a fiddle, and a drum. When the music stopped, all the couples graciously parted with thank you's and gracias's amid great merriment.

When the music resumed, women formed a line to the left and men their own line on the right. At a signal from the guitarist, the two lines approached each other and met in the middle. The dancers paired off as the two lines met, each with the partner randomly across from them.

And off they went. This time the band played a light vendetta.

The dust kicked up from the boots and sandals rose into the air to mix with the smoke and the candlelight, creating a dusky, romantic glow. After watching several dances, Damours joined the middle of the men's line.

The music began, and the two lines converged. Damours found himself face to face, then arm in arm, with an immense New Mexican woman well into her sixties who spoke no English. She was a very good dancer, a wonderful laugher, and she loved to waltz. She told him her name was Beatrice, but indicated she couldn't understand his. No matter. She called him her Pocolito Gringo. And laughed merrily.

To Damours' surprise he heard the guitarist sing a refrain about Mama Beatrice and her Pocolito Gringo. When the music stopped Beatrice curtsied her rough farmer's dress, kissed him on the cheek, and laughed her way quickly back to the bench.

Damours danced the night away. He danced with beautiful, black eyed young women, aging farm wives, both beautiful and not so beautiful farmers' daughters, one of the girl's from Maria's, a wealthy rancher's wife, Hattie from the hotel reception desk, a now-giggly Beatrice again, and, to his astonishment, the Governor's wife, who wore more silver jewelry than he'd ever seen on anyone before.

Some women wore splendid silk, some calico. Some had expensive silver jewelry and some were wearing colored glass necklaces and bracelets.

He took special care not to flirt with any of the women. He'd heard the stories of women's knife fights and men getting shot at fandangos. He had no desire to find himself at the wrong end of a husband's or a vengeful girl's wrath. At least not at his very first fandango.

The music began again, and he moved forward in the men's line to receive one of the oncoming girls.

He stopped dead in his tracks as a grinning Lily Smoot walked into his open arms.

"Having fun, Auggy?"

How long had Lily been here? He hadn't seen her. How had he never realized how beautiful she was? Or was it the champagne? Or the smoke and the candlelight?

As they danced a waltz together, he realized he hadn't said a word.

He looked straight into her eyes. "Good evening to you, Lil."

He felt her body move under the bright red silk dress. Noticed the glass necklace against the white of her neck.

They smiled at each other, somehow wordlessly agreeing that there was no need to talk. They just danced.

As if they'd danced together for years.

When the dance ended, they didn't pull apart. Just kept looking at each other. Finally, Damours released her, stepped back, bowed.

"Thank you, Miss Smoot."

She laughed and whirled away back toward a bench on the other side of the room, looking once back over her shoulder.

He couldn't remember the next several dances, trying, and failing, each time to pair up with Lily. He could see her intentionally just missing him. Making a game of it.

Looking at him while she danced with an ancient old priest, a fat Mexican farmer, a young New Mexican boy in moccasins. Once he found himself dancing with Hattie again, but by then Damours wasn't present. He was physically dancing with Hattie, but his heart and soul were on the other side of the room, being danced 'round and 'round by Lily Smoot.

When he saw Lily leave the dance floor and enter the dining room, he broke free and followed her. He came up behind her and said, "May I buy you a glass of champagne, Miss Smoot?"

She turned and said, "You certainly could if it weren't already free, Mr. Damours."

They stepped out into the cold night air, each with a fresh glass of champagne.

He leaned against the wall of the building. She stepped in front of him. Moved very close, but not touching.

"I don't think they allow dancing in the streets here in Santa Fe," he said.

"If you're right, they should certainly change the law."

She reached up and clinked her class to his. Put it to her red lips and sipped. Never taking her eyes off his. Then she moved and stood next to him, on his right, leaning against the wall. Their arms were touching and she made no move to pull away.

"You are very beautiful tonight, Lil."

"Just tonight, Auggy? How very disappointing to hear."

He saw her nose crinkle but saw no need to take the bait.

In their previous times together they had just been friends. Breakfast buddies after she got off work early in the morning when the poker games died off. She'd always been tired and he had wanted a friend in town. Neither of them thought to make anything more of it. He knew that she thought he was younger than she was, and he had let that stand.

She knew he frequented the whore houses. Did she now also know that Cummings had told him she'd been a whore? Did it matter? He realized that it did matter a little to him, but would it bother her that he knew?

"Hey. It's morning now, Auggy. A new day."

And suddenly Damours realized that he wasn't thinking like a man having a nice time at a dance anymore. I'll be damned, he thought, can I really have fallen in love with Lily Smoot?

"Look, Lil. The semi-circle moon just rising over the Governor's Palace and the golden color of the adobe walls over there in the moonlight."

"It's the same color as the smoky candlelight in the dance hall," she said.

They clinked champagne glasses again and looked at each other.

"It's magical, Auggy."

"Yes, it is."

7

February 6, 1861

Having failed to head off the morning stage, the Apache raiding party spotted five wagons headed toward Apache Pass from the west and split into two groups to attack.

Geronimo and five others lay in the ravine completely hidden while Nahilzay and a young brave approached from above signaling that they came in peace.

The driver of the lead wagon pulled his laboring mules to a full, rough stop. He and his partner riding shotgun sat stock still, looking at the two Apaches. All the Territory's drivers knew there was no danger of an ambush in Cochise country. But that didn't mean they would be reckless with two oncoming Apaches.

"I don't see any sign of anybody else," the driver said.

His partner just peered more carefully into the surrounding rocks and Mesquite, swinging his rifle from side to side.

The driver jumped down from the seat and headed, rifle at his side, toward Nahilzay who stood in front of the steaming mules. His partner stayed put and continued surveying the scene. After a moment, he backed down the side of the wagon one handed, with his rifle held aloft.

Just as his right foot reached the ground, he and the driver were each struck by a war club and knocked senseless. Soundlessly, the seven Apaches surrounded the other four wagons, rifles aimed at the remaining eleven men, nine of whom were Mexicans.

The six women and children in the wagons were too scared to make a sound. The Apaches grimly motioned them all out of the wagons, lancing one of the Mexicans in the chest to pull him off the wagon. Cochise hadn't said anything about not killing Mexicans.

The Apaches quickly cut the mules from the train and lashed the whites onto them, linking them all together in single file.

They then tied the nine Mexicans to the wagon wheels and took turns torturing them with their lances and knives, until they were barely conscious. They then burned the wagons and used their lances to make sure each Mexican was dead.

Nahilzay let out a long whoop and raced the group back to camp. The Chiricahuas made fun of their terrified prisoners all the way up the mountain, exulting at their easy success.

The raiding party clambered back into camp well before their promised deadline.

Cochise came out of his wickiup as Nahilzay rode up. "Have you come back with three White Eyes?"

"Ten." Nahilzay gestured back at the captives, still on their mules, shivering from both fright and cold. "It is a beautiful day for the People."

"Any killed?"

"No White Eyes. But we tortured nine mexicano and burned them with the wagons and the provisions. We also brought back the mules."

Cochise looked out over the valley. "Just like before. In the days of war."

And he and Nahilzay let out a long war cry together, which was picked up by the rest of the gathering Apache camp.

Much to the terror of the captives.

Arnold reported the discovery of the wagon train to Bascom. "Cochise has attacked a wagon train, killed nine Mexicans, stolen all the mules, and captured all the whites."

"Are you sure it was Cochise?" Bascom said.

"Yes."

Bascom looked unconsciously up the hill to where he'd last seen the Apaches. "You sure are confident about a lot Captain."

"Yes, I am."

"How can you be so sure Cochise has all these Americans and so sure he doesn't have the Ward boy?"

"Why would he risk his men to capture a wagon train if he could get the same result by simply handing over the Ward boy?"

Bascom seemed to think about that.

"What would you do in my place Captain Arnold?"

"Nothing."

"Nothing?"

"There's nothing we can do, Bascom. It's in Cochise's hands now."

Nahilzay argued for dividing the four white men among the successful raiders.

Cochise silenced him with a gesture with his lance. He stood among the assembled Apaches and said, "We will kill no White Eyes unless the boy soldier gives us no choice. We will not give up our peace and our people unless we have to."

"But the captured White Eyes belong to those who fought and killed for them," Nahilzay said.

"The captured whites belong to the People," Cochise said.

He swept his arms over the whole camp. "To all of us. Until we know the boy soldier's response. The soldiers hold five Chiricahuas who they captured under a flag of truce like cowards. Bring me the four White Eye men tightly tied up so they cannot move or make a sound."

The four captives were brought around, secured on three painted Apache ponies. The captives were wide eyed, spooking the ponies who sensed their fear.

"I will take four braves and we will go down to the boy soldier. Nahilzay, bring twenty men with you. But well behind us. Do not let the soldiers see you. If you see that we return with our people, we will meet you here. If you see that we return with the white captives, then find a weakness in the soldiers' camp and kill two of the soldiers as we return. But I want no Apaches lost, understand?"

"Yes," Nahilzay said as he raised his lance and yelled out twice, once for the celebration and once for all the time that he had had to wait for this moment.

"Now we will see. We will see in what direction the Life Giver wills the People to go," Cochise said as he reached for his horse, pulled himself up, and led his small band down the mountain.

There was no joy in his heart.

"Here he comes," Sergeant Wilson said.

"So what did he choose, Captain?" Bascom said.

Arnold looked through the glasses up the hill. "It looks like Cochise, four braves, and...," here he paused and held the glasses out to Bascom. "And four hostages."

Bascom looked up at the party as Arnold said, "Four drivers I recognize from Las Cruces."

Cochise and his party stopped, well out of range of the soldiers' rifles, and stood still. Looking down at the camp.

"So he holds fewer hostages than the Chiricahuas we have?" Bascom said.

"We don't know if these are his only hostages," Arnold said. "And any one of the drivers is worth more than all the Apaches we have."

"Do you see the Ward boy?"

"No."

"Then there'll be no exchange."

"Bascom?" Arnold said.

"Yes, Captain?"

"He's going to ask for a fair exchange and repeat that he does not know the whereabouts of the Ward boy, sir. My recommendation is that we say 'yes,' and move on without starting a war with the Chiricahuas."

"I have my orders, Captain Arnold," Bascom said. "Sergeant Wilson, mount up. You and I are going up there to tell Cochise to release those four men and the others that he holds. Then, when he also brings the Ward boy, we will release the Chiricahuas."

"That is a death warrant for hundreds of people in the Arizona Territory, Lieutenant," Arnold said.

"Mount up Sergeant Wilson," Bascom said. "Let's move out."

"I'll need a moment, sir."

"Let's go now Sergeant."

"Cochise'll wait, Lieutenant Bascom."

And, at that, Wilson turned his back on the startled Lieutenant and led his horse back into camp.

Bascom watched furiously as Wilson made the rounds to his platoon, shaking hands with each man in turn. With some, it was just a quick handshake. But with a couple, he had more poignant messages. In each case it was delivered quickly and followed by a salute. When he was done, he mounted his horse and rode back to Bascom.

"What was that all about, Sergeant Wilson?" Bascom said.

"They're good men, Lieutenant. I told them it was an honor having served with them. Let's go talk to Cochise."

The two soldiers worked their way up the hill at a professional pace. The Apaches above and the soldiers below never took their eyes off their progress.

When they reached Cochise's party, the two soldiers waited for Cochise to speak first, but Cochise just nodded to Bascom in recognition.

"I apologize," Wilson began in his broken Apache, "for my poor language, but you are holding our interpreter."

"I understand, Sergeant. He is being taken care of by our women and young boys. Soon he will rejoin his family and the mexicanos we killed today in the mexicano sky."

He looked up at the crystal blue Arizona sky and let out a satisfying grunt that was echoed by his braves.

"Cochise," Wilson said. "You and I have much experience together. It is... er, has been, good. We trust each other. Our soldiers below," and here he swept his arm to encompass the camp below, "Have been friends to the Chiricahua. They respect your people. They want no war with you."

Cochise nodded for him to continue.

"The Lieutenant is not experienced. He is making a grave mistake. You are a wise man. You must see some way to avoid a war here."

"What are you telling him Sergeant?" Bascom said.

"I have told him that you believe he has the Ward boy and that you, and the soldiers below, will settle for nothing less."

"And what did he say?"

"Only that my Apache is very bad and that your interpreter is still alive. But unavailable."

"I told the boy soldier we do not have the Ward boy," Cochise said. "And that we do not know where he is. We want to join the soldiers to find him for his red beard father."

Wilson sighed. He pushed forward in resignation, knowing he was signing his own death warrant. He pointed to the terrified hostages.

"Lieutenant Bascom wants us to take the four hostages back to camp now. Then he will wait below for you to bring any other Americans your warriors took today and the Ward boy. Then he will give you the five Apaches."

"The hostages are the possession of all Chiricahuas. I will trade these four for my family. We have no knowledge of this Ward boy, and we have been called liars for the last time by the nantan."

"Is there no other way?"

"No," Cochise said as he gestured emphatically toward the ground with his free arm, startling all the horses.

Wilson reported Cochise's response to Bascom.

Bascom pointed to the white hostages, stood up in his stirrups, and said, "Hand those people over to me. Now."

Cochise sat impassively on his horse and stared at the Lieutenant. "Sergeant Wilson, many whites and many soldiers have been good to our people. I am sorry."

"I am also very sorry, Cochise."

Cochise said something sharply to the Apaches that Wilson could not understand, and they turned their horses in unison.

Just as the day before, two shots rang out and both soldiers' horses fell. But this time, Bascom had prepared himself. He rolled off his horse and came up with his service revolver in hand. He got off two wild shots before an Apache shot the pistol out of his hand.

Bascom stood helplessly watching the Indians gallop up the hill, with Wilson dragged, face down, through the rocks and brush at the end of a twisting turning rope. Then he heard rifle fire off to the left. He saw soldiers firing up into the hills at several fleeing Apaches. And Bascom could see two of his soldiers laying inert near the Springs under the Cottonwoods.

The American's peace with Cochise's Chiricahua Apaches was now officially ended.

8

February 7, 1861

Cochise had spent a sleepless night alone high up in the mountains above the camp. His hatred for the White Eyes, so long held below the surface, was now back in all its fury.

He watched as dawn came up over the vast desert below. It was cold, yet clear, perfectly matching his mood. He had tried all he could do. Against a large part of his nature and the advice of many of his warriors, he had lived in peace with the Americans for many years. He had dealt patiently with greedy prospectors, paranoid ranchers, arrogant stagecoach operators, and careless wranglers. But now this prideful, inexperience boy soldier had brought it all to an end.

He leapt on his pony, let out a wailing scream, and headed down to talk to the People. The People he had led against the Navajo and the mexicanos into a now-ending period of peace and prosperity, he would now lead against the White Eyes.

But it was the Life Giver's will, and, like an avenging god, Cochise would now lead the People back to the ways of before. His father-in-law had been right all along.

He rode into camp to find the shamans expecting him. Despite a steady snowstorm, they had already gathered the band for a blessing ceremony. The medicine men and the warriors, a hundred and fifty strong, were gathered in the front. The women and children with the white hostages were on the sides and in the back of the camp. The warriors and their ponies, penned off to the side, were already decorated, wearing their ceremonial beaded leather and covered with war paint.

The only sounds from the camp as he dismounted was the crackling of the fires that fought the morning cold, the moans of the hostages, and the sounds from the tethered, but excited ponies.

"For many years," Cochise said. "We have lived in peace with the White Eyes. Despite the counsel of many of you," and here he paused to gesture honorably to Nahilzay, Geronimo, and several others seated near them. "Now a boy soldier comes to challenge the People. We have done the Americans no harm. Yet he has taken our people from us and he has called us liars. Now we must go to war to rescue the Apaches he holds in Apache Pass. Bring the American soldier forward."

Two braves dragged what was left of Sergeant Wilson and laid him at the feet of Cochise. Except for his uniform, in tatters, he was all but unrecognizable. His face was a mess of broken bones and skinless features. His lips, eyebrows, and ears all gone. Nothing at all was left of his full beard. Both arms were broken. But he was still conscious. Cochise signaled to one of the shaman to come forward.

"Sergeant Wilson, can you hear me?"

The bloody form nodded in acknowledgement.

"Is there anything left for us to do to get the boy soldier to release our people."

As if in a trance, Wilson's bloody head moved back and forth. No.

Cochise turned to the shaman.

"Bless this American soldier. He has been a friend, and he is brave and he deserved a better fate."

While the shaman performed a brief blessing ceremony over the still, but breathing form, Cochise turned back to the assembled band.

"You five go to Mangas Coloradas. Tell him that we are now prepared to join him in his war to rid our land of the White Eyes. Tell him that, today, the Chiricahuas are raiding the American soldiers at Apache Pass. Ask him to bring his warriors and to meet us at his camps in the Tres Hermanas Mountains on the new moon. Tell him we will avenge the killing of my father. We will avenge his torture by the miners. We will avenge all the injustices at the hands of the Americans. Take one of the white girls with you to give to him."

He turned to Nahilzay and said, "Give the other three girls to those who captured them."

He gestured to the back of the camp.

"Give the rest of the white hostages to the women and boys. Let them work their revenge for my father's death at the hands of the White Eyes in Mexico."

He remounted his pony, raised his rifle over his head.

"We will have a proper war dance against the White Eyes soon enough. With Mangas Coloradas and the Mimbres. But today," and here he pointed to the assembled medicine men, "bless the warriors for a raid today to Apache Pass."

As the blessings began, in one motion he wheeled his pony around and leaned down for one clean kill shot into the head of Wilson.

The Sergeant's bravery had been rewarded with mercy.

Apache style.

9

February 8, 1861

Kit Carson, the Indian agent in northern New Mexico Territory since 1853, had agreed to this meeting with the leaders of his Utes and Jicarilla Apaches.

Carson was the most famous of the early 19th Century explorers, trappers, scouts, adventurers, and Indian fighters. After his important contributions to the American victory in the Mexican-American War, he had settled with his third wife, Josefa, and their children just off the main Plaza in Taos. Previously he had been married to two Indian women, an Arapaho and then a Cheyenne. Dour, a half foot short of six feet, with thinning silver blond hair and moustache, looking much younger than his 51 years, he looked nothing like the larger than life, storied frontiersman legend that had grown up about him in the 19th Century American culture.

But his Indians respected, almost loved, him.

"Thank you for inviting us here tonight," Carson said, gesturing toward his nine-year old son, William, who was seated next to him.

"No, Agent Carson, it is we who are thankful to you and Chief William for traveling here to our homes," Yellow Horse, a Jicarilla chief, said. "We," and here he gestured to the entire encampment. "We need your help again. No matter how patient we are, the Inltane, Navajo, continue to raid our homes and take our children as slaves. Not only we Haisndayin, Jicarillas, but also those of our friends the Utes."

"Yes, Father Kit," Kaniache, a Ute chief, said. "Yellow Horse speaks the truth about the Navajo. We have not always been friends of the Jicarillas," and here he nodded deferentially to the Jicarilla leaders. "But the Utes have always been enemies of the Navajo."

Kaniache looked to the assembled Indians for approval. They all nodded. "You white men have asked us to respect your laws and stop raiding the Navajo in the west. And also the Cheyenne and the Comanches in the east."

Carson nodded to Kaniache to continue. In 1854 Kaniache had saved Carson's life when one of the Utes had tried to shoot him at his Taos home. Carson certainly owed him patience in getting to his point.

"We Nuche, Utes," Kaniache said, "Have always tried to live in peace with our neighbors. To stay on the path given to us by Senawahv. The path between here and our sacred mountain retreats. Now, with the arrival of so many white men, the bears have fled and it is impossible to live our traditional lives. Out of respect for you, Father Kit, we try to live in peace here. But the Navajo will not allow it. They take advantage of the weakness that you have forced upon us."

Carson sat silently. His Indians knew that he knew all this. That he, himself, had been involved for decades, fighting the Indians in general, then in defeating the Jicarillas and Utes in particular, and now as a successful Indian agent.

He waited. There would be a point to all this. He suppressed a smile as he noticed William starting to fidget out of the corner of his eye.

"It is getting very difficult to keep our young men from fighting back," Yellow Horse said. "We cannot control the behavior of our young warriors like you whites can. Their grandfathers and fathers have raised them on stories of defeating the Inltane. They think we are weak. That the white man has made us weak. It is becoming very difficult."

And here Red Cloud, the Utes emerging young new chief, said, "You provide very well for us Father Kit. All our needs are met. Except, of course, for those needs that our traditions require."

All present knew that Red Cloud had been kidnapped by a Navajo war party twenty years before. The Navajo had attacked his Chiricahua Apache encampment, killing all but the young women and the four year old boy. On their journey home a Ute hunting party had surprised the Navajos, massacring them and taking the women and the boy as their slaves. The Chiricahua boy had grown up to become one of the Utes' best hunters and most feared warriors. Now, the twenty-four year old chief addressed Carson.

"The white man," Red Cloud said. "Asks that we summer here instead of in our natural summer home to the north. He asks that we not move from season to season as Senawahv instructed us. We were created to be the strongest of all men, but the white man's orders weaken us. And the Navajo ignore you to take advantage of our weakness."

Red Cloud looked to Kaniache for a nod of approval to continue, and got it.

"When the Navajos attack us, our warriors do not see why our wives and children must then be Navajo slaves while we do nothing. When the thieving, murdering Navajo attack white ranchers, the white man takes Navajo slaves in retaliation. We have all met William's little Navajo brother in Taos that you and your wife took from the Navajo. Since you do not retaliate when the Navajo attack us, we only ask that that we be allowed to. It should be as Senawahv demands of us still."

Carson sat and pretended to think about what Red Cloud had said. But it was nothing new. Carson was becoming increasingly comfortable that the only solution was to isolate and support each tribe away from each other tribe and the white settlements. But where would the resources come for that?

"I understand your position," Carson said. "You each speak the truth about the nature of the Dine. But you know that the Navajo say they were at peace with all the tribes until the Spaniards enslaved their people eighty years ago. And they say the same things about you and that they also cannot control their young braves. They say, and we all know it is true, that the Jicarillas and the Utes raided the Dine homes, and brought twenty-one small Navajo girls and at least fifty of their horses to this very place. They believe they are still today looking for either their daughters, granddaughters, horses, or revenge."

Carson looked pointedly at Red Cloud. Red Cloud, who had famously led the most successful raids against the Navajo; whose English was better than any Indian in the agency; and who understandably looked more like an Apache than a Ute.

"And we all know that many of you, while certainly Jicarillas and Utes today, were not born into your tribes," Carson said. "Slavery among the various tribes is poisonous to us all. Just as it is among the white men and the New Mexicans and even the Mexicans. We must all learn to live together. It is the policy of my country to help you live in peace. Here, near your homelands. Somewhere in this circle of violence and stealing and killing, some must learn to stop. We will continue to provide for you if you adopt the new traditions and learn to live in peace with the Cheyenne and the Comanche, and yes, even with the Dine. And I will make it my job to work with your young braves so that they can learn to live in peace with the Navajo."

The Indians, having expected this answer, sat quietly for a while.

William took advantage of the silence.

"Chief Yellow Horse. Will you please tell us a Coyote story?"

The assembled Indians chuckled indulgently. Smiling because Yellow Horse was a master story teller and they loved hearing the stories, even though they'd all heard them many times before.

"How about 'Coyote Hides in Gopher's Mouth'?" Yellow Horse said.

"No. I don't like that one."

William made a face that caused Yellow Horse to laugh.

"How about 'Coyote and the Talking Tree'?"

"Yes. Please? I don't know that one."

"You will like it Chief William," Yellow Horse said. "The Jicarilla people were talking amongst themselves about the famous talking tree. A tree very far away that makes sounds when the wind blows through it. And Coyote overheard and wanted to meet the talking tree. So the people told him where it was. But Coyote didn't believe them. So, since Coyote was not going to believe them, the people decided to lie to Coyote, pointing to trees and telling him that each one might be the talking tree. And Coyote went from tree to tree through all the forests in all the mountains, talking to the trees. But none of the trees would talk back to the foolish Coyote."

Here, Yellow Horse looked to the other Jicarillas to make sure he'd left nothing out.

"After talking to all the trees he could find and finding none of them willing to talk to him, Coyote gave up. But, even from this experience, Coyote did not learn to believe the Jicarillas when they first answered his questions."

"Coyote is always so foolish," William said.

"As are many when confronted by Jicarilla wisdom, my son."

"But where *is* this famous talking tree, Chief Yellow Horse?"

"The talking tree is very far away, Chief William. It is in the Chiricahua Mountains, among a different clan of Apaches."

William thought about what he had learned while Yellow Horse turned his attention back to the other chiefs and William's father.

"We know how you feel Father Kit," Kaniache said. "But we believe the Dine will never do as you ask. They will continue to raid and steal from our people and your people."

He looked at the other two chiefs before continuing.

"There will come a day when the white man will have had enough from the Dine. Just as all Indians have over time. So, we ask only this of you, Father Kit. When the day comes that you decide to hunt down the Dine and bring them to justice, will you allow the Jicarillas and the Utes to be at your side for that great campaign? If you grant us this, we will do all in our powers to bring our young braves under control."

Stunned, Carson reached absently down and rubbed William's head. He realized immediately that his nod, while unintentional, was interpreted by the assembly as his agreement to their request.

10

Lily smiled up at Damours, her black hair spilling out over the pillow. Some of it, wet with sweat, was stuck to her cheek.

"That was nice," she said, touching his cheek with her right palm. "Ya' feel better about things now, Auggy?"

"Is it better with someone you like or is it better with a paying customer," he said.

"I wouldn't say 'better.'" She frowned up at him. "It's more special with you then it was with a guy who was just paying me to show him a good time. That's work. Fucking you is fun."

Why do all the guys need it to be special, she wondered for the millionth time? She remembered sitting up nights in Virginia City, all the girls laughing about it. Did they each really think the girls remembered them after they walked out the door?

They each walked in thinking they were God's gift to women. And the only thing the whores saw on the front of their heads were dollar signs. If you were good at the work, you made 'em feel special. Just like any job and any customer.

Nobody ever made a good living telling their customers what they really thought of 'em.

She pulled his head down onto her naked breasts.

"I want you to get over this, honey. You're my guy. There's no one else. I stopped being a whore six months ago. I don't do that anymore. I just made more money than I could've any other way is all."

"How do I know?"

"C'mon Auggy. I needed the money. I met Cad when I was in Virginia City, and she made me comfortable. Promised to take care of me. And she was just great. She had guards at the Brick House all the time to protect us from any rough stuff."

"But after what Cummings said, I can't help but see you with sodbusters and gunslingers when you're with me."

"C'mon Auggy. I'm not the first girl you ever fucked."

"Sure, but none of them ever paid me for it."

She looked up at his face, above her breasts, and saw that he was now kidding. She reached down and slapped his butt.

"Stop it," she said.

"Okay, but, seriously, if it's so different, what's it like with some guy you're only gonna know for ten minutes?"

"I guess it's a challenge to find out what each guy wants to do. But, unless you already know the guy, you're never relaxed. So you have to be careful and pretend to have fun all the time. It's actually harder with you. The challenge with you is to learn what you want and then give it to you 'cause I want to. And 'cause it feels so good to get loved at the same time as I'm relaxed and giving it."

She rubbed her hands through his hair.

"Besides, what's it like for you? With whores?"

He looked sheepish. "It's more fun. No. I didn't mean that. It's not that it's more fun, it's just that there's no obligation to 'give,' as you put it. You just take what you want until your time's up."

"So it's better?"

"You never have to worry about the girl liking it or not. You just meet 'em and try to have a good time. And when they're being happy, you know they could always just be pretending."

"So you enjoy it more?"

"I guess. No. Of course not. C'mon, I know I got lucky findin' you. For most guys, except at the whorehouses, you're just lucky to find a girl who'll talk to you out here."

He looked down at her. Deadly serious now. Propped up on his elbow.

"How come you and Pepper don't want to be whores anymore? Danson says you're both still after money. Why not work at one of the cribs here?"

"Well, he's right about Pepper." She was surprised to see his eyes widen. "You didn't know? Where'd you think she worked, Auggy?"

"I just thought she was your friend and was working, like you, as a dealer somewhere in Santa Fe."

"Sorry, honey. Pepper works over at Manuela's. I thought you knew. We're just friends. She likes it and doesn't think she can do anything else. Truth is, like most whores, she doesn't have the brains to do much else."

"And you do?" Damours said.

She made a face. Saddened.

"Sorry you could ask that Auggy. I like sex. I like men. And it was the quickest way to get cash. Unlike most of the girls, I saved some money in Nevada. Enough to get me here. But you can't get rich whoring unless you run the place, and I have no interest in dealing with all the girls' problems."

"So what dya' want then?"

"I want to be rich. Really rich. And I want to be rich with the right guy. And then I want to get away from all the roughness and violence out here, and me 'n the guy are gonna live the kinda life worth living. On our own ranch. In the Washington Territory. It's my dream."

"And I'm the guy?"

She kissed the top of his head as she wrapped her legs around him. He wasn't as dumb as some, and he was quick to be trusted. Not bad to look at and as dependable as a puppy.

"Yeah Auggy. You're the guy. God love ya'."

She reached down and put him back inside her.

"You're most definitely the guy."

11

February 19, 1861

It was bitter cold, but morale was good among Bascom's troops in Apache Pass. Cochise's warriors hadn't attacked or been seen in the two weeks since Captain Arnold and his platoon had departed for Fort Marcy at Santa Fe. The Chiricahuas had initially attempted a half dozen sorties to try to rescue the hostages, but each time, were unable to break through.

The American ranchers in the Territory were less lucky. Scores had been killed and their horses and cattle scattered. The head of the Butterfield mail runs, Tom Jeffords, full red beard flowing off both sides of his head like fire off a tree hurtling to the ground in a forest fire, had galloped in one day to report that the Tucson to Fort Bowie mail run had been fully stopped by the Chiricahua raids. He requested the Army's support in order to keep up any type of mail service at all.

But Bascom's mission here was over and the Army was now going to have to organize itself to fully engage the Apaches.

The sentries could hear what sounded like cavalry coming through the Pass.

A scouting patrol appeared, leading three captured Indians.

"We need to speak with Lieutenant Bascom," the Sergeant in charge said.

The Corporal gestured to the Lieutenant's tent as he looked curiously at the three captives. "Over there," he said.

As they arrived at the tent, Bascom emerged. He looked at the soldiers, then at the three Apaches. "What can we do for you, Sergeant?"

"I have orders for you to return to Fort Buchanan, sir."

"And these three Indians?" Bascom said, gesturing to the three expressionless prisoners.

"We caught them red handed with captured horses and cattle from a burned out ranch east of here. We're under orders to execute all warring Apaches we encounter."

"Okay, we need to hang three of ours before we head back, anyway. Cochise has tortured and mutilated the bodies of eight citizens that he refused to turn over to us. They dumped what was left of them on the other side of the Springs last week in the dead of night." He looked over at his own captive Apaches. "Sergeant. Bring your prisoners. We may as well finish this business."

That afternoon, Lieutenant Bascom led the entire contingent of soldiers out of Apache Pass toward Fort Buchanan. With him were Cochise's wife and young son, Naiche.

Left behind, hanging from six separate Cottonwoods, were the six dead Apaches, including Cochise's brother, Coyuntura along with his two sons, Cochise's nephews.

Several hours later, when scouts said the White Eyes were not coming back, Cochise and ten of his men, in loin cloths and full war paint, rode down into the Pass.

The Indians stopped at the bottom of the hill and looked at the six men hanging from the trees. This was an unimaginable desecration of their home. The ten warriors rode toward the stage station, leaving Cochise alone with his grief.

He dismounted and walked over to his brother and nephews, swinging slowly back and forth on their ropes from the wind in the trees. He reached up and tenderly touched the legs of each nephew. He then grasped his brother's left calf and looked toward the Springs, pondering how this had all come to pass.

What could he have done differently? And, if nothing, then what did the Life Giver intend to come of this? Perhaps the priests were right and the nantan was a witch. If not, then were the Chiricahuas being punished for not avenging the torture of Mangas Coloradas? Or for something else? This was their home and the White Eyes were wrong to do this to the People.

Still gripping Coyuntura's lifeless calf, he sadly signaled for his men to come to the Cottonwoods.

He directed them to carefully cut his family down.

"What of these other three," Nahilzay said.

"They are White Mountain Apaches," Cochise said. "Let's give them the respect of a neighboring clan's funeral."

Cochise held each of his dead nephews for a long time while his men watched, their grief mirroring his.

He ordered them back to their camp with instructions to prepare a full ceremonial funeral for his family. He then ordered five of the men to each place a dead Apache respectfully in front of him on his horse. Cradling each with their left arm as they guided their horses reigns up the hill and into the Chiricahuas.

Cochise remained behind, holding his brother in his arms, grieving and thinking about what he needed to do next. Finally, he mounted his horse, and with his brother cradled in front of him, he began the sad ride back to his home.

After returning his brother's body to the camp, Cochise rode silently and alone high up into the Chiricahua Mountain passes to his camp. He spent three full days staring out over the land to the West. All the way to the Dragoons and his Western Stronghold.

He watched the sun set three times over his homeland and the home of all the People.

He did not think it would end well, but no matter how much he tried, he could find no alternative to his decision to join with Mangas Coloradas and all the People in an all-out war against the White Eyes. The White Eyes were so plentiful and the People's homeland so vast, that he had thought whites could learn to live with a mere twelve hundred Chiricahuas.

He knew his wife and son were with the boy soldier at the fort. He would kill all the White Eyes he could. He would like the chance to meet the boy soldier again, so he received no satisfaction from the prophecy that the boy soldier would soon die at the hands of his own people.

The plans of the Life Giver were not known to Cochise. Nor would they ever be. He could only do now what he had to do. The path was as clear as that of the sun travelling over the People's land.

12

February 27, 1861

Major Edward Canby stepped into the Carson household a block up from the Plaza in Taos and tipped his cap to Carson's wife at the door.

"Mornin' Josefa. How ya' doin'?"

"Fine Major. How's your family?"

"Fine. Near's I can tell, they're bearing up well with all the rumors about a coming Civil War. How's your family?"

"We're well. We're very much looking forward to Kit's retirement."

It was an old joke between the two of them. Kit was always retiring and Canby and Josefa both knew the former mountain man wasn't going anywhere.

"Yeah, me too," Canby said. "Soon as the New Mexicans and the Indians are getting along and things settle down in Washington, I'll be looking for his replacement."

Josefa smiled up at the Major, whose unlit cigar was, as always, clamped between his teeth. Canby was second in command of the U.S. Army in the New Mexico and Arizona Territories. Tall, thin, boyish looking because of his clean shaven face, Canby was a career Army officer. West Point class of '39. He was a veteran of the Mexican-American War and Indian wars in Florida, Utah, and now New Mexico, in the futile attempt to reign in the Navajo.

"I'll get Kit," Josefa said. "He's playing with the kids."

Canby again tipped his cap and sat down to wait. He looked fondly around the familiar, sparsely decorated, but warm room as he waited. Two overstuffed chairs were set by the fireplace. The low ceilings accented the coziness of Josefa's touch. It was not hard to see why Carson dreamed of retirement here in Taos, in this home, with his wife and children.

"Don't get up Major," Carson said, entering his favorite room. "How'd it go with your Navajo headmen?"

"They agreed to move all their people east of here," Canby said. "Far to the east. Near Canyon de Chelly. They claimed they would control their young braves. Stop attacking the settlers. Stop taking slaves and stop stealing livestock."

"First time the chiefs have ever agreed on anything," Carson said. "They agree to stop attacking my Utes and Jicarillas?"

"Not too likely. When I asked, they said the Apaches still had their horses and their daughters. Said the Utes and Apaches can't control their young braves, so they need to defend themselves."

"I met with my Indians. They said the same thing about the Navajo."

Canby just nodded.

"But they said something new," Carson said. "They said that we'd have to eventually go after the Navajo because they'd never leave the New Mexicans and the whites alone."

Canby looked surprised. "And?"

"And they want in on the fight when it comes."

"Interesting. Did you hear about the Chiricahuas?"

"Yes," Carson said. "I heard some damn fool West Pointer singlehandedly started a war with Cochise".

Always digging at his friend about the Academy.

"I'm afraid that's precisely what happened. A lot of settlers are going to die over this."

"I'd say more'n a lot," Carson said. "We'd better hope he doesn't hook up with Mangas Coloradas and the Mimbres. The old man has been waiting for his son-in-law to join him."

Carson's looked out into the courtyard as he tried to remember something.

"General Kearny and I met up with Mangas Coloradas fifteen years ago on our way to California during the Mexican-American War. Back then he wanted to join us to kill Mexicans, but we disappointed him. Told him no."

Canby didn't respond.

"What's the latest news from Washington, Major?" Carson said.

"Lincoln's set to be inaugurated in less than a week. Several southern states have already seceded. There's talk of southern sympathizers coming here to take Colorado and New Mexico and Arizona. Every conversation among the officers is who's staying and who's going with the rebels."

The room descended into silence. Neither man wanted to ask the next, obvious, question.

Characteristically, the ex-mountain man waited out the impatient officer.

"Okay," Canby said. "I'll ask you direct. If it comes to it, are you going to join the New Mexico Volunteers or join the rebels?"

Carson smiled as he caught a glimpse of his children, mouths and fingers full of the candy he'd used to bribe them , headed out of the inner courtyard toward the Taos streets.

"It's time for me to retire, Major," Carson said. 'Hell, I'm an old man now. Fifty-five years old. I've fought bears, individual Indians, whole tribes of Indians, gunslingers, Mexicans, and now I'm helping the Indians live in peace. I don't want to kill boys from Kentucky and Texas. Or from Massachusetts or New York, neither."

Canby smiled thoughtfully. "And you've been married almost twenty years and barely know your wife and kids."

"Yeah," Carson said.

"Fifty-one."

"Fifty-one what?" Carson said.

"You're only fifty-one years old, Kit. None of us know who we can and can't count on if war comes. If the rebels really do secede, then the 'boys' as you call them, will be killing each other whether we're involved or not. Nobody's giving any thought to how the Indians are going to react if the Army gets distracted and the Agents stop being able to support them. And now damn Cochise is back on the warpath."

"Who can you count on, Major?"

"Truly?" Canby said. "I don't know. Even Major Sibley, my own brother-in-law, told me himself last summer when we were chasing the Navajo all over the

Territory, that if Lincoln got elected, he wanted me to go to Texas with him and come back here with an Army to make Colorado and New Mexico slave states. Who could have thought it might come to this, me fightin' my own brother-in-law?"

"Sir, if I may?"

"Sure, Kit. What?"

"Major, do you have any idea how bad your officers are? I don't know this damn fool who started the Chiricahuas up again, but if it's not drunkenness and bringing their whores along with them into battle, then it's damn incompetence."

"That's why I can't let men like you retire, Kit."

"I'm from Kentucky, Major. I just don't know."

"Bull, Kit. *I'm* from Kentucky. You moved to Missouri when you were two and lived your whole life out west. There's no way you're gonna sit and allow this Territory to be torn apart and your Indians, poor as they are, left to drift back into chaos."

"It's a lot to ask, Ed. I'm tired. It'd suit me fine to let it all go to hell. Nobody agrees on a solution to this Indian mess. And a war would make it worse."

"I know this, Kit. We need you to help with the Indian mess. And, if in the meantime, we have to work to keep the Territory from falling apart, Colonel Kit Carson will be there for us."

Carson looked up at that.

"Colonel Kit Carson of the New Mexico Volunteers," Canby said.

With that, Major Canby stood, shifted his cigar to the left side of his jaw, and held out his hand.

A thoroughly resigned Kit Carson stood and unenthusiastically shook Canby's hand.

"If you're right, Major, this is going to be one hell of a mess."

"Agreed. One hell of a mess, Kit," Canby said.

And he walked out the door.

13

Cummings and Danson walked into the general store on the south side of the Plaza, down the street from the Exchange Hotel. Cummings looked around, then walked up to a small, bearded Jew behind the counter. "Friend of mine said that you could help us."

"Help you with what?"

He had a very thick European accent.

"We're looking for a partner to help us sell some merchandise we're bringing in."

"What kind of merchandise?"

"She said we could trust you."

The Jew looked more closely at the two men. 'Who is this friend of yours?"

Cummings stepped back and looked more closely around the store. He stepped back up to the counter and held out his hand. "Name's Cummings. Joseph Cummings. This here's my partner Jim Danson."

The Jew didn't even look at the hand. "Nice to meet you. What's the name of your friend?"

"What'd you say your name was?" Cummings said.

"I didn't say," the small shopkeeper said. "You just assumed I was this person your unnamed friend said you could trust. You don't seem to be a very cautious man, Mr. Cummings."

The three men just stood looking at each other. Cummings slowly lowered his hand. "Whaddya think Danson? Are we sure this is someone we want to be in business with?"

The Jew just looked at them. He looked patient. In no hurry.

The shopkeeper had found that it was too easy for a Jew to get in trouble in this country. He and his brother had found that out the hard way in New Orleans almost ten years earlier. And now there was just him. He had learned to be less trusting after his brother's lynching.

Lily had told him that these two would be coming and that they couldn't be trusted. Well, not trusted to do anything but look out for themselves, anyway.

"Look," Danson said. "Joseph here didn't mean anything by his ill manners. We have a shipment of goods coming in from Arizona. Lily Smoot said you were the best possible partner in town."

"Lily would know," he said.

"So," Danson said. "What's your name?"

The Jew looked thoughtful, as if his name was just another product for sale. He finally held his hand out to Danson. "Name's Zapico. David Zapico."

He shook hands with each of the men in turn.

"What kind of a name is Zapico? For a Jew?" Cummings said, failing miserably at regaining any social grace.

Zapico smiled. "You wouldn't believe what it was before the people at the dock in New Orleans took a stab at it."

"Sounds Greek," Cummings said.

"No. It's just an Americanized version of the original German. Look, let me try to make this a little easier... Jim? Joseph? Right?"

"Joseph is fine," Cummings said.

"I'll talk to Lily," Zapico said. "I trust her. If you have a legal claim to the merchandise, we can talk tomorrow night at dinner about what you have in mind."

He looked back and forth between the two men.

"Is that soon enough for you?"

Danson nodded.

"And Lily has to be there or no deal," Zapico said.

"That was just what I was about to say to you, Zapico," Danson said. "You can be sure it will be a very profitable dinner."

"Thank you for your time," Cummings said, tipping his hat. "I'm sorry I wasn't more polite there when we first came in."

Zapico never took his eyes off the two men as they walked casually out of his store, crossed San Francisco Street, and strolled into the Plaza.

Lily came out from the back storage room.

"What do you think?" she said.

"You were right about two things. They aren't smooth and they aren't gun slingers. And Sylvester Mowry was right to ask me to wait until Cummings introduced himself. Cummings might be fine as Mowry's arm in New Mexico and maybe even in the Army, but I need to be his eyes."

"As long as we are careful, David, very, very careful, you and I, this'll work."

"Should, anyway," Zapico said.

14

March 11, 1861

"Is Zapico who we want?" Danson said.

"It's really up to you," Cummings said. "That's your end of the deal. Mowry and I will deliver to whoever you're comfortable with."

They both looked over at Lily.

She just shrugged.

"The Jew said all the right things," Cummings said. "He knows who out here he can trust. You heard him, as long as his side is legit, he'll play."

"Lily," Danson said. "You?"

"I told you before I introduced you that he was your guy. You can trust him as long as he feels he can trust us."

Danson uncorked the bottle of whiskey, took a shot, and passed it over to Damours. He looked thoughtfully at each in turn. "Auggy, how easy is it going to be to get Mowry's equipment through the Jew, into the Army, and then out again, using the Jew to then resell it?"

"Once I'm in the Army, it'll be pretty easy. The Army keeps track of everything. Just not very well."

"And Zapico won't notice it's the same rifles and ammo he sold before?" Danson said.

"Whether you think so or not, I'm pretty good at my job,'" Damours said. "We're good here."

After the meeting finally ended, Lily headed toward work in the gambling hall in the back.

"Hello Lily." A voice behind her and to her right.

An officer at the bar touched his cap as she turned. The voice was familiar but she couldn't place it. And then she saw him.

"Captain Arnold," she said. "You came to Fort Marcy as you promised. It's nice to see you. I'm surprised you found me."

"It's a small town. Pretty easy to find a poker dealer if you know where to look."

"There are dozens of gambling halls in Santa Fe. Not so easy, Captain. I'm flattered you bothered to look."

"Please call me John, Lily. Reserve formal titles for formal occasions."

She laughed.

"Okay, John. It's nice seeing you again. But I have to go to work now. Thanks for making the effort to find me."

He pretended to not have heard the dismissal. "Have you heard that Cochise is at war with the whites now, Lily? And that the Army stole Naiche and Dos-teh-seh from him and have them imprisoned at Fort Buchanan?"

"No." She said. "What happened?"

"It's a long story and you have to go to work."

He winked.

She made a face. "Sorry about that. I have a break in two hours. You want to buy me a drink?"

"Where can I find you?"

"You found me in the town, John. I think you'll be able to find me in the bar."

And she walked into the gambling hall.

15

March 25, 1861

Carson walked into Canby's Fort Marcy office. "So, Canby, how do you think you'll like being the District of New Mexico's new Commander?"

"Pure speculation, Kit."

Carson knew better and he was pretty sure Canby did, too. But he waited for him to answer his question.

"Let me see," Canby held out his hand as he counted fingers. "Lincoln was inaugurated three weeks ago today. Already seven states have seceded from the Union. There are rumors that my brother-in-law Sibley is already headed here with the entire Texas Army. The fine citizens of Tucson and Mesilla met in their secession convention and voted to have the Arizona Territory join the Confederacy nine days ago and elected an idiot as their territorial governor. And the Utes just took 125 horses from some trappers north of here."

He looked at Carson as if he expected some sort of response. Getting none, he went on. "That's six problems before we even get to your opinion of my officers, and thinking about who's staying, who's leaving to join the rebels, and who's even qualified to serve after a few months of drinking and whoring here in Santa Fe."

"Has there been any declaration of war back East?" Carson said.

"No. Virginia, North Carolina, and Maryland are still in the Union. Rumor has it that Lincoln has asked Lee to be the commander of the U.S. Army. I'm sure my brother-in-law is happy as a hog in a briar that Texas seceded."

"Do you think there'll be a war?" Carson said.

"Certainly if the Charleston plantation owners get their way. The wind in Washington blows back and forth. Say what you will about that baboon in the White House, he's a damn good politician. If he can find a way to get Lee to be his General and get the South Carolinians to agree to a compromise, there might not be. But, yes, Kit, I think we're headed for war."

"Then my recommendation to you is get things settled with these Indians here as soon you can. If war comes among white men, those Indians that've trusted us will be left out in the cold. And when the Chiricahuas, Comanches, and Navajos see us fighting 'mongst ourselves, heaven help the settlers, the towns, and the Agency Indians that we've weakened. Heaven help them all."

Lily and Damours were riding back to Santa Fe from the Pojoaque Pueblo. They had been feeling suffocated by their secret relationship, and had needed to get away for a day. They had ridden up in the morning to see what had once been a sizeable pueblo before the Spaniards had come, but now was a sparsely populated shadow of its former self.

They had ridden, talked, and occasionally raced their horses through the sage and Piñons in the morning. The Pueblans had been surprised to see white visitors, especially a woman. The little children were especially curious about Lily. Unable to communicate, Damours and Lily walked around the largely vacant Pueblo. They eventually accepted some meager, indeterminate lunch offerings in exchange for some onions and chilies they had brought.

They were now about an hour into their return ride. Damours occasionally took the lead, but mostly they plodded along side by side.

"What don't I know about what your planning, Lil?"

"I think you know pretty much everything I know. You and Cummings in the Army stealing supplies that Zapico is going to sell for us. Most of it's not going to work out like we plan anyway, Auggy. It's gonna be like herding half wild horses. We know the final destination, but how we're going to get there is a mystery."

"And we don't know who all's going to still be around to show up at the final destination, anyway," he said.

"There's that, of course. Why do you need to know, Auggy? Seems like a waste of time to me."

"Mostly I'm just used to beating people at poker or working small cons with Danson. Not too many loose ends or things I don't control. I feel like someone else is pulling all the strings this time. I'd be comfortable if I knew it was only you, but you've got Mowry who we've never met, Cummings who I don't trust, at least two Indian wars going on, and maybe another really big war coming."

"Once you're in the Army, Auggy, I think it'll feel more like a plan."

"Once I'm in the Army, you and I'll have even less control, Lil. That's partly what's bothering me. Being told what to do and where to go and not being able to see you and being shot at isn't going to make it feel like a plan to me."

"If you want to go back to nickel and dime poker scams, all you have to do is tell Cummings, and he and Mowry will move on to their next plan, Auggy."

"And you and me, Lil? What about your ranch?"

She didn't answer.

He shrugged, pointed, and said, "Race you to that mesa over there."

She laughed and took off before he could. It took him a half mile to pass her, but when he did he just flew by. The only thing between him and the mesa, was a stand of thick Cottonwoods, which he approached at a dead run.

As he passed the trees, seven Mexicans rose up out of a hidden ravine and blocked his way. Lily was too far behind to be seen as he reigned in.

He tipped his cap to the Mexican who rode toward him.

"Hello amigo," the Mexican said. "What's your hurry?"

Damours frowned and cleared his gun on his right hip. "I'm not in a hurry. I'm just breaking in my new horse."

Two of the Mexicans looked over Damours' shoulder, as the lead Mexican suddenly drew on him.

Damours froze. He felt the old, familiar fear go straight up his back. His right hand was useless at his side. He'd never been any good in a fight. Just couldn't get up the nerve to follow through. Nerves of steel at the poker table or when he was conning a mark, but when it came to physical force he was always paralyzed at the moment.

And now he could hear Lily's horse galloping toward them. He felt useless, and feared that all the good and all the expectations of the past three weeks was about to fall dead at his horse's hooves.

"Friend of yours?" The Mexican grinned and nodded over the sweating Damours' left shoulder. "Don't go for that gun, amigo. Let's see what your lady friend has to say before you get yourself killed, okay?"

"Like I said, senor, we're just out breaking in these two horses," knowing he sounded weak as soon the word "senor" left his mouth.

He could hear Lily slow down as she approached, pulling up about thirty yards abreast and to his left.

"Friends of yours Auggy?" she said.

"Very funny, senorita," the Mexican said. "Buenas tardes. Your friend here has not had too much to say."

Damours started to say something and the Mexican cut him off by holding his gun vertically up to his lips in the universal gesture to shut up.

Damours clenched his teeth.

"I'm talking to the senorita. You had your chance cowboy."

Fear gripped Damours' every nerve, as the other six Mexicans now drew their pistols.

"You have nothing to gain by bothering us, sir," Lily said. "We're just riding by ourselves on to Santa Fe. We've got nothing worth taking. Certainly nothing worth having the U.S. Army come looking for you."

"I think, senorita, that I will decide that. You would make a grand prize back in Sonora. And I don't think the U.S. Army is going to risk having to fight the Mexican Army and the Arizona Apaches just to bring back one senorita. Do you?"

"You have no idea who we are."

He smiled. "Okay, bonita senorita. Who are you?"

"I am a very close friend of both Kit Carson and Captain John Arnold."

"And him?" Pointing to Damours and laughing. "Is he also a good friend of the famous mountain man, Kit Carson? We are all very terrified, senorita. All seven of us."

Lily looked over at Damours, as if seeing him for the first time.

"Well," she started....

"No, senorita, let me guess. He is a famous gunfighter and poker player. Senor Carson hired him to protect you, but, as it turns out, he's not such a good gunfighter."

Damours turned as red as his kerchief. He was furious at himself. He thought he'd long gotten past this, but he was frozen in place.

The Mexican turned in his saddle and said to one of his men, "Maybe this gringo could teach some of you to play better poker once we get home, while I play with the senorita."

They all laughed.

Damours was helpless to do anything, so he just sat, getting more and more depressed as the scene unfolded. He looked plaintively at Lily.

"Either you're gonna get around to killing us," she said. "Or you're gonna let us go. I don't think any of the nine of us here think you can really ride with two healthy, resisting hostages in the saddle for two weeks all the way to Mexico."

"You make a good point," the Mexican said. "Your beauty on the outside is not matched by your mouth, senorita."

"I don't see much point in you sitting around making fun of us, senor," she said. "Decide and let's get on with it."

He motioned three of his men over in front of Lily and the other three in front of Damours. He then rode up to Lily.

"It's too bad about your mouth, senorita. You would have lived a little longer if not for that. I would have enjoyed you in Senora."

He raised his pistol and aimed at her chest. Damours started to turn his horse and found himself staring into the barrels of three revolvers.

The leader waved his pistol as he held his hand out.

"No," he said. "He is a coward. Make him watch what we do to his senorita first."

Again, he raised his outstretched pistol toward Lily's chest.

And then he gagged. Blood rushed down his chest and arched toward Lily. His pistol shot harmlessly at the ground as the tip and front ten inches of an arrow protruded from his neck.

The other six Mexicans whirled around, too late. A fusillade of arrows took all six of them and two of their horses down. One of them tried to pull himself and his horse back up and a lone rifle shot drove him back into the ground.

Twenty Utes, half on foot the rest on horseback, came rushing up to Lily and Damours.

"You okay?" said the first Indian that reached them.

Both Damours and Lily nodded.

"Where did you come from?" Damours said, realizing immediately that there were several better openings. Even "thank you" might have been a better start.

"These mexicanos robbed our village yesterday." He pointed back behind him toward the northeast. "They surprised you from the ravine. It was not very difficult for us to do the same."

"They were actually about to kill us," Damours said.

"No doubt. You would have been a nuisance as captives, and you would tell the soldiers at Fort Marcy if they let you go."

"Is there some way we can repay you?" Lily said.

The Indian shrugged. "I don't see how. You should be all right from here back to Fort Marcy, but we can go with you if you like."

Lily looked at the dead Mexicans and horses, and shuddered.

"No," she said. "We should be okay. What is your name? And how do we find you to repay you?"

"I am Red Cloud, from Agent Carson's reservation. Agent Carson can always find us."

And with that, Red Cloud took the five living Mexican horses and turned back with his men toward the ravine.

Lily and Damours took one last glance at the seven dead Mexicans left unceremoniously in the dust, and headed wordlessly back to Santa Fe.

16

"Hey, Auggy," Lily said. Damours was spooning her in her bed when the two of them woke up from their naps.

He kissed the back of her wet neck. "Um, what, Lil?"

"I think I solved our problem," she said.

"Which one?"

"The only one I know of." She rolled over and looked at his face. "I think I solved how to get you a non-fighting position in the Army."

"That's not *our* problem, Lil. That's my problem."

"We don't have any unshared problems, Auggy."

He sat up, put his hands together at the back of his head and stared out the window.

She put her head in his lap. "It's okay, honey. We already went through this. I'm not looking for a fighter. I'm looking for a lover. And a ranch builder."

"I've never been much of a carpenter either, Lil."

"You know what I mean, Auggy. When we're done here, we can buy all the carpenters in the Washington Territory. I can't do this without you, so it's gonna be our ranch, not mine."

He stroked her hair absently.

"You're the best con man ever. So you're not so good at shootin' people? Nobody's perfect."

She bit his stomach until he laughed.

"Okay," he said. "I'll bite…." And she punched him lightly. "How are we getting me into an Army where I don't have to fight?"

"I know a priest here at the church who is looking for help with the church's books. I told him I knew the perfect guy for the job."

"And?"

"And he just happens to know the priests who are close to the key officer of the New Mexican Volunteers, Rafael Chacon."

"And?"

"C'mon. You have to do something, Auggy. I can't do everything."

He rubbed her head while he thought. That just might work. Worth a try anyway. Bookkeeper for the Union Army? It had a nice ring to it.

"You ever hear of a bookkeeper getting shot, Lil?"

"Sure, Auggy. Happens all the time. Just keep your books over your chest, 'n you'll be fine."

17

April 12, 1861

Lily and Captain Arnold were having lunch in a café off the Santa Fe Plaza.

"If there's a Civil War John, what will happen here?"

"Maybe nothing. Southern sympathizers in the Arizona Territory will side with the rebels, but they have no ability to bother us here in New Mexico. Our only risk is if the Texans try to take the western Territories for the rebels. But I think that's a long shot. If there's a war, the rebels will probably have their hands full back East."

"It would be a mess to be here in the middle of a war," she said. "I probably wouldn't have come if I'd thought much about that. I don't think there'd be much protection for bar maids and poker dealers."

"First there has to be a war, Lily. And I think you'll do just fine. The rebels aren't likely to have anything against pretty poker dealers."

He smiled as she went back to eating.

"What about your wife and sons in Maryland, John? Will they be okay?"

He shrugged. "Like I keep sayin', first there has to be a war. Then it has to reach up to Maryland. And I have no idea where I'll be by then. I can't worry about it."

The two worked on their dinners, lost in their thoughts.

"I was hoping tonight," Arnold said. "To get around to discussing where you're thinking of going next? After dealing cards in Santa Fe?"

"I don't have a clue. This conversation sounds like I'm finally getting the father I never had. You looking for a daughter, John?"

Peering up at him from her steak, she expected him to look surprised or hurt. But instead he looked thoughtful. He looked out over the Plaza.

"Perhaps I am, Lily. I've never had one. I enjoy our time together. I'll think about that."

Lily sat at the end of the table, with her back to the window. She'd been quiet most of the night. Cummings and Danson, as usual, did most of the talking. And almost all the drinking.

The noise level in the saloon was so loud that there was little danger of being overheard. But the men relied on her for security, so she pretended not to listen to them while she looked continuously around the room.

Everybody knew the whores were upstairs, but that didn't stop the men in the bar from trying to get her attention. Especially the soldiers.

Spending the night looking around a Santa Fe bar, you can hardly expect the guys not to look back, she thought. None of the men in the saloon expected a woman to be at the tables who wasn't a working girl.

"Danson," Cummings said. "Did Zapico sell the stuff down in Albuquerque when and where he said he would?"

"Yes. And at our price, not his."

"Mowry says we can expect the next shipment next week," Cummings said.

All three men sipped at their whiskey.

"How does Mowry get his stuff through when everybody else is stopped by the Apaches?" Danson said.

"Back way," Cummings said.

"Is this next shipment the illegal stuff for the Army, or is that the next one," Damours said.

Cummings looked around, but Lily signaled him that it was safe to talk openly. Nobody was paying them any attention. "No. We need at least one more dry run with the Jew before we can start to process that stuff through him. Also, you and I have to be in the Army for that to work. Last time I checked you hadn't joined the Volunteers yet, Auggy."

"I'm workin' on my introduction to Chacon through the priests, just like we discussed. Waddyathink, the priests are just gonna introduce me because I ask them to? Getting close to Chacon is critical, and that's not happening unless the priests really believe in me."

"Lily, you and I continue to play Zapico from the outside," Danson said. "Ultimately, we use him to hide our guns and whiskey shipments going in, and our money coming out?"

"And Zapico knows about this?" Lily said

"Not now," Cummings said. "Maybe never. Depends on how it plays out. How he plays it."

"When do you go into the Army, Cummings?" Lily said.

"Maybe a month yet for me," Cummings said. "More like two for the kid unless we can find a way to speed up the priests."

"If you ask me," Lily said. "This whole thing is going too slow. You got contingencies for who's gonna be a rebel and who's not? You ready to deal with the Texans when they get here if you're backing the wrong horse and they blow your plans all to hell?"

"That's why I'm taking it careful," Cummings said. "Last I heard, there was no war. Not yet, anyway. We'll be ready to deal with it if it comes. We've got contingencies for everything."

Lily smiled to herself. Well, all except for the two or three that you ain't gonna see comin', mister.

No, make that four.

18

Word had reached Santa Fe that the Civil War had begun. Predictably in Charleston. At Fort Sumter, some eleven days before.

"In light of the War news, you comfortable with how things are developing with these guys so far, Lily?" Zapico said.

"I think Cummings has the right idea after all," Lily said. "Play it both ways until we see how it goes. He's got Damours going into the New Mexico Volunteers while he waits to see which way it's going before he chooses sides. That way we're covered either way."

"Well, that's the way Mowry told me he wanted Cummings to play it."

"The Rebels might or might not let the Texans come up here to take New Mexico and Colorado. We'll have to wait and see," she said. "Tell me, Zapico, do you think Cummings is good enough for this job? Mowry's putting a lot on this one guy."

"I don't know. If Mowry's just trying to make money, then probably. But if Mowry's thinking higher, politics? Inserting himself into the winning military picture? A governorship? A country separate from either the Rebels or the Union? Who knows? But if that's what Mowry's ultimately after, then, no, I don't think Cummings is good enough for what he's after."

"Do you think Cummings knows we have a direct line to Mowry?"

The big Jew laughed. "None of 'em are that good, Lily. No. Cummings couldn't hide it and there'd be no point. Cummings thinks he's playing me for Mowry and he's got his hands full with Danson and the kid."

"And the two of them?" Lily said.

"The kid's perfect. He's already wormed himself into the Church and the Governor's offices, and he's a natural con man. He'll get into the Army soon enough. As long as the Texans don't run over the Army here, the kid'll have most of the Territory's money for us in two years."

He laughed again. "The weak link is Danson. Danson could screw the whole thing up without half trying. Whether Mowry's after power or merely money, Danson will always be the one I worry about."

"So," she said. "Money or power? Which is it for Mowry?"

"I think all Mowry wants is the money for now. Depending on the outcome, he'll decide what's next after the war."

"Then my answer to your question," she said. "Is that we're doing fine. It's going just fine. It's my job to take care of Danson. You can consider it taken care of. Say hi to Sarah and the kids for me."

Without another word she walked out the side door into the alley, and disappeared into the Plaza.

At precisely that moment, seventy miles to the northeast, Kit Carson and a dozen men were raising the American flag in the main square of Taos. As word of the outbreak of war back in South Carolina had spread through the town, most of the citizens had gathered to cheer for the Stars and Stripes.

A few southern sympathizers openly jeered.

Carson and the others agreed to divide up the watch, setting a round the clock guard at the base of the flag pole. They intended to fly the flag all day and all night.

The tension, if not the fight, had arrived in the New Mexico Territory.

19

May 12, 1861

Even back in his mountain man days, Carson had loved nothing more than to compete with Indians on horseback. And, oh how *they* loved competing against him.

Today, Carson had taken forty of his Utes and Jicarillas out to the plains west of Taos for a relay race on horseback.

The hardest part about getting his Utes and Jicarillas to compete, though, was that the two Jicarilla clans preferred competing with each other rather than working together. The Jicarilla Apaches were composed of the llaneros, moon/plants, clan, and the olleros, sun/animals, clan. The two clans were in continuous competition with each other, culminating in an annual festival and relay race between the two every Fall.

As a result, Yellow Horse and Carson had to work with the Jicarillas to get them to work together, Carson insisting that they not divide up by their usual tribal clans.

Kaniache and Red Cloud quickly ordered their twenty Ute horsemen into two lines, and then turned to watch in merriment as Carson worked to get the Apaches organized.

Once the Jicarillas were finally ready, the first two competitors took off at Carson's sign. Each had, of course, been chosen for their speed, and there was no strategy. They matched each other stride for stride like twin bolts of lightning across the plain toward their waiting ten tribe members. There wasn't an inch of difference between them across the entire distance of more than half a mile.

And so it went for the first three pairs of riders. The thunder of hooves accompanied by the whoops of the young men. The lust for competition filled each of them with a need to outrace his opponent.

At this point, Red Cloud pushed in front of the next Ute in line. As the onrushing two horsemen reached the waiting Red Cloud and his Jicarilla opponent, Red Cloud suddenly pulled his horse straight at the surprised Jicarilla, and then took off. He reached the waiting horseman a full three lengths in the lead.

In the midst of organizing his Apaches around this new situation, Carson noticed that Red Cloud had not come back to the line of Utes. He was now a few hundred yards to the west, kneeling by his horse and staring across the plains.

Carson motioned to Yellow Horse to reorganize his men to try to regain the lead, and then galloped to Red Cloud.

Red Cloud signaled him to be cautious.

When he reached Red Cloud, Carson dismounted and joined the Ute chief.

They searched the horizon together in silence.

"There. Did you see that?" Red Cloud pointed to a spot on the horizon.

"I see it," Carson said. "How many are there?"

"Ten. Maybe more."

"Who are they?"

"Dine."

He spat in the dirt at his feet.

"You can't tell that from here. I was chasing Navajos before you were born, Red Cloud. You just have Dine on the brain."

Carson expected him to laugh along, but he just received a baleful stare from the Ute chief. Without a word, Red Cloud grabbed his horses reigns with his left hand, vaulted onto its back, and took off at a gallop toward the now empty horizon.

Carson lifted himself onto his saddle and galloped off after the stubborn Indian.

When they reached the Rio Grande canyon, Red Cloud was sitting on his horse looking down at what was indeed a party of Navajos on horseback, now deep in the canyon. Maybe a dozen or so.

"What the hell are they doing out here," Carson said, more to himself than to Red Cloud.

"We can go and find out. There are forty of us."

"They have too big a lead. We're out here for a party, not a fight. We aren't armed nearly enough if they are joining up with others somewhere down there."

Carson leaned out over the edge looking down into the canyon. "So, what are they doing here?"

"What they're always doing," Red Cloud said. "The Dine warriors have no respect for the promises of their chiefs. They're looking for women and children and sheep. You whites are naïve. You don't understand the Navajo."

He turned his horse around to head back. "We will all pay a heavy price some day for the white man's ignorance of the Dine."

Then he had second thoughts. He turned back and slid down the canyon siding to a ledge about twenty feet below where they had been standing. To a spot where he could see the descending Navajo and their horses.

Before Carson could react, Red Cloud had fitted an arrow and released it in an arc high and to the left, toward the gliding Rio Grande below.

Seconds later there was an eruption of yelps from below and Red Cloud rose and pointed at the war party that was now looking up at him. He stood in full view of the Navajos and unleashed one more arrow.

He then climbed up to rejoin Carson. Both now on the edge of the canyon, invisible to the Navajos below.

Carson turned his horse to ride back to his Indians and the announcement he had come here to make.

Red Cloud joined him and the two rode in silence for several moments.

"Red Cloud, what do you consider to be your home?" Curious to see how the Ute would handle this unanswerable question.

"Home is a white man's concept, Father Kit. You force the Utes to live in this place. It is not our choice to be here. Why do you ask me this?"

"But I know, proud as you are, that you are no Ute."

"You are wrong, Agent Carson. I have reached manhood among the Utes and they are my people. I am as much a Ute as your adopted Navajo son, taken from his Ute enslavement, will someday be a white man."

"But many whites will always see an Indian when they look at my son. So, in some sense, he will not be a white man."

"In all senses I am a Ute, Agent Carson. And I have no home in the white man's sense."

"Have you no curiosity about your Chiricahua ancestors? Living in the land of the Talking Tree? I'm told that you are cousin or nephew to Cochise."

"I am a Ute, Father Kit. Mother Earth belongs to all of us, yet you whites feel a need to wrongly own parts of her. Watch the Dine and see how they are going to respect your white man's concept of home."

He stopped his horse and turned to face Carson.

"Father Kit, you are a good man. For a white man. I think you feel you are doing the right thing by caring for the conquered Jicarillas and Utes. But penning us in is destroying us. The Jicarillas are resorting to begging in Santa Fe for their livelihood. And the Dine will now make all of us pay for your misguided belief that creating a home for them will work."

Red Cloud looked over at the Indians, waiting for them to return.

"Now, Father Kit, come tell us what you brought us here to tell us. What is to happen to us now."

He rode off, leaving an astonished Carson sitting on his horse, looking after him.

He had told no one that he was here to make an announcement.

Carson looked at his assembled Apaches and Utes. They sat impassively in a semi-circle around the fire before him. The collection of bedraggled Jicarillas and gloating Utes made any questions about the outcome of the relay race unnecessary.

Carson hesitated before speaking. Hell, it had been easier to tell Josefa. He still wasn't sure how much to tell them. Wasn't sure how they would make sense of what was about to happen out here.

"I am going to leave for a while. For a great long while, actually. Maybe forever. There will be a new Agent taking my place, as I have resigned and am joining the Army. You will have to move to Cimarron. Once a new agent has been hired, he will come to arrange the move so that all of your peoples will still be together. Nothing else will change."

Characteristically, after an appropriate silence, Yellow Horse spoke first. "Father Kit, thank you for coming to us with this news and congratulations on your promotion."

It was not unusual for the Jicarilla to make jokes when he was starting serious negotiations. All the Indians smiled and looked back and forth as Carson acknowledged the joke with a nod.

"But," he said. "Why do you join the Army? Is this about a great war on the Chiricahuas?"

"No, my friend, this has nothing to do with any Apaches."

"Then," Red Cloud said. "Is this the war against the Dine that we have discussed? Have you come to honor our request to join you in fighting the Dine?"

"No, Red Cloud, we are not fighting the Navajo. We white men are fighting each other. Many Americans back East have broken with The Great Chief Lincoln."

Carson then stumbled through an explanation of the issues in the Civil War, knowing he was raising more questions than he was answering.

"Why do some whites care if others have slaves?" Kaniache said. "Why stop someone you don't know from having a slave you don't know?"

"Yes," Yellow Horse said. "Can't the slaves' own families fight to get them back?"

"Why," Red Cloud said. "Would you whites kill your own people to free slaves you don't know when you won't even let us fight to get our own people back from the Dine?"

He explained the issue of African slaves as best he could, then moved on to the moral issue. "Many whites believe people should not be slaves. That is one reason we are stopping the Navajo from taking your people. And you from taking theirs."

"So," Kaniache said. "Chief Lincoln believes it is wrong and he is willing to have white people kill other whites to prevent this?"

"Yes."

"Then why is it we are enslaved here," and he waved his right arm over the plains. "And not allowed to be free to follow the bear during the seasons? Why must we be forced to live with the Jicarillas? Why does not Chief Lincoln send you to kill those whites who enslave us here?"

Why indeed, Carson asked himself, not surprised that his Indians saw through the hypocrisy of the American policies. "You," and here Carson used a Ute word that indicated all the people, "are here so we can protect you from white men who see killing you as their only alternative. As we've discussed, there are good and bad whites, just as there are good and bad Navajo."

He stood to leave.

"And now," Carson said. "The whites will fight each other rather than you. Be thankful for that. Be safe and trust yourselves to your new Agent. I look forward to when next we meet and when, hopefully, all the killing and fighting will stop."

He turned, mounted his horse, and started the ride back to Taos.

The mountain man who became Indian fighter who became Indian caretaker, now rode off to become a killer of Texans.

PART II
THE TEXANS

20

The advanced force of two hundred fifty Texas Cavalry arrived at Fort Bliss in El Paso, Texas in the blistering heat of the Texas desert.

A little over 300 miles north, Kit Carson entered Canby's Fort Marcy office for the first time since Canby had taken over the Department of New Mexico and Carson had been made head of the New Mexico Volunteers.

Canby looked up at his old friend and smiled. "How's Josefa?"

"She's fine. Sends her regards. Wanted me to especially thank you for talking me out of retirement again."

The two sat down across from each other in Canby's Fort Marcy office.

"Where do things stand with your Volunteers and with things here?" Canby said.

"The soldiers sympathetic to the Confederacy resigned and rode down to Fort Fillmore two weeks ago. We expect them to pick up more on their route down to Mesilla and then probably Fort Bliss. All the New Mexico Volunteers will be loyal to New Mexico, and most of your remaining soldiers should be fine. Those who wanted to join with the Rebels already had their chance."

"What will we need, Kit, to defend New Mexico from the Texans?"

"More forces."

Canby frowned. "How much recruiting have you done, Kit?"

"The New Mexico Volunteers have been volunteering and disbanding and volunteering and disbanding for hundreds of years. Fighting against the Cheyenne, the Comanches, the Navajo, then Kearny and me and the U.S. Army fifteen years ago, and now the Rebels. Probably against the Spanish before there even was a New Mexico."

"So you're avoiding telling me you haven't done any recruiting."

Carson smiled at his friend. "Recruiting's never really been necessary. Whenever their homes and farms have been threatened, New Mexicans have stood up."

"So when did you and Chacon start the training?"

"None of us were sure which way the Federals out here would go until now, sir. To have mobilized too soon risked losing manpower that might have been ordered to join the Rebels."

Canby nodded.

"It'll take two, three months to get them mobilized and ready," Carson said.

Canby shifted his cigar to give Carson time to reduce his estimate, but he didn't. "And when do we expect General Sibley and his Texans?" Canby said.

"Last we heard Sibley was still back in Virginia with Jefferson Davis. Still trying to convince the Rebels that he should be allowed to move against us. If he gets permission, he'll bring the Texans here January, February at the earliest."

"And the advance force of Texans?" Canby said.

"I wouldn't call two hundred fifty cavalry much of a force," Carson said. "At most they'll be a minor nuisance. It's commanded by that idiot, John Baylor. He hates Indians more than he does Lincoln. Maybe Cochise will turn out to be a blessing in disguise for us, finish off Baylor."

"Excellent plan, Kit."

"Well," Carson said. "Baylor's Texans will have their hands full with the Apaches in any case. Even with the deserters and the southern sympathizers in Mesilla added to his two hundred fifty, these advance Texans aren't much of a threat."

"Any other possible reinforcements, Kit?"

"There are rumors that the Colorado Volunteers are organizing to come down here and that Carleton is organizing an Army in California to march here."

"Unfortunately," Canby said. "There is no way that the Californians can organize, get across the desert, and then through the Apaches to us before next Spring. It's going to have to be you, me, and the Coloradans, Kit. How quickly can you get Chacon's New Mexicans here?"

"A week at most. We'll need to send someone to Denver to let Colorado know we need their help."

"Yes," Canby said. "Have them take Tom Jeffords with them to Colorado, one of the best scouts from Arizona. He'll see them through any Indian problems."

Carson stood.

"One more thing, Kit. Make sure that Chacon double times on getting the Volunteers here and organized. We aren't likely to have your three months."

A little over a mile below them, a block off the Plaza, Lily and Damours sat with Zapico.

"No question but that the Army is starting the resupply process in earnest," Damours said. "I should have those supply orders for you by tomorrow. The next day at the latest. And our stuff from Arizona is now being delayed. Apaches or encroaching Rebel armies are both being blamed."

"I thought you weren't in the Army yet, Auggy," Zapico said.

"I'm not. Father Ussel keeps putting me off. Says there's no point until Chacon starts mustering in the Volunteers. Besides, the more I work with the quartermaster guys, the closer I'm getting to 'em. I'll be in the Army at the right time in the right place and long enough for everything we need. You two have nothing to worry about from me."

"Who then?" Lily said, teasing him.

Damours laughed. "The damned Rebels, the drought, and Danson. Not necessarily in that order."

21

July 21, 1861

Cochise's war party entered Mangas Coloradas' Cooke's Canyon camp at midday, having ridden almost two hundred miles from the Santa Cruz Valley south of Tucson.

After dismounting, Cochise approached his father-in-law. He knew the 70 year-old chief had been wanting this moment for months, so he was very direct. "The Chiricahuas accept the Mimbres' invitation to join you in throwing the White Eyes out of the land of the People. Our gift of cattle and mules we took from the soldiers at Fort Buchanan will be here in two days."

"Any news of the boy soldier who killed your family and took my daughter and grandson?"

"We attacked Fort Buchanan and fought a skirmish with him, but he ran away. We killed many of the soldiers that the coward left behind. But, our priests continue to tell us that he cannot be killed by us. That he will die at the hands of the White Eyes themselves."

"Ours tell me the same," Mangas Coloradas said. "I am also told that the White Eyes have since abandoned Fort Buchanan. You have done well, my son. The soldiers know they can no longer keep our land. A runner told us yesterday that Dos-Teh-Seh and your son are now safely back at your Stronghold."

"I will see them then when I return home. But I will not stop trying to kill the boy soldier. He deserves a long and dishonorable death, and I will not rest until he and his White Eyes are gone from our home."

"Do you know the fate of the miners in Apache Pass three weeks ago?" Mangas Coloradas said.

Cochise motioned to Nahilzay who threw a satchel to the ground in front of Mangas Coloradas.

"It's all the gold and silver they had on them," Cochise said. "They all lie naked under the trees where the boy soldier hung my brother and nephews. Like the soldiers, the miners are learning it is no longer safe to be here."

There was a long silence between the two warriors, as Chiricahuas and Mimbres waited together for the word that it was to be the all-out war they had been seeking.

"It is the time of reckoning for the White Eyes," the older chief said.

That afternoon, one of the Mimbres scouts galloped into camp and spoke briefly to the two chiefs. The three Apaches then went among the warriors gathering all who were ready to fight, and left for the canyon.

A half mile from the eastern entrance, Cochise saw a wagon pulled by four mules accompanied by five mounted men moving toward them, the sun setting in their faces. He organized the men so that half hid out of sight, overlooking the rocks where they all now lay, silencing their horses. He directed the rest to the other side of the pass where they would be level with the encroaching wagon, but hidden by the trees.

Within hours of joining forces, the Life Giver had presented the Apaches with a clear signal. This war against the White Eyes would be successful.

And it would not be difficult.

The wagon, preceded by three of the riders and flanked by the other two, came abreast of the trees that hid the Apaches. Cochise could see that there were two men on the buckboard, one driving and the other holding a shotgun and looking intently into the trees.

All were miners or hired guards. There were no soldiers. He could not see what was in the wagon that was trailed by two spare mules.

After allowing the wagon to pass the trees, Cochise and Juh shot the two mules on the right side. The lead mule fell dead on the spot, but the second mule was only wounded.

He reared and bucked and roared and pulled back desperately, the streaming blood and whites of his eyes visible all the way up into the boulders.

As the miners and guards wheeled to the right to shoot up into the boulders where the gunfire had come from, the invisible Apaches in the trees, came whooping low on their horses from the other side. The two trailing riders and the left lead guard went down before they even knew they were being attacked from the trees.

The two on the buckboard were thrown from the wagon. The one with the shotgun landed hard and was immediately jumped by two of the Mimbres who clubbed him unconscious.

After releasing the mules in hopes that would satisfy their attackers, the driver and the remaining two scrambled to set up a defensive perimeter in the rocks around the wagon. They kept up a continuous fusillade through and around the wagon at the Apaches who kept racing in and out of the trees and firing down upon them from the boulders.

The three desperate survivors kept up a continuous gun battle with over two hundred Apaches. For their part, the exultant and confident warriors kept up a relentless barrage of arrows and rifle fire.

One by one, the white men were wounded, and then eventually mortally dispatched before the fighting finally ended early the following day. The Apaches suffered twenty-three dead and nearly a hundred wounded.

In exchange for their heavy losses and expended ammunition, the Apaches gained four healthy mules, five horses, dozens of rifles and pistols, a small amount of ammunition, and seven dead White Eyes.

Cochise designated three warriors to scalp three of the dead guards. All seven men were stripped where they lay and the Apaches set upon them with knives, clubs, and pistols. Each was shot in the head for good measure.

Mangas Coloradas surveyed the scene and the damage. He turned to Cochise and said, "If all the People were as brave and as strong as these seven White Eyes, we could conquer the world."

Cochise nodded in agreement, and gave his father-in-law one of the scalps.

There was nothing of value in the wagon. They galloped back to camp with the lead rider of each of the two clans triumphantly carrying a scalp aloft on his lance.

The all-out war had started. The blessing of war ceremony would now be long and would begin in triumph.

But the two chiefs were sobered by the high cost of their first battle.

22

July 22, 1861

Damours entered Father Ussel's Taos office. Father Gabrielle had assured him that all proper introductions had been made, but Damours' limited experience with the New Mexico Church left him necessarily uncomfortable.

One slipup with this priest, who had put him off for weeks, and they had all wasted six months.

"Are you Augustine Damours?" the ancient priest said from behind his desk.

"Yes, Father. Father Gabrielle suggested that I meet with you for an introduction to Rafael Chacon."

"Yes, he told me."

The old priest looked at the papers on his desk and began to search for something among them.

For a minute, Damours feared he had been dismissed, or, worse, that the old priest had simply forgotten him. Unsure what to do, he decided to just stand there.

Eventually, the priest looked back up at Damours. "What do you know of Chacon, young man?"

Damours was surprised. He had expected Father Ussel to ask him about himself and had prepared an elaborate lie that would assure the introduction they all felt he needed. "Not much I'm afraid, Father."

It seemed a potentially useful answer. Its main virtue was that it was the truth, and, whereas Damours was often out of his league when resorting to the truth, it felt right here. His likeability was going to be his lone asset. Either Father Gabrielle had obtained Ussel's prior approval, or most likely Damours was going fail here.

"Most of us here are products of the Spaniards and the native Pueblo Indians who are scattered throughout the Territory," Father Ussel said. "Rafael included. Both he and his father fought the Americans and General Kearny just outside of Santa Fe in Apache Canyon in Glorieta Pass when they came here fifteen years ago to conquer us. Rafael was a mere thirteen year old boy. The Chacons come from a long line of fighting, oppressed New Mexicans. They have been fighting Navajos, Apaches, Comanches, Cheyenne, Spaniards, and, finally, Americans for as long as they have a memory."

The priest again shuffled through his papers, peering as if he was having trouble reading something.

"Rafael joined with Kit Carson to defeat the Muache Utes and Jicarilla Apaches after the 1854 massacre at the Fort Pueblo trading post. He and Carson have been inseparable since. And now that the Americans have tired of fighting everyone else and are now fighting each other, Rafael and Carson will now fight together against the Texans when they come."

"When does Chacon expect to finish forming the Volunteers, Father?"

"I think events are pushing them all now. Maybe a week. Maybe ten days."

"Father, I have written this letter laying out how I can help Chacon. Father Gabrielle suggested that you might consider making the introduction on my behalf."

He handed him the sealed letter, and the fate of Joseph Cummings' and Lily Smoot's plan passed from his hand to the Father's.

"Son, why are you involving yourself in all this? Chacon and Carson and the regular soldiers and Volunteers have been fighting bears and Indians and each other since before you were born. It's in their nature and they live for it. Their homes, families, and, for some, their careers are at stake. And, besides," and here he actually chuckled, deep down in his throat, "They all like fighting. These are very rough men you suddenly want to be a part of. Much tougher than what you have experienced in the gold mines and the gambling halls of California and Arizona, young man."

Since lying was what he did best, Damours had no choice now but to resort to ingratiating himself with Ussel.

"Father, as I explain in my letter to Chacon, my family is Spanish and comes from just outside of Albuquerque. My mother, Alita Martinez, made a mistake and married a traveling French financier who, sadly, is my father. He just left with her with no word. I returned to find my family no longer in New Mexico. I've decided to remain in the Territory. I feel a duty to help the Volunteers keep New Mexico from becoming a slave state. And becoming slaves to the Texans."

"Then why did you not tell Father Gabrielle of your heritage?"

"He never asked and I didn't think it mattered until you just questioned my motives."

He couldn't remember ever lying to a priest before. Were there, he wondered, worse consequences for lying to a priest than, say, to a General or a Marshal?

Ussel stared silently at the young boy before him from under his dark eyebrows. Like some predator lying in wait in the mountains. Damours knew from experience not to turn his back on predators. Not to speak out of turn or out of weakness. He just stared back, all innocence.

"Father Gabrielle said you are talented with numbers. With tracking and saving money. Is this what you wish to do for the Volunteers? Or do you wish to fight for them?"

"My impression is that 'choice' is not a word in the Army language," he replied.

Ussel smiled. "I will deliver your letter to Chacon," he said. "God be with you, young son of Senorita Martinez. No, Senora Damours, of Albuquerque."

23

August 3, 1861

The civilian standing before Canby and Carson had arrived to describe the events of the past ten days at Mesilla and Fort Fillmore.

"You're our first eye witness," Canby said. "The rumors of a total disaster at Fort Fillmore are hopefully unfounded."

"You have no eye witnesses from the Army, Colonel Canby. I doubt battle news gets much worse than that."

Canby indicated he should proceed.

"On July 25th, the Texans marched north, right past Fort Fillmore and arrived in Mesilla. Major Lynde followed them and offered them the opportunity to surrender. We lost three men plus several wounded in the skirmish that followed their refusal. Upon the first Rebel shots, Major Lynde ordered a retreat back to Fort Fillmore. That night he ordered preparations to abandon Fort Fillmore and retreat west, to Fort Stanton."

"Fort Stanton?" Canby said. "Why not the shorter march north to Fort Craig? To reinforce the troops there?"

"Sir, with respect. Major Lynde feared that the Texans, being already between us and Fort Craig, would prevent our march up the Rio Grande."

"Lynde outnumbered the Texans three to one? Why retreat at all?"

The witness merely shrugged.

Canby looked at Carson. Then turned to the man and indicated he should continue.

"All day the 26th, preparations were made for the abandonment of Fort Fillmore. Women and children, arms, munitions, whatever supplies we could reasonably carry. Many of the officers and men were furious. Some were terrified. All was in disorder. Then, at some point the men discovered that the liquor was going to be left behind."

Carson and Canby looked perplexed.

"I'm afraid the men decided this was too much to bear. They began drinking the liquor and, sadly, emptying their canteens of water and refilling them with liquor."

Carson couldn't help himself. "And none of the officers stepped in to stop it?"

"I'm afraid the officers participated, sir. We left the fort at first light on the 27th, and were proceeding as quickly as possible toward San Augustine Pass, the mountains, and then hopefully on to Fort Stanton."

"And the Texans?" Canby said.

Carson noted that he was no longer taking care to disguise his discouragement.

"You could see their cavalry coming once daylight came. Most of us made it the twenty or so miles to San Augustine Pass, but many of the soldiers were left along the road, drunk, dehydrated, and unconscious."

"What happened at the Pass?" Canby said.

"The Rebels offered unconditional surrender and Lynde accepted the terms, sir."

"But he still outnumbered the Texans," Canby said. "Even then. His soldiers were well trained, disciplined. Some of our best. Did no one object?"

"Yes, sir. Several of the officers. But in the end they all followed orders. Lynde surrendered unconditionally and there was no one prepared to mutiny, sir."

"We lost everything?" Canby said. "The guns? The horses? The ammunition? The stores?"

Carson couldn't help himself. "Well, Ed, everything but the liquor. And probably the whores in the wagons."

"Was there no attempt by the soldiers at Fort Stanton to reach Lynde to stop the Texans?" Canby said.

"Sir, I'm sorry to report that it is even worse than that."

"How so?"

"I was told by a scout in the waiting area on my way in that your troops abandoned Fort Stanton to the New Mexicans and the Mescalero Apaches. They are headed to Albuquerque with everything they could get out of the fort."

"So our southern forts are now in Confederate hands with hardly a shot being fired?" Canby said.

The witness had no answer to that.

"Thank you, sir. That will be all."

"Oh, There is one more thing, Colonel," he said. "If I may?"

"Yes?"

"Well I thought it was odd and don't know if anyone has told you yet. The Texans, sir. They are mostly armed with shotguns."

Canby looked thoughtful. "Thank you. That will be all."

"So," Carson said. "Baylor hasn't brought regular, fully equipped, Confederate forces. He's come only with Texas Rangers and Volunteers armed with shotguns. And Lynde just ran for it?"

Canby didn't answer.

"Is there now a threat to Fort Craig or any of our northern forts, Colonel?" Carson said.

"Not from two hundred Texans, Kit."

"Well, Colonel, let's hope that you had only one Lynde under your command. And let's hope that President Lincoln and General McDowell are faring better against the Rebels in Virginia."

"Baylor has now declared himself the Territorial Governor," Canby said. "And declared southern New Mexico and Arizona as The Confederate Arizona Territory."

"I'm sure," Carson said, "That John Baylor will make a fine politician, sir."

Canby laughed grimly. "Just get your Volunteers ready, Kit. And let's hope that we get help from Colorado by the time Sibley gets here with the rest of the Texans."

24

August 10, 1861

Lily listened to Cummings and Damours. Cummings, once again looking for a reason to stay out of the Army. Keeping Cummings penned was becoming a full time job. Like having a steer that wouldn't stay inside your ranch's fence, she thought.

"Is it too early to ask again if we're on the wrong side of this damn thing?" Cummings said.

"It's too late for me," Damours said. "I'm essentially in the Volunteers already."

"Well," Cummings said. "We just heard from Mowry that the Apaches have Tucson and Tupac in virtual siege. Mowry doubts that the Texans can protect the entire area between Tucson and Fort Bliss against Cochise. And the politicians in Washington are refusing his calls for aid. And now we get word that the Rebels have routed the Union Army just outside of Washington. In Virginia. Some place called Manassas. I hear it was worse than Lynde at Fort Fillmore. Much worse."

"C'mon, Cummings," Lily said. "This was all your plan. Yours and Mowry's. You've come up with excuses every step of the way for not personally committing to your part. You know as well as the rest of us that the Texans and Arizona Guards won't be able to bother the Union forces for months."

"How 'bout if I go down to Tucson," Cummings said. "To see Mowry. And then join up with the Texans. Then when Damours is with Chacon and the Volunteers, we're covered both ways?"

"Cummings," Lily said. "How do you propose to keep supplying and selling stuff for Zapico if you're running around fighting Apaches?"

"I could always use Mowry as an excuse to take leave for business up here in Santa Fe?"

"You start doing that, and eventually somebody's going to shoot you down as a traitor. One side or the other. Either side might see it that way. C'mon Joseph, try to be sensible here."

"This is a lot of work for nothing if Canby gets routed soon," Cummings said. "That's all I'm saying. The Federal troops are obviously no Army."

"By the way," Damours said. "I keep hearing that you killed a soldier in a duel at Fort Marcy two months ago. But Lily tells me it wasn't you."

"I got in a heated argument with some drunken Sergeant. He challenged me to a duel on June 15th, but it never amounted to anything. Nobody shot anybody."

"Okay," Damours said. "But I hear he disappeared after that. It only matters when you join up and start having to deal with his friends who think you killed him."

"It never happened. Nobody's going to make anything of it."

"Don't give him any more excuses to back out, Auggy," Lily said.

"Look Lily," Cummings said. "I'm not comfortable with a plan that depends on Canby's Yankees lasting out here."

"Dammit, Cummings," she said. "From what we hear, it'll take a year or more for additional Confederate troops to get here. Jefferson Davis has a few more priorities than New Mexico and Arizona. In the meantime, the New Mexico Volunteers will be ready more than soon enough and the Colorado Volunteers will be here long before the Texas reinforcements."

"Cummings," Damours said. "I'll be joining Chacon's Company under Kit Carson in three days when we're all mustered in. Everybody's optimistic that the Volunteers and the federal troops will be more than enough to drive the Texans back where they came from."

"Are these the same troops who ran for their lives two weeks ago from two hundred Texans?" Cummings said.

Damours and Lily didn't take the bait.

"Joseph," she said. "Auggy will be inside in three days. Just focus on doing your jobs with Mowry and Zapico. Let's deal with you joining the Army when you're more comfortable with the concept. But in the end, you're going to have to be on the inside. Just as you planned it."

"The plan was to be inside the *winning* side, Lily. Not just inside any old army that came along."

"We'll know soon enough, Cummings. Just do your job."

Jeez, she thought. This is much harder than whoring. It's much easier making men think you're happy in their bed than it is getting 'em to do what should be obvious that they need to do.

Hopefully, in the end, it'll be more profitable, too.

Being respectable was sure harder than it had sounded.

25

August 15, 1861

Canby shifted the cigar from one side of his mouth to the other as he looked at the two officers standing with Carson in front of him. One was a

Lieutenant unknown to him. The other was Captain Rafael Chacon. Chacon, 28-years old, was smaller than Carson, and was dwarfed by the youngish looking Lieutenant. Chacon was more than a half foot short of six feet and well under a hundred and fifty pounds. His jet black, military cut hair and perfectly groomed Spanish military moustache accented his military bearing. Chacon took care to always carry himself like the proud New Mexican officer that he was.

"Who is this Lieutenant with you, Captain Chacon?"

"Sorry, Colonel," said Chacon. "This is Lieutenant Augustine P. Damours."

Canby looked back and forth between Carson and Chacon, waiting for an explanation.

"He recently joined us at the recommendation of Fathers Gabrielle and Ussel," Chacon said. "I received a July 22 letter stating his wish to join us. He's fluent in English and Spanish, and he could be the accountant needed by the Company."

"Why is he here today Captain?"

"Kit and I thought he could also be helpful to us in administration or possibly as quartermaster. The Fathers think he can be immensely valuable."

"Lieutenant Damours, why do you want to join the Volunteers?"

"Sir, my family is from south of here. But when I came here recently from California, they were no longer there. I couldn't find them. I feel strongly about preventing the Texans from taking New Mexico, sir."

"Are your loyalties to New Mexico then son, or to the Union? This is not a regional skirmish."

Carson suppressed a smile as Canby tried to have a little fun with the boy, appearing to like him already.

Damours looked confused, not sure what the truth was, let alone the best lie. "Well, Colonel. I've just joined the New Mexico Volunteers. I expect to be fighting Texans. But if President Lincoln orders us to fight Rebels back East, then I will certainly follow my orders, sir."

"Excellent answer, Lieutenant. Excellent answer." Canby looked thoughtful. "And what are your experiences with fighting? With killing Texans?"

Damours was now on much more comfortable ground. He could lie through this with impunity.

"Indians in California, sir. Claim jumpers in the Gold Rush. Actually, Colonel," he turned toward Carson, "Major Carson and I met in San Francisco in '53. I didn't want to mention it that first day we met."

"We did?" Carson said. "I have no recollection of it."

"Well, you wouldn't. It was in a restaurant and everybody was crowding in and wantin' to meet the famous mountainman and Indian fighter. No way you'd remember me among all them people."

"Well, thanks for reminding me. I've tried to forget all that."

Canby laughed good naturedly. "Aw c'mon Kit, you mean you don't want to tell the kid here some of your 'blood and thunder' exploits? All the Indians ya' killed? All the ladies you saved?"

"You know damn well I don't, Ed," Carson said without taking his eyes off his hands in his lap.

"Okay, then," Canby said in the awkward silence that followed, "Lieutenant Damours, I think you were telling us about your experience killin' Texans."

"No Texans yet, sir. That I know of. I think I might've killed a couple of Apaches on our way here, sir, but I can't be sure."

Carson winked at Canby and Chacon. "That's the whole trouble with Apaches, kid. You never know."

But Canby wasn't done with him. "One more thing, Lieutenant. Has anybody ever told you that you bear a remarkable likeness to that actor in Baltimore? John Wilkes Booth?"

"It comes up now and then, sir."

Canby looked at Carson, then at Damours. "We'll give some thought to an appropriate job for you, Lieutenant. In the meantime, Kit, let's get your Volunteers ready to kill Texans sooner rather than later."

26

August 28, 1861

Cochise and three of his warriors perched on their horses, peering down at the western edge of Cooke's Canyon. The Life Giver had once again been good.

Heading slowly into the canyon was a wagon train, accompanied by hundreds of horses, sheep, goats, and cattle. They could see nine wagons of various types. And there were no visible soldiers.

Each of the four Apaches carried a rifle and had a band of white war paint across their faces, from cheek to cheek across their noses. They each also wore headbands across their foreheads and the front of their hair. One wore a black porkpie hat he had taken off the body of one of the seven White Eyes they had massacred in this same place one month before.

Moses Carson, half-brother of Kit Carson, rode alongside Felix Ake at the head of the wagon train as they entered the canyon. Ake owned everything in these wagons and his entire family was in or riding next to them. He'd had enough of the Arizona Territory and had hired Carson to take them back East.

"You see 'em, Moses?" Ake said, peering up at the four Indians on the mesa. "Are they Navajos?"

"Chiricahuas, Felix. We told you that the best way from Tucson back East was through this canyon. And, for that reason, this is where Cochise and Mangas Coloradas have set up business."

"I thought leavin' is what they wanted from us."

"They want you gone Ake. They want me gone. They sure as hell want the soldiers gone. But your sheep and cattle? I'm thinking they'd just as soon keep those for the four or five hundred warriors they're feeding."

"Will they attack?"

"We've gone all through this, Felix. Those bodies and bones we've been passing for the past few days didn't die of old age. He's almost certainly figured you for more than twenty-five men. From up there he can't tell the difference between women, teenage boys, and men on horseback or driving wagons. If we're lucky, he'll send about fifty braves to cut out some cattle, horses, and sheep and let you go on to Mesilla."

Turned out they weren't lucky.

After a lengthy discussion, Cochise and Mangas Coloradas decided to send their entire force into the canyon. They wanted the livestock. They wanted whatever was in those wagons. They wanted the White Eyes dead. And they wanted vengeance for all the men they had lost in this canyon a month before.

They sent two hundred warriors to each side of the first blind spot between the western end and the middle of the canyon, and prepared for what they intended to be a quick massacre.

"I'll ride back to make sure that all the women and children are in that last wagon where they need to be," Carson said.

"Should we stop here?" Ake said.

"Felix, you stop here and we're all dead. This spot is indefensible. You keep moving forward. That's your job. My men and I'll get your people set for an attack and keep an eye out for the best place to stop if we need to. That's our job."

Carson turned to head back toward the rear wagons, and trotted back to two of his scouts.

"Go up with Ake and lead us through the canyon. Apaches watched us enter. Let's not give them time to figure out what they want to do with us."

He ordered all seven children and sixteen women to immediately get into the ambulance at the back of the wagons. One little girl was walking alongside a wagon, so he reached down and plucked her up on onto his saddle.

"What's your name sweetie?"

"Sarah. And I know yours."

He laughed. "What is it then?"

"You're Mr. Carson, aren't you?"

"I am."

"Is it true that you were a mountain man and that you beat the Utes all by yourself?"

He laughed again and hugged the little girl. "No honey. That's my brother, Kit. Kit Carson."

"Oh."

Her body sagged in clear disappointment, and they were both quiet until he delivered her up into the ambulance.

"Good luck Sarah."

And he watched her peer out from under her bonnet down at him just as he heard the hysterical whooping and the beginning of gunfire at the front of the train.

He turned his horse around.

"Shit."

The Chiricahuas came with everything they had. There was no strategy.

No tactics. Just hundreds of screaming warriors on horseback hurtling toward twenty-four men defending whatever and wherever they could.

All effort that wasn't directed at shooting the onrushing Apaches was thrown into circling the wagons. The first wagon was strategically abandoned by the retreating vanguard of men. Three men turned the ambulance with the women and children around as ordered and raced it westward out of the canyon and back toward the Mimbres River.

Four of the defending men turned tail and raced after the women and children, leaving seventeen to confront several hundred mounted Apaches.

The second wave of Apaches came from the opposite direction of the first. The fighting intensified for over an hour, and the battle raged until well past noon.

At one point Carson was surprised, then annoyed, and finally relieved that one of Ake's daughters had stayed behind and was feverishly reloading guns non-stop under the protection of one of the double wagons.

The ranks of the circling Apaches began to thin slowly after noon. The experience the previous month had dampened Cochise's enthusiasm for bearing the high cost of all out victories. When one of the attacking Apaches was shot in the head from point blank range, the Chiricahuas had had enough.

Out of range of the defenders' rifle fire, the Apaches gathered over 1,000 of the cattle and sheep, and, firing a volley into the air, herded their booty eastward out of the canyon.

Carson took off his hat, swept his long white hair back off his face, and surveyed the damage. One woman and eight men unhurt. Four dead. Five wounded, two badly enough that they had not been able to fight the last two hours.

"Well I reckon they got more'n half of us in just a few hours," Carson said. "They were going to have to pay a very heavy price to wipe us out."

"Why aren't they content to just take the livestock, Moses?" Ake said.

"Cochise is madder'n hell. The Army just wouldn't leave him be in peace."

He swept his arms to encompass the circled wagons.

"This is the price. But only a very small part of the price. Arizona is going to be a living and dying hell for a very long time now"

He turned and doffed his cap to Ake's daughter, sitting exhausted and filthy on the ground.

"Ma'am, you should be very proud of what you did here today. I don't know if you know those four cowards who ran away, but I sure hope you and I never have to see them again."

He spat on the ground.

"Cowards. They're going to have to live the rest of their lives knowing they left a little girl and their family here to die. I'll tell you that Cochise and his men out there deserve this place. It's their home and they'll defend it with everything they have. That we go on killing these brave people so that cowards like them can stay here is disgusting."

She was crying now.

"Sorry, ma'am, but it's the damn truth. And it's just a damn shame."

Mangas Coloradas watched his Mimbres herd the cattle and sheep out of the canyon toward Mexico.

"Many of the White Eyes are cowards, eh?"

"Yes, some." Cochise said. "But most are better fighters than either the Mexicans or the Navajo."

"And better than the People?" his father-in-law said.

"No Mangas. The People are better fighters than the White Eyes. Much better. But I'm worried that there are not enough of us to save our home. I think we must now change our tactics. We lose too many of our bravest men by trapping small numbers of White Eyes in long battles."

"What do you suggest, my son?"

"The Life Giver told us this place would be our home forever, that it would care for us if we took care of her. The Chiricahua must strike the White Eyes on the run when they are least able to defend themselves. We must drive the miners out. The farmers out. The ranchers out. One small group at a time. Striking and running to fight other small groups."

They both gazed down into the canyon at the dust cloud from their newly acquired livestock.

"As for the soldiers," Cochise said. "We should harass them. Hitting them from behind and then vanishing with their livestock. Have them waste their bullets as though we were ghosts."

"I think we may already be winning, Cochise," Mangas said. "They are already abandoning their forts. Burning when they leave."

"These are signs from the Life Giver that we will prevail," Cochise said.

"When the White Eye soldiers abandon their forts, I think we should harass them and chase them from behind. We must repay the Life Giver by driving the White Eyes out of our lands forever."

27

September 22, 1861

Canby greeted the newly promoted Colonel Carson in his Fort Marcy office.

"You said you wanted to see me about something, Colonel Carson?"

"Yes, Ed. The New Mexico Volunteers are trained and ready. I'll lead these Volunteers against the Texans any time, but I wouldn't give a bucket of piss and sweat for your untried Federals at our flanks. I'm concerned your soldiers aren't any better than Lynde's at Fort Fillmore or McDowell's at Manassas. Make that Bull Run."

"I think you can trust me and George McClellan to do a darn sight better job training our soldiers than our predecessors, Colonel. Lincoln has relieved McDowell and given the Little Napoleon the Army of the Potomac. McClellan and I served together in Mexico. He'll organize and train a true Army. With Grant having just taken the Tennessee River at Padukah and George heading the Army, this should be the short war we all initially expected."

He looked out the window at his soldiers on the parade grounds. "Then, Kit, it'll be like old times. You, me, and Sibley can go after the Navajo instead of fighting each other."

Nope, Carson thought. Retirement. I'm done fighting Navajos. But he said, "You served with all these guys in Mexico. And the last time we had this conversation, you said McClellan could train soldiers just fine, but was always reluctant to use them, Grant was a drunk, and Lee the man you thought would make it a short war."

"We'll be fine, Kit."

"This is all a game for you West Pointers isn't it? You all schooled together, taught each other tactics, and served together killing Mexicans and Indians. You and McClellan and Grant against Lee and Johnston. Competing against each other to see who learned the most at the Point. Or in Mexico. Or against the Seminole. Or wherever."

Canby chewed on his cigar and frowned. "There certainly was an element of camaraderie down in Vera Cruz and Mexico City, Kit. But none of us thought it was a game losing our boys to Mexican fire. And I don't think any of us think beating up on these poor Indians is much fun either."

"I think Baylor does," Carson said. "And I think our old friend Carleton does. They both hate Indians and want them gone."

An uncomfortable silence rose over the two friends.

"Did I ever tell you," Carson finally said. "That I ran into Robert E. Lee coming out of Camp Cooper, Texas about five years ago? He was heading up some cavalry units to try 'n chase the Comanches out of Texas. Present company excepted, Lee made the biggest first impression on me of any officer I ever met."

"Oh? Strong enough to talk you into helping him chase Comanches?"

"He wasn't that impressive," Carson said. "But he knew what he was doing, what his limits were, and what he didn't know. You sure General Lee's gonna let this be a short war, Ed?"

"Tell you what, Kit. I'll wager you a week of horse's rations that the war will be over by the time Sibley gets here."

"You gonna be disappointed then, Ed?" Carson said.

"I'm sorry this War has come and I want no part of it, Kit. I think Lincoln could have avoided it. But we can't have states just leaving every time we have a disagreement, and then wanting back in when the British or someone come to carve us up."

"You think slavery is a 'disagreement', Ed?"

"C'mon Kit. Grant and his wife have slaves. Hell, you have slaves."

"Well, there're pretty incidental to whites out here. There are only about twenty Negro slaves in the whole Territory. And the Indians take slaves out of vengeance, not out of dependency. We solve the Indian problem out here, the slavery goes away."

Carson stopped to give Canby a chance to reply. When he didn't, Carson continued with his point.

"Slaves aren't incidental in South Carolina and Virginia and Texas. The southern plantation owners depend on them. If Lincoln could find a way to enable the plantation owners to earn the same living without their Negroes, slavery would become incidental there, too."

"There are those, Kit, who feel strongly that it's not morally right."

"Then have the moralists figure out a way to solve the problem without killing all the twenty year old boys in the country. But enough. Sorry. Let's just hope it turns out that you're right and it is your short war. Just a game among all you West Pointers that unites America and makes it stronger and rids us of slavery."

"You can count on it, Kit."

"Well, then you all can go back to chasing Navajos like you say. And like my Utes want you to."

"And chasing Chiricahuas," Canby said. "I have a feeling that Cochise is going to be a bigger problem than all the Confederates they can send our way."

28

September 27, 1861

Cochise and Mangas Coloradas said their good-byes late that afternoon.

"The Mimbres will now go to the Gilas to rest and take care of our families," Mangas said.

"And we will go to Mexico," Cochise said. "To replenish our stores of ammunition and guns. We also need the rest."

"And you will bring the other Chiricahuas from Mexico?"

"Yes. We will rejoin you near Tucson and Tubac."

"And finally drive the White Eyes from our land?"

Cochise thought carefully before answering. "Yes, I think so. The White Eyes now have little stomach for being here in Pinos Altos. I think when they leave here, all that will be left of the White Eyes will be at the Tucson mines. The soldiers have been abandoning their forts, and the wagons have all been going East. All leaving. None coming anymore."

"And Tucson, my son?"

"Any whites foolish enough to be there when we arrive in four months will be easy to drive out. But I think there will be none left."

The two chiefs turned their horses and headed off in different directions as each wished the other well, looking forward to their reunion.

Cochise was to be proven right about Pinos Altos. The miners abandoned it. The Apaches had convinced the miners that the cost of mining had become too high.

He would, however, prove less prescient about Tucson. Upon his return to Southern Arizona in February, it would have become the center of a mess that the Apache chief could not possibly have imagined.

29

September 29, 1861

Damours was disciplining one of the Corporals on the parade grounds.

"Lieutenant Damours. Stand down," Chacon said.

"Yes, sir."

"Lieutenant Damours. We have discussed this. You are to cease poking the 'Mexicans,' as you call them, with sticks and prodding their legs with your sword in order to speed up their marching and straightening their shoulders."

"Yes, sir."

"The men tell me that you continue to abuse the New Mexicans verbally and physically in front of the whites, as I just saw you do. Lieutenant, these people are not Mexicans. They are New Mexicans. We have been fighting the Spaniards and the Mexicans for generations here in our home..."

"I…"

"Do not interrupt me Lieutenant. Be silent."

Chacon was working himself into a rage. Across the parade grounds a group of other officers were starting to glance their way.

Chacon stared at Damours.

"We," and here he swept his arms toward the other officers and the barracks. "We have been fighting foreigners and Indians here in our home forever. We haven't needed your help, Lieutenant. And we don't need you treating the men as your inferiors. God help you if you go into battle with men who resent you. Do you understand what I'm telling you?"

"Yes, sir."

"I'm now told that you have been suggesting to the men that they elect you Captain instead of me. Is this true?"

"Yes, sir."

"I have been fighting with these men and their fathers for fifteen years, Lieutenant. And they and their fathers fought with my father. I have been fighting with Colonel Carson and Colonel Canby for a decade. What in the hell are you thinking Lieutenant?"

Silence.

"Answer me, dammit."

"With respect, sir, it's a free country and my right."

"True enough, Auggy. And I have my rights as well."

In one motion, Chacon picked up two boards at his feet and, seeing Damours begin to draw his sword, slammed first one, then the other into each of the Lieutenant's shoulders. Knocking him backward, but not off his feet.

As Damours slipped and tried to regain his footing Chacon fell upon him repeatedly slamming the boards against his shoulders and across his back.

Damours, still trying to get to his sword, fled across the parade ground.

One hour later there was a knock at Chacon's door.

"Yes?"

Damours entered the room, fresh from a meeting to denounce Chacon to the Major. The Major had told Damours that it was he who was out of line and that he, the Major, was expecting Chacon to bring charges against Damours for conduct unbecoming an officer and a gentleman. The Major left no doubt in Damours' mind that he was in official, if not mortal, peril.

Chacon noticed the prominence of Damours' sword and stood.

"Yes Lieutenant?"

"Captain Chacon, I am deeply sorry for my actions."

Silence.

"I regret my inexperience at training and my lack of appreciation for the work and courage of the New Mexicans. You have my deepest apology. You may have, from this moment forward, the utmost confidence in my support, my professional behavior, my public loyalty as one of your officers, and my private loyalty as your friend. I swear as an officer and a gentleman."

Danson had taught him well. Rule Number One for a con artist is to always know when the cork is out of the bottle and when it's time to begin the next con.

No better opportunity to apply that Rule had ever presented itself to Auggy Damours.

30

October 14, 1861

Damours slipped his hand under Lily's skirt as she lay on her stomach next to him. They were on the bed in her room. She stretched her legs and arms and turned her head slowly to look over at him.

"I wasn't asleep Auggy."

"Just thinkin'?"

"Yeah," she said. "Just thinkin'."

He slid his hand up the inside of both her thighs and got the expected low moan and separation between her legs.

She smiled up at him. "How's it going with Chacon, Auggy?"

He slid two fingers into her and felt her slide down them, and said, "You need to know now? Right now?"

"Yes, Auggy. I want to know right now. Your fingers'll wait till we're done talkin'."

"I think things are fine, now." Not moving his hand. "Chacon appears to believe that he and I are now good buddies and that he can trust me. Both professionally and personally."

Lily shifted her bottom to envelop his hand. Murmured.

"Why is that?" he said.

"Why is what, Auggy?"

"I just never understand why everybody always trusts me. From the minute they meet me. From the minute I clear up a dispute. Always. I'll never understand why."

Lily lifted her head and kissed him softly on his ribs. He leaned down and she opened her mouth and kissed him long and soft on his mouth.

"Dunno," she said. "Why ask? Just enjoy it, honey."

"I mean we're looting the Church, the Territory, and the Army. I'm in the middle of all of it. Nobody trusts anybody. You don't trust Cummings or Danson, and they don't trust each other. Hell, they probably don't trust you. The Fathers don't trust the Governor and he doesn't trust them. Nobody trusts Zapico. And there I am, robbing everybody. And everyone knows I'm robbing the others, because they're in on it with me. And still, everybody trusts that I'm looking out for them. Been true ever since I was a little kid. I just never understand it."

Lily lifted up her head and propped herself on her elbows. Looked out the window over Damours' body up at the crystal blue October sky.

"Well, I can only tell you why I trust you Auggy. Men probably trust you because you appear to not be a threat to them. Ol' Rafael always felt he could put you in your place if he needed to. And, in his eyes, that's precisely what happened. As for me, you're adorable and come across as guileless. And so far you've never done anything that would suggest to me that I can't trust you. We're always working together on the angles against the others and you've always come through for me."

She stretched and rubbed herself against his fingers.

"I can trust you, right Auggy?"

"You had me the minute you told me I was 'that guy,' Lil. You would crush me if you let me down, but you'd still be able to trust me."

He kissed her.

"See. Guileless," she said.

She laughed. Then squirmed.

"In answer to your question, Lil, Captain Chacon has taken it upon himself to conclude, correctly of course, that I would be a hindrance in battle. Therefore, he is recommending to Carson and Canby that I be removed from harm's way. As Canby's aide de camp."

He grinned down at her.

Her eyes widened. "Seriously?"

She burst out laughing.

He winced as his hand was squeezed.

"Even if we'd had the thought ourselves," she said. "We wouldn'ta had the audacity to try to get it put into place. It's perfect, Auggy. It puts you right in the gun sights of all the Army's money and out of the gun sights of the Texans. It's practically like asking a wolf, just because he acts all tame like, to guard your sheep. We couldn'ta ever come up with an idea as good as this. It's the mother lode, Auggy."

"Careful Lil, as far as I know, Canby hasn't approved the appointment yet."

"Oh, he will. Nobody ever says no to Augustine P. Damours."

She laughed again, kissed his shoulder, and reached into his pants. "Okay, Auggy you can slide those fingers a little deeper. Like I like it."

"Lil, my whole hand and arm are numb. I didn't even know they was still in."

"Well then, big boy you got anything that's workin'?" She rolled over on top of him.

"'Cause I'm done talkin'."

31

October 20, 1861

"Colonel Carson, we need your Volunteers to leave for Albuquerque," Canby said.

Both Carson and Chacon looked up, surprised by Canby's order. They both looked over at Captain Arnold to see if he was equally surprised.

"We're still training the Volunteers," Chacon said.

Canby frowned. "Continue their training down there, then. We need you to be in one of the southern forts when the fighting starts. May as well head out now."

"There's nothing going on up here," Arnold said. "And there are increasing reports of robberies around Albuquerque. You could be helpful on the way down to Fort Craig."

"We have until after mid-January," Carson said, "Before the Texans get down there. And the Colorado Volunteers should have reached Fort Laramie on their way here by now and will be there with us ahead of the Texans."

"Nothing ever happens the way you plan, Kit," Arnold said. "That's a pretty brutal march through the winter mountains for the Coloradans."

"Luckily," Canby said. "My brother-in-law has his Texans running late. But Arnold's right, there's no point waiting and pushing our luck. Best guess is General Sibley himself will lead the rest of the Rebels out here in about a month."

Canby chewed on his cigar for a while.

Carson finally said after getting a nod from Chacon, "Okay, we'll have the Volunteers start south tomorrow."

The three officers all stood to leave Canby's office.

"Kit," Canby said. "Can you please stay for another minute? There's another issue I'd like your thoughts on."

The two friends sat back down after Chacon and Arnold left.

"Kit, with the War now practically here, I've been trying to decide what to do about the damned Navajo. Half of them are always angry about some incident or other, frankly perpetrated by the soldiers or the New Mexicans, and the other half finally seem amenable to moving west and finally leaving us alone. I'm concerned we can't afford to waste soldiers chasing them around."

"I'm where I've always been, Canby. You need authority from the Bureau of Indian Affairs to force the chiefs to agree to permanently go back to their homeland, west of here. Away from all the New Mexicans and our soldiers. Get the Bureau to agree to pay them to move and convince the Dine their people will now be killed if they stay. The Bureau should see you can't fight both the Texans and the Navajo."

"I was hoping you had come up with something else, Kit. They're a pain but I'll just have to work with the Bureau to get this done before we have our hands full of Texans."

Carson stood and looked out the window, down at Santa Fe. Another beautiful New Mexico Fall day. Thinking about the approaching nightmare.

"Will that be all sir?"

"No, Kit. One more thing. Chacon has recommended I take Lieutenant Damours on as my aide de camp. What's going on there?"

Carson laughed.

"It turns out the kid has absolutely no military aptitude at all. He and Rafael had a, well, let's call it a meeting of the minds."

"Something I should know about?"

"No, sir. These things happen. In any case, Chacon now agrees with Father Ussel and, it turns out the Governor, that young Mr. Damours is great at finances and organizing information and getting things done, and…well, not so good with rifles, pistols, or enlisted men."

"And you agree, right?" Canby said.

"I have no idea, Ed. He seems like a very earnest kid. The Governor and the Fathers oughta know, right? But I can't read or write. Makes it pretty hard to evaluate paper work. You're on your own on this one."

"Okay. I'm inclined to bring him in. Tell him and Chacon that Damours is not going to Albuquerque with his unit. That we need him here more."

"You and the State and the Church," Carson said. "How wrong could you all be?"

32

November 4, 1861

Danson had asked to meet with Lily and Cummings.

"This isn't the way I thought this was going to work," he said.

"Look, Danson," Cummings said. "I'm not sure I get your point. Things are working better than we planned. Damours is Canby's right hand man and has been helping both the Governor and the thankful Fathers with their finances. The money he's been funneling to us from all three is just the beginning. And your trades through Zapico can't be going any better. What is it you're not comfortable with?"

"Mostly I just sit around and wait for you to tell me what to do with the Jew. I have nothin' else going on at my end but sittin'."

Danson looked over questioningly at Lily.

"Honey," she said. "You're winning at cards and your business with Zapico couldn't be better. I know it isn't as much fun for you as you and Auggy constantly up to one con or another, but we're all making much more money this way."

She looked quizzically at Danson, waiting. What had she missed? She thought she'd played him right.

"It's just that...well... Never mind. You're right. Auggy and I are making more money this way. I guess that's all that matters."

Cummings stood up to leave. Said, "Anything else?"

Lily and Danson both shook their heads.

Cummings tipped his hat toward Lily and walked out the door.

They made love desultorily, neither of them having much energy for it.

Afterwards, Danson lay on his back, quietly smoking a cigarette. He glanced over at Lily and placed the cigarette in her outstretched hand.

Finally, he said, "You sure Cummings is leveling with us? You still believe we'll get our fair cut? Hell, Auggy's doin' all the work and it feels like I'm gettin' steadily cut out."

"But *I'm* not honey. And you're not either. You gotta trust me to watch our end. Cummings has the direct line to Mowry, but I've got Zapico in my pocket. So long as you've got Auggy's loyalty, Danson, you have nothing to worry about."

She took the cigarette back. Took a long drag. "You're still good with Auggy, right?"

"Sure. Damours will never be our problem. It's always going to be Cummings."

"Well don't worry about Cummings, hon. Until he joins the Army, he's Mowry's problem. And then he'll be Canby's. In each case, I've got him covered with either Zapico or Auggy."

"No," he said. "In the end, Cummings'll be our problem. Trust me on that."

They both stared up at the ceiling.

So now you're gonna overplay your hand and fuck this all up, she thought to herself? I should have seen it coming. You probably don't even trust me you sunovabitch. But she said, "I guess we're going to have to find something to keep you busy, so you don't get us all into trouble, huh, Jim?"

While we find a way to cut you out.

Unbeknownst to both of them, Danson would soon solve each of their problems.

Permanently.

33

November 15, 1861

One hundred of Captain Chacon's New Mexico Volunteers had completed the two day ride to Chilili only to find virtually nobody at home.

"Where is everybody, Rafael?" his Sergeant said.

"They're hiding in the hills. They think we're here recruiting for the Volunteers."

"Damn patriotic of them. Maybe they'd rather be killed by the Texans."

"Texans, Mexicans, Union regulars, Rebels, Navajos, Apaches, bandits, us?" Chacon said. "Farmers traditionally aren't too picky about who they don't want killin' em. Or stealing their crops. Or raping their women. They've learned over the years that hiding in the hills from approaching armed soldiers is a practical strategy."

"I guess they don't know that the famous Kit Carson has sent us here to capture the bandits they've been complaining about."

Chacon looked at him to see if he was being insubordinate. Decided to let it go. He ordered four of the men to ask around the village for information about the killers of the Los Colonias family.

"Sergeant, let's go find the Sheriff and do what Colonel Carson sent us here to do."

Since the Sheriff and Justice of the Peace were sitting outside the jailhouse waiting for them, it didn't take them long to find them.

The two Volunteers didn't even bother to get off their horses. Chacon tipped his cap, though.

"Gentlemen," he said.

They both nodded. Said nothing.

"We've ridden down from Albuquerque under orders to bring the killers of a family up at Los Colonias to justice."

The Sheriff looked over at the Justice of the Peace, then back up at Chacon.

"Over by Anton Chico," Chacon said.

Chacon, now puzzled by the silence and lack of apparent cooperation by the two, started to ask them if there were a problem, when the Justice of the Peace said, "You don't have far to look, Captain. But if it's recruits you're looking for, you've come to the wrong place."

"No," the Sergeant said. "Just bandits and murderers. We'll catch them and then be on our way. We don't cotton much to hanging around where we're not wanted."

"Our boys," Chacon added. "Are perfectly happy in Albuquerque and Santa Fe. The girls and the fandangos are a far sight better than what Chilili seems to offer."

"What do you know about the boys you're looking for, Captain," said the Justice of the Peace.

"I've got the names right here," Chacon said, leaning down to hand him a piece of paper.

"There are about twenty of them we think. From here, Tajique, and Manzano. All New Mexicans."

The Justice of the Peace looked at the paper.

"Well, Captain, somebody did their homework for you. We hadn't heard they'd killed a family, though. You sure of your information?"

"Yes. We're sure of it. By the way, my men are asking around for information. Are they likely to be wasting their time here in the village?"

"Likely. Look, the villagers are hiding from you over there."

He pointed toward the foothills several hundred yards from the town.

"And the men you're looking for just might be on the hill over on the top of that mesa behind me."

He made a point of neither gesturing nor looking in that direction.

"We don't have the manpower here to deal with this sort of thing."

The mute Sheriff nodded in agreement at this.

"I'd recommend you go hunting for these men at night. When they're drunk and asleep up there. Without bothering the townsfolk."

"We could sure use a guide."

"That'd be me."

"And it might help if somebody could let the villagers cut us a little slack and come back into town. Let them know to stay inside and expect some fighting tonight."

"We'll take care of that, too, Captain."

"Okay. Sergeant, set up camp outside of town out of sight of the mesa."

He looked down at the two lawmen.

"Name's Chacon, Captain Rafael Chacon of the New Mexico Volunteers. How about if we meet over behind this side of town at around ten 'oclock? That suit you?"

"Yes, Captain. I'll be waiting there for you at ten."

"Pleasure meeting you, sir. Thanks for the help. You, too, Sheriff."

He tipped his cap to the two. They turned their horses and rode off to organize the men.

"You suppose," the Justice of the Peace said when they were out of earshot. "That they can get this done, Sheriff?"

"A hundred trained soldiers against a dozen drunk kids and their girlfriends? If they can't, we're sure as hell all gonna be a part of Texas pretty damn soon."

"Don't you think some of the soldiers'll be pretty drunk themselves?"

"I doubt Chacon accepts that from his men. He doesn't look like he takes much from anyone," the Sheriff said.

Now a hundred yards down the road, the Sergeant said, "You suppose that the Sheriff is a mute and that those boys don't have any names?"

"No. I suppose that they have to live here after we leave and that their cover story will hold up better if we can't report any knowledge of the two of them. These people out here don't hold much truck with soldiers."

"Unless they need their help," the Sergeant said.

"Even then," Chacon said, "only reluctantly."

That night at ten o'clock Chacon had his men circle around to the back of Chilili where the Justice of the Peace was waiting as he'd promised. No sign of the Sheriff.

He led them up the mesa to the base of the hill. The robbers campfires were all extinguished. Some still smoking.

Chacon ordered half his men to dismount for an assault on foot. The other fifty took the horses and silently rode to surround the base of the hill.

Chacon and his men headed as quietly as possible up the hill. The Justice of the Peace paid his respects and disappeared back toward the village.

The men were under orders of silence. They were to apprehend bandits without alerting the others, threatening death to anyone who sounded an alarm. They were not to shoot unless fired upon. Swords, knives, and bayonets had to be used in lieu of firearms if they were to capture the bandits alive.

They crept up the hill in silence.

Chacon heard some quiet whimpering from among the roots of an old cedar tree toward the top of the hill. He and one soldier crept to the tree. They found a woman, almost dead, with wounds on her neck and back. She was gagged. As Chacon tended to her, his companion came upon her captor from behind. He was hiding in the roots of the same tree and was startled when confronted by a soldier. He had a serious wound in his own shoulder and started to shout out, but was silenced by the sword across his throat.

The wound turned out to have been inflicted by the captured woman. She still cradled a bloody pair of scissors in her hand. The man was weak from loss of blood.

Chacon immediately seized on the situation.

He asked the terrified man, "What's the camp password?"

The man shook his head, eyes white with fear in the moonlight.

"Kill him, Sergeant," Chacon said, stepping aside so that the Sergeant could get in front with his sword.

The man shrank back, turned his head, and whispered the three word password. "La Cabra. La Oveja. La Vaca." Goat. Sheep. Cow.

"In that order?"

The man nodded hurriedly.

"It'd better be, or you'll wish you'd been hung like the rest of your friends are going to be. At least it'll go quicker for them."

He nodded again, more energetically. They gagged him, secured him to the tree, and did the best they could for the girl, who didn't look like she'd make it through the night.

They hurriedly spread the word of the password to the other men, who fanned out looking for the rest of the robbers.

They found them in one's and two's. Mostly drunk around the various still-warm campfires. One pulled a gun and was immediately stabbed in the chest and arm by three soldiers. One tried to run but two soldiers fell on him as he tripped, the only sound the wind bursting out of his throat as he hit the ground.

Two of them had young women hostages, or, as it very quickly turned out, two girlfriends who had the sense to pretend to be hostages.

One soldier grabbed one of the young men from behind, threatening to stab him if he didn't release the girl. The bandit whirled on the soldier with his own knife and jumped the surprised soldier, stabbing him in the left arm as they went down together.

Despite his wound, the soldier quickly gained the upper hand.

Another soldier tried to intervene, only to be jumped by the girl, who bit him on the neck and knocked him to the ground. A general melee ensued. Strange to watch. A pantomime, with five soldiers subduing the young robber and, with considerably more effort, the fighting girl.

The other man dragged a hostage, who, again, turned out to be a girlfriend, behind him, threatening her with a drawn pistol. By now it seemed to the soldiers that most, if not all, of the bandits had been discovered, so a couple of them risked violating orders and drew upon the man with their rifles.

When the bandit stopped and pointed his pistol at one of the soldiers, he was clubbed senseless from behind.

The girl immediately jumped up and ran through the line of soldiers screaming epitaphs at them. With the silence broken, all hell broke loose. Two soldiers took off after the girl, several of the previously subdued bandits tried to escape, and several more rose up from surrounding piles of leaves and discharged their pistols.

Chacon shot one through neck and another in the thigh. The shooting lasted only moments.

Two bandits dead, three wounded, and one soldier wounded slightly in the arm.

Two soldiers brought the struggling and screaming girl back to Chacon.

"Stop. Stop that screaming."

She spit at him and scratched one of the soldiers.

Chacon clubbed her with the butt of his rifle. She fell unconscious.

Chacon ordered the captives tied up and told the men to search the area.

"No need for quiet, any more. We gave them a chance. Warn any you find, but shoot them if you have to. The others await any that run down the hill. Use your bayonets in the piles of leaves," he shouted loudly.

Immediately, three bandits jumped out of hiding under the leaves with arms raised high above their heads.

Bayonetting the piles of leaves netted another two robbers. Chacon entered a ditch containing piles of leaves and began methodically stabbing his sword randomly about. A sudden cry emanated from one pile just as he was starting to thrust downwards.

An arm was held up, frantically waving. When they pulled the pathetic bandit out of the ditch, it turned out he had two deep wounds in his leg from Chacon's earlier sword thrusts. He had taken it soundlessly until he saw the sword headed toward his belly.

"My compliments, sir." Chacon said. "You're very brave. I hope to see your bravery on display again on the Albuquerque gallows in two days' time."

Pleading for his life, one of the bandits told them that their leader had gone on to Manzano earlier that afternoon. Chacon sent ten men on the one day ride to Manzano with orders to find him and bring him back dead or alive.

The rest of the Volunteers rounded up the bandits. Dead, wounded, whimpering, and blustering alike. They loaded them onto wagons and headed out for the ride to Albuquerque. On their way, they delivered the severely wounded and unconscious girl who had saved her own life with a pair of scissors to the only doctor in Chilili.

Nobody, not even the doctor or the attending priest, expected her to survive till morning.

Upon their arrival in Manzano, Chacon's men found that the bandit leader had headed to Mexico the night before.

"Do we follow him to Mexico?" the Sergeant said.

"We were ordered to bring him back," the Lieutenant said.

"From Manzano."

"Excellent point, Sergeant."

Both men looked around the town, calculating their options and their odds.

"I think Captain Chacon would expect us to try," the Lieutenant said.

"He also expects all of us to return. And alive, I would think."

"Another excellent point, Sergeant."

"It's a very long ride across the desert."

"Twice." The Lieutenant said. "There and back."

"And there are our horses to think of."

"We have an important responsibility to save our horses for the coming war with the Texans."

"And I think we have no authority in Mexico."

"And there are only ten of us," the Lieutenant said.

"Against the entire Texas army between us and Mexico," the Sergeant added.

"And the Chiricahuas."

"And the Mescaleros."

"Do we even know that this bandit is alone?"

"You make a convincing case, Lieutenant. Let's thoroughly search Manzano and then head back to Albuquerque."

"Yes. Maybe we don't return with the bandit, but at least our Major will be pleased to see that all ten of us are safe. With our horses. With no casualties. Still ready to take on the Texans."

"What will Chacon think?"

The Lieutenant looked thoughtfully to the south. Toward Mexico.

"Fuck Rafael."

The ten New Mexicans searched Manzano to confirm that the bandit was indeed no longer there, and then turned back and headed directly to their unit in Albuquerque, safe in the knowledge that they had tried but had found no bandit leader.

After the three day ride, they arrived in Albuquerque to discover that Chacon had delivered the nineteen bandits to the Albuquerque jail the day before, and that all the bandits, including the two girls and the four severely wounded men, were taken out that night and summarily hung from telegraph poles around town.

Two months later, Chacon was astonished to receive a note from the scissors-wielding girl, thanking him for saving her life, and informing him that she had, miraculously, recovered fully.

34

November 18, 1861

"Gentlemen," echoed across the San Antonio parade ground.

General Henry Hopkins Sibley raised himself full in his saddle to address his men, who he intended to soon be the Confederate Army of New Mexico. Fully two thousand five hundred Texas Mounted Rifles, if you also included those who had earlier gone on ahead with Baylor to Fort Bliss.

"We leave today fully prepared to do our duty for Texas, President Davis, and the just cause of the Confederacy."

They roared back as one with the rebel yell he had taught them from his Louisiana home.

"From Fort Bliss, we will march up the Rio Grande as a grand conquering Army. The New Mexicans and the Federals are no match for the Texas Mounted Rifles. We outnumber them, you are better than they are, and they have already run from our tiny advance force. On to Colorado. And then on to California."

He started his horse toward the west, raised his right arm, sword held high and headed toward the long expanse of desert between himself and El Paso.

The chilling chorus of the rebel yell behind him roared through the Texas hill country.

An hour later his second in command, Colonel Tom Green, joined Sibley out ahead of the Army. Green looked at his commanding officer and friend, famous long, moustache flaring out to both sides, now whipping toward the back of his head in the wind. The general was drunk. Earlier than usual, but not by much.

"You are right about Canby's regulars and the New Mexican Volunteers," Green said.

"Well, my brother-in-law has been a fine officer fighting Indians and Mexicans, but I don't think he's much of a match against a real Army. There's a little too much Quaker still left in ol' Ed for the rough stuff. I worry about Carson, though. I've never fought with anyone who knew better when to attack, when to wait an enemy out, and when to negotiate. I never imagined me'n Kit on opposite sides. All those romantic novels about him are poppycock, but Kit will be a challenge."

"And the Volunteers from Colorado and California?" Green said.

"I don't think the Coloradans matter much. They'll either be there or they won't. Carleton's Californians would have been another matter, though. But Carleton's got too much on his hands to leave California before early in the year, and we'll already be at the Rio Grande. If things go as easy as we think from there, we'll be in Colorado before Carleton even leaves California. And Carleton likes killing Indians as much as Baylor does, so he'll get distracted when and if he ever gets to Arizona."

"And," Green said, "The small force of Californians that showed up at Fort Yuma a couple of weeks ago will be at most a nuisance. Even for Baylor."

The two rode on in silence for a long while.

"I had a dream last night, Tom," Sibley said.

Green gestured for him to go on.

"I dreamt we won every battle in New Mexico easier'n we expected. And then somehow we found our asses back in Texas instead of continuing the fight."

"Why, sir?"

"Damned if I know. That wasn't in the dream. I've been worryin' at it all morning and damned if I can figure what it meant. I worry that Lee is having such an easy time of it back East, that maybe Lincoln surrenders and Jefferson

Davis brings us home? Maybe the Indians drive us back out of godforsaken New Mexico? Maybe it doesn't mean anything? Maybe none of the dream is true?"

"Well, General. Let's hope the first part's true anyway. We could certainly deal with anything that came up after that. We win the New Mexico battles 'n you can count on being in California in short order, General."

35

November 28, 1861

Damours entered Canby's office.

"Two things, Auggy," Canby said. "First, where are you on accounting for the funds that Chacon says are missing? For his horses and rifles?"

"We're pretty sure we've found the missing funds, sir. The men will have their weapons and the funds will be found."

"Okay. Make sure, Auggy. That's an order."

He looked at Damours to emphasize its importance. Got the nod he was looking for. "Second, I got the Navajo authorization from the Bureau of Indian Affairs. Draft up the orders: The leaders of the Navajo Nation and the U.S. Army have agreed that all Navajo are to move west of Fort Fauntelroy immediately. Any Navajo found in violation are to be considered at war with the United States."

He paused while Damours wrote this down.

Damours looked up. "Colonel. With the Texans coming, do we have enough forces to protect the Navajo out there?"

"From what, Lieutenant? Thanks to Cochise, the white farmers, ranchers, and miners have all left the area. The New Mexicans have never had much appetite for the high desert that far west. The Utes and Jicarillas are safely at Cimarron for the winter. Cochise and Mangas aren't going to pick a fight with the Navajo that far north. No, they're safe there. That's the point, Auggy."

"I just worry the Navajo will find something to justify coming back here, sir."

"You're from here, Auggy. Do you have any original thoughts on how to deal with the Indians?"

"Well, sir, I'm not one of those who feel we should just kill them. I think that a lot of Indian problems are created by them and a lot of it's created by us. Maybe it's just the nature of people not to get along, sir."

"Not much of an answer Lieutenant. It's a damned difficult problem. It's not the Indians' fault that we came here. And it's not their fault that they don't see adapting to our ways as being better."

He pulled his cigar out of his mouth and looked at it. Decided to toss it and put a fresh one in, then continued his lecture.

"Kit taught me that you have to understand each tribe's unique ways to be effective with them. They believe in dispatching Old Testament justice, or vengeance, quickly. And they can't fathom our concept of land ownership."

"Why not just bribe them to stay where we want them?" Damours said.

"Kit believes if we work out an area where they can live the way they want to with our support, without interference from hostile whites, it can be made to work."

"How is that any different than back East, sir?"

"It isn't. This has been going on now for over seventy years. Washington and Jefferson came up with Kit's solution at the beginning. The problem with their idea is that the Army never enforces the treaties against encroaching whites."

"That's not the problem with the Navajo," Damours said.

"Right. No whites want to live on their sacred lands. They're their own worst enemy, raiding everyone for food and slaves. They're friendless out here. And for good reason."

He glanced at someone entering the adjoining room, then went on.

"Chivington's on his way here from Colorado and he hates Indians the way Baylor does. Carleton hates all Indians too, and his solution to Jefferson's dilemma is to put them on land that the whites don't want. Which is easier to do out here."

"So, are we going to kill Navajos found east of Fauntleroy?" Damours said.

"Good point. Let's draft two versions of the General Orders, Auggy. Read back to me what you've got so far."

Damours read it back.

"Okay. Draft one set of orders after that background summary with orders to round up any straying Navajos and send them on to Cubero. If they return, they are to be arrested on the spot. Send those orders to the regular Army commanders both here at Fort Marcy and in the field."

"And the second set of orders, sir?" Damours said.

"Use the same background summary. But order them to take no errant Navajo men prisoner. They are to shoot them on site. And then send their families back to Cubero."

Damours looked up from writing. "Who gets those orders, Colonel?"

"Carson. Send only the first set to the Army, and both orders to the New Mexico Volunteers. Carson can then quit complaining that all he's doing is police work."

"What will Colonel Carson do, sir?"

"His duty," Canby said.

Damours understood immediately from past discussions with Carson that he would ignore the second set of orders.

But now nobody could claim that Canby had been too soft on the Navajo.

36

December 7, 1861

Chacon had set out three days before with seventy of his Volunteers to round up some Navajo who had come back.

He had his orders.

Chacon had ridden west to where the Navajo were reported to be, but they were already gone and their trail now headed east, back where Chacon had just been. Toward the Zia Pueblo on the way back to Albuquerque. Precisely where they were not supposed to be. The seventy Volunteers arrived at the base of the Zia Pueblo with a couple of hours of daylight left, and Chacon led them single file up to the top of the mesa and into the Pueblo.

Once up top, they dismounted. They received the expected stares from the Pueblans. Children looking around corners, people stopping their work to stare. The Pueblans, intentionally, didn't get much opportunity to see soldiers up here.

Chacon singled out two men and made known his intentions to meet with either the head or the head of justice for the Pueblo. The Pueblans had no interest in doing anything that kept the soldiers there any longer than necessary. Even if the Navajos had done nothing directly to hurt the Zia, bringing the soldiers would be reason enough to wish for their departure.

A very old, very small Zia came around the corner after a brief wait and approached Chacon. The old man's head did not even come up to Chacon's chest. He couldn't have been five feet tall.

The two spoke in a combination of pigeon Spanish and pigeon Zia.

"Yes, some Dine arrived here yesterday and asked for our hospitality," the old man said.

"Do you know where they are now," Chacon said.

Once the old man understood what Chacon was asking, he said something to the Zia who were crowding ever closer to them.

Immediately, the assembled Zia disappeared. As if by magic. Men, women, children, everyone but the old man. Disappeared into the low stone buildings, around corners. Gone.

The old man turned back to Chacon, and said, "Si."

He walked Chacon around a corner and pointed to a solitary building off a plaza. "The Dine are there. In that house."

"Are there any Zia in there with them?"

"No. Just the Dine."

"All the Dine?"

"Yes. All of them. They were afraid you were following them and are hiding in that house."

He turned, and, without another word, disappeared down a street away from the house with the Navajos.

"Well, I hope I'm never to depend on the hospitality of the Zia," Chacon said.

One of the Corporals volunteered that he spoke enough Navajo to at least try to communicate with them. The New Mexicans surrounded the building. Chacon approached the building.

"We would like to talk to you," the Corporal said to the door.

Silence.

"Maybe your Navajo is not so good," the Corporal's brother said. A big grin showing his teeth through his beard.

The Corporal tried again. Louder.

Nothing.

"Tell them we don't want to harm them," Chacon said. "We just want to take them back to their homes in peace."

Both brothers laughed.

"His Navajo is not so good, Captain. My brother knows how to barter with Navajos for food and clothing only."

The first Corporal said something to the door in Navajo. Something different, but louder.

"What did you say that time, Corporal?" Chacon said.

"I asked them if they wanted us to share some of our cebolla and corn after their hard journey."

"Apparently their answer is 'No'."

The Corporal yelled his initial message, practically at the top of his lungs. Nothing but silence.

"The Texans can't get here fast enough for me," Chacon said to his men.

There was a wooden bench in the square across from the house. Chacon sent the brothers over to pick it up. He and a Sergeant used the bench to attack the door.

The two of them, followed by the brothers and three of the larger Privates, burst into the room.

Gunfire immediately exploded from the darkness in front of them, and the Volunteers opened fire.

One of the Navajo shoved a rifle in Chacon's chest and pulled the trigger. Chacon twisted away from the rifle just as it discharged and stabbed the Navajo with his sword.

Most of the shooting was now coming from an adjacent room. A young Navajo man ran out the back door, shooting at the soldiers who were waiting there. But they shot and killed him before he could get by them.

The New Mexican return fire eventually brought order and silence to the building.

The Navajo at Chacon's feet was dying. Nothing could be done for him.

One Volunteer had a flesh wound in his shoulder.

The only other casualty was Chacon's shirt and jacket, both of which had been burned beyond repair by the shot at his chest.

The next day, having received no thanks from the Pueblans, the Volunteers started the two day ride back to Albuquerque, where they delivered the sad-looking bunch of Navajos to the regular Army soldiers at the central garrison without incident.

Chacon rode over to Volunteer headquarters and reported the details to Carson.

"A sad business, Rafael. A very sad business," Carson said.

"Why don't the Navajo just go home as they have agreed, Colonel?"

"There's nothing for them there, except for their home, Captain. Those Navajo who have been terrorizing the other tribes and the New Mexicans here, left their homeland because there is not enough there for them all to survive. They've come to depend on their raiding for their existence."

"What happens to them after we are done with the Texans?" Chacon said.

"If they go back to raiding," Carson said. "The U.S. Army will have to deal with them once and for all. I will want no part of it. Fighting the Texans is all I have left in me. This will be a very sad business with the Navajo."

37

December 12, 1861

General Sibley completed his three and a half week march and led his Texans into Fort Bliss.

On that very same day, four hundred seventy-five miles due north, Alonzo Ferdinand "Lon" Ickis and Company B of the Second Colorado Volunteers mustered into Federal service at Fort Garland, Colorado. The 25 year old Ickis had rushed to Colorado with his brother two years previous for the gold rush. Tall, thin with a head that was covered with chestnut curls and was filled with dreams, the failed gold miner had joined the Colorado Volunteers six weeks before in search of his next adventure. The lack of any successes to date had not dampened his idealist's sense of enthusiasm for everything and everyone.

Halfway between these two groups of Volunteers, nestled along the Rio Grande River, lay the little agricultural town of Belen. The Spaniards had named Belen for Bethlehem in 1740 because they felt it shared a similar climate and terrain with that Biblical city.

The Rio Grande River worked its way south from Colorado, passing by Taos and Santa Fe, then nearer to Albuquerque, and by the farmers and ranchers of Belen.

From there it continued on for fifty-five miles southward, by Valverde Mesa, and then Fort Craig and Fort Thorn, before flowing on to El Paso, and then along the entirety of the Texas-Mexico border.

The New Mexicans from such towns as Belen and Albuquerque and Santa Fe, normally worried about droughts, drunks, and raiding Navajos, were about to be subjected to three months of armed conflict.

The American Civil War was coming to the New Mexico Territory.

38

December 23, 1861

"Are we ready for Sibley, Kit?" Canby said.

"Ed, you know I'm not too enthusiastic about this adventure. You've got my Volunteers marching around the desert chasing after bandits and Navajos. Your officers are drunks and worse. Your troops are not battle ready or trained. We have no idea who or what is coming down from Colorado. Or even if they can get through the snow in the mountains. And we know that Sibley is damn good at training troops."

"On the other hand," Damours said, "We just heard that another 1,300 Colorado Volunteers will be headed here in February under Major Chivington and somebody named Slough."

"Ah," Carson said, "That should supplement Canby's amateur soldiers nicely. A minister and a lawyer, both from Ohio."

Carson turned to Canby. "The Colorado Volunteers and my New Mexicans, combined with your worthless Union regulars, Colonel, are not likely to be enough to stop Sibley's Texans. And I don't like your strategy of just sitting here, waiting for them."

Canby chewed his cigar before responding. "There is another piece of good news, Kit. Three companies of Carleton's California Volunteers under Joe West arrived at Fort Yuma November 3rd to keep the Texans from controlling the Colorado River."

"Colonel Joseph West?" Carson said. "Nice for us Yankees to now have a future General from New Orleans on board."

"By the way" Arnold said. "Speaking of Baylor, did you hear he killed the editor of the Mesilla paper in cold blood? And he has now officially ordered his Texans to kill all Apaches. Men, women, children, even under a white flag. 'Kill them. Just kill them all.' is what he ordered."

Carson looked at the floor dejectedly, then up at Canby. "On the subject of your officers, I just met Captain Bascom down at Fort Craig. Now there's a fine officer for you Ed."

Neither Canby nor Damours took the bait.

"How'd he ever get promoted to Captain?" Carson said.

"West Point." Arnold said. "Time passed. Time for a promotion."

Carson just shook his head. "When do we now expect the Texans?"

"Soon Kit," Canby said. "I shouldn't think he'd need more than a couple of weeks to organize. All the food he needs for his men is up here. If he's going to feed three thousand soldiers, he needs to come through here to get it. It won't be long now."

In fact, Sibley and his twenty-five hundred Texans would leave Fort Bliss, headed for Fort Craig, in eleven days.

39

December 25, 1861

"Merry Christmas, Auggy," Lily said.

She was standing in his doorway with flowers and a box.

He was sitting up in bed, naked from the waist up, sheets covering his legs and stomach. "Oops. I forgot about Christmas."

He frowned, but she didn't believe him.

He signaled her to come to bed when she closed the door.

"It's Christmas, Auggy. I'm not getting into that bed. Certainly not without a proper meal, and certainly if you didn't get me anything for our first ever Christmas."

She feigned a pout as she sat in the room's lone chair.

He reached out his hand and laughed.

"Your hand or the box, beautiful lady."

She handed him the box, taking care to make sure he couldn't grab her hand.

He smiled at that and took the offered box. He opened it.

Tissue paper.

He unwrapped it.

Another box. More tissue paper.

He looked at her as she pretended to be fascinated by something outside the window.

Another box. A very small box.

He opened it.

A set of cuff links. Jet black. In the shape of diamonds. Jet black amethyst diamond cuff links.

He was amazed as he cocked his head and smiled over at her. "Where did you get these, Lil? They're simply stunning. Are they *his?*"

"No. I had them made by a jeweler off San Francisco street."

"But they're identical to the ones Canby said John Wilkes Booth wears."

"I thought you'd like 'em, Auggy. Just be careful and don't wear them in front of the Colonel, okay?" She blew him a kiss. "Now, mister. What'd you get me? Really?"

"It's under the pillow."

She frowned. "My pillow or yours?"

"Yours."

She looked skeptically at him. "No tricks?"

"No, Miss Smoot. No tricks."

Suspicious, she walked around the bed and slid her hand under "her" pillow. She felt around. Found an envelope and slipped it out.

Walked back to the chair and sat.

She looked thoughtfully at Damours. "It worked?" Lily said as she cocked her head. Suspicious again.

"It worked," he said, grinning from ear to ear.

She slipped over $600 in cash out of the envelope. Almost $650. Her eyes widened as she looked over at Damours.

Damours had taken a letter from Canby's mail pouch the day before. It was from a businessman in Albuquerque and had contained a government draft for $750 on its way to pay a merchant in Colorado. Zapico verified that it was as good as cash, but he was uncomfortable cashing it and thus being so directly linked to Damours.

Especially if this turned out to be a one-off swindle.

Lily had suggested that Damours go to one of the saloons on the east side of town, somewhere he'd never gambled before. He should, she said, "lose" at poker, then use the draft to pay off one of the winners. The cash left after paying his losses would then be his.

Had it really worked? Was Damours really that good?

"Any problems?"

"None at all. I even forged a letter of payment from the issuer to me to make it look more authentic. The gambler took it and gave me this cash without a second thought."

"You used your real name?"

She held her breath.

"Ah. I guess I never showed you my California papers. A very Merry Christmas to a very beautiful lady from Mr. Billy Rome."

She beamed. "Auggy, we're gonna be the wealthiest ranchers in all of Washington Territory. You really are the best con man ever lived."

"Ah. We're well-matched, lady. I'll take it as a compliment if you'll come to bed now, and then accompany me to Christmas breakfast."

And she did.

That evening, Lily agreed to let Captain Arnold take her to dinner. New Mexican food off the Plaza.

"Feeling lonely, John?"

"Are you teasing me, Lily?"

"No," she said, her teasing obvious. "All alone on Christmas, two thousand miles away from your family. And stuck with me for dinner."

"I'd rather be in Baltimore with my family for Christmas, Lily. But this is the life I've chosen. We understand that this is the way it is."

"Is this your first Christmas away?"

"Hardly. I doubt Beth and I have spent anywhere near half our holidays together in the twenty-six years we've been married."

She cocked her head as she listened. Thought about it. Was there any stability in *her* future?

"On the bright side," he said. "This is the first holiday I've ever spent with my 'daughter'."

She smiled. She liked John and was happy to stick with the fiction that she was "family." But it only worked on one level for her, and she doubted he really meant it. More like a mentor than a foster father. Still, it was nice to not always be on your guard with a man.

"You able to save money dealing poker, Lily?"

"Some. Not as much as in past jobs."

He let it go. Lily had made it clear that her past jobs after she left Utah and Mormonism were off limits.

"Enough?" Arnold said.

"Sure. I like Santa Fe. Dealing poker, the guys pretty much leave you alone. The town's full of whores, so I don't have problems with anybody refusing to take 'no' for an answer. I make more than I spend. I'm here until the War is done out here anyway."

She sipped her whiskey.

"John, how much longer you all going to be in Santa Fe?"

"A few days yet. We're headed down south to Fort Craig. It's a week's ride.

We'll no doubt be dealing with the Texans around there within two months. Why?"

"Just thinkin'. Always good to know what's going on. Can't hurt."

They both sipped the whisky. Waiting for their dinners.

"Lily, do you know this young Lieutenant works for Canby? Looks like Booth the actor from back in Baltimore?"

She looked into the distance like she was trying to remember. She had known this was likely to come up eventually. There was always the risk that Auggy might mention her to someone. And she didn't want to get caught in a lie with Arnold.

"I think so. If he's who I think he is, he plays a lot of poker. He came in from California. Damours, right?"

"Right."

"I thought he joined the Volunteers. He works with Canby now you say?"

"Right."

"Why do you ask, John?"

"No real reason. Just a feeling. Canby is very high on him. Depends on him. But, as you say, he came from California and joined the Volunteers. Just seems odd, and he seems an unlikely soldier."

He took a sip and lit up a cigarillo. Gave it to Lily, then lit one for himself.

"Anything bother you about him, Lily?"

She took a long drag. "He seems more honest than most. Seems pretty open and earnest. He does seem awfully young, without much military experience for Canby to have so much faith in him, I guess."

"He's older than he looks, Lily. And he seems slippery. Very few men out here are as guileless as he appears to be."

Lily looked at Arnold. "Well, John, I guess he either is or he isn't. We'll probably never know."

40

December 29, 1861

Danson sat on the edge of his bed, facing Pepper, Angela, and the three he had brought in from Arizona for this job. He had just briefed the five of them.

Since Lily and Cummings had nothing for Danson to do but sit around and wait for the money to roll in, he had decided it was the right time for him to do something on his own.

He and his gang were going to rob a Santa Fe bank.

Two hundred yards northwest and two floors below, Cummings sat silently in the Plaza with Lily, people watching mostly. It was one of those spectacular Santa Fe winter days that regularly seem to come immediately after a snowfall.

Yesterday, a foot of snow had turned the city into a winter wonderland. Even though four days too late, the trees had been decorated as if for Christmas. And here today it felt like Spring. Not a cloud in the sky and everybody in shirts with no jackets. Only the muddy puddles in the streets marred an otherwise perfect setting.

Walking under trees could still be perilous, though.

"Any idea what Danson's up to Lil?" Cummings said. Coming out of his silent reverie.

"What do you mean?"

"I haven't heard a word from him in weeks."

"I don't think it's much of a mystery," she said. "He's waiting on you to get into the Army, like the rest of us. It's on you, Joseph. Everything else is working, right? Damours is Canby's aide de camp. Zapico's selling Mowry's stuff and selling the Army their own things back to them. We're all just waiting for you to join up now."

She looked across the Plaza at something, but decided she was mistaken.

"Auggy thinks Jim might have something else going on," she said. "But he's not including us in on it."

At this point, there was a commotion at the other end of the Plaza.

Cummings looked over and saw Kit Carson riding over to the Governor's Palace, a mounted Indian on each flank. Carson had brought Red Cloud and

Yellow Horse in to meet the Governor to discuss their unhappiness with the new Reservation at Cimarron.

Cummings walked over to where his horse was tethered to get a better view of the famous Indian fighter turned babysitter turned military commander. As he took hold of the reigns, one of the Indians looked down at Cummings' horse and said something to Carson.

Carson turned and looked down at Cummings.

"Sir, Red Cloud wants to know where you got that Apache quiver. With the bow case."

Cummings pulled his horse around to inspect the quiver.

"Why is it any business of a Ute, sir?"

Carson looked curiously at Cummings and then turned toward the Indian and spoke to him. Then turned back.

"He just wants to know how you came to possess it. It caught him by surprise is all. Me too, now that I look at it."

"A year ago June I was commanding the security forces for Mowry's mines down below Tucson when some Chiricahuas attacked us on their way back from raiding the herds around Tubac."

Neither Red Cloud nor Yellow Horse showed any signs of understanding. They both sat impassively on their horses, looking down at Cummings. Either not comprehending or just letting Carson carry the conversation.

"In the course of the fighting," Cummings said. "I just missed one of the Apaches and shot his horse out from under him. He came off the horse running even faster, like they do, and ran off into a ravine. After a few minutes they all came thundering back, angrier than hornets. Trying to get to the horse. It seemed odd to me."

"I know any number of good men who would risk their lives for their horse," Carson said. "By the way, what's your name, if I may ask."

"Cummings, sir. Joseph Cummings."

"Go on with your story, Cummings."

"Not much more to tell. They couldn't get back to the wounded horse through our gunfire, so they ultimately rode back to the rest of the band and the cattle they'd stolen."

The three men looked down at Cummings, apparently waiting for him to answer the original question.

"After they ran, I walked over to the horse and finished it off. One of the miners came running over and told me that I had shot Cochise right off his horse. So I took that quiver there off his dead horse as a memento. And that was that."

Knowing better, Carson said, "I thought the Chiricahuas were at peace back then."

Cummings snorted. "Sure, Colonel. They were at peace. Just so's you don't count the raiding they do to earn a living off the Mexicans and the whites in southern Arizona. They don't consider it war, so I guess we didn't either. Come to think of it, I almost changed the history of the Territory that day."

His short laugh was not returned by either Carson or the two Indians.

Red Cloud said something to Carson after hearing the translation.

"He says he'll buy it from you, Cummings."

"It's not for sale."

Carson didn't translate and nobody said anything for a time.

Cummings looked up at the Ute chief.

"What business is a Chiricahua quiver of yours? Why do you want it?"

Red Cloud looked steadily down at Cummings.

"No hablo Ingles."

"What are you doing here in Santa Fe, Cummings?" Carson said.

"Actually, on business for Mowry. But I'm considering joining the Army if they'll have me."

"You can come see me if you're interested in joining the New Mexico Volunteers."

Carson started to turn his horse back toward the Palace when Cummings said, "Tell me Colonel, what are you going to do with these Indians when the Texans get here? These Utes and Apaches gonna help us against the Rebels? Or are they gonna scatter back where they came from and start making all our lives miserable again?"

"That's less of your business than Cochise's quiver is of Red Cloud's, Cummings," Carson said. "Maybe you'd better talk to Colonel Canby or the Governor rather than me about a job. I hear they're looking for a Marshal here in Santa Fe. Might suit you better."

And he touched his cap and nodded as he turned his horse back across the street toward the Palace, summarily dismissing the grinning Cummings.

Red Cloud, though was now distracted. He noticed the woman across the Plaza, the woman he had saved from the Mexicans. She was looking directly back at him. He nodded to her in recognition and she waved back. It was just a moment, but it was a memory shared by each of them.

The moment passed and Red Cloud looked back down at Cummings. Neither he nor Yellow Horse took their eyes off the confessed "horse killer" as they trotted behind Carson toward the Palace.

I didn't expect him to remember me, Lily thought to herself as she watched the two Indians follow Carson, while Cummings sauntered back toward her. If he was going to remember her, she owed Red Cloud. Maybe someday? Who knew?

Cummings walked up.

"You're an idiot, Joseph." Lily lit into him when he walked back.

She, along with everybody else around the Plaza had watched the entire incident.

"Red Cloud has killed any number of people over the last decade for doing less than you just did to him in public. You're supposed to be getting people to trust your judgment, especially people like Carson. Not annoying everybody."

"Well, Cochise's quiver is mine. It's not for sale."

"Neither is Red Cloud's pride. When he's not being a cold blooded killer, he's one of the most respected and trusted Utes in New Mexico. And just for your future reference, he understood every word you said. You're a complete, total fucking idiot, Cummings. Just an idiot."

Jim looked out his window down at the Plaza at the entire scene. From this vantage point nobody could tell what had just happened between Cummings and Carson and the two Indians.

He looked over at Pepper. As they'd agreed before the meeting, she nodded to indicate she was fine. She hadn't seen or heard anything that bothered her during the discussion.

"Any questions?" Danson said.

"You sure you don't want us in disguises, too?" one of the men said. "By now someone may associate us all together."

"No," Danson said. "Not necessary. The two girls and I will be unrecognizable, and you three will be gone the second we're out of the Bank. Even if somebody recognizes you and tells the Marshal to check on us, our alibis will be airtight. And nobody in the Bank will have recognized us three. You can wear bandanas over your faces if it makes you feel better. More like real bank robbers. You three just take off. Leave our half of the money buried under that wagon in the arroyo southwest of town. One of us will pick it up after you're long gone."

"Our only risk is you three talkin'," Pepper said.

"There's nothing in it for us to talk, Pep," the bank robber said. "Nobody up here would believe our word against Danson's anyway. And nobody in Tucson cares."

41

January 2, 1862

Danson pulled his right boot on, looked over at the two girls snuggled together on the bed under the covers, and smiled. He reached down and snagged the left boot, almost falling off the bed. He stepped into it and reached over and slapped Pepper on the ass.

She looked up sleepily and frowned.

"You leavin'?"

She snuggled up closer to Angela.

"Yeah. I need to talk to Cummings about a couple of things."

He nudged Pepper hard on the shoulder. Did it again until both girls were looking up at him.

"Everything okay?"

They both nodded. He picked up his hat and left the two girls where he'd found them an hour before.

"You think Lily's right?" Pepper said. "That I can't trust Danson."

"Of course you can't Pep," Angela said. "You can't trust any of these guys. Take your share of the money and then see where it goes."

"He's assured me that after the bank job I can quit working and that he and I are gonna get outta here. I'm not going to have to work anymore."

"Pep, you can't be as naïve as you sound. Lily's right."

Pepper crossed her arms over her chest. "I know what he told me. It feels like the truth to me Angela. This is all going to work out just like we've planned."

And then it all went to hell.

42

January 3, 1862

Pepper left the parlor house near 4:00 am. It had been an exhausting night. At first she couldn't believe all three of Danson's Tucson bank robbers had wanted her.

She'd tried to talk them into Angela and Tina, but they insisted they only wanted her. They said it would help them all work better together at the bank job later in the morning. But it became clear that they were disdainful of Danson and this was just a sporting form of disrespect. Hiding disgust came with the territory if you were going to be a successful whore. Probably in the bank robbing business, too, she laughed grimly.

But Danson needed to know about this. He needed to know everything she'd learned.

But he wasn't in his room.

She decided, spur of the minute, to retrace her steps and wake up Lily. Lily knew she was anxious about both Danson and the bank job, and never minded her late night visits.

She entered the boarding house from the side entrance and headed through the sitting room back toward Lily's room, only to be brought up short by the sound of footsteps and Lily's door closing. She froze and shrunk back into the darkness of an armoire's shadow.

And then her heart stopped.

Danson walked within a step of her as he headed toward the back entrance and out the back door into the alley.

She just stood there unable to breathe. Unable to think. After a few minutes, she gathered both her physical and emotional self and walked quietly to Lily's door.

Knocked.

"Yes," Lily said, sounding annoyed.

"It's me. Pepper."

After a moments' silence, Lily opened the door and Pepper's heart sank. It was obvious in Lily's eyes and in her disheveled appearance.

Pepper pushed her way in. "I just wanted to talk," she said. "I didn't know you were busy."

It came out as an accusation.

Lily gestured toward a chair and then suddenly rushed forward to take her friend in her arms.

"I'm so sorry, Pep. I told you that you couldn't trust him. I warned you."

Of course I never told you that you couldn't trust me, Lily thought.

"But you knew how I felt about him," Pepper said. "You knew what he's told me, what I was counting on. How could you do this to me?"

They were both in tears now. They separated and sat across from each other.

Silence.

"Well," Pepper said.

Silence.

Her eyes were like daggers digging into Lily's head.

"Look," Lily said. "I'm so sorry. I can't undo this now. Jim is who he is. He's just another guy we can use. We talked about this, hon."

"And me? I'm just another whore *you* can use?"

Silence.

"Okay, Pep. When is the bank job?"

On her guard now, Pepper just sat. Wringing her hands and glaring at her friend. Her former friend. "Did you tell Jim that I told you about the bank job?"

"No, of course not. I'm not an idiot, Pep."

Pepper got up to leave.

"Don't leave, Pep."

Lily reached out for her and Pepper pushed her away. She put her fist to her lips and walked out, biting her knuckle. Into the hall and then into the cold Santa Fe night.

She wandered the streets in a light snowfall, now five hours to the bank robbery, and she had nobody to trust.

10:00 am.

Time to go.

Pepper took a deep breath and crossed the street toward the Bank. She nodded tightly at their lookout, standing there holding the horses as planned.

He gaped at her in astonishment.

Her job was to come in last. In disguise. Checking outside to make sure nobody was coming into the Bank for the next couple of minutes.

She paused at the entrance.

Nobody was approaching the Bank. She took one more look around Santa Fe.

She stepped over the threshold into the Bank.

There were a dozen people lined up against the far wall. Arms raised. A couple tried to warn her away with their body language.

To her left, guns drawn, were the two other guys from Tucson. Both with bandanas over their faces.

To her right was Angela, barely recognizable in her disguise. She looked just like any other strange cowhand just come into town. Gun drawn, hair hidden under her cowboy hat and blue bandana. Just your normal high desert bank robber.

All three of the robbers looked at her in shocked surprise. Eyes wide.

Pepper had come in dressed normally. She had failed to put on her disguise. Just walked in as if she'd come in for a normal visit to the Bank. Like she'd forgotten all about the robbery. She was recognizable to everyone in the Bank.

Angela failed to hold back a gasp.

"Pep?"

Also at 10:00 am, just as the Second Colorado Volunteers received their orders to start their march southward from Fort Garland, Colorado to Fort Marcy in Santa Fe, General Henry Hopkins Sibley rode out to the parade grounds at Fort Bliss.

Sibley had planned for this day from the minute Texas had seceded from the Union.

He sat astride his horse looking out over the Fort Bliss parade ground. Over twenty-five hundred of Texas' finest. Recruited by him, trained by him, and as ready to kill Yankees as they would ever be.

Headed for New Mexico, Colorado, and then California.

In ten short miles they would leave Texas and instantly be transformed into the Confederate Army of New Mexico. They were under orders to use Texas scrip to "pay" all farmers and merchants for food and provisions all along the Rio Grande. Their cattle herd and their empty wagons waited outside the fort to bring up the rear of the column. The wagons would not be empty for long.

"Lieutenant," Sibley said.

The Lieutenant rode over. Both he and his horse excited from all the preparations.

"Take your platoon, Lieutenant. Ride on ahead to Mesilla. Tell Governor Baylor that the Confederate Army of New Mexico will be arriving in eight days."

"Yes, sir."

Sibley turned and handed his sword to Green. "Tom, why don't you do the honors?"

Green raised the General's sword high, glinting in the morning sun. "On to California," Green said.

"On to California," came back the shout from twenty-five hundred throats, followed immediately by the rebel yell, reverberating off the walls of Fort Bliss.

Green led the Texans northward toward what would was intended to be a brief, triumphant march through New Mexico.

Sibley stood and watched. Beaming.

As drunk as he'd ever been.

Pepper looked frantically around the Bank.

She looked left, then right, desperately trying to find Danson.

One of the robbers suddenly yelled, whirled around, and shot one of the tellers.

Pepper and Angela both screamed.

The noise immediately died down when he let loose another shot into the ceiling and pointed his revolver at the people along the wall. Waving it back and forth.

Danson shouted, muffled, and barely recognizable. "Dammit. Dammit all to hell."

"He was pulling a gun on you. I had no choice."

"Those're his keys. He's unarmed, you damn fool," Danson said, still not visible.

"Nobody's coming," Pepper said. Just to say something.

Danson emerged from behind the counters with a bag, presumably filled with money.

He was unrecognizable in his fake red beard and overalls and straw hat making him look, well, like a farmer. Nobody in town would recognize him. Even his voice was disguised.

He stopped and stared at Pepper for a brief second.

"Where the hell's your outfit? What's going on?"

One of her regulars against the wall said, "Pepper. You know this farmer?"

The look on his face indicated that he immediately regretted his outburst.

The jumpy robber pointed his gun at the guy, but Danson pushed his arm toward the floor.

"Let me think, dammit," Danson said. "Hold off."

"We're fucked, Jim," the other robber said. "Everybody here knows she knows us and they'll figure out who you are in no time."

"Shut up, dammit." Danson pointed his gun at the man against the wall.

Danson shot the man twice in the chest.

He looked around and pointed his gun at Pepper. "What the fuck were you thinking?" he said.

"C'mon, let's get out of here," Angela said, just as the lookout said, "Here comes the Marshal."

The two robbers grabbed Angela's arm and pulled her out the door.

Danson was still staring incomprehensively at Pepper with his gun pointed at her. He looked back at the people lining the wall and turned his gun on them as they screamed and fell to the floor. He hesitated and then headed out of the Bank.

Pepper looked him in the eye as he walked by her, and drew two items from her satchel. She swung the hunting knife in her right hand into Danson's neck as he passed by.

He stumbled and his gun went off into the floor.

One of the robbers, in the doorway, yelled and turned back into the Bank. He saw Danson, looking perplexed, fall. Pepper walk over to him. She raised her left hand toward Danson. The robber took a step toward her to help.

Pepper calmly shot Danson in the back of the head with the small derringer held in her left hand.

The kid in the doorway, stunned, reflexively shot Pepper twice in the chest and then ran out to the other three, jumped on his horse, and, returning gun fire at the Marshal, heard himself yell, "I was fucking her just six hours ago? That's just fucking amazing."

43

January 4, 1862

"You okay, Lil?" Zapico said.

"Sure. Why not? Stuff happens. Plans fall apart. I'm fine. Danson was a fool. But Pepper deserved better."

He handed her a bottle of whiskey. She took it. They were in the back of his store. It was Saturday and the store was closed.

"Since when do you close on Saturday, Zapico?"

"Since I started getting religious again. Came on me all of a sudden."

She laughed. Handed him back the bottle. "Thanks, I needed that."

"The whiskey or the joke?"

"Both. Thanks for both. How many Jews are there in the Territory, David? "

"Why do you ask?"

"Always been curious. Maybe it's the shock or the whiskey. Just need something to talk about."

"A few in Taos and Las Vegas," he said. "More here. Even more in Albuquerque. Maybe fifty in all."

"It okay for you all out here?"

"No problems here. There was a recent anti-Semitic assault and theft by the Colorado Volunteers against some Jewish sutlers outside the fort in Las Animas. But here, several of the Jews are in the Masons. My cousin Solomon joined up as a Captain with Canby."

Maybe being respectable is worth shooting for, she thought.

Zapico looked curiously at her as she stifled a laugh.

"Okay, are we still okay after this fiasco?" she said, getting back to the problem at hand.

"You tell me, Lily. I just buy and sell stuff Mowry and you and Damours send my way," he said.

"It's a little late for innocence, Zapico. It wasn't his intention, but Danson kept us in the clear on this by cutting us out."

"What do Damours and Cummings know?" he said.

She paused. Excellent question, David Zapico. What did that fucking idiot Cummings know?

"Look, Lily. Up to now, I've been fine with you playing everybody. Even me. But if this is going to come back at us, we need to deal with it."

He poured her a little more whiskey, then said, "Mowry and I can't afford to be bushwhacked from behind. My livelihood depends on my business staying legit. That's important for all of us. I'm not willing to take any risk on that. I'm dead if my sales are dirty. Literally. Dead. Do you understand?"

"Yes, Zapico, I understand."

Neither spoke for several minutes.

"Look, David. I'm also dead if this thing blows up. The life I want depends on this continuing to work. We depend on each other here."

"Convince me."

She exhaled. Then looked at him. Men. They're all different, but, unless they're just plain bad to the bone, they can always be manipulated. Their egos ask for it.

Zapico. Zapico just wants to be treated like who he sees himself to be. Successful. King of his new world. Able to lever his new freedoms like his fathers before him could not. Respected like the king they wanted themselves and him to be.

Cummings. Cummings wants to make the big score without making the tinyest commitment. And feeling like everyone dances to his tune while he plays the music and makes the score. He confuses opportunism with patience. Thinks that he's just been unlucky. Opportunities all around and he just has no luck. Luckily, luck is always just around the next corner.

And Auggy. Auggy's such a dear. A true artist who doesn't see it. Has no need to even be paid for his art. Just the need to be loved back by those who he wants to love.

Dear, sweet Auggy.

She looked up at Zapico. Eyeing her patiently, but curious.

Damn, I'm so close. So close to getting everything I want. Time to get back to work.

"Waddya want to know, David? Ask away."

He laughed.

"What does Auggy know?"

Men are so predictable, she thought.

"Absolutely nothing," she said. "Nothing at all."

Less than a hundred yards away, across the Plaza, unbeknownst to Lily, Damours was having a similar conversation with Canby.

"This bank robbery yesterday, Auggy?"

"Yes, sir."

"I'm told that you knew this Danson fellow. Is that true?"

This could go in any of a hundred different directions. Damours knew he needed to be careful. It was a situation that he was peculiarly adept at handling. But he needed to be careful. He tried to remember what that damnable Chacon did and didn't know about him and Danson.

"Yes, sir. I knew him."

"From where, Auggy."

"I met him in San Francisco. During the gold rush days. We played in some of the same poker games. Other than that, not very well. I worked a lot of jobs back then, but never any with Danson. It was purely social."

"And is it merely a coincidence that you're both here in Santa Fe? At the same time?"

Excellent question Colonel, Damours thought. Who, besides Lily and Pepper knew of their relationship? Angela? Could Canby have talked to Angela already?

"Partly. He had mentioned New Mexico to me several times in San Francisco. I came here on…" and then he remembered his earlier lies. Damn. How stupid. Amateur.

"…and since I was originally from here, I decided to come back."

Canby stared at him, chewing on his cigar.

"I was as startled to see him as he was to see me. Since then, poker games occasionally. Then I joined the Volunteers and haven't had much occasion for social life since."

They were interrupted by a Private knocking on the door.

"Colonel Canby, they just sent someone in to tell you that the Marshal died from his wounds at the bank, sir. Nothing could be done for him."

"Thank you, Private."

Canby sighed. "Well, Auggy, you got any ideas for a new Provost Marshal?"

"Auggy? Auggy is a total dear, David," Lily said. She suppressed a smile at how transparently Zapico tried to mask his real interest in Cummings.

"Everybody wants to be Auggy's friend. Look how quickly Canby grabbed him. Even after Chacon had that run-in with him."

"Maybe that cinched the deal for Auggy," Zapico said. "Nobody much likes that little greaser. Wait until he and Cummings have to work together. If, I suppose, Cummings ever commits to working with anybody."

"Ah. And there lies our problem, Zapico."

"Joseph," they said together.

"Okay, then," Zapico said. Finally getting to it. "So what does Cummings know?"

"What does he know," she said. "Or what does he think he knows? Or what is he planning? If anything?"

"For starters, I can tell you what Mowry has told me," he said.

"Okay. That's a start."

"Mowry told me from the beginning that he trusted Cummings, but that I couldn't. He sent him here in an attempt to generate a pipeline for his and my business interests. Also as his eyes on the ground to get a feel for who might come out on top if the Texans come. He tells me that Cummings has been useless as an informant, and he knows his only contribution so far was his success in getting Damours into the Army."

"In truth," she said. "That's been a pretty big contribution. The biggest by far. And Cummings does keep claiming he's going to share his poker winnings with us."

"Not funny, Lily. Four-fifths of his poker winnings, assuming he's being straight with us, is poor payment for a fifth of our total action. If that's all he contributes, we should cut him out. Do you think he'll ever come around and join the Army? Or do we just move on without him at some point? And can we?"

"I think Cummings is terrified of being on the wrong side," she said. "Partly because he then fears that Mowry will cut him out."

"Plus, he could get shot," Zapico said.

"I think even Cummings has figured out you can get shot on either side. My guess is he enlists when the shooting stops. Or takes Carson up on his suggestion to become a Marshal."

"Especially now that they're one Marshal short."

"There's that."

"Can we cut him out?" Zapico said.

"I don't see how, David. He knows too much, and it'd spook Mowry."

"But it wouldn't spook Damours?"

"Never worry about Auggy, David. Never. You're his partner, not his target."

"I thought Cummings controlled him."

Lily just looked at Zapico like he was the biggest idiot in the world.

"Okay. I get it," he said. "By the way, Mowry asked me a question I couldn't answer. He wanted to know who you were, how you came to be a part of the gang, and what your role is in all this."

44

General Sibley sat in front of his fire with Colonel Green and Jack Swilling of the Arizona Guard in his Mesilla office. Sibley had taken almost two weeks since his arrival in Mesilla to sort through how he wanted to proceed.

He was now ready.

Swilling, a Lieutenant in the Arizona Guard, had been protecting the miners and ranchers from the Apaches for years before the Texans got there. However, he was better known throughout the Territory as a saloon and dance hall owner, a teamster, and a prospector.

"When we march north," Sibley said, "I want Governor Baylor to stay down here and do what he likes best. Chasing and killing Apaches with his Volunteers."

He looked over at Green and got the expected nod, and said, "Swilling, I want you and your Guard unit to escort one of Baylor's Companies to Tucson to secure the western frontier of Arizona. I don't want any unexpected Californians coming up my backside. Understood?"

"Yes, sir," Swilling said.

"Will that be sufficient to hold Tucson, Swilling?"

"More than enough, sir. Colonel West and a tiny force hold Fort Yuma for Carleton two hundred forty miles from Tucson, on the other side of the Colorado River, sir. He'll have no appetite for marching all that way through the desert."

Swilling waited to be dismissed. Nobody said anything, so he said, "My men asked me to ask you how the War is going back East, sir?"

"What looked like a quick Confederate victory is now bogged down," Sibley said. "Grant has been terrorizing Tennessee, and nobody has followed up the early routs in Virginia. It's damned disappointing. But I think we'll be fine once President Davis finds a way to put Lee in charge. In the meantime, they'll have something to celebrate soon enough. We'll be in Colorado and on our way to California in less than three months."

"When do we head to Fort Craig, sir?" Colonel Green said.

"Canby and his New Mexicans think we're going to mount a frontal assault," Sibley said. "But I'm inclined to just march around them and go up the Rio Grande to Albuquerque. If they try to chase us, it will have to be with a small force and it'll be a short battle indeed. Are we set to go in two weeks?"

"Less, sir," Green said.

"All right then. Gentlemen, you have your orders."

Having been told that Cochise had stolen a hundred Texan horses, Baylor rounded up as much of his command as he could after Green gave him his orders and headed after them that afternoon.

The Apaches had, characteristically, headed straight for Mexico. South and west.

The Texans caught them a little over a week later, a hundred miles south of the border at a Chiricahua rancheria, near the town of Corralitos. The Apaches had followed their usual pattern of bringing the horses to sell to the Mexicans for food, ponies, and blankets.

The Confederate forces attacked the rancheria at dawn and were able to secure the horses, but not before virtually all the Apaches had fled.

Baylor was disappointed to capture only one Chiricahua man, three women, and five small children. Per his previous orders to kill all Apaches, Baylor ordered the man and the three women executed, and the small children bound and taken prisoner.

Over a week later, Baylor and his Texans returned triumphant to Mesilla with what was left of the horses and the five captured Chiricahua children. But Sibley and his Confederate Army of New Mexico had left him behind and were marching north.

45

February 12, 1862

Damours, at Canby's direction, sat down to start the Fort Craig war briefing with Carson, Chacon, Bascom, and Arnold. Ickis represented the Coloradans.

"Sibley might attack us here at Fort Craig sometime around the 20th," Damours said. "Everybody's here who is going to be here. Ironically, President Lincoln has asked all federal troops to celebrate George Washington's 130th Birthday by beginning a general advance on the 22nd. If the Texans have not attacked by that date, Canby wants to obey the President's order and drive them back to Texas on the 22nd."

"Do we still estimate the Texans at twenty-five hundred, Auggy?" Carson said.

"Our spies say thirty-five hundred," Arnold said.

"And Baylor?" Chacon said.

"Twenty-five hundred, Arnold," Damours said and looked quickly at Captain Bascom and then back at Chacon. "And it seems Baylor is down in Mexico chasing Cochise's horse thieves."

"Nice to know, Captain Bascom," Carson said. "That we have fewer Texans to deal with as a result of your fiasco with Cochise."

Bascom ignored Carson's comment and said, "We have twelve hundred regular, seasoned Federal troops."

Carson snorted.

Arnold turned to Ickis in the ensuing silence.

"You're what, Lon, a hundred?"

"Yes, sir. A hundred Colorado Volunteers. But the rest should be arriving within the month."

"Then they'll either be here to congratulate you or bury you, Private," Chacon said. "Depending."

"We intend to welcome them with open arms, Captain Chacon," Ickis said. "How many gr...... How many New Mexicans do you have, sir?"

Chacon bristled at the slip, but Carson held out his arm.

"We have about twenty-five hundred New Mexico Volunteers and Militia under arms, Private," Carson said. "They have been training since Summer, and there's two generations of history here between the New Mexicans and the Texans. We are certainly grateful to you and your colleagues for making the trip down to help us out."

"This is my first time to New Mexico, sir," Ickis said, trying to cover over his previous near slur. "And.....my first time I ever got a chance to meet my idol, Kit Carson."

Everybody stared at Carson, who just looked at something in his hands.

"When did you get to Fort Craig?" Chacon said, more to fill the silence than anything else.

"About ten days before you. You arrived two days ago, right? We got here February 1st, through the mountains from Fort Garland to Taos, then to Santa Fe, then Belen in that beautiful little valley, and then the final three days to here."

"We know we have them outnumbered," Arnold said. "But nobody here really knows for certain if we have them outgunned. The scouts tell us that Sibley may be headed this way as soon as a day or two. Canby saw their advanced units yesterday on the west bank of the river just south of here. It's a two day march from Fort Thorn, so Damours is right, we expect to see them soon, certainly before the 22nd."

"Private Ickis," Damours said. "What do you boys think of your first trip to New Mexico?"

Damours couldn't help but grin now at the earnestness of this kid, out in the world for his first adventure.

"Boy, the women and fandangos in Santa Fe were something. Best we've ever seen. All the women here at the fort left by escort to Fort Union the day before you arrived, Chacon."

Arnold laughed . "Ickis, I think the Lieutenant wanted to know what you thought of our fortifications. Are we ready for the Texans?"

"Well," Ickis said. "I'll leave that to Colonel Carson and you to determine. Just point me at which Texan you want me to shoot and I'll do my damndest to do my duty for my Uncle. But I'll tell you this. I feel obliged to keep the Texans away from those villages up north of here. Those gr…. Sorry, those farmers offered us food and blankets, but told us they'd bury everything in the mountains if the Texans got by us. And, if you need reinforcements, just arm all the whores in Santa Fe, the odds would sure improve in our favor."

Even Chacon laughed at this.

"Don't worry," Damours said. "The girls of Santa Fe can take care of themselves, Ickis. They'll tell you they're rooting for your return. But if the Texans come calling, they won't be shooting any potential paying customers."

And then he thought about Lily up in Santa Fe.

He suddenly realized this wasn't fun and games any more. Their money was safe. But was Lily?

The war was now here.

46

Sibley had arrived within three miles of Fort Craig, and spread his forces out in a line of battle.

And there they sat. The Texans had tired of minor skirmishes and sorties, and were pretty much ready to force the issue.

"Let's see how Canby wants to play this, Green," Sibley said as they sat on their horses early in the morning behind the line.

Fort Craig sat between the Texans and their first real provisions since they had left San Antonio three months earlier. El Paso was not the garden spot of the West. And southern New Mexico and Arizona wasn't much better.

He planned to see if he could draw Canby out and defeat him south of the fort.

Fortified by the arrival of seventy wagons of provisions from Fort Union, Canby sent a third of his men out in force to engage the Texans.

"Do not," he said at the dawn meeting, "Allow your forces to be drawn into a pitched battle. Let's see how Sibley wants to play this. Understood?"

Carson and Arnold nodded in turn.

A thousand cavalry marched south out of Fort Craig at 8:00am, with Canby at the head. In a matter of minutes, the Texans were visible below along the river. After a half hour, they were in rifle range and Arnold and Carson stopped their advance.

With the Yankees on the high ground, the Texans began an orderly, slow retreat out of rifle range. Arnold ordered Bascom to lead two Companies in an attack. They were under orders to engage by fire, but not make physical contact.

Canby sat implacably on his horse, above the field, working his unlit cigar from side to side as his cavalry rushed the Texans, discharging their weapons. Sharpshooters from each side rained fire on the other.

Sibley oversaw an organized withdrawal under protective fire. The Texans lost on the order of a dozen men, about half killed. One of Bascom's Lieutenants was wounded slightly.

Bascom pulled up short as ordered and rode back to Canby and Arnold.

"Up to them now, Arnold," Canby said. "If they want to attack they have the provocation. If they want to sit, well here we are."

Sibley looked up through the haze at his brother-in-law up on the hill.

"You want to attack General?" Colonel Green said.

"Not now. Not now. There will be plenty of time. I want Canby to commit his main force. I don't want to engage and then deal with defending against his reinforcements. Let's give him time to succumb to his natural instincts for doing nothing."

They both looked up at Canby.

"He'll prefer to just sit and wait," Sibley said.

47

February 18, 1862

Lily looked Cummings in the eye and asked him point blank, "What's your plan, Joseph?"

"C'mon, Lil. Same as at the beginning. Mowry and I thought Santa Fe would be a nice place for us to make a fortune and keep my ear out for news that might interest him."

"So all this about joining the Army was just bullshit?"

"Not necessarily. If that's the best way, that's the way I'll go. Getting Canby to let me Marshal up might be better. We'll see if and when he comes back."

"And your move on Danson and Damours was what? A diversion? A scam?"

"No. C'mon Lil. I ran into them and started running with it from there. The kid's the best con artist I've ever seen. Danson is, er was, an idiot. He was always a risk to screw up Damours for us. Pepper did us a service, shooting him."

Lily frowned at the mention of Pepper.

"Like it or not, Lil, I'm staying flexible, Just going with this for now. I never saw any value in joining up with the wrong side. Where's the profit in that? And why do I owe you an accounting anyway. What's *your* plan, Lil?"

"I have Zapico. And I have Auggy. Without them, you have nothing but a chain of supplies with nowhere to go with 'em."

"I can go around you to either of them any time I want. Money talks for the Jew, and the kid can be his own man. He'd have to be if something happened to you. Ever think of that?"

"Yes, Joseph, I've thought of that. But if the 'something' that happened to me came from you, both Auggy and Zapico would see to it that you were out."

"You sure about that?"

"Deadly, Joseph. Deadly."

They stared at each other.

"Look, Lil. Don't take any of this the wrong way. You've helped set this up nicely."

"Without any help from you, Joseph."

"With nothing to sell, the Jew would be of little value to you."

"That's a joke, right? Auggy's fed more stuff, at better prices, than you 'n Mowry by a mile. And he's provided a ready market for resale. You fed us a line of bull about going into the Army as cover. Unless you ultimately do that, your contribution is minimal. Ultimately Mowry will figure that out and you'll be all alone out there."

There. She'd said it. It was out now. His Mowry connection was all he had, and without leveraging off it, Cummings was a spare part.

And a replaceable spare part at that.

Cummings looked like he was trying to work it out in his head. "I think my relationship with Sylvester is closer than you think, Lil. But you may be right. I'll grant you that he's looking for more from me than he's gotten so far."

"Add to that," she said. "His world has gone to hell over the last year. Cochise and the Mexican bandits are running him into the ground, and the Texans have too much on their hands to help him out. He has much more at stake than you do on who wins this War. You're ducking and covering to try to avoid being on the losing side, while, from where he sits today, there doesn't look to even be a winning hand. The winners, whoever they are, are probably going to hang him for treason and take his mines. That's where he's gonna need help. You're gonna need to be in a position to deliver for him."

She was running right over him. She had guessed right, he hadn't thought of any of that. He changed the subject. "Where's the money that Zapico and Damours have already saved up?"

"Auggy's got it. Some in jewels. Some in cash."

"Damours has all that money down at Fort Craig? With the Texans a mile away and planning on taking the fort? What if Damours gets killed down there? Are you all crazy?"

"No, of course not. Zapico and I would never have allowed that."

"Then where is it?"

"I know where it is," she lied. "If something happens to Auggy, you, Zapico, and I will meet to decide what to do. What to do with the money and what to do going forward."

"And if something happens to you?"

"Then you're fucked, Joseph. You're simply fucked."

Lies are always best when they can't be checked, she thought to herself. Then said, "But you changed the subject, Joseph. What's your plan? I think we've come to the part where you need to come up with one, don'tcha think?"

"Let's see whether or not Canby can send the Texans back to where they came from, then I'll tell you my plan. That good enough for you, Lily?"

48

February 20, 1862

Characteristically, Sibley tired of waiting for Canby's officers to talk him into coming out to fight.

The skirmishes over the previous few days were amounting to nothing except for spent ammunition and a few casualties on both sides.

The Texans crossed to the east side of the Rio Grande on the 19th and rode to a point opposite the fort.

Sibley had intended to rain artillery down on the fort from the opposite heights of El Contadero Mesa, but Canby had previously set up artillery defenses of the hill and Green failed to secure it.

The Texans had to satisfy themselves with firing into the pickets around the east side of the fort on the opposite bank.

Sibley spent the 20th marching his forces past the fort.

As dusk fell, the Confederate forces stretched the six miles along the eastern side of the river, northward. Sibley had decided to move north and cut off Canby's communications and supply lines to Fort Marcy in Santa Fe and Fort Union in Las Vegas.

At Green's urging, Sibley had decided to let his brother-in-law decide whether to come out and fight, or to leave the Texans clear sailing to the rest of Canby's Federals waiting a hundred and fifty miles to the north.

There was no risk that Canby would head south to Texas itself, leaving the New Mexico Territory to the Confederacy.

The Texans made camp at Valverde and prepared for the next day's march to Albuquerque.

Colonel Canby, Colonel Carson, and the newly promoted Major John Arnold stood together at the top of the fort, watching the Texans settling in for the night.

"It doesn't look like Sibley has much of an appetite for an assault," Carson said.

They had watched all day as the Texans supply train, a mile and a half long, had moved north past the fort on the east side of the river.

"They're gonna just leave us here and head out for Santa Fe," Arnold said. "We've got nothing between here and there to stop them."

"We have Lincoln's orders to start an assault in two days, on the 22nd," Canby reminded them.

"You can't do that Colonel," Arnold said. "They'll be halfway to Belen by then. Sibley will be able to prepare and choose any number of places for a battle. All to his advantage. It's either now or never."

"I agree with Arnold," Carson said.

"We could send half our forces to the west and then north to wait for them on the 22nd," Canby said. "With the rest of us coming at them from behind. They'd be surrounded."

"Too risky." Carson said. "He could simply head out tomorrow morning.

Then when his scouts told him you'd sent forces west and north, turn around and successfully defeat whoever is left at the fort before the others could return."

"I agree," Arnold said. "It's precisely what we'd do.'

"You and Sibley did that many times against the Navajo, Colonel." Carson said. "Whenever they split their forces and tried to fool us."

Canby chewed his cigar. Surveyed the banks of the river in the dwindling light. Campfires starting up here and there on both sides.

It was starting to look like the stars were both in the sky and on the ground. Soon, there'd be no horizon and it would be impossible to distinguish between them.

"What a damn shame," Canby said almost as if to himself. "Bunch of boys gonna die here in this godforsaken place. Boys who a year or two ago were hunting together, mining together, whoring together in Canon City and Santa Fe and Tucson and San Antonio. Makes no sense coming here to kill each other. Hell, Kit, it was just a little while ago you 'n Henry 'n I were riding around here on this very spot, killin' Navajos. Trying to civilize these parts."

"Well, Colonel, I guess movin' on to killin' each other is more civilized."

"Tomorrow's as good a day to die as any, I suppose," Canby said. "Let's go get this over with. It's the only choice Henry's given us. Let's make Honest Abe proud. Give him an early birthday present for President Washington."

Two hours later, three miles north of the fort, two New Mexico Volunteers led two of the most broken down mules they could find across to the east bank of the river as quietly as they could, dragging two heavily-laden sacks behind them.

There, they loaded boxes of 24-pound howitzer shells on the backs of the hapless animals. Once secured, they inserted the fuses and began walking them toward the Texans' campfires.

When they had worked themselves as close as they dared, they lit the fuses and slapped both animals on the butt, propelling the doomed mules forward.

They ran into no interference or unexpected challenges on their hurried run back to the river.

But, as they neared the river, they heard the sound of approaching hooves behind them. They pulled their revolvers, turned and prepared to defend themselves from the alerted Texas pickets.

Much to their horror, the two mules were following them back. They succeeded in stopping them and turning them back around before plunging themselves into the welcoming frigidity of the river.

Moments after they ran, freezing, back into their camp, sixty-three hundred armed men on both sides of the Rio Grande in and around Fort Craig were suddenly startled into high alert by twin deafening explosions that reverberated off the mesa walls around them. Hundreds of Confederate cattle stampeded instantly, across the river and straight into the Union lines and, eventually, into the corrals of the Union forces.

The only two casualties, the two mules, were the first to die at Valverde.

49

February 21, 1862

Valverde.

Green Valley. It is the southern end of a long, meandering, beautiful green valley along the Rio Grande as it heads down to the bleak deserts of southern New Mexico and, eventually, down to west Texas.

On this date, it was to be the site and the name of the first of the only two major Civil War battles fought in the Western Territories.

The Texans awoke with orders to head north to Albuquerque on their way to Colorado. They also awoke to discover that they would have to so without 164 of their mules, as Union pickets had stolen them under cover of the early morning darkness.

As a result of intelligence from Tom Jeffords, Canby chose the Valverde ford crossing as the best location to pick his fight. As the sun threatened to rise over the mesa, under cover of artillery fire he sent Major Arnold out with a significant force of regulars and Volunteers to cross the river.

An advance line of Texans, surprised, opened fire on the Union forces.

Carson ordered Chacon and Bascom to lead their respective cavalry units into a fire fight with the Texans.

It became clear to Carson early in this fighting that Bascom was drunk. Not too drunk to fight, but too drunk to lead effectively. It turned out not to matter, as Arnold's artillery inflicted serious damage on the Texans, who ultimately withdrew back to their readying main force.

Bascom wasn't alone. As the aggressors, the Union regulars and Volunteers had a two hour head start on the Texans on drinking whisky from their canteens. But the Texans now began catching up quickly. The vast majority of soldiers on both sides, as was common, were soon fortified in the fight by very poor whiskey.

Over the ensuing two hours, Arnold directed up to five more companies to cross to the east side of the river, where the regular soldiers and New Mexican cavalry and infantry were now joined by the Coloradans.

On command from Arnold, they charged through the swirling snow flurries. Under support of the artillery on the far bank, fixed bayonets, lances, swords, revolvers, rifles, cavalry, and infantry hurled at the four Companies of advanced Texan cavalry units. In what seemed like hours, but actually took fifteen minutes, the Texans sustained significant casualties, were routed, and fled to rejoin the main force of the Texas Cavalry.

Despite superiority of force at this point, the Union forces held back, choosing to continue harassing and flanking the main Rebel forces. Arnold decided against the pitched full attack being urged by Bascom and Carson.

"Canby will be arriving with the rest of the army shortly," Arnold said. "There will be plenty of time for a full assault. It'll be our day soon enough. Continue harassing the Rebels."

Just after noon, the Texans hauled up one howitzer and began shelling the New Mexicans on the east bank of the river. The Federal howitzers on the west bank were out of range. The barrage became enough of a nuisance that Chacon decided to show some initiative.

"Let's go get us a Rebel cannon," Chacon said as he and ten of his Volunteers lit out, straight at the howitzer and the Rebel artillerymen.

"Look at those greasers go," whooped Ickis, as the Coloradans and regular Army shouted their support for the charging New Mexicans.

As shots rang around them while they were reloading, the Texans looked up.

The Rebel Lieutenant in charge of the battery grabbed his horse's reigns, leapt into his saddle, and led his troops along the mesa, hell bent on reaching the main force of Texans.

Upon reaching the cannon, one of the Volunteers lassoed it like the cowboy he was, and three of the men on horseback dragged it and its ammunition back to the Volunteers' position.

They urged a couple of Union artillerymen to come on over to the east bank of the river, show them how to work the gun, and then cheered as the Texans were bombarded and pushed back by their own weapon.

Several hours later, the Coloradans' cannons were brought through the ford to the east bank, and the entire artillery unit began firing grape and canister at the Texans.

Additionally, Canby himself accompanied the rest of those forces he was willing to commit to trying to defeat Sibley once and for all.

He left a small reserve force of New Mexico Volunteers back at Fort Craig. He also left six cavalry companies behind with orders to charge from the fort down to Valverde when Canby ordered the first charge of the battle.

Canby and Arnold now positioned the Colorado artillery and Volunteers, a Company of New Mexicans, and the regular Army infantry and cavalry to the far north of the line along the east bank of the river. In the middle of the line were Carson and Chacon's Volunteers, reinforced by the Coloradans. The rest of the New Mexicans and regulars' artillery were on the southern end of the formation, to Carson's right.

Sibley was nowhere to be seen on the other side. He had claimed illness and sent Green to lead the offensive. But Canby and Carson knew better. As did Green and the Texans.

Sibley was drunk. Unfit for command.

Green sent a lancer company at what he thought was an inexperienced New Mexican company on the extreme left of the Federal lines. But it was in fact Colorado Volunteers, not New Mexicans, who awaited the charge.

"Hold your fire. Stand," came the orders.

At forty yards, "Fire."

And the Coloradans let loose a staggering volley of buckshot and mini balls. The Texas lancers stumbled and fell back. When they charged again, the Coloradans had reloaded and slaughtered them at even closer quarters. The survivors who weren't instantly killed or bayoneted, turned and dashed back under artillery fire into the Cottonwood trees by the mesa.

"That was fun, boys," Ickis said at the sight of the fleeing lancers.

This would prove to be the only time Green and Sibley would send lancers against armed Union troops. In fact, as Sibley was to learn years later as the butt of many a joke, it would be the only lancer attack of the entire Civil War.

The Texans then attacked the center of the line with the force of a thousand cavalry. The shelling and fighting were so ferocious that Canby's horses were shot out from under him three times. But he never left the field and never lost his unlit cigar.

After several such assaults had led to a stalemate, Canby sent Carson orders to attack the flanks of the next assault.

The time had come for the Quaker to take the role of the aggressor.

The Texans came in full force straight at the center of the right flank, targeting Canby and the Coloradans artillery.

A thousand strong.

Cavalry, some with rifles and revolvers, some with swords and lances, and some, with astonishing ferocity, with double barreled shotguns. The shotguns were a nuisance at a distance, but they were deadly close up. Close-in fighting immediately became a death sentence for the Union forces.

The beauty of Canby's idea to send the New Mexicans at the right flank of the charging Texans was that they neutralized the otherwise lethal shotguns. Shooting straight at someone with a shotgun as you advanced was one thing, but trying to aim off to the side or behind you, one-armed, was as likely to unhorse the shooter as the target. Or worse, a fellow Rebel.

Carson and his New Mexicans charged at the flank as ordered, driving the Texas cavalry back in a withering attack that seriously damaged the ability of the attacking companies of Rebels to reorganize and attack again.

The Federal reinforcements and six cavalry companies sat in the fort and watched. Their commander had misunderstood Canby's orders. Waiting for a direct command, they did not charge when their comrades crossed the river.

And Carson's charge now exposed the Union infantry, Coloradans' artillery, and Bascom's cavalry on the left flank. The Texans, among their other growing problems, were now desperate for water. There was no way to the river except through the Union Army. And the opening they had been waiting for now presented itself.

Green had positioned seven companies of Rebel cavalry in the Cottonwood trees back against the mesa for just this opportunity. He ordered them now to attack Canby's dangerously exposed position. They came in three waves, several minutes apart. Straight at the Union left flank.

And still no reinforcements came out of the fort.

Out of the trees the Texans came, screaming the rebel yell, firing their revolvers, and waiting for close quarters to unleash their shotgun attacks.

The Union line broke even before the Rebels closed. The Coloradans were horrified as they were abandoned by the two hundred New Mexico Volunteers who had been assigned to support them.

While reloading, Ickis nudged the man next to him and pointed out the fleeing "greasers." Their prejudice had been confirmed. Neither man had to say a word. Just reload and shoot, reload and shoot. Just kill Texans was all they could do until ordered otherwise.

Many fell on both sides in the charge. But it was absolute carnage when the Texans got close. For both sides. The booming of shotguns could be heard up and down the collapsing line. Dozens of cavalry and infantry on both sides were blown to bits. Five of the Colorado artillery men were killed while reloading their cannons.

The drunken Captain Bascom gave orders on horseback, riding back and forth behind his men. Two Rebels broke through the line. Bascom shot the first out of the saddle as they charged him. The second headed straight for him.

As Bascom desperately yelled orders and fired his revolver from his whirling horse, the second Texan closed on him. He discharged his shotgun at point blank range, but missed. His horse shot past the unharmed Bascom.

The Texan reached the river and, while his horse desperately drank, he reloaded both barrels. The horse wanted no part of returning to action, but the Texan finally turned him around, rode up the bank of the Rio Grande, and charged Bascom again. Alerted by one of his wounded men on the ground, Bascom turned to confront the charging Texan. He got off several shots, but missed. The Texan missed with his first shot, but aimed again on the dead run, and, from point blank range, hit Bascom full in the face as he rushed by and back through the Union lines. The shotgun blast almost blew Bascom's head clean off his shoulders, spattering the nearest soldiers with brain matter and blood.

Bascom's horse took off north along the river bank with the nearly headless Captain's body snagged in its reins.

Chacon and his Volunteers, whose charge had seriously exposed the left flank to this deadly outcome, were triumphantly herding several companies of Texas cavalry back toward the Rebel rear. Their rifle and revolver fire was relentless in their pursuit.

"Rafael," Carson said, cutting him off on the run. "Stop. Turn your men around. We have to get back."

Chacon wheeled, looked back to where Carson was pointing and saw the imminent disaster behind him.

"Halt. Back to the river," Chacon said.

The New Mexicans turned back from their triumphant charge, and now headed back to try to save their comrades.

New Mexicans and regular Union forces were crossing the Rio Grande in panic by the hundreds.

One young New Mexican artillery gunner returned to the field from hauling a cannon back across the river. He and several Texans arrived at the remaining ammunition at the same time. As the Texans raised their shotguns, the New Mexican raised his revolver, yelled "victory or death," and fired into the ammunition.

The explosion blew the Texans and the New Mexican to pieces.

Carson and Arnold turned the forces they could muster around to chase and shoot at the Texans to provide cover for the retreat.

At one point, Arnold had a clear shot at Green, but missed him with his last shot.

"Where's your General, Tom," he shouted at the retreating Green.

Green reigned in his horse and looked back at him. "Where's your Army, John?"

Carson took a shot, but Green was safely out of range.

Canby, on his fourth horse of the day and still chomping his first cigar, was urging the retreating troops across the river.

"Leave the cannon, Ickis. We'll come back for it. Grab some men and try to help Carson protect our rear."

"Yes, sir. Best I can." He looked at the disconsolate Canby. "Don't worry sir. The Texans're hurting, too. We'll get them the next time. Up in Santa Fe."

But neither man would be there to make good on that promise.

50

Under a white flag the evening of the battle, Canby had requested permission to return to the battlefield the next day. He was rewarded the next morning by a visit from two hundred Texans under a white flag.

"Yes, Colonel, what can I do for you?" Canby said.

"General Sibley offers you an unconditional surrender," he said.

Canby was visibly angry at this affront. After he regained his composure he responded to the offer. "You may tell General Sibley that he is welcome to come and try to take the fort if he likes. But I seriously doubt that he has either the manpower or the stomach for it. You can tell my brother-in-law that his absence from the field was duly noted yesterday. I doubt seriously he is any more sober today."

The Texan officer winced. "I will convey your message in full, sir. I have too much respect for you, sir, to respond."

He led his men back across the river to give the news to Sibley.

Canby thus wound up celebrating Washington's birthday walking among the dead and dying horses and mutilated men on the bloody, bloody field of Valverde.

There were arms, legs, and heads thrown about the battlefield as if they had been left by callous boys maliciously destroying their sisters' dolls. And, of course, torsos with missing heads and limbs all over the field. Both sides collected their dead and dying into carts and took them behind the lines.

Canby was personally saddened to discover what was left of the wounded, and dying Captain Ben Wingate. They had fought together in the Mexican-American War, and it had been Wingate who had placed the American flag on the Mexican National Palace.

Wingate, as he had in Mexico, refused surgery for his ghastly leg wounds. This time they were fatal.

Chacon and Ickis entered the room in the fort piled high with dead bodies.

"Welcome to war, Private," Chacon said, seeing the obvious distress the younger Coloradan was experiencing as he climbed over bodies looking for his friends.

"There's not much original one can say at a time like this, is there?" Ickis said. "The blood, guts, and wounds are everywhere. On the dead, the wounded, and the dying alike."

"No, Lon. Not much different from one war to another. A dead Coloradan or a dead Texan is pretty much not very different from a dead 'greaser'." He stared expressionless at Ickis. "And the wounded and dying all call to their gods and their mothers. It's all the same to us, fighting the Americans or the Mexicans or the Apaches."

"It's a shame that any of us have to share scenes such as these, Captain."

"Si, Private. You make the same observations we all make. They are all the clichés of war."

"I think," Ickis said. "The next time I hear the 'Old Man' or Kit speak about not wanting to fight anymore, I will now understand."

Chacon laughed. "Another cliché. And then you'll fight again anyway. We all do. There doesn't seem to be any other way. It's just the way it is."

Ickis wiped the gore off his hands thoughtlessly on some anonymous dead soldier's pants. "It's just horribly degrading is all. I didn't expect it to be degrading."

Counting the New Mexican desertions, Canby had lost close to five hundred men. The Texans had lost nearly two hundred and, perhaps as devastating, untold numbers of horses, mules, and cattle. As a result, even after commandeering all the horses out from under the 4th Texas Cavalry, Sibley had no choice but to order the burning of those supply wagons he could no longer take on the march to Santa Fe. The 4th Texas was transformed, de facto and unhappily, into an Infantry Company.

Sibley, despite the victory, was not in a celebratory mood.

He had two days rations for his remaining forces.

Maybe.

He ordered the immediate march northward, on the hunt for the needed materials to fight decisive battles in Santa Fe or Las Vegas.

Canby, instead of his plan to celebrate Washington's birthday by driving the Texans back south and ending the war in the Territory, had now to retreat back to Fort Craig.

He was disappointed in the comportment of all his troops save Carson's New Mexicans. Canby, too, had lost his stomach for a continued fight.

He settled on the convenient strategy of reinforcing the fort against possible future attacks, and preventing further Confederates from heading up the Rio Grande. He would block Sibley's communications with other Rebels, but he would not chase him northward.

Canby told Carson that he expected Sibley's Texans to outrun their supplies and, essentially, defeat themselves. This would require him to do nothing but stay at the fort for now, and await the Texans' inevitable return on their retreat southward.

That did not sit well with Arnold and Carson, but it wasn't their decision to make.

In the meantime, Canby sent Jeffords to alert the authorities in Albuquerque and Santa Fe to the fact that the Texans were coming. All civilian and military personnel were to use all means necessary to keep provisions away from the Texans.

And for God's sake, use all means possible to get Chivington's Coloradans to Santa Fe as quickly as possible. Before it was too late.

Canby sent Arnold and four Companies of regular Army cavalry to outflank the Texans and get to Fort Marcy ahead of Sibley.

Sibley did indeed have his initial victory. But it didn't feel particularly victorious to the undernourished and exhausted Texans. Not yet anyway. It occurred to Sibley as he and Green led the troops up the valley, that, so far at least, his dream was turning prophetic.

And, of course, Mangas Coloradas' and Cochise's priests had been right about the boy soldier.

Bascom was killed by his own people.

Mangas would not live to find this out.

It would be a decade before Tom Jeffords would think to tell Cochise. And it would, of course, be a totally different world by then. The old Chiricahua chief would look impassively at his by-then old friend Jeffords, and just shrug at the news.

51

"The Texans are coming," Lily said to Zapico. "It has a certain ring to it."

"I'm not as light about it as you are, Lily. The ring is ominous to me."

"How about Mowry?" she said. "I've always suspected that's where his sympathies lay."

"Sylvester's a businessman. Same as me. War itself is good for Mowry. Which outcome is best is less clear."

"Yeah, and I'm a poker dealer and a bar maid and I never viewed any man as anything but just another paying customer, too."

"Cute, Lil. Save your 'aw shucks' lines for someone you can profit from by using 'em. Do we know if Damours is okay?"

"Jeffords didn't know. He said that the aide de camp doesn't usually come out for the battles. Stays back in the fort to attend to Canby's orders. But the dead and wounded weren't accounted for when Canby sent him up here."

"No point on dwellin' on it," Zapico said. "The kid is either dead or alive. My money's on alive. But even then, we won't be seeing him any time soon. Canby's staying in the safety of Fort Craig and leaving us to deal with the Texans all by ourselves."

"The Army is still here and at Fort Union, Zapico. Arnold's coming with more, and the Colorado Volunteers are supposed to be headed here, too."

"Well, either way our business is shot to hell. For a while, anyway. Damours, Cummings, and Mowry aren't going to be getting me anything to sell until this is over. If the Texans take the Territory then the kid is a POW. He'll be lucky to be able to go back to playing poker for a living. And if the Federals ultimately send Sibley packing, and I don't see how that happens now, the war's over here. And so are we."

"You've got it backwards, Zapico. Either way, we're back to equipping whoever's army is fighting the Indians. Just like six months ago. Mowry and

Cummings will go with the winner. And we've got what Auggy has already salted away."

"Unless he's already dead."

That brought her up short. "Auggy's not dead, Zapico. He's sitting back in the fort counting Canby's supplies and Chacon's horses. I agree if the Texans win, all we have is what he already has for us. But that's a lot. He stashed away almost fifteen thousand dollars in poker 'losses' from those three government drafts he lifted before they all headed south. And we've got your money from the sales and re-sales, right?"

Zapico nodded.

"But even if the Texans win," she said, "Mowry's business will continue. And maybe Cummings will prove to have been right. If he's a Marshal or officer for the Confederacy, maybe he will take over on the inside for Damours."

"Maybe," Zapico said.

"And," Lily said, sarcasm evident in her body language, "Cummings already has his poker winnings ready to be delivered to us, right?"

"Smart money says you see Sibley's departing backside before you see any of Cummings' money."

Chacon couldn't believe his eyes.

Five days ago he was in a pitched battle with the Texans.

And now he sat suddenly face to face with the hundred and fifty Navajos he had been tracking, boldly shepherding the six thousand sheep they had stolen. Right where they weren't supposed to be.

Down Chacon's Volunteers charged.

It had taken Swilling's Arizona Guard and the two Companies of Texas Volunteers two weeks to organize for their march from Sibley's Mesilla Headquarters to Tucson. They had left the day after Sibley left for his march to Fort Craig, and were now passing through Dragoon Springs. Sixteen hard, but uneventful, days of riding behind them and now only two days from Tucson.

Cochise and Geronimo sat on their horses looking down on the White Eye soldiers marching westward toward Tucson. About a hundred on horseback, with their wagons, horses, cattle and sheep. The two Apaches had believed that all that now stood between them and ridding their homeland of the White Eyes were the Tupac miners.

"Those aren't the blue coat soldiers," Geronimo said.

"No. Who are they? What do they want? There is nothing left for them to protect, except for the Tubac mines," Cochise said.

"There are new soldiers at the fort at the Colorado River. Maybe they go to join them?"

"But why? There are no hostilities near the fort? It must be for the mines. There is no other reason. We will have to drive them out."

"Do you want to take their horses now?" Geronimo said.

"No. there will be a better time."

The two continued staring down on the White Eyes. Why were they back, Cochise wanted to know. There was nothing to the west for them. It bothered him.

"You see them, Captain?" Swilling said.

Looking up into the sun and shading his eyes.

"Yes," the Rebel Captain said. "Up top there. They've been watching us since we got to the edge of the mesa. I see two. You?"

"Yup. Only the two. Impossible to say how many there are. Have to be Chiricahuas, though. They'll go back to Cochise. See what he wants to do about us."

"He has two days to decide. Not much point in his attacking a force this size. He'll wait. Time's on his side."

"It always is Captain," Swilling said. "Lucky for us that they get impatient. Otherwise there'd be none of us out here and more of them."

The Captain looked back up. "They won't bother us when we're marching all together. Even on this route. We'll get to Tucson with no trouble."

He was right.

The return trip, however, would prove to be a very different story.

52

The Texans were now only a day's ride from Albuquerque. They had followed the Rio Grande sixty-five miles through the valley, largely small farms with an occasional tiny town or village. All New Mexicans. No whites or Indians. The Rebels were desperately seeking provisions. The New Mexicans were unhelpful.

It was clear that the farmers and villagers had hidden everything they could from the marching Rebel army. Despite the clear Confederate victory at Valverde, the New Mexicans believed the scrip being offered for goods was of no value. Many wouldn't take it, just threw it back at them, and called the soldiers ladrones. Thieves. Or worse.

Previously harvested fields and orchards were plentiful, but there was no food to be found.

The Rebels were furious that they were being treated so badly by their nearest neighbors. They felt they had come as a liberating army, delivering the New Mexico Territory from the Yankees. Instead they were being treated as hated conquerors.

Sure there was bad blood between the New Mexicans and the Texans, but, with a little cooperation, they felt that they could be compadres again.

The Texans had no beef with the New Mexicans. They were at war with the Yankees.

At times, the search for provisions turned ugly. Sometimes the soldiers became frustrated out of anger and hunger. They had seen many of their friends blown to bits at Valverde to rescue these people from the Yankees, and in return the locals hid their food.

When threats didn't work, the Texans beat some of the villagers, and when they found hidden stores they beat them again.

Upon being informed that Belen was named for Bethlehem by the Spaniards, one Sergeant ordered the destruction of several of the farmhouses.

"Let them sleep in mangers then," he said, as his men torched one of the houses.

Frustrated and angry, leading a desperate instead of a victorious army, Sibley and Green led the men on toward Albuquerque in silence. They could hear the curses of the men, the braying of the hungry mules, and the groans of the wagons behind them.

And, worse, they could hear the taunting sound of empty wagons as they bounced along the roadway.

"Well at least none of us are going to die of thirst," Sibley said.

"Ironic, after the long dry march from San Antonio," Green said, looking over at the roiling Rio Grande.

And then anger turned to horror, as the two men looked to the northeast horizon. They could see the smoke. The sky black with it low on the horizon. But the wind was carrying it east and up, higher and higher into the sky. And it was increasingly clear this was no ordinary, isolated fire.

Sibley had spent enough time in the Territory to know what he was looking at.

He could barely make out the silhouette of the mountains behind the smoke, but there was no mistaking it.

Albuquerque was burning. The Federals were burning anything of value in Albuquerque. All the provisions the Texans so desperately needed.

The Yankees had beaten the Texans to the prize, and now there would be no prize.

"No wonder Canby didn't follow," Green said. 'He is waiting in Fort Craig for our return".

Under a clear, crisp Colorado February sky, the Private rushed into Colonel John Slough's tent.

Slough and his second in command, Major John Chivington, were the commanding officers of the 1st Colorado "Pike's Peaker" Volunteers. "The two John's," as they were known behind their backs, had been delaying their departure for New Mexico in hopes of more troops, more training, and, more importantly, word that Canby's defeat of the Texans had made their march unnecessary.

"Yes, son," Slough said. Slough, a 42 year old, balding, overweight lawyer and legislator with a long black beard to compensate for his lack of hair, was from Cincinnati. He had left for Colorado two years before after beating a fellow Ohio legislator, and had jumped at the first chance to join the Union in the War.

"The Texans defeated Canby and the Colorado Volunteers at Fort Craig, sir."

"Were you there?"

"Yes, sir."

"What happened? Slow down, son. Just tell me what happened."

The Private caught his breath and spent the next fifteen minutes telling Slough what had happened.

"How did the Colorado Volunteers do, Private?"

"Very well, sir. It was the greasers who ran. They abandoned the artillery to the Texans and ran for the hills. Just like Ickis and the other fellas said they would."

"What does Canby want us to do, son?"

"You are to get to Fort Union as fast as possible. He thinks that's where Sibley is headed on his way here, sir."

"Is Canby chasing him?"

"No, sir. Canby's Federals and New Mexicans stayed back at Fort Craig."

"He say why?"

"He didn't discuss strategy with me, sir. He just wanted me to ride to you as fast as I could."

Slough smiled at that. "Okay, then. Let's go to New Mexico. Sergeant, tell Chivington we leave for Fort Union at daybreak. Let's go kill us some Texans. Sounds like we're scheduled to meet up with the ol' drunk Sibley after all."

He would be wrong about that part.

53

"Ten hut."

The 4th Texas snapped to attention. Sibley had given them the honor of raising the Confederate flag over Albuquerque as recompense for forcibly turning them into infantry.

A few brave New Mexicans looked out their windows through the still-acrid smoke at the ceremony. Some waved Confederate flags.

On command, the six Companies saluted as the flag was raised, and, as one, they let out the rebel yell.

Green turned to Sibley.

"I'll wager more than a few of these greasers were waving the Stars and Stripes yesterday."

"Maybe their banners got burned up in the fires," Sibley said.

Both men were grim. Their victory was pyrrhic. There was precious little for their victorious men here in Albuquerque.

"Here's what we do," Sibley said to his assembled officers. "Major Pyron, in a week you take the bulk of our forces up to Santa Fe. Gather whatever provisions you can from the locals before you leave. Keep foraging all the way up the Rio Grande to Santa Fe. Kill the greasers if you have to. Them withholding food and provisions from our men and animals is just the same as killin' 'em. The New Mexicans are going to help us. Willingly or unwillingly. Their choice."

"Yes, sir," Pyron said.

"Green, put together two companies. Send ten wagons with them. Our spies tell us that in December Canby did what he and I always did when we were chasing the Navajo. He sent his supplies to Cubero, where they'd be ready for him and Carson when they resume chasing the damn Indians. I guess he didn't really believe we were coming. We'll accept his gracious offer and take those Cubero supplies and use his own provisions against him."

"Where do we take them, sir?" Green said.

"It's a three day ride from here to Cubero and another three days back. Once you get back here with the Cubero supplies, Pyron can take them to Santa Fe."

"And Colonel Scurry, I want you stay back here with the rest of us. Let's rest the 4th for a few days before you follow Pyron up there with your cavalry and half the 4th."

"Yes, sir," Lieutenant Colonel Scurry said.

"What are our orders in Santa Fe?" Major Pyron said.

"If the troops from Fort Marcy and Fort Union come out to engage you, I'll be surprised. But if they do, you have superior force and better men, so end it right then and there."

"And if they run?"

"Then we'll join you at Fort Union in Las Vegas shortly with the rest of the 4th and the cavalry. We'll chase them to wherever they go and put an end to this, and then head on to Colorado."

"And Canby?" Green said.

"Ed's instinctually holed up in Fort Craig, expecting us to return. Let him sit there. He and Carson's New Mexicans will miss the decisive battle. I'd rather finish this off with Carson sitting back there. Maybe someday they can welcome Carleton there, and then they can all re-cross the desert together to come after us in California."

He took a sip out of his canteen, and then finished. "Or, better yet, they can fight the Apaches and the Navajo while we take the entire West for the Confederacy."

54

March 4, 1862

Zapico and Lily had been watching in silence from the Plaza as the Governor directed the hurried evacuation of the Governor's Palace.

Everyone in town knew what was happening. The Texans were rumored to have already left Albuquerque and would be here in two days.

At most four.

Surrounded by hills, Santa Fe was indefensible. Even if the Army had wanted to make a stand here, there were no strategic reasons to do so. The saloons and bordellos would do fine without the Yankees. The Texans had no reason to harm Santa Fe.

The Coloradans were expected at Fort Union in a fortnight. Everybody had known that the Army would eventually abandon Fort Marcy and head to Las Vegas and Fort Union through Glorieta Pass and Apache Canyon.

Zapico nodded at Lily, pointing with a nod of his head. "Fort Marcy's commanding officer. In the flesh. This must be it, then. He hasn't left Fort Marcy to come down here in weeks."

While the officer met with the Governor, Zapico pointed to the sky above the Palace to the northeast. Smoke. Growing billows of smoke rose into the Robin egg blue Santa Fe sky. The soldiers at Fort Marcy were now burning the supplies and papers that couldn't be transported to Fort Union.

The citizens of Santa Fe, both good and bad, were being left to their fate.

Lily got up and walked over to the two men as they prepared to mount their horses.

"Mornin' Governor."

"Mornin' ma'am."

Both men touched the brims of their caps.

"Anything you want to share with us, Governor? Major?"

The Major looked at the Governor, deferring to him.

"I guess it's pretty obvious." As if for emphasis, he looked up at the smoke for a moment. "We're evacuating the fort and the town. We're moving west. The government to Las Vegas and the Army to Fort Union."

"And what are your plans for us?"

She gestured to the growing crowd in the Plaza. Some watching curiously. Others anxiously.

The Governor looked at his citizens. The Major mounted his horse.

"I'm guessing you'll all be fine. Give the Texans what they ask for. Give them access to the saloons and the fandangos and the poker games. They're soldiers, ma'am, not devils. The more you distract them for us, the longer the Coloradans and Canby have to get to Fort Union."

Easy for you to say, she thought. Maybe she and the Governor could sit down some day and discuss the major differences between soldiers and devils.

Probably not.

So Canby was coming after all. And Damours.

But the Governor was wrong about that. Canby wasn't going anywhere.

Arnold came by the saloon and spotted Lily. She was dealing five card stud to a a group of six. He caught her eye and she indicated it would be a few minutes.

She joined him at the bar on her break.

"I hear you get to take a three day ride to beautiful Las Vegas, John."

"Yeah. I see your customers aren't fleeing at the news."

"They're talking about it. Some'll go to Taos. Most'll stick around. The Governor's right, most businesses don't have a rootin' interest in this War. It'd be one thing if it were Indians or Mexicans coming our way, but these are Americans."

"Used to be, anyway," he said.

"Somebody'll win, somebody'll lose, John. It'll sort itself out in the end one way or the other. The Texans don't gain anything by turning whores, bartenders, and poker dealers against them. If they win, they'll be *their* whores, bartenders, and poker dealers when they come back through."

"Fair enough, Lily. So you're not coming with me to Las Vegas?"

She could tell he was kidding, but played along anyway. "Obviously, Major Arnold, you've never seen Las Vegas. Nothing there for you or me. Any predictions on what happens next?"

"We shoulda ended it at Valverde, but for some tactical errors. But you and I discussed all that the other day. Canby is convinced Sibley will outrun his supply lines, and maybe he will. We'll sit at Fort Union and there won't be anything Sibley can do about it."

He lit another cigarillo, gestured toward Lily. She shook her head.

"Sibley can't afford to wait us out and his backside is too vulnerable if he leaves us alone in the fort and heads north to Colorado. My hunch is we sit around staring at each other for a week or two, and then Canby arrives and we defeat him then and there."

"And if not?"

"Then, Lily, you can visit me at the stockade. I'll be a POW and you'll be a newly minted citizen of the Confederate States of America."

"How nice. I always wanted a Dad I could visit in prison."

55

A little over a week later, Arnold, second in command at Fort Union, met with Slough after the Coloradans' had had time to settle in at the fort. "We're relieved to see you, Colonel. We were concerned you wouldn't be here for another week or more."

"Our pleasure, Major Arnold," Slough said. "Thanks again to you for lending us provisions until our wagons could catch up."

Arnold nodded. "We were counting on you for a thousand Volunteers Colonel."

"And we've brought you thirteen hundred."

"That gives us a total of seventeen hundred men here then. We have the Texans outmanned, outgunned, and outmaneuvered. And Canby will bring the rest when he is sure there are no more Texans coming up his backside."

"And that would trap Sibley exactly where, Major?" Slough said.

Arnold looked surprised by the question. "We're under specific orders not to leave Fort Union, sir. Canby wants an undersupplied and outmanned Sibley to surrender without a fight right here against the odds and the practical realities."

"And what if the General is impractical, Major? What if he decides to take defenseless Santa Fe, finds his needed resources, and Canby is wrong about your ability to hold the fort?"

"I have my orders, Colonel."

"Major Arnold, where are the Texans?"

"Our scouts tell us that the advance companies almost certainly arrived in Santa Fe today..."

"Three days ride from here, right?"

"Yes, Colonel. But, as I was saying, the advanced companies arrived this morning. The rest of Sibley's Texans are riding in three groups, all expected to be in Santa Fe in ten days. Probably more than eleven hundred in total."

"My job, Major Arnold, is to protect Colorado from the rebels. Why don't we just ride to Santa Fe now, destroy the Texans' advance troops, and then take each group as they ride up the Rio Grande?"

"Orders, sir. I have my orders. We're to defend the fort."

"And allow Sibley to mass his forces? That's insane. Let's take the battle to the enemy Major," Slough said.

"As I said, Canby believes we will win this battle and end the Civil War in the West without having to risk your troops, Colonel Slough. Santa Fe is nestled against the hills and can't be defended against a thousand Texans. And there is no strategically advantageous location where we could fight a pitched battle between Santa Fe and Albuquerque, sir. I believe Canby knows what he's doing, Colonel."

"In my experience, Major, battle plans never work the way you think they will. I think the chances of you winning by sitting here waiting for Sibley to give up, while you both wait for Canby to show up, isn't going to happen. With all due respect, Major."

Arnold chose not to respond.

"What's in Las Vegas, Arnold?" Slough said.

Arnold look surprised at the welcome subject change. "Essentially nothing, Colonel. It's a very small impoverished collection of a few hundred New Mexicans. It's off limits to my soldiers, mostly because the only available women are scraggly, dirt poor, and unappetizing. There's too much smallpox. They hardly speak a word of English. There's some good bread, but virtually no available supplies in the town. The few whites are Jews and standoffish. There's nothing for any soldier who hopes to keep his self-respect in Las Vegas."

"My men have reported the same," Slough said. "The greasers in town are miserable and seem drugged. Accordingly, and not surprisingly, Major Arnold, my point is that my Volunteers are now even more eager to get to Santa Fe. A few Texans aren't going to keep them out for long."

"They'll get to Santa Fe soon enough, Colonel. More of 'em'll make it, if you wait Sibley out here."

"That may or may not be true, Major. I outrank you, your commanding officer, and Canby, and I'm under no such orders. My men aren't going to sit here waiting for Sibley to start pining away for Fort Bliss and just go away. Not when he has the Colorado gold fields and the California shores in his head."

Slough looked out over his troops, then said, "No, Major. We marched all the way here to drive the Rebels back to Texas, and by God that's what we're going to do. You and Ed Canby can sit and watch if that's what you've a mind to do."

"So," Lily said. "What's your new plan, Joseph?"

"I'm working on my Texas drawl."

He mimicked his idea of a Texas accent.

Lily and Zapico both laughed.

"That's Cajun," Zapico said. "Stick to what you know, Joseph. Getting caught with a fake Texas accent might be a capital crime in the Confederate States of America for all you know."

"Being suspected of being a Yankee spy definitely is," Lily said. "Seriously, Joseph, you need to decide what you're going to do. The Texans are already checking out Fort Marcy. They've commandeered officer's quarters three blocks northwest of the Plaza on Johnson Street. They told me the rest'll be here in ten days or so."

"Your options," Zapico said. "Appear to be faking an injury, enlisting in the Confederacy, or getting out of town."

"Look, Joseph," Lily said. "If the Rebels defeat the Coloradans and the Federals at Fort Union, it'll be perfect if you showed up with Mowry's introductory letter. You could lever that into a job with them either here or in Colorado. Sheriff, maybe? Marshal?"

"Either's fine with me," Cummings said, as if he were at a job interview.

"You were right," she said. "There's no need for you to go getting' killed in a war or getting hung as a spy. If the Texans win, they'll need men in the conquered Territories. That'd suit you fine. And us."

"Where do I go in the meantime?"

"Taos," she said. "Enjoy the girls and what's left of the poker. Either way it comes out, just remember to come back."

"What about you two?"

"The Texans'll rob me blind, but I'll be fine," Zapico said. "They need me and, either way it comes out, they won't be here long. I'll be fine."

"As the Governor so nicely pointed out," Lily said, "all us girls'll be fine. The Rebels need me more'n they need Zapico. We'll both be fine."

"I like your Taos and Marshal ideas, Lil. Better than enlisting with the Rebels."

Does this guy have any idea what a coward he is, Lily asked herself? Said instead, "It is indeed, Joseph."

"You gonna ask him?" Zapico said to her.

"Cummings, where's our money?"

"You mean my money, don't you?"

"No, Cummings, I mean the money we're all splitting."

"It's safe. We all agreed to split it up when we're done. We're not done."

"I didn't ask for it. I asked where it was."

"It's safe, Lil. That's all you need to know."

"And if the Rebels shoot your sorry ass? Or hang you after all?"

"Well, Lil, President Lincoln will be happy to hear you finally have a rooting interest in his War."

He saluted Zapico and got on his horse.

"I'll be in Taos until the Texans have beaten Canby's butt or are headed back to San Anton'. You two be careful. Either way, I'll be back soon enough."

56

March 17, 1862

Fifty Coloradans on a mid-day scouting expedition two miles north of Fort Craig could hear shooting and shouting upriver.

"The Texans returning?" Ickis said.

"Could be. It's certainly something," the Sergeant said. "Let's go."

The Coloradans charged, guns drawn into they knew not what. As they emerged around the bend in the Rio Grande, there were three hundred Navajos stealing the Army's herd of mules that a dozen New Mexicans were guarding.

"Look," Ickis said. "The greasers are actually fighting back."

"Just chase the Navajos, Lon. Let's go boys. Charge."

The Navajos were everywhere. Racing in and out, separating the mules into packs of a dozen or so. Shootin' at the New Mexicans, who were shootin' back on foot. There were Indians racing in for mules and Indians running off with mules. The mules were braying like mad and the Indians were whooping and shouting. Some to scare the New Mexicans. Some to herd the mules.

The Coloradans took off after them at full gallop. The Navajos split into seven groups, each about the number of the total Coloradans, and sped off in different directions, with a handful of Coloradans in hot pursuit of each group of Indians.

Ickis stopped to help a wounded friend. It took him time to get some New Mexicans to take him back to the fort. He then, belatedly, rode out to meet the returning Coloradans.

"How many did you get," Ickis asked his Sergeant.

"They outran us, Lon," the Sergeant said. "We only caught up with two of the groups. We killed six. Looks like they got away with forty of the mules."

Ickis noted the scalp on the Sergeant's belt. "We're not supposed to be scalping down here, Sergeant. Carson's orders."

"I know. I took it off one of the boys."

"Well, I'd put it away. Carson and Canby don't want the Navajos mad. They want 'em to give up friendly and stay home."

"Well then, Lon, I'll just tell the Old Man and Kit that these fellas didn't seem too friendly."

57

Arnold and Slough had agreed upon a clever strategy to circumvent Canby's orders. They had left four hundred soldiers to defend Fort Union, some from each of their commands. The thirteen hundred combined force under Slough that would now march to confront the Rebels were the best of the seventeen hundred men.

They had left the fort the previous day to start their march toward Santa Fe and camped at what passed for the little town of Bernal.

"Private," Colonel Slough said.

"Yes, sir?"

"Find Chivington and tell him he's to leave to engage the Texans within the hour."

"Yes, sir."

The Private galloped toward the camps on the other side of town.

Slough rode first around, then through, Bernal, rounding up the Coloradans and the Federals from their campsites and their sightseeing. Chivington would lead his four hundred men the dozen or so miles toward San Jose today, and Slough and Arnold would follow with the rest of the men tomorrow.

Slough and Chivington were confident that, even if Canby sat down at Fort Craig for the duration, the thirteen hundred "Pike's Peakers" and Federals could defeat all of Sibley's Texans.

And now they were going to find out.

It was a three day march from the current capital of Las Vegas to the former capital of Santa Fe. If the Rebels were already coming toward them from Santa Fe, the inevitable confrontation would be somewhere around Apache Canyon and Glorieta Pass, the very site of Kearny's definitive battle in the New Mexico Territory in the Mexican-American War sixteen years before.

Most of the Coloradans were miners, hunters, farmers, adventurers. They had experienced their share of violence in the West. But most of it had been bar room brawls, individual shootouts, and Indian skirmishes.

This would be their first war.

Lieutenant Colonel William R. Scurry, a Texas lawyer and former member of the U.S. House of representatives from Gattlin, Tennessee, and Major Charles L. Pyron, a Texas rancher by way of Marion County, Alabama were both veterans of the Mexican American War and both impressive looking, full black-bearded Confederate officers. The two stood looking back together at their eleven hundred Texans. They could see Santa Fe over the heads of their assembled troops. They both knew this place very well from their time with Kearny in the successful war against the Mexicans.

"Go into the canyon, Major Pyron," Scurry said. "I'll follow with my eight hundred tomorrow."

"I figure three days to Fort Union, Colonel," Pyron said.

"My guess is that we'll see action well before then," Scurry said. "I suspect our skirmishers will report back soon enough that some of the Yankees have already started our way from Fort Union. In any case, I'll be right behind you by a day. Green should be in front of you with the rest of the 4th presently. I urged him to go the back way to Fort Union. That way if the Federals have already left, he'll be at their backs when we meet them."

The two shook hands.

"It's going to be their choice," Scurry said. "A pitched battle in those canyons up ahead, or a siege and eventual attack on the fort. My bet is tomorrow or the next day right up ahead. Either way, it's just a matter of time until they run for it. Then California."

"When do we expect Sibley, Scurry?"

"Frankly, Major, I think the General has in mind our finishing this off before he gets here."

"If you're wrong and they're just sitting there waiting for us at Fort Union, how long a siege can we lay in," Pyron said.

"With the haul we took from Cubero, we're good to outlast them, no matter how long it takes."

Both men looked back at the seemingly endless columns of wagons that flanked the Texans. Eighty wagons of provisions nicely solved Sibley's supply problem. Morale among the Rebels was as high as it had been since they had left San Antonio.

Pyron ordered his three hundred advance unit out, south and east into Glorieta Pass and Apache Canyon with their now-standard order of, "On to Fort Union, Colorado, and California."

And they moved out to the echoing rebel yell.

As Scurry turned his horse around to rejoin the rest of his men and make preparations to bring his part of the Confederate Army of New Mexico to Apache Canyon in the morning, they believed they were about to deliver a Confederate West to Sibley and President Davis.

58

March 26, 1862

Chivington, a very heavy, almost comically large figure on a horse, was a 40 year old Methodist minister from Ohio. His short, black beard was also somewhat comically framed by his unkempt hair out to both sides of his head. His comportment as a minister was so confrontational that his congregations had kept him on the move, from Ohio to Nebraska to, finally, two years earlier, Colorado.

He now set out with his four hundred men, cavalry and infantry at 8:00 am sharp. After the march from Bernal the day before, they had camped at Kozlowski's Ranch, about twenty miles from San Jose. Kozlowski, a Polish immigrant, was an Army veteran and a strong Union supporter.

Anticipation was high among the men. Pickets had captured four Texans the night before near Pigeon's Ranch. Among the four was a member of Canby's staff at Valverde who had switched sides and now would be hung.

They also had received information that a force of Texans was definitely in the Pass just ahead of them. This was being repeated by scouts reporting in along the route.

As they marched past Pigeon's Ranch, there was a hubbub as the men discussed the origins of the Ranch's name. The owner, a French immigrant, was famous for his singular and notable style of dancing at fandangos throughout the Territory.

He had proudly adopted "Pigeon" as the name the women of Santa Fe had given him.

For their part, Pyron's three hundred Texans had camped the night before at the western end of Apache Canyon, at the very edge of Glorieta Pass. Pyron had sent fifty men with two howitzers to the summit to his east to prevent a surprise attack.

Pyron's Texans marched eastward through the canyon. Advance pickets were under strict orders to hold off any Yankees, send for help, and fight a retreating action if it came to that.

And it did.

Just as the Texans were getting through the Canyon, Chivington's Yankees approached the summit on the road into Apache Canyon. Their scouts came racing down the hill with a captured Confederate officer yelling that the Texans were over the hill.

All talk of fandangos, Santa Fe women, and the beautiful New Mexico mountains was replaced by shouted orders and scrambling soldiers.

Horses and men raced into formation waiting for Major Chivington's orders. Chivington sat on his horse looking back at the men as the officers shouted more orders over the din of the men taking up the chant of "Pike's Peakers, Pike's Peakers."

"Remember their shotguns, boys," Chivington said to his officers over the growing din. "Tell the men that if they come at you on horseback with their shotguns raised, use your pistols and shoot for their gut. You don't have time to aim your rifles."

At the sound of "Charge" from Chivington, the four hundred men, as one, hurled themselves up the hill, littering it with all their belongings that they flung to the side to ready themselves for whatever lay ahead.

Two howitzers fired shells over their heads as they crested at full gallop. Mounted Texans and howitzers awaited them a mere two hundred yards down the hill into the canyon.

The Union forces organized flanking attacks on both sides and then attacked straight into the center of the howitzers.

The noise was deafening. Confusion reigned over the field. The Texans pulled the artillery pieces and retreated back into the canyon, their cavalry covering as best they could against the furious Coloradan onslaught.

The horse-drawn howitzers made good their escape and the Rebels broke and ran. The cheers and mock rebel yells from the Union forces bounced off the canyon walls all around them.

Not satisfied, Chivington reorganized his troops and led a march further west, following the fleeing Texans.

"Major Chivington," a Lieutenants said. "Do we know for certain that there aren't a thousand Texans waiting for us at the end of this road."

"No. Not for certain. But if their entire Army were around that bend, I would have thought they would have counterattacked by now. They haven't. Either way, we came to take the fight to the enemy and that's what I intend to do. If there are a thousand men at the other end of this canyon, then we'll be in a real fight, won't we?"

"Yes, sir."

"Something to tell your grandchildren. You were there when...."

The infantry had now caught up with the cavalry, and Chivington gave the order to charge again. Morale was high. They had just given the Rebels their first defeat of the War and they intended to keep on rolling them back.

But Pyron's three hundred Texans awaited them at the western edge of Glorieta Pass, and they had no intention of retreating another inch without a fight.

Chivington again sent his cavalry against both the Texas flanks, while the bulk of his forces went straight at the middle of the Rebel line. The cavalry charged the artillery at the middle of the line repeatedly. The fighting was furious. Hand to hand combat, shotguns, mini-balls, and pistols.

Pyron organized his troops in a gradual retreat throughout the battle until they found formidable defense positions a mile and a half east of their previous evening's encampment.

"What do you think now, Lieutenant? How far away are the rest of the Texans?"

"I don't know, sir. My fear is that they are drawing us into a trap. And it'll be dark soon. We may regret pushing too far ahead of Slough."

Chivington peered through the fading light.

"I don't think we have enough to get them to surrender. And their defenses are too strong along those two ridges."

He pointed over to both sides and slightly above them.

At that moment, the howitzers boomed and the Lieutenant took a direct hit to the chest. His arms flew from his body and blood burst over Chivington.

Both the officer and his horse fell dead on the spot as his head rolled over to the edge of the road.

The right Reverend Chivington gritted his teeth at the sight, brushed savagely at the blood on his chest, and calmly ordered his forces back to Kozlowski's Ranch at the other end of the canyon. There was nothing to be gained by further attacks.

Pyron was dug in, and somewhere out there were a thousand Texans.

The Lieutenant had been right though, they would need Slough's nine hundred whenever the full force of the Texans arrived.

Chivington and his officers were in a mood to celebrate when they returned to Kozlowski's. This had been the first Union victory of the Civil War in the West. And the victory was theirs and theirs alone.

When word reached Canby, he'd certainly bring the rest of his troops up behind the Texans to finish the job. They had lost only five killed and thirteen wounded, with three soldiers unaccounted for. They figured the Confederates for fifteen to twenty dead, thirty to forty wounded, and they had captured seventy-five and had sent them back to the fort for imprisonment.

The Coloradans around the campfire felt happy to have survived their first battle. They had received withering fire for what seemed like hours, and all agreed it could have been much worse. All felt happy to have survived their first battle.

And to have been victorious.

But there had been nothing glorious or brave about it. It had been continuous and unrelenting noise and confusion and terror.

All around the campfires you could hear the soldiers in great spirits. Some singing. Some mocking the Rebels. Most drunk. Once Slough and Canby get here, they all thought, they'd make short work of the Rebels. You could hear it all around the camp.

But Canby wasn't coming.

And a thousand Texans were.

59

March 28, 1862

Since the battle of Apache Canyon two days before, Colonel Scurry had arrived with his remaining eight hundred Texans to swell the Confederate ranks to eleven hundred at the western edge of Glorieta Pass.

They still hoped that Colonel Green and the rest of the 4th would arrive momentarily, but had no idea if they were coming up their rear to reinforce them or up the Federals' rear to surround them.

Or even, for that matter, if they were coming at all.

Not to mention if General Sibley was with them.

Just as Scurry was arriving with the rest of the Texans to the west, Colonel Slough and his nine hundred Union troops arrived to reinforce Chivington at Kozlowski's ranch to their east. There were now thirteen hundred Federals and Coloradans and a handful of New Mexico Volunteers in place.

If Canby was coming it was going to be a big surprise now. They had to assume at this point that he would miss this next battle, as he had the one in Apache Canyon two days before.

And they had to assume that today's battle would be decisive.

"Chivington," Slough said. "Let's go now. Let's finish this thing. I want you to take four hundred fifty men immediately. Skirt to the south of the road in the hills along the edge of the Pass to the top of Glorieta Mesa. I want you hidden and ready to attack from above. The rest of us will head up the Pass straight back at the Texans' defensive positions. Where you left them night before last. Understand?"

"Yes, sir," Chivington said. "When do I attack?"

"You should position your men unseen, above them. When I hit the center of their line, you should attack from above. If they haven't yet been reinforced, we have them vastly outmanned. And it will be clear sailing to Santa Fe from there."

"And if they have been reinforced, sir?"

"Then your position assures us of victory. We will engage and hold and you will sweep them away from above? Any questions Major?"

"None, sir," Chivington said.

"Then go. I want to get started and we have to give you a head start."

Chivington immediately moved his men out. To the south and into the hills of the Pass.

Scurry strode to Major Pyron's tent. "Let's go Charlie. I want to attack the Yankees now, not later."

"What's the hurry Bill? Are we now sure the rest of the 4th isn't coming?"

"Damned if I know. We've heard nothing from Sibley or Green. The Coloradans couldn't have had more than four hundred men two days ago. My guess is that they know you've been reinforced and are retreating back to Fort Union."

"What if the Coloradans have already been reinforced?" Pyron said.

"Well, unless Canby's entire force from Fort Craig quietly slipped by Sibley and Green and you last night, we should still have them outgunned. And attacking now is the right move either way, Major."

Scurry slapped Pyron on the back. "Let's go."

"Yes, sir." Pyron said. "Sergeant, put together a detail to take the supply train around that way."

He pointed out the route through the south edge of the Pass.

"Toward Canoncita and the Johnson Ranch we scouted. Take one of the howitzers and enough men to discourage skirmishers."

"Yes, sir. We'll hide it in the hills near the ranch."

"Okay, Colonel Scurry, let's go kill us the rest of the damn Yankees."

Scurry and Pyron formed the Texans and led them east at a gallop. Toward Fort Union, the Coloradans, and the Federal troops.

Galloping to their last battle in the West.

After a short charge though the Pass, scouts reported to Scurry that the Yankees were just ahead.

He prepared the men for an all-out assault.

"I guess they're not retreating after all, Colonel," Pyron said over the bugles and the din of the troops readying for the charge.

"So much the worse for them, Major," Scurry said. "Besides being outgunned, they'll now be out of position. Get those howitzers over against those hills over there."

The Coloradan skirmishers saw them coming and raced back to Slough, Arnold, and the Union force that had just passed Pigeon's Ranch. The battle was to be much sooner and well east of where Slough and Arnold had figured.

This fight would be short of the Pass itself. On the positive side, Chivington would be coming straight up the Rebel rear. Slough had them surrounded.

Slough ordered the charge. It was a repeat of Chivington's charge two days earlier. But with twice the numbers.

Bugles sounded the charge straight into the teeth of the Texas artillery and cavalry.

The two sides attacked each other a half mile west of Pigeon's Ranch.

The Texans had hoped for a battle site somewhere near this location, but had expected to be hitting a much smaller force from behind as it was retreating back to the fort.

Slough and Arnold had hoped for a battle in the canyon far west of this spot, also against a much smaller force. Both sides now saw the need for the reinforcements that they had hoped for, but that were now far too late.

The battle was a ferocious confrontation between two charging armies.

Artillery was thrown into place in the melee of charging cavalry and infantry. Owing to the rough, hilly arroyo-choked terrain, much of the cavalry fought dismounted. Howitzer shells and rifle fire whistled over the heads of both sides. The continuous rattle of Sharpe rifles and pistols echoed across the field.

Horses and soldiers in full flight fell alongside those crouching among the Mesquite and the Cottonwoods.

Despite his artillery superiority, Slough's Coloradans and Arnold's Federals fell begrudgingly back, little by little, continuously expecting Chivington's charge at the Texans rear to turn the tide.

The Texans advanced cautiously, not trusting that the Yankees were indeed retreating. They were content to keep moving forward and not gallop into any ambushes.

"Orderly retreat," Slough ordered. "Orderly retreat back toward Pigeon's Ranch. Ten Texan dead for every yard backward."

Slough looked over the heads of the charging Texans. No Chivington. He rallied the Coloradans and Federals around him. Shotgun blasts from the charging Texans could be heard over the booms of the cannons throughout the field. The effects of the shotguns on the mounted Coloradans was horrible to see. Men and horses lay dead or rolled screaming on the meadow and in the ravines.

After an hour, the Yankees had retreated the half mile back to Pigeon's Ranch under an unrelenting rain of artillery and rifle fire. They were now in defensive positions all around the adobe houses and outbuildings.

Scurry readied his Texans for an all-out, artillery-supported attack on the Ranch. He would lead the attack on the Yankee center.

Pyron poised for an attack on the Coloradans' right flank with those of the 4th Texans who had made the initial march from Albuquerque.

Three hundred Rebels were sent at Arnold on the Union left flank.

"Pyron, send twenty of your best riflemen up to the top of that ridge. There to the north of the ranch," Scurry said.

He pointed up to a hill off to his left.

"Tell them to eliminate the artillery units, and then start on any officers they see. Now, Major. Send them."

Slough organized the Union defense. He had to get word to Chivington.

"Lieutenant," he called out to the Coloradan next to him. "Take two men and get to Chivington at Glorieta Mesa as quickly as possible. We need him to come at the Rebels' rear. Now, Lieutenant. Ride."

The three men galloped off to the southeast to outflank the Texans.

Slough saw all three men shot dead off their horses by sharpshooters at the same moment he turned toward the sound of a rebel yell from a thousand Texans bearing down on him and his men.

No Chivington. No Canby. Canby's strategy to stand at Fort Union now depended on Slough alone stopping the Texans.

"For the Union," Slough yelled. "Kill them all. Send every last one of the Rebels to hell."

The battle at Apache Canyon two days previous had involved only about a third of the forces now engaged on the field. It had been all about constant motion and confusion and surprise and terror.

Today at Pigeon's Ranch was just offensive brute force meeting defensive brute inertia.

In each of the repeated assaults, the artillery fire reigned on the ranch, while the Texans used their shotguns to devastating effect whenever they got in to close quarters. Otherwise it was rifle fire and hand to hand, squad against squad in repeated assaults by the Texans against the entrenched Yankees and Coloradans.

Initially, Pyron's attack on the Union right stalled out as Slough rallied the Coloradans. Similarly, Scurry could make no headway against the entrenched Yankee center near the main ranch house. Arnold's Federals and Coloradans on the left actually succeeded in routing the Rebel attack on that flank, killing the commanding officer in the initial skirmish and driving the Rebels back up the road toward the southern edge of the canyon.

After several hours of repelled attacks on the ranch, the sharpshooters and Rebel artillery began to take their toll.

Pyron, despite his loss of the 4th's commanding officer, succeeded in driving the Coloradans right flank back, past the ranch, eastward, back toward Kozlowski's.

The continuous, withering fire was taking a great toll on the Yankee defenders.

Slough, as he had earlier in the day, now ordered a controlled retreat, this time to a defensible point about a half mile to the east of Pidgeon's Ranch. He pulled Arnold's forces back with him as reinforcements.

And here they took their stand. Skirmishes erupted all the rest of the day between the two armies. Slough and Arnold ordered a general retreat back to Kozlowski's under cover of these skirmishes across a broad front.

As the shooting ebbed and finally stopped. Scurry raised himself in his saddle and looked at the dead and wounded that surrounded him. Each side looked to have lost around a hundred men during the day. Dead, wounded, and missing. He took in the groans of the men and the screams of the horses.

He looked up at the ridge to the north and saw the twenty sharpshooters all raising their rifles in triumph. "Sharpshooters' Ridge," he shouted as he raised his own rifle in salute.

He signaled for Pyron to ride over to him. "Charlie, gather the dead and wounded. Accept their white flag when it comes so they can do the same. There's no need to take any prisoners. Let their wounded go back to the fort. There's no fight left in 'em."

He slapped Pyron on the back. "This war's over," Scurry said.

"On to Colorado," Pyron said.

"I wish I knew where Sibley and Green were with the 4th," Scurry said. "Send some men to the southeast and around the back way, and another group back to Santa Fe and then to Albuquerque to give them the news.

"New Mexico is now part of the Confederacy. We march to Denver as soon as they arrive."

Chivington's Coloradans were sitting on Glorieta Mesa as ordered. They'd never seen any sign of a fight below them.

"Major Chivington," the New Mexican Colonel said.

"Yes, Colonel? What is it? Where the hell is Slough? How can he not of engaged the Texans by now?"

"We told you of the shooting we heard and the smoke there, to the east, sir."

"Skirmishers, Colonel. I told you those were skirmishers. Slough is coming to attack the Rebels right over there. I don't report to you, I report to Slough."

He pointed down the hill for perhaps the tenth time this afternoon.

"Yes, sir. I know that was his plan. But maybe his plans changed, sir?"

"I don't think so," Chivington said. "He would have sent someone with new orders."

"Yes, sir. Now can we please talk about the other thing, Major?"

"What 'other thing'?" Chivington said.

"I told you about an hour ago that we think we discovered the Confederate supply train. Over there, by Canoncita."

He once again pointed vaguely toward a point on the horizon to the west and below where they sat.

"And I asked you to confirm it, Colonel."

"And we have. It's hidden in the hills near the Johnson Ranch."

"If I violate my orders and leave this mesa, I leave Slough vulnerable to the Yankees."

"The wagons are essentially unprotected, sir. Take a small force and leave most of your men here. But I recommend haste. I would expect the Texans to reinforce the protection of their supplies as soon as they can."

The two officers lay on the crest of a hill, looking down on the ill-concealed supply train.

"There's about eighty wagons, Major. And at least five hundred horses and mules. I think this is all of the Confederates' supplies, sir. We have seen no trace of any other supplies between here and Santa Fe. Much of this looks like what they took in Cubero."

"How large is the force protecting it?"

"One howitzer and a handful of Texans, sir."

"How long have you been watching them?"

"About two hours, sir."

"What do you recommend we do, Colonel?"

The New Mexican just looked at him. Not hiding his disdain.

The silence finally grew uncomfortable enough for the Colonel to answer. "I recommend, Major Chivington, that we get on our horses and ride down this hill and destroy that supply train."

He managed to say it with a straight face.

"Okay, Colonel. Men, mount up. Let's ride."

The Coloradans and New Mexicans on horseback galloped straight down the hill, while the rest followed at a run. They took the Texans totally by surprise. The shooting was brief and the howitzer and the Texans were taken captive all but immediately.

The suddenly decisive Chivington was all over his men. "Destroy that howitzer, Private. Tie these men up to those trees over there. Burn the wagons Sergeant. Every last one of them. To the ground."

"And the horses, sir? The mules?"

"Kill them. Massacre their stock. Drive them into that canyon and then slit their throats."

"You can't do that, sir," one of the Texans said.

"Shut up, son." Chivington said. "I view you as treasonous traitors. You deserve to have your throats slit, too. Just like your mules. Why don't you run toward them so I can kill you while you're trying to escape, Rebel? Then I can slit your throat too."

He threatened the man with the butt of his pistol, but didn't strike him.

"Take them away, Sergeant. Burn the wagons. Kill the mules and horses. Release the ones that we don't have time for."

Two hours later, scouts raced back to Scurry and Pyron. They reigned in their horses after a dead gallop. Dust spiraling into the air.

"The smoke to the west, sir? That you asked about?"

"Yes, Corporal? What is it? Calm down, son. What is it?" Scurry said.

"The Yankees, sir. They've destroyed our supply train."

"Everything? All of it?" Pyron said.

"Yes, sir. Every wagon burned totally. Destroyed. All the horses and mules dead or gone, sir. It's a total disaster."

"All the food? All the ammunition." Scurry was in shock. "Everything?"

"Yes, sir." Both scouts nodded their heads and looked at the ground.

"Is it Canby?" Scurry said.

"That's the rumor, Colonel. But if it is, there's no sign of a large force of Federals, sir."

"How could it be anybody else, Colonel?" Pyron said. "We'll have to get back to Santa Fe and then back to Sibley in Albuquerque."

Scurry and Pyron looked at each other. They both knew that Sibley would be left defenseless in Albuquerque if Canby trapped them here.

Unbeknownst to them, Canby still sat safely in Fort Craig. Awaiting news from Fort Union.

The Confederate Army of New Mexico stood victorious on the field. They had won at both Valverde and Glorieta. There was nothing between Jefferson Davis and a Confederacy that could now span the continent between the Atlantic and Pacific Oceans.

Except that his troops were in dire straits. It was virtually certain that if they stayed, they would starve to death in their now-conquered New Mexico

Territory. And if they chose to advance to Colorado they would face similar defeat and starvation.

If the victory at Valverde and Albuquerque had been both literally and figuratively pyrrhic, then the victory at Glorieta had been disastrous.

In fact, with the loss of all their supplies, the victory at Glorieta would go down as a defeat.

They had won all the battles and lost the war.

The Texans would now have no choice but to go back to Texas.

Those that didn't starve along the way, anyway.

60

March 31, 1862

Three days later, a thousand Federal troops and Volunteers from both Colorado and New Mexico mounted up and, led by Colonel Canby himself, headed north from Fort Craig toward Albuquerque.

"Feels good to finally be headed into action," Carson said.

"Always glad when you're happy, Kit." Canby said. "Any news from Taos?"

"The Rebels had no reason to bother with Taos."

"You still have guards around the clock up there to keep Confederate sympathizers from lowering your flag?"

"We do," Carson said.

"Couldn't we use those men against the Texans?"

Carson ignored him. "Any idea who that might be up ahead, in such a hurry?"

Canby sat up in his saddle, looking into the distance. "Riding hard to raise that much dust. How many?"

"Five. Maybe six."

"Well we'll know in ten minutes or so," Canby said. "Maybe Indian trouble?"

They didn't change their pace as the men up ahead kept racing toward them.

"What's our new plan, Colonel?" Carson said.

"By now, either Fort Union needs our help or we're needed to escort the defeated Texans back to Texas. I figure it's about time to find out which."

"Maybe that's your answer galloping toward us," Carson said.

The five men slowed their horses to a cautious walk when they got within a hundred yards.

Canby halted his column as the two groups came together.

"Colonel Canby?" said an exhausted and filthy Federal soldier.

"Yes, soldier."

His rank was indistinguishable under all the dust and grime. "Colonel Slough, Major Chivington, and Major Arnold have defeated the Rebels at Glorieta, sir. The Texans are retreating back to Sibley in Albuquerque. Chivington burned all their supplies, sir."

"How could that happen? They were under direct orders to defend Fort Union. And not to attack."

"Don't know anything about that Colonel. I only know that I was ordered to find you and tell you what happened."

A second soldier broke in.

"Maybe that explains why Colonel Slough resigned. I heard that rumor, sir, but didn't understand it. Maybe that's it, though."

"Funny War, Colonel," Carson said. "Commanders in the field quitting after their victories, and commanding officers not happy to hear that they've won."

Some eighty miles to the north, three soldiers rode into Sibley's Albuquerque command center. They dismounted and entered his office. They were as dirty and exhausted as their Federal counterparts.

"Yes, gentlemen? Any word from Scurry or Pyron?"

"Yes, sir. They've lost everything, sir."

"How do you mean, Sergeant?"

"We defeated the Union handily at a place called Glorieta. But the Federals found our supply train and destroyed it."

"How much did we lose?"

"Everything. They burned and killed everything we had. Scurry said to tell you he's headed this way. No longer has any resources to fight a war. He awaits your orders, sir, but respectfully urges you to consider an immediate retreat to Fort Bliss to avoid disaster and starvation."

"And what, Sergeant, does Colonel Scurry propose to do about Colonel Canby who is between us and Fort Bliss."

"He didn't say, sir. He just thought you needed his assessment."

Sibley sat down. Stared out the open door. "Dismissed, Sergeant."

Sibley took a slug from his canteen. His dream had been right. He had won all the battles, but his dreams of conquering the West for the Confederacy were dead.

How could a General win all the battles and lose the war?

His dream had been right, and his dreams were now dead.

61

April 12, 1862

Canby and Damours, at the head of their thousand troops, were watching Sibley and his Texans' southward progress on the west side of the Rio Grande from their perch on the east bank.

"You really think they're leaving for good, Colonel?" Damours said.

"I do. They're exhausted. Starving. They have no supplies and are practically out of ammunition. They've left nobody behind, Auggy. They're harmless. Put out general orders to follow the Texans. But stay on the east bank of the river. Orders are to attack any Rebels found on the east bank. Let the Coloradans and the New Mexicans satisfy their eagerness for battle if Sibley is dumb enough to send somebody back across. Have the men follow them all the way to Fort Bliss if they have to."

"Yes, sir."

Damours rode off to draft the command and pass the order.

Canby sat and watched his brother-in-law pass out of sight and out of history. He felt no satisfaction from the victory. There was work yet to be done while waiting for Carleton.

Now the Apaches and the Navajo had to be dealt with once and for all. He needed to get the situation in better shape in preparation for Carleton's arrival.

Carleton hated Indians as much as Baylor did. He had missed the Civil War. Now let him finish off the Indian problem.

Somebody had to.

62

April 13, 1862

Cummings walked into Zapico's store just before noon. Tipped his cap.

"How was Taos, Cummings?" Zapico said.

"Fine. How'd the Texans treat you?"

Zapico grinned. "Fair to middlin' as they say in New Orleans. They robbed me a little and didn't notice when I did the same to them."

"Lil?"

"They're big on drinkin' and poker and fightin' and taking stuff. Not so big on tipping or asking for stuff. Sorta like men everywhere. Taos?"

"The fandangos are tamer than in Santa Fe. The ladies friendlier than here. Mostly folks were worried the Texans might show up. The Pueblans stay to themselves, but Carson's Utes and Apaches come and go around the Plaza. Rations are scarce and the Jicarillas are clearly starving. I ran into Red Cloud again. I don't think he likes me much."

"Wonder why, Cummings," Lily said. "After you told him you killed Cochise's horse and stole his things."

"Don't see why it's any of his business."

"He thinks you made it his business in front of Carson."

Cummings seemed to think about that awhile. "Word in Taos is that the Texans are gone for good."

"I would think so. Unless they learn to fight without bullets," she said.

"Or food." Zapico said. "Speaking of food, Joseph, with the War over, we were thinkin' you've run out of reasons to put off earning an honest living."

"Where's the kid?" Cummings said.

"He made it okay," Lily said. "Still Canby's aide de camp. Still down at Fort Craig."

"I agree with you," Cummings said. " It's time for me to get to work. Good thing I didn't join the Rebels. Mowry's going to be disappointed with Sibley's defeat, but relieved that the four of us are still working together. I'm now liking Carson's suggestion that I become the Marshal. They need one. I can work with both the Governor and Canby, and work with Damours officially without raising suspicion."

"Why not just join the Army instead, Joseph?" Lily said.

"Actually, with Zapico's help, I was thinking of doing both."

63

May 1, 1862

Cummings walked into the Governor's office precisely at 10:00 am.

"Good morning, Cummings."

"Morning, Governor."

The Governor motioned him to sit down across from him.

"It says here that you would now like to be the Marshal here in Santa Fe."

"Yes, sir. That's right."

"What brought you here to Santa Fe originally, Cummings? And why do you want the job now?"

"As you know, I've lived variously here and in Taos for going on a year and a half now, sir."

"And before that?"

"I worked in security and guarding for the last twenty years. The California gold mines, San Francisco, Virginia City. Tucson and Tubac most recent."

"Ever do any pure law work before? Or has it all been private?"

"Deputy Sheriff in both Sacramento and Virginia City," he lied.

The Governor looked thoughtfully at the piece of paper on his desk and then looked back up at Cummings.

"Have you ever fought in the Army at all, Cummings?"

"I served briefly as a kid in the Massachusetts militia before I came out West. We had some skirmishes with Indians. We also had some pitched battles against Indians in California about ten or twelve years ago. We were deputized as an armed militia there, sir."

"We've had quite a late, great unpleasantness here the past few months, Cummings. How'd you miss out on that?"

"I've been back and forth on some business interests between Tucson, Taos, and here, sir. Every time I started to approach Canby or Carson they were too busy or I got called away. Once I approached Carson about the Volunteers and he suggested I see you about the Marshal job. Then you went to Las Vegas, and here we are."

"You have an impressive list of local business people down here as references. Including all the Masons in town. Are you a Mason?"

"No, sir. I was invited to join in San Francisco just as I was headed to Arizona. It didn't feel right to accept just as I was leaving town."

"Well, I can talk to Carson and Carleton on your behalf when they get here if you'd like."

"Yes, sir. I'd appreciate that. I'd be a fool to miss the opportunity a second time."

"If you worked security in Tucson and Tubac, why isn't Mowry on this list? I would've expected to see his name."

"Well, sir. That's a good question. If you ask Sylvester I'm sure he would be quite positive about me. We left on very good terms, actually. The Arizona Territory is still in the Confederacy isn't it? At least until Carleton gets there and drives the Rebels out, right? I didn't bother to include anybody living and working in the Confederacy, sir. But I'm sure Sylvester would be happy to speak for me if you asked him."

"I think Carleton is due at Fort Yuma around today or tomorrow, actually. I would expect the rest of the Texans to be heading back to Texas very shortly. We'll let Carleton sort out who's a Rebel and who was loyal."

"Sounds right to me, sir."

"Any hobbies, Joseph? Passions? Anything else I should know about? Uh, besides poker, of course."

He looked at Cummings with a smile that let him know he'd done his homework.

"Actually, when I was a young boy, I used to love to play base ball. I really loved it. Then as a young man we played teams all over the East coast."

"Who'd you play for? What position?"

"The Boston Tri-Mountain club. Mostly I played in the outfield. I pitched once against the Niagara's from Buffalo. Boy, that was a big deal for me at the time. A lot has happened since then. I hadn't thought of base ball for a while. A few of us tried to put together a set of San Francisco Base Ball Clubs, but there wasn't enough interest by the time I headed to Tucson."

"Too much fightin' going on in these parts for anybody to play games yet, Cummings," the Governor said. "Maybe you can talk Kit Carson into teaching it to his Indians."

"I might do that, Governor," Cummings said.

The Governor looked thoughtful, then once again shifted through his papers. Looking for something else to ask.

Finally, he looked up. "It was brought to my attention that you and one of your merchant friends on the Plaza have made some donations to the, uh, Territory's General Welfare fund, right?"

Cummings looked surprised at the Governor's directness.

"Yes, sir. It's the least I could do, given that I didn't do any actual fightin' against the Texans, sir."

The Governor looked back down at his stack of papers.

"I think it's a little light, Cummings."

"What is, sir? I don't understand."

Now it was the Governor's turn to look uncomfortable. "The donations, Cummings. They're a little light for this appointment."

"Oh. I see. I'm pretty sure we can double them, Governor. In fact I'm sure of it."

The Governor smiled broadly. "Okay then, Joseph. When can you start?"

Cummings frowned in thought. "I can push a few things around I'm sure. In fact, Governor, I guess there's nothing preventing me from starting now."

"You do know that the job here in Santa Fe includes Provost Marshal?"

"Yes, sir."

"I think you'll have more authority if you're also appointed as a Major in the regular Army. Canby won't mind now that the War's over out here. Carleton either if he ever gets here. You okay with that, Marshal?"

"Yes, Governor. But I think I like the sound of 'Major' better. Marshal's gonna take a little more getting used to."

64

May 5, 1862

It had been only a little over two months since Swilling's Arizona Guard and the two Texas Companies had arrived in Tucson to protect Sibley's rear. Two months in Tucson spent by the Rebels on meaningless skirmishes with the Federals out of Fort Yuma, listening to Governor Baylor bitch about the Chiricahuas, and dealing with Mowry's whining about the Rebels' ineffectiveness.

They'd learned only yesterday morning that Carleton and his two thousand Californians had arrived at Fort Yuma. Their choices were then to hang around Tucson and surrender, get killed by the Californians, or flee and try to rejoin the Confederate Army back East. They had chosen to head east away from Tucson, back toward Fort Bliss.

Swilling and his Guards were given the choice of going to Texas with the Rebels and then east to fight the Yankees, or staying in Arizona and playing it however they wanted with Carleton. Most of them chose Arizona, preferring to help whichever Indian-hating Colonel from whatever Army dropped in to try to tame the Territory.

"Remember," Swilling said when the Texans had departed, "Baylor failed to even hurt Cochise. He only made him more angry, killing his women and children. Cochise will be watching you. And remember the two Apaches we saw watching us on our way here on the mesa above Dragoon Springs? They'll be watching you again. But this time they're madder, 'n they'll see you as retreating, wounded prey."

Now, two days into the Texans' retreat, Cochise and Geronimo indeed sat on their war ponies on the mesa. They had been looking down on the Texans' progress since morning.

"The White Eyes have finally had enough," Geronimo said.

"Did any of the soldiers stay behind?" Cochise said.

"No. The wagons contain all of their belongings. They left nothing behind."

"Then you're right," Cochise said. "They've given up. They have left the miners and remaining white ranchers to us."

"And we have won," Geronimo said.

"And we have won."

Cochise turned his horse toward the rest of the Apaches waiting down on the desert floor. "Let's now make sure that their parting memories of our homeland are so painful that they tell all White Eyes the folly of ever returning."

The Texans' Captain watched the two figures suddenly melt away from the top of the Mesa.

"Sergeant," he said, pointing up ahead to the pass between the mesas. "Double time through that pass. And prepare to defend against an attack on the run. Protect the wagons and the horses."

"Do you want us to circle the wagons if they hit us?"

"No, we'll be better off in a running battle."

He turned back to the rest of his men.

"Lieutenant," he said. "Take your dozen best shooters to the rear. Deploy them against the Apaches at any points of attack as they come."

The Texans galloped double time.

They got through the pass without incident. Then slowed to a normal march, keeping watch in all directions.

An hour and three more miles of desert went by.

Nothing.

The God forsaken Arizona desert stretched as far as they could see in every direction. Only occasional Saguaros and flowering Brittlebush to break the monotony of sand. The two mesas a disappearing mirage to their rear.

The Apaches came silently and unexpectedly out of a series of ravines to the rear. Like phantoms in a nightmare.

There was shouting, then a rattle of rifle fire. The distinctive continuous popping of Sharpe rifles. The Captain turned his horse a hundred and eighty degrees. He saw what looked like a hundred Apaches, in war paint, attacking the Lieutenant's dozen riflemen at the rear of the train.

"Sergeant. Don't stop. Orders are to return fire on the run and to outrun them. Forward. Let's go."

The Apaches peeled off and let the Texans run for it. They followed just out of range from behind. They would gallop up in twos and threes, attacking periodically at their flanks.

The Texans were like sheep or deer being herded by shepherd dogs. The Captain looked toward the front to see if they were being run into an obvious trap.

There was nothing but desert ahead.

The trailing Apaches increased their pace and started a withering rifle attack aimed at the trailing soldiers.

Two of the men pull up wounded and the Captain headed back at a full gallop to support them, telling the Sergeant to keep his pace.

Apaches now came out of the ravines on either side, raining rifle fire on the teamsters and horses pulling the wagons. All the teamsters went down and several horses pulling each wagon were killed or wounded. The wagons came to a halt. The soldiers broke ranks and converged on the developing massacre in their center. Their herd of horses broke free and ran through Apaches and Texans indiscriminately.

"Lieutenant, get your riflemen up there to the wagons," the Captain said, then raced ahead firing both pistols at the Apaches descending on the wagons.

Reaching the wagons, he saw the Indians overrunning the wagons.

"Sergeant, move us out. Get us back on course. Let's get out of here. Due east."

"But the men around the wagons, sir?"

"They'll follow, Sergeant. Get us out of here. Lieutenant, get your men out of here. On the double. Everybody move out."

"But Captain......"

"No buts, Lieutenant. There's no point in all of us dying here. Get your asses out of here. Now."

The Texans galloped after the rest of the men, turning back and firing in fury at the celebrating Apaches behind them, now falling upon the wounded soldiers.

Cochise watched the White Eye soldiers in the distance galloping east, back where they had originally come from. He was intentionally letting them go. They would spread the word of their disgrace.

He watched his men torturing the four wounded White Eyes. Keeping them alive to punish them for the atrocities committed by their countrymen.

The White Eye soldiers were now all gone. Ultimate victory was now his, but there was no sense of satisfaction for him. It was his job to reclaim his homeland, and he had done that.

As he listened to the fading last screams of what he mistakenly thought were the last White Eye soldiers he would ever fight, he knew is father-in-law should know. He would send Geronimo to tell him.

He watched the wagons burn. And listened to the last soldier die.

65

May 14, 1862

At Canby's Fort Marcy headquarters, Canby, Carson, and Damours were enjoying the beautiful Spring evening as they overlooked Santa Fe just below them. They could smell the flowering Mesquite and see the open Poppies everywhere.

Damours, with his ever-present sheaves of paper, was keeping track of what they'd already agreed to. Canby had increasingly become dependent on his young aide de camp, and Carson had come to trust Canby and Damours completely. Being illiterate, Carson either deferred to Canby or had Damours read him the orders.

"While you were up in Taos, Kit, we heard that McClellan took Yorktown. Coupled with Grant's victories in Tennessee and Kentucky, it looks like the Union may finally be taking advantage of the lack of Confederate leadership. But this War is just a great tragedy now, no matter how it comes out. There were twenty-three thousand casualties in one battle, at a place called Shiloh. Incomprehensible. The politicians should be hung for not avoiding this War."

Nobody had any response to that, as Canby just shook his head. He then said, "And Carleton got his promotion to General."

"Sorry, Colonel," Carson said. "I guess, McClellan, timid as he is, didn't like you letting Sibley go back to Texas."

Canby just shrugged. "We're done with the War now. Back to dealing with the Indians."

"Look Canby," Carson said. "At some point I do have the right to retire. And the time is now. I have a wife and family. I'm an old man. I'd rather keep my promises to my Jicarillas and Utes than go after the Mescalero and then the damn Navajo again. Not to mention Cochise."

Canby looked at his friend. "We all eventually have the right to retire, Kit. But the job isn't done here and you know it. After all these years, let's get this done before Carleton is ordered here to do it."

Carson just slumped in his chair. Torn as always between his desire to be done with this and his fear that officers such as Carleton and Chivington would be in accord with Baylor's orders, "Kill them. Just kill them all." If Carleton rather than Canby was in charge of this, it would go badly for the Indians. Carleton just didn't have the wisdom to work toward saving these people and their cultures.

"Carleton hates Navajos as much as Baylor hates Apaches," Carson said. "When do you think the ol' Calvinist gets here?"

"Say a month in Tucson. A month traveling here, maybe with time wasted on Cochise? Late July? Early August? Major Arnold is waiting for him at Fort Craig to escort him up here."

"Unless McClellan orders him here sooner," Carson said. "Okay, Colonel, tell me what you want us to do."

"I've reorganized the Army under your command. You need to go to Fort

Stanton, rebuild and reoccupy the fort and then bring the Mescalero in. They've done nothing but killing and thieving since the Texans arrived and we abandoned that fort ten months ago."

"The Mescalero are the least of your problems. Where do you want them to go?"

"I'm going to issue you an order to kill all the men that resist, Kit. And bring the rest back to live under the protection of the fort."

"I'm not going to kill all the men, Ed."

"I know you're not. But the orders give you all the authority you need."

"Okay then, but then I'm retiring. Put that in those notes, Auggy."

"No, Kit. Then we finish this business with the Navajo. You and me."

"With my Utes and my Jicarillas."

"Yes, Kit. Just like old times."

"And then I will retire."

"And yes Kit, then you can retire."

The three men then discussed the final disposition of the wounded Texans and rebuilding the towns along the Rio Grande before calling it a night.

As they got up to leave, Canby said, "By the way, do either of you know the new Marshal? Name's Cummings. Joseph Cummings."

"I don't know him," Carson said. "I remember running into him once. This Cummings fellow asked me about joining the Volunteers. As I recall he was in possession of something he took off Cochise, and he infuriated Red Cloud somehow. I think I wound up telling him he should look into a Marshal's job."

"Well then, we know he's a good listener."

"He's a good poker player, too," Damours said. "I've played against him some around town."

He knew better than to say another word.

66

"Hey Lil." Damours was lying on his side, his back to her, right hand dragging the floor.

"Mmm…."

He sat up. Sipped the wine. Drummed his fingers on her butt. First the left cheek. Then the right.

"Mmm…"

Waiting for Lily to decide between more fun or more planning, he began to add it up. The thefts of the three drafts before he went to Fort Craig with Canby last February, plus the letter from the Fort Craig sutler he had stolen two weeks ago from the Express mail when they had arrived back in Santa Fe. It included a draft for $2,800 on its way to Leavenworth.

He looked down. Lily was looking up at him.

"Whatcha thinking' about, Damours?"

"Your future fortune, Smoot. What would you rather I was thinkin' about?"

"Mmm. That'll do nicely for a start. Does it include our ranch?"

"Unless you change your mind, Lil."

"Did you hear that President Lincoln signed a law that gives anybody 160 acres of free land to farm?"

"Really? Wherever we want?"

She snuggled up to him, spooning him with her right hand on his arm. "Yup, wherever we want. It's nice to have you back in town, cowboy."

He smiled. Always good to hear. "So I hear Cummings finally got a real job."

"Yup," she said." You're both finally on the inside now. Frankly, I'm surprised."

"Have you talked to him since he bought the Marshal job?"

"Yup. He and Zapico and I got things pretty much back on track. Cummings is helping throw more of the business Zapico's way now, and has finally produced some of his gambling money to toss into the pot. We figure Cummings should spend his time with your old quartermaster scam while you continue finding the serious money."

"I have a surprise from the mail."

He showed her the $2,800 draft from the sutler.

She looked at it thoughtfully. "It's as good as cash," she said.

"I think this is safe enough to pass through Zapico, right Lil?"

"As long as it's only one time he can always say it was official. Paid for legitimate purchases for the Army. Whatever he could get for it would be pure profit."

"We both need to be more careful now. It's getting close to the end for me here. When Carleton gets here in two or three months, he's likely to replace Canby. Within a week, Carleton's aide de camp will know everything I've done."

"It's that easy to discover?"

"For somebody who's looking. I'm going to have to start getting all I can as quick as I can, Lil. And I'm going to have be ready to leave in a hurry. Once Carleton's here, I'll have less than that one week, plus whatever cushion Cummings gives me if they ask him rather than someone else to find me."

"Auggy, Cummings isn't going to go after you if they ask him."

"He won't have a choice. It'll be an order. He's the Marshal."

"If Cummings comes for you, Auggy, he'll be at risk of you talking. I think he's gonna feel he needs to kill you."

"Not 'til he has his money, Lil."

"Well, there's that."

PART III
"KILL THEM.
JUST KILL THEM ALL."

67

General James Henry Carleton and his California Volunteers had arrived in Tucson on June 1st. A week later, he declared martial law with himself as the military Governor. He immediately levied taxes on gambling and saloons to ferret out those who were going to object to a strong Yankee presence. The first to object had been Sylvester Mowry.

This was his first meeting with his staff at the Tucson headquarters. The nearly fifty year old Carleton was imperious, with his signature mutton chops meeting his jet black moustache and covering his cheeks down to his bare chin.

"General," Colonel West said. The forty year old West was bald except for two oversized tufts of hair on each side of his head that, curiously, matched Carleton's puffed out mutton chops. West's already-graying full beard was in sharp contrast to the older Carleton's jet black facial hair.

"Yes, Colonel."

"I arrested Mowry yesterday as you ordered, sir."

"How'd he take it?" Carleton said.

"He wasn't too happy, General. He kept blustering about what was going to become of his silver and his four hundred employees. But he was aware there was no appeal."

"Has anyone learned anything about any remaining Rebel dispositions in the Territory?" Carleton said.

"We know the Texans who were in Tucson headed toward Mesilla six weeks ago," the boyish looking, blonde Captain Tom Roberts, who was called "Captain Kid" by the men behind his back, said. "And we know that Jefferson Davis removed that despicable John Baylor from all his positions. Even dishonorably discharging him from the Confederate Army. Something about killing women and children."

"You mean the Apaches he ordered killed?" Carleton said.

"Yes, sir. 'Kill them. Just kill them all.' Is what Baylor actually ordered," West said.

"I guess it's okay to lynch Negroes in the Confederate States of America, but not kill Apaches," Carleton said. "Good to know."

Carleton looked over at West. "Do we know if the Texans got through the Apaches and made it back to Texas?"

"We do not, sir."

"Colonel," Carleton said. "I want you to take a hundred and forty men and proceed to Mesilla. Let's try to find out if there are any Rebels out there before the rest of us follow you. Your first priority is to find and clear out any remaining Rebels. Second, we will refortify the Rio Grande forts in case the Texans decide to try again. And then we'll go to Santa Fe."

"What about the three scouts you sent that way two days ago?" West said.

"They're supposed to get to Canby with our plans. We later discovered that the Apaches still control that route. Hopefully you won't find three dead scouts."

"The three of them should be okay," Captain Cremony said. The forty-seven year old Captain John C. Cremony, a very imposing figure, well over six feet, stocky with a heavy black moustache and full head of hair, was an experienced soldier in the southwest. He was fluent in Spanish and several Apache languages. He had lived among the Indians and knew them well.

"I talked to them before they left about how to approach Apache Pass," Cremony said. "They won't be in uniform and Cochise is more likely to be curious than threatened by them. West's force will have to be more cautious, though. Cochise isn't going to like soldiers coming through."

"What do we think about the Arizona Guard?" Carleton said. "I met Jack Swilling yesterday. I liked him and I think we can use him."

"All those Arizona Guards fought with the Texans, sir," West said.

"Could be, Colonel," he said. "But my sense is that the Arizona Guards' sole interest is to try to bring civilization to the Territory. Swilling struck me as a businessman. He wants to get the Apaches and the Civil War behind him, and get back to making money off the miners."

"Well he musta been disappointed to hear you were arresting Mowry," Roberts said.

"As matter of fact, he was. But he was even more disappointed when I told him that the Rebels had named Lee as Commander of the Army of the Potomac two weeks ago. He agreed with us that means the War's not going to end any time soon."

"Are you okay then, Colonel?" Roberts said. "Working with men who fought against our own troops."

"Look, Roberts. Frankly, we don't have time to Court Marshal every Guardsman somebody has a grudge against. Swilling was eager to get back to driving Navajos and Apaches out of the Territory. I'd rather leave him than your cavalry behind to do that. Swilling and the other Guards are downright ecstatic that we're committed to ridding the Territory of hostile Indians."

"Ridding the Territory of Cochise isn't going to be so easy, Colonel," Cremony said. "If you go after him, he'll just take all his Chiricahuas into Mexico. Then come back after he's traded everything with the Mexicans to do more of his business with the Americans."

"Swilling, Baylor, and I are more optimistic, Cremony," Carleton said. "You each have your orders. Let's get to the Rio Grande and then to Santa Fe. I want to meet with Kit Carson there. Then we can discuss how best to dispose of our Indians."

"Can I tell you a story, Colonel?" Cremony said.

Carleton nodded.

"One day I was escorting an Apache captive back to a fort in west Texas. This was the single meanest, toughest man I have ever dealt with. And I haven't led a sheltered life. Meaner than any Sergeant in your Army, Colonel. Meaner'n any cattle rustler or bar room brawler I've seen before the law arrived out here. This was the third time we had captured him. He hadn't killed anybody escaping, but he was impossible to keep subdued and he just outfought and disarmed any three or four soldiers we assigned to him. And then he just fled."

"You shoulda just shot him," Carleton said.

"Patience, Colonel. It's my story."

Carleton grunted.

"So I'm escorting him back, with three guards riding behind us, practicing my Apache on the way. And we're talking about how whites are amazed at how hard it is to find Apaches and how we can't figure out why they can always surprise us. And he asks me for an example. Suddenly friendly as all hell."

"Friendly," Carleton said, skeptical rather than questioning.

"So," Cremony said, ignoring him. "I tell him about the time I'm guarding a herd of Army horses and a lone pony comes out of nowhere and just walks over to the herd. The horses all gather together, like they do when they're being neighborly and curious. This goes on for a time, so I take little notice of it after a while. Suddenly the pony bolts, with, incomprehensibly, four of our horses roped to him coming out of the stockade. Not a human in sight. I leap up, aiming my rifle just to be doing something as I race over to close the stockade. When the five horses are safely out of range, I see a lone Apache rise up, now astride the pony leading the horses off into the distance." Cremony slapped his thigh and shook his head, as if he still couldn't believe such a thing could have happened to him. "Well," Cremony said when nobody responded, "He laughed when I asked him how it was done and said he couldn't tell me."

"Couldn't or wouldn't?"

"He wasn't inclined to make that distinction, Colonel."

"You shoulda shot him," Carleton said, having fun with it now in front of all his officers.

"In any case, about a mile of total silence later, he suddenly says he wants to show me something and leaps off his horse. He just stares impassively into the barrels of the three pistols and one rifle aimed at his chest. When I ask him what he wants, he says he wants each of the three guards to retreat behind the three hills surrounding us. He only wants me to see this."

"Don't tell me you were damn fool enough to let him loose."

"Well, as you might guess, none of the three of guards were too happy about it. But they finally agreed, saying that if I'm fool enough to do it, they'll give me ten minutes alone with him. When they're gone, he has me unshackle him on his word that he won't run away, and has me turn my back to him and count to ten."

"And you did it?"

"I did. When I turn around, of course he's gone. There's not a trace of him anywhere. Each of the hills is a half mile or more away. There's nothing but sand 'n cactus 'n small Mesquite within a thousand yards of where I'm standing. Let me tell you, I was stunned. I'm no stranger to Indians, but this was truly amazing. I walked all around where I'd stood and couldn't for the life of me figure where he'd gone off to."

He looked at Carleton and West and Roberts as if wanting someone to ask him to finish the story.

Carleton signaled him to continue.

"While I was looking around like an idiot, he suddenly rose up out of nowhere, not more'n fifty feet from where I had been standing all along. He dusted the sand off himself, and held his hands out for the shackles. In less than ten seconds, he'd completely covered himself with sand and had become a part of the desert landscape. He made himself completely invisible in ten seconds."

"Fascinating Cremony," Carleton said. "But what's your point?"

"My point, Colonel, is that if you plan on killing 'em, you're going to have to find 'em first."

68

June 18, 1862

"I'll raise you five dollars," Damours said.

He was sitting on another pair of Kings, the King of spades in the hole, looking into three spades on his right and a pair of Jacks on his left.

He loved five card stud. In truth he was better at it than he was at the cons. The cons paid better though.

He had cashed one of the stolen drafts to pay off his losses three hours earlier at a small private game where he was known only as "Bad Luck" Billy. They loved him there. Everybody always loves to have a perpetual loser and complainer as a regular in their game.

Now he was at the biggest gambling saloon on the poor side of Santa Fe. No chance he'd be recognized here. He had started the night winning big. Nobody ever felt sorry about taking money from a winner. Problem was, he was trying to lose, and these drunks were making it difficult.

"I'll call," said the young blond cowboy on his left.

"Me too," from the ancient rancher on his right.

The trick was going to be getting one of the two wealthy New Mexican ranchers sitting between those two to cash his second draft. He had to lose and lose big, but not to these two and not on this hand.

The dealer flashed the next three up cards. The cowboy paired his nine's and the old guy actually got his spade, the Queen. Damours got no help for his pair of Kings.

Damours couldn't even call. He couldn't have anything that beat the cowboy's two pair.

"Your bet, kid," the dealer said to the cowboy.

The cowboy, drunk, fidgeted. He couldn't take his eyes off the four spades. He finally bet ten dollars and the old rancher immediately raised him.

Damours folded in heartfelt disgust.

The cowboy called and then swore when the old guy flipped over his fifth spade.

The old rancher, now well ahead on the night, looked to be quitting, but tossed in his ante instead. Chasing his new winning streak.

Damours now sequentially folded the winning hand twice to wealthy rancher number one, and then two more to wealthy rancher number two.

Within the hour, he was down to close to nothing.

"I'm gonna have to go unless somebody can cash this draft for me," Damours said. He was sure that nobody wanted him leaving this table the way he was bleeding money.

"How much is it for?" wealthy rancher number one said.

"Billy" pulled it out of his pocket and peered at it.

"Three thousand three hundred dollars. It's for some equipment I'm on my way to Denver to pick up for the Territory."

"Too rich for my blood," the first rancher said.

Damours shrugged, stood up, adjusted his gun on his hip, and reached down to pick up his chips.

The cowboy and the old rancher flinched when they thought he was reaching for his gun, so Damours moved very deliberately.

"Let me see that thing," the dealer said. "You sure it's legit, Billy?"

"Of course I'm sure. I do business with the Territory all the time."

"And if you lose?" the second rancher asked.

"Then it comes out of my pocket. It's the business I'm in. I cash these all the time."

"Hell, I'll give you two thousand eight hundred for it Billy," the second rancher said.

The first rancher looked unhappy that he hadn't thought of that.

"Make it three thousand and you've got a deal. I'll have the difference back in an hour," Damours said.

The second rancher bargained him down another $100 and "Billy Rome" signed it over. The trick, of course, was now to keep playing without winning any money from either of the wealthy ranchers. Getting the money was one thing. Getting out of the gambling hall without arousing any suspicions was another.

Forty-five minutes later, he had won enough back on two winning pairs and a straight bluff to start relaxing. Three hands later he then lost to a new player just in the game.

The dealer flashed the seven up cards for the next hand. Damours had paired his hole Queen.

"I'll bet two dollars," trying to drive out the two wealthy ranchers, each of whom had a black six. They both folded, but the other four called him.

His next card was a nine and there were no A's, King's, or pairs on the board.

"Five dollars," Damours said.

All four called. The new guy, showing 10, Jack, started to raise and didn't.

Four more cards. Nothing for Damours' Queens, but an eight to the new guy's possible straight. Three nine's had already appeared.

"I'll bet ten," the new guy said.

Damours raised him twenty dollars and was promptly raised right back. It was an obvious attempt to drive Damours out, so he raised fifty back at him and got a hundred raise in turn.

He could have a pair of Jacks or a straight draw if he had the last nine in the hole. Damours was willing to bet he didn't have the case nine and raised again. After hesitating, the new guy finally called.

The dealer's hands flashed. A seven to each of them. He either had his straight or he didn't. Damours was willing to bet against it.

"I'll check," Damours said.

"Thirty," said the guy. An obvious bluff. Pair of Jacks or 10's.

"I'll raise a hundred," Damours said, tossing in the chips.

The guy stared at Damours as he reached for his chips with his left hand. Since he was right handed, everybody knew what was coming next. As the guy reached his right hand under the table, the dealer shoved him. Damours rose up, right hand on his gun.

Nobody said a word. The two players flanking the new guy stepped away and one of the bartenders came over. Stood over the guy.

"We have a problem here?" he said.

"He check, raised on the last card," the new guy said.

The bartender looked at the dealer, then at Damours. "Anybody say that wasn't allowed in this game? Anybody got a problem with the kid here checking and raising?"

Everybody shook their head except Damours and the now enraged new guy.

"It's your bet, mister. You can call, fold, or raise," the dealer said.

"I'll call you Billy, but either way, you better watch your back."

Damours shrugged and flipped over his Queen.

The guy picked up his chips, put the knife back in his belt, and stared at Damours.

"Where I come from, kid, people get shot for that."

And he walked out of the saloon.

Damours sat down. Bluffers always bluff, he thought to himself. Even when they're out walking in the street. He'd never known anyone to advertise an ambush. And this guy wasn't likely to be the first.

Ten minutes later, he drove everybody out of a hand except the rancher who had cashed his draft. Damours had a pair of eights showing with another one in the hole. The rancher had Ace, King, four showing and was betting like he'd hit the mother lode.

On the fifth card, the rancher caught another four. Two pair or trip four's, second best to Auggy's trip eight's either way.

Damours bet fifty, knowing he'd get a raise. And he did.

"I'll raise you two hundred, Billy. Just for fun."

Damours looked long and hard at the table and at the gloating rancher. This was exactly what he'd spent the last hour waiting for.

"My two pair ain't good enough this time," he lied.

He folded the winning hand, trip eight's.

"G'night gents. Always a pleasure donating to your well-being."

He doffed his hat at the bartender as he walked out of the saloon.

Another hard night spent building Lily a ranch.

69

Damours and Lily were eating dinner.

"Two more, Lil." Damours said.

"Two more what?" Lily said through a mouthful of cebolla, cheese, and chicken.

"Two more stolen Government Drafts cashed by the unbelievably unlucky Billy Rome last night at poker."

"Can't you at least give that poor boy a lesson or two? Before he becomes a Santa Fe legend and everybody wants him at their table?"

He just smiled at her and shook his head no.

"How much this time?"

"A little less than five thousand."

"Just last night?"

He nodded.

"Anybody you know there?"

He just stared at her.

"Auggy, are you going too fast here? Are you taking too much risk?"

"You don't have to take the money if you don't want it, Lil."

She made a face.

"Cummings give us the rest of his take yet?" he said.

"Nope. He's now saying 'it's in a safe place.' Zapico thinks he knows where, though."

"Zapico want another one of these drafts yet?"

"No. Too risky, Auggy. Zapico's sticking with selling Cummings' stuff for now."

"Any word from Mowry?"

"Nothing since the Californians got to Tucson, lover. Why all the questions all of a sudden?"

"The Californians are coming, Lil. We're pretty close to the end game now."

70

June 20, 1862

Twenty hours later and a hundred and fifty miles to the southwest, Lon Ickis and the Coloradans were on a routine overnight reconnaissance north of Fort Craig. Both Major Chivington and Major Arnold had come with them.

The men were bored numb. There had been nothing to do for months since Valverde, Glorieta, and the Texans' disappearance into the mountains.

Sibley was now at Fort Thorn, a hundred and fifty miles to the south, so the newly promoted General Canby had ordered them all to stay at Fort Craig. They were ordered to let the Californians have the job of reoccupying the southern forts to discourage any further aggression from the Texans.

Suddenly two soldiers came hurtling toward them from down river.

"Major. Navajos. A ton of 'em. Stealing at least a thousand head of livestock."

"Ickis," Arnold said. "Take five Volunteers and find out where they're headed. We'll be a mile behind you, Lon. Once you know exactly, get back here on the double without being seen."

The six men took off to the north.

"Let's move out then." Chivington said. "Everyone. Now"

Everybody seemed electrically charged.

Something to do. Finally.

Less than an hour later, Ickis rode back to Arnold and the main force.

"They're on the other side of that hill, sir. Just on the other side of the river. Maybe a hundred of them. Maybe a thousand sheep, a dozen cattle, and a dozen or so mules. They're counting on us not being able to cross the river to get 'em."

"I can understand," Arnold said, "That the Utes and the Apaches and even the Cheyenne and Comanches, are fighting against subjugation and the destruction of their way of life. But the damn Navajo could just stay in their homeland between their four sacred mountains and nobody would ever bother them. Yet here they are, three hundred miles from home. Stealing from the New Mexicans. Even under the threat of death."

"As I've been saying," Chivington said. "Kill 'em. It's the only way to bring civilization out here."

"Well, let's start with these, for now." Arnold said. "They're clearly stealing. We can discuss philosophy later, Major."

Arnold turned back to Ickis. "Lon, race ahead upriver with half the men and ford the Rio Grande ahead of the Indians. We'll wait until they've passed us, and then cross over behind them down here. When we hear you shooting, we will attack from behind. First priority is to shoot to kill. Second priority is to chase the survivors so far to the northwest that they won't think to come back. We'll round up the livestock on the way back or over the next few days."

"Let's move out," Chivington said. "'Bout time we had some action."

The Coloradans hit the Navajos with a full force frontal attack. They came at them, rifles firing and horses speeding straight at them all at once.

The Indians initially scattered in every direction with sheep and cattle and mules racing back and forth among the attackers and the defenders. The Indians' initial attempt to retreat met with an equally stunning attack by Arnold and his cavalry at their rear.

The battle was shorter in the execution than it had been in the planning. Immediately knowing all was lost, the Navajos sped to the northwest, abandoning their stolen livestock and their dead tribesmen.

After a brief, futile pursuit, the Coloradans pulled up and headed back. Playing cowboy to the frightened livestock, doing their best to round them up.

There were two wounded and one dead Coloradan. Two dead Navajo.

By the time the soldiers arrived back at Fort Craig with over a thousand recaptured head of sheep, cattle, and mules, their accounts had ballooned to upwards of fifty Indians killed or wounded.

71

The advance unit of West's hundred forty man cavalry entered Apache Pass at daybreak. Cremony had recommended that they travel at night as much as possible to minimize the chance of interference from the Apaches.

There was evidence of recent Indian activity at the abandoned stage station, but no Indians. As each platoon arrived, the men spread out, watered their horses at Apache Springs and rested under the Cottonwood trees. They were sobered by the Texans' skeletons and destroyed wagons back on the trail, but encouraged that there was no evidence of a similar fate for the three scouts Carleton had sent first.

Cochise, Mangas Coloradas, Geronimo, Victorio, and ten braves looked down at the assembling cavalry. The Apaches were on foot and without war paint.

"So the three scouts were what we feared," Geronimo said.

"We thought the White Eye soldiers were all gone," Mangas Coloradas said. "That we had won."

Victorio said nothing. Just looked menacingly down at the scene below.

"Are they here to punish us for killing the soldiers a month ago," Cochise said. "Or are these the Californians the White Eyes talk about, going east for some unknown purpose?"

"Only two ways to find out," Mangas said. "Ask them. Or kill them and see what happens next."

Eventually, three of the soldiers wandered off, away from the Springs. Just before West arrived at noon, four shots rang out on the bluff southeast and above the Springs.

Cochise had ordered rifle fire rather than arrows and lances. He wanted the White Eyes to hear it. He then waited to see what would happen.

As the shots echoed through the Pass, the soldiers sprang up. A Sergeant organized a defensive perimeter and ordered for an accounting of all men. Three men were missing, their horses where they had left them.

The Sergeant reminded the men that they had seen no Apaches and that they were under strict orders to avoid fighting the Indians.

Cochise had arrayed his men in a semi-circle around the Springs. They were invisible to the soldiers. Cochise was very conscious of the fact that his last meeting at this very spot with the boy soldier had gone badly. The boy soldier had determined how things went over a year ago. He would now let these soldiers choose how today would go.

Colonel West arrived and was briefed.

"How long were they missing before the shots, Lieutenant?" West said.

"Nobody noticed they were gone until after the shots, sir."

West looked up at the surrounding hills and mountains. Looked at the flat ground between the Springs and the stagecoach station. It was an indefensible position. Attacking from here would be irresponsible. And the soldiers could see nothing to attack.

"Bascom was really a fool," West said. "Why on earth would he try to arrest Cochise and his family on this spot? He was lucky that he and his men weren't massacred."

The Sergeant shaded his eyes and looked up into the hills. "I'll be damned if I can see a single Indian, sir."

"Well, I doubt that our three missing soldiers had a gunfight to the death with each other up there. Let's see what we can find out."

West had his interpreter bring a long stick with a white flag. "Have you met Cochise before?" he said to the interpreter.

"Yes, sir. Before he was on the warpath he was friendly with all the whites in this area. He never liked Mexicans much."

"Yeah, I knew better than to bring a Mexican interpreter. Let's go see how Cochise wants to play this."

The two men walked fifty yards toward the hill where the shots had come from, carrying the white flag out in front of them. A thousand eyes could have been on them. Watching their every step.

Nothing happened.

The two men stuck the pole with the white flag into the ground and sat down.

Cochise stared impassively at the two white men.

"Shoot them," Victorio said. Let's see what the White Eyes do then," Victorio said.

Cochise said nothing.

The two soldiers sat patiently below them. Like lambs awaiting the slaughter.

After an hour, at a signal from Cochise all the Apaches miraculously became visible. Showing their rifles and lances and bows above the bushes and rocks that had been concealing them only seconds before.

Seventy to eighty armed men. One minute not there. The next, fully armed and threatening.

The soldiers were unnerved. But they held their ground. It was all up to West at this point.

Finally, an additional ten to fifteen warriors appeared and walked down from the top of the hill side by side. They were all armed to the teeth and all had covered themselves with white and red war paint.

"That's the most impressive sight I've ever had the opportunity to see before a possible battle," West said. "The Chiricahuas might be murderous savages, but they sure arrive in style."

"That's Cochise," the interpreter said. "The big one in the middle."

Coming down straight at them, Cochise looked even bigger than his full six feet. He led a magnificent pony, carried a rifle in his left hand, and had two pistols in his belt.

Cochise knew his men were ready to kill the two soldiers. He, himself, was prepared to kill, but preferred to talk.

When the interpreter stood, West remained seated, looking up at the Apache.

Cochise sat.

"We come in peace, Cochise," West said through the interpreter.

"In my experience, all White Eyes tell us this lie."

"We are travelling from the ocean to the west." He pointed to the trail they had come in on. "We are travelling in peace to the Rio Grande on the other side of your home. We mean you no harm."

"Are you from the place you White Eyes call California?"

"Yes, we are the California Volunteers."

"If you mean no harm to the People, who do you intend to harm? You bring many soldiers and horses for such a peace mission?"

Cochise was toying with West. Enjoying himself.

"We come wishing to be friends with Cochise. My chief, General Carleton, has brought us from California. He is in Tucson with twenty times my men." He gestured toward his men. "He wants to meet with all the Apache chiefs. To make friends finally and forever with the Apache tribes."

"The last White Eye soldier who sat here said the same thing. Then he killed my family."

"Yes, I have heard of Lieutenant Bascom. I have heard of his injustices toward you and your people. General Carleton and I have come many miles to start the peace process with all the Apaches."

"All of my people are also peaceful," and here he gestured to the armed Apaches standing behind him and above the bushes and rocks all around the soldiers.

"We have been waiting for decades for the White Eye soldiers to come in peace."

He stood.

West rose with him.

"I will go now and tell my people of your peaceful intentions and will return at sundown."

He turned on his heel, took his horse's reigns, and led his men back up the hill.

When they were out of earshot, West asked the interpreter how it had gone.

"He thinks you're either naïve or stupid, sir."

West looked up at Cochise talking to two of his men.

"Victorio," Cochise said. "Strip the three soldiers, and drive spears into their necks. Leave them on the other side of the Springs. In a place where even the stupidest White Eye will look. Geronimo, gather all the men and head quickly to the Chiricahua Mountains without the White Eyes knowing we are leaving."

"When do we attack the soldiers?"

"We don't. There will be more here soon. We will kill the rest when they come here through Apache Pass."

Two soldiers discovered the three naked and mutilated bodies an hour later. Each had a ten foot spear through his neck, painted red at the bottom and blue at the top. Bloodied eagle feathers were still attached to the spear points.

West sent all available forces out after the Apaches. But there were no Apache targets available. They were looking down at them, unseen, from the mountain peaks overlooking the pass.

West took his command to the San Simon River, two miles to the east of Apache Pass for the night. He could not know that he was camped in the precise spot where Carleton's three scouts had been attacked one week before.

The naked, mutilated body of the Mexican scout lay decomposing not two hundred yards from their camp sight.

72

July 10, 1862

Padre Guerrero looked affectionately down at Damours.

"Lieutenant. You have done very well for the Church."

"Muchas gracias, Padre. It is my pleasure."

"Father Ussel and Father Gabriel are happy that their confidence in you was well placed."

Damours, in his finest uniform, just stared at the Padre.

He never knew if the friars ever joked or were ironic. Damours was out of his element with both Spanish priests and Indians. White men trusted him. Always taking him at face value. Most women, too. But the Franciscans and the Indians were simply a different species.

Damours always felt that he had to be on his guard at all times with them.

"Con mucho gusto, Padre Guerrero. How are the Fathers?"

"They are well. They asked me to convey their best wishes. 'Please tell the young Lieutenant we are very proud of him,' they said to me."

Damours nodded.

"Do you have work for me on the Church's books, Padre?"

"No, I am told they are fine until September."

Damours knew he had been asked here for some reason. He decided the best way to find out was to shut up.

So he did.

After an appropriately long silence for a priest, Guerrero said, "Is it true that the Californians are now coming?"

More small talk, Damours thought. Let's get to the point, can we?

"Yes, Padre. We are told that many of the Californians have left Tucson and some have even reached the Rio Grande near Mesilla. We are told that General Carleton and the rest should be here next month."

Why do you care, he thought, but said nothing.

"And will General Canby then stay, Lieutenant?"

"Quien sabe. Nobody knows."

He shrugged his best possible inscrutable shrug. The one that worked with white women.

The Padre looked skeptical. "Lieutenant Damours. The Fathers asked me to ask you as to the whereabouts of our purchases. They said that they gave you vouchers in the amount of..."

He shuffled though the papers. Peered at them, then looked over his glasses.

"...Nine thousand two hundred fifty-four dollars for provisions for the monasteries and Churches in the Territory. They say they gave you these over the past six weeks. They asked me when we can expect delivery?"

Damours was back on solid ground again.

"The War is delaying many things, and sadly, the Army is insisting on priority. General Canby and I have requested your goods from Kansas, Colorado, and the East along the Santa Fe trail. We expect you to see some deliveries in September. Until then, I'm sure the local merchants will take the Church's credit."

"Yes, they do that already. September will be fine."

The Father again shuffled interminably through his papers, then finally said, "In the meantime, Lieutenant Damours, here is a list of important purchases that we will also need. Before October if at all possible. And here's four thousand dollars more in quartermaster vouchers to pay for them."

More Billy Rome losses.

"I will order these things for you," Damours said. "We will try to expedite the delivery."

Guerrero now seemed distracted. Damours realized he had been dismissed.

"Gracias," Guerrero said absently.

"De nada," Damours said as he left the room.

73

July 14, 1862

Ceremony couldn't get the line out of his head. "It was a dark and stormy night."

The line from Washington Irving's satire, *The History of New York*.

He looked out at the bizarre scene. They had left Tucson four days ago. One hundred twenty-five soldiers with two hundred forty horses, cattle, and mules, plus supplies and artillery wagons, had marched through the parched, unforgiving alkaline desert. It was already past midnight. So it was now the 14th and they had left Carleton on the morning of the 10th.

Good God. Merciful Lord in heaven. All the water needed by all mankind for a year was plummeting down on them from the heavens.

It was like a plague. A river of water pouring down on them in the pitch black. He half expected to see fish swimming through the air at every blinding flash of lightening. How on earth the horses and the mules were going to survive this deluge he had no idea. Streams rushed through the campsite where only the desert and a few Gila Monsters had been at dusk.

First the floods of California. Then the merciless march across the desert to Tucson. Then the smothering heat of Tucson and the three-day march through the desert to here. And now this.

How do the Apaches survive in this environment? Why do they stay? Why would anyone want to claim this as their home?

Cremony covered his head and tried to sleep through the wind, the thunder, and the screaming of the horses and the mules.

He was awakened before dawn by one of his lookouts.

"Captain Cremony. Come look at this."

The two crouch-ran to a spot on the periphery of the camp, sloshing through the mud and the running water. The rain had stopped.

They looked up at the surrounding hills. Burning torches being carried by men could be seen running around and over the hills. More than a dozen in all. Maybe twenty. It looked like fireflies in the trees.

"Shall I wake all the men, sir?"

"No, Sergeant. Tell Captain Roberts and make sure all the lookouts are on full alert. They are no threat to us. Apaches never signal an attack."

"Then what are they doing, sir?"

"Damned if I know, Sergeant. I've never seen anything like it. They wouldn't let us know if they were watching us. I have no idea. But there's nothing to worry about."

"The runners have all been sent out," Nahilzay said to Cochise and Mangas Coloradas. "They are carrying torches to all the People within three days of here, summoning them to Apache Pass to massacre the White Eye soldiers who are coming."

They had just completed their war dance in the Chiricahuas and been blessed by the priests of all the clans. The Mimbres had come from Pinos Altos when Cochise had told Mangas of the number of soldiers West had said were headed to the Pass.

To the west, they could see the lightning from the storm, but could hear no thunder.

"We have eight hundred warriors here now," Cochise said.

"There will be a thousand in two days' time," Geronimo said.

"More than enough."

"I agree," Mangas Coloradas said. "It is now time to stop the small fighting and running and time to stop the White Eyes forever. Right here."

"And the White Eyes still in Tucson?" Geronimo said.

"If they come," Cochise said. "We will let them see what's left of these men who are about to die. Let them decide between death or returning to the place they call California."

He looked toward the lightening in the dark western sky.

"This is our home. They can die here or return to their own homes. It is up to them. It is a good time for them decide."

Roberts awoke at dawn. The river was now a swollen torrent. Streams from the rains still flowed through the camp.

The men were breaking camp and were amazed to find the camp filled with all sorts of frogs, toads, and salamanders. One of the Corporal's dog, Rucker, was chasing them, catching them, and eating them to the merriment of the men.

"Where did the frogs come from?" one of the Lieutenants said.

"They're desert toads, actually," Cremony said. "They live under the sand forever, almost in hibernation. When it rains, they emerge. Either that, gentlemen, or we have been visited by a Biblical plague sent by the Chiricahua priests. Let's move out. We've got a nine hour march. Toads or no toads."

His laugh wasn't even comforting to him. The entertaining Rucker aside, there was no way the amphibians they saw hopping under their horses' hooves for the next few hours could be a sign of anything good. Certainly not in the desert.

They arrived in Dragoon Springs at midafternoon.

"Set sentries, Sergeant," Roberts said. "Tell the men to get as much sleep as they can. We leave at dark for Apache Pass."

He turned to Cremony. "We'll just be getting there a little after dawn, and

I don't want any Apaches to see dust announcing our arrival."

"They know you're coming," Cremony said. "You can count on that. Cochise let West through. He knows there's more of us. They're up there watching us now. Only thing we don't know is what his plans are for us."

The two Captains looked silently up into the hills.

74

Roberts' exhausted, parched one hundred twenty-five men arrived at the stagecoach station at the entrance to Apache Pass just after dawn.

Dragoon Springs was forty miles behind them and Apache Springs was a mere six hundred yards in front of them. Smelling the water, the horses snorted and pranced, pulling forward against their reigns. Like thoroughbreds itching for a race.

Not an Indian in sight.

The Californians now faced what every white man before them had faced in precisely this spot. The Springs were hidden just ahead in the Cottonwoods. Over the centuries they had sunk into a nice stream bed, some thirty to forty feet below the level of the plains where the station sat, and were thus invisible from the meadow.

This high desert meadow, was indefensible. Hills rose above it to the northeast and the south. If there were hostiles, you couldn't get from the meadow through to the east. And you damn sure couldn't get to the Springs.

Roberts sat in his saddle, reigning in his thirsty horse with his left hand and running his right hand through his sweaty, blonde hair as he looked up into both sets of hills. Peering into the trees six hundred yards away. This is where Bascom had started this mess. Where West had lost his three men to unseen foes. And who knows how many more.

"What do you think Cremony?" Roberts said. "You see anything that remotely suggests an Indian?"

"No sir. But that doesn't mean a damn thing."

"I count more than a hundred and twenty," Geronimo said.

"What are the two wagons at the back?" Cochise said.

"Food maybe," Victorio said.

"Perhaps ammunition?" Cochise said. "We have nine hundred Apaches on the hills and in the trees. More between here and the Chiricahuas if we need them. The runners did well."

The Apaches had crept down to their places in the hills and trees before dawn. Invisible to the soldiers, as they had been for West's forces.

This time Cochise wanted to avenge the shooting of his father and the execution of his family members by the boy soldier a year and a half earlier at this very spot. There would be no mercy for the soldiers.

The days of small attacks on small groups of White Eyes and then running back to Mexico were now over. This was their home.

Today would be the end of the White Eyes in the home of the People.

"Forward to the Springs," Roberts said. "Very carefully. But forward."

"You won't see a damn thing coming, Roberts," Cremony said. "Think about sending a smaller party to the Springs."

"I would fear for their safety, Captain."

Roberts characteristically led the men from out front. Tired, hungry, thirsty, the Californians spread out and slowly walked toward the Springs.

The horses were eager, whinnying and difficult to control. And there wasn't an Indian in sight. Rucker trotted back and forth behind the horses.

They had advanced to within two hundred yards of the trees, when, simply out of nowhere, hundreds of arrows and bullets rained down on them from the two hills and the Cottonwood trees in front of them.

Where a moment before, there had been two empty hills and a grove of peaceful Cottonwood trees, there were now puffs of smoke and a continuous hail of descending arrows.

There had been innumerable skirmishes and fights over the decades in Apache Pass. There had been murders, lynching's, and even a few massacres. But this volley now started the biggest and longest battle that would ever be fought there.

Rucker yelped as an Apache arrow clipped off one of his toes, the first casualty of the battle.

The soldiers returned fire, shooting at an unseen enemy in front of them and above them on both sides. The howitzers were back at the station. But there was nothing for the soldiers' or the howitzers to shoot at. Not an Apache in sight. Just puffs of smoke and volleys of arrows.

"Re-form. Back to the station," Roberts said, then led an orderly retreat under a continuous blizzard of arrows and bullets.

Once at the station, both sides continued firing from behind cover. The cavalry in and around the station and the Apaches, some now visible up in the hills, behind natural and man-made rock formations.

They rained down hell throughout the morning. The increasingly desperate and thirsty soldiers returned fire at their largely invisible enemy.

For the soldiers, the thought of spending all day without access to the Springs and possibly the night in the station, surrounded by well-armed, confident Apaches, and starving and thirsting for the nearby water, presented Roberts with the prospect of a defeat of unprecedented magnitude.

"Set up the howitzers," Roberts ordered.

"Roberts," Cremony said. "I think a coordinated three-pronged cavalry assault at the Springs and up each hill will be more effective."

"There may be a thousand Apaches up there, Cremony. Twenty horsemen going up that southern hill will be cut to pieces. It looks to be at least three or four hundred Indians in those rocks and behind those escarpments. The horses will be dead within minutes and the men helpless."

"Apaches never stand their ground in the face of a cavalry charge," Cremony said.

Roberts looked toward the Springs. Then up at each of the two hills.

The arrows and rifle fire continued. Several of the men had been wounded, and all were parched almost beyond endurance. Whatever they were going to do, it was going to have to be soon.

"We can't see them, Cremony," Roberts said. "Their arrows and bullets suggest a much larger force than you think. They aren't going to run from forty of you charging up a hill when they outnumber you ten to one."

"They don't outnumber us ten to one, Roberts."

"Cremony, you don't know that. Cochise knew how many we were when he picked this fight. Put the howitzers into position. Now. Let's blast them back to where they came from."

"Captain," the Lieutenant said. "Cremony's point is that this is their home. They aren't going anywhere if we don't chase them."

"Your orders are to set up the artillery and commence blasting these Indians back to Mexico. Either obey your orders or remove yourselves back to your horses and await arrest."

"Yes, sir."

Both officers leaped to their duty. After several false starts, Roberts finally got his two howitzers in place, pointing up at the Apaches' firing positions in each of the hills. With time of the essence, the batteries opened up on the dumbfounded Apaches. Under cover of a fierce fusillade into the hills and into the Cottonwoods, the gunners placed a howitzer aimed up at each hill, and fired again.

Up above them, Cochise met with a small group of his warriors, watching.

Mangas Coloradas had been wounded deep in the chest, perhaps mortally. Several Mimbres had just left with him, racing him to a doctor in Janos, Mexico.

Fearing the worst now both for his father-in-law and his Chiricahuas, Cochise turned to the disaster in front of him.

"What are in the "fire wagons"?" Cochise said.

"Very large rifles," Victorio said.

"Magic," Juh said.

"No," Cochise said. "Victorio is right. They are very large rifles. We have ten times as many men as they. Kill the White Eyes who shoot from the wagons and we kill the wagons."

He had Geronimo and Victorio select a hundred warriors to kill the men at the "fire wagons" so that they could then have their way with the soldiers.

Geronimo and Victorio raced down to direct their warriors to lay down fire on the gunners at the "fire wagons."

Several of the gunners fell. Cavalry officers continuously replaced them as each fell, learning how to fire the guns as they went along. The next two cannon shots boomed out and echoed back off the mountains. Adjusting for the distance to the rocks where the most shots were coming from, the cannons burst again as one. The Apaches had rarely seen cannons before, let alone seen the havoc that a flying missile can wreak on rock and man alike. Honing in on the positions, thundering crash after thundering crash reverberated through the pass.

And then again. And then again. The cannons wrought hell on the Apaches, blowing apart men and rocks alike.

The Indians had no idea how to defend or counterattack. Many began fleeing the "fire wagons," back up the hills.

Rucker put his toad practice to excellent use, driving startled Apaches from cactus, rock, and brush cover.

The Chiricahuas now began leaping out from behind bushes and trees and rocks in larger and larger numbers. They jumped and dashed out of the Cottonwoods and up, across, and over the hills.

If it hadn't been such desperate business it would have looked humerous. The soldiers could finally see their adversaries and commenced shooting at will. When not firing over and over again at the fleeing warriors, the soldiers felt they were watching mountain goats cavorting across a mountain slope.

Cochise and Nahilzay watched as their warriors fled up and over the hills and swarmed out of the Cottonwoods, away from the Springs. They were powerless to stop the retreat of their terrified warriors. The Chiricahuas, who backed away from no man, had nothing with which to answer the "fire wagons."

"We had defeated them before the wagons began shooting," Geronimo said as he trotted over to his chief.

"Yes. We had a great victory," Cochise said.

The three watched sadly as the world they had known and hoped to preserve swarmed up and away from them.

Back toward the safety of the Chiricahuas.

"Tell the priests about Mangas," Cochise said. "Their prayers are stronger than any mexicano doctor. Mangas was right. We can't stand against the "fire wagons". And we can't make the 'fire wagons' run from us. So we can now only fight and run."

Cochise stood alone, looking down on the disaster. This was their home. These soldiers were thieves. They had taken his home. And his father's home. And all their fathers' and children's home for generations.

"Now take your cavalry, Cremony, and chase the bastards," Roberts said. "Chase them back to their mountains."

The cavalry units mounted up and gave futile pursuit. They caught and killed a few wounded Apaches, but the rest had fled to the safety of their invisible arroyos and canyons and mountain hideouts.

Roberts set up rigorous defense pickets and let the men and horses have access to the Springs. When they were done, Roberts ordered them east, to camp at the San Simon River.

Just as Roberts and Cremony started to lead the march out of Apache Pass, they were surprised by five men riding up the stage trail from the east. The five men rounded the hill and stopped at the sight of the stage coach station and the Californians.

"We heard all the shooting, Captain," said the red bearded soldier at the head of the five. "Looks like you didn't need our help."

"Who the hell are you?" Roberts said.

"Tom Jeffords. General Canby sent us to Tucson to see if we could talk General Carleton into finally coming to the Rio Grande. You, I take it, are the Californians."

"Yes," Roberts said. "We are the second advance of General Carleton's forces. Colonel West was through here three weeks ago. We assume he's at Mesilla and Fort Thorn by now."

"Well," Jeffords said. "Canby got word about three weeks ago from someone claiming to be a California scout that Carleton was coming. But the Rebels had captured him and we didn't know if it was reliable or not."

"Were there three men or only the one?"

"The scout claimed that the Apaches killed the other two and that he escaped only to be taken by the Rebels when he got near Mesilla."

"Yes, that's Carleton's scout. His report was accurate."

"We had no way of knowing. I do think your Colonel West got to Mesilla, though. That would explain why Sibley just fled from there to Texas."

Jeffords looked around the hills.

"What happened here, Captain?" He said.

"Cochise had us pinned down," Roberts said. "We blasted him out a couple of hours ago. We lost four men, though."

Jeffords looked up into the hills, saw a lone Apache on a glorious pony, looking down at them. "Is Carleton really coming?"

"He should be here in two weeks on his way to Fort Thorn, Jeffords," Cremony said. "Do you know Cochise? Would you recognize him?"

"As a matter of fact, yes. I used to ride for Butterfield through here. Cochise and his people were at peace back then. Before the Bascom fiasco. I can assure you that nobody shed a tear when Bascom was killed at Valverde."

"Bascom is dead?" Cremony said.

"Beheaded by a Rebel shotgun blast."

Nobody knew what to say to that.

"Actually," Jeffords said. "If you want to see Cochise, that's him right there."

He leaned forward in his saddle and pointed up to the mountain above the southern hill, where Cochise sat on his horse looking down on them. He stared at them for another minute, then turned his pony and headed out of sight, deeper into the Chiricahuas.

They all looked up at Cochise as Jeffords pointed to the man who would eventually become the closest friend he would ever have.

75

July 28, 1862

Damours entered the Governor's office.

"General Canby asked me to come by, sir. Said you wanted to see me."

"Yes, Lieutenant. We're seriously short on supplies and are having a devil of a time getting any deliveries at all. Canby said you could help us."

"When do you need them?"

"Early October at the latest. Preferably before the end of August if possible."

"Do you have a purchase order?"

Damours, the model bureaucrat.

"Yes. Right here."

He handed Damours several sheets of paper and two official Government Drafts, each in the amount of $3,800.

Sometimes Damours felt like the ant lions he'd watched out in the desert. If you just sat at the bottom of your sand pit trap, the damnedest things just wandered by and spilled down on top of you. Tumbling down the precarious sandy slope into your waiting jaws at the bottom.

Well, into your waiting wallet at the bottom, anyway.

But the Governor? Some things were just too big and needed to be thrown back.

Well, maybe not.

Damours pretended to read the lists carefully. Carleton was now due here in August. How long would it take to cash these? And where? And how long 'til it all starting to come to light? His mind was spinning.

He looked up at the Governor and gave him his best Auggy Damours earnest look.

"I'll get right on it, sir. You'll have delivery and some returned change before October. I guarantee it, sir."

The Governor looked at him curiously.

"Okay. Thanks. By the way, Lieutenant. Has anyone ever told you that you bear a remarkable likeness to the actor, John Wilkes Booth?"

"Yes, sir. It does come up every now and then."

"If he ever played a soldier on stage, he'd look just like you."

"Not from what I hear Governor. I hear he'd be wearing a grey uniform."

"More, Auggy. More"

He reached down and kneaded Lily's toes as he moved his tongue back down between her thighs.

Her toes curled hard into his palms as her stomach pushed even harder into his forehead.

It hurt good for Damours.

"Harder. Harder, Auggy."

He came up for breath. Looked for her face, but could only see her breasts and erect nipples. One of which she was squeezing between her fingers just like she always did.

"Which?"

"C'mon, Auggy. Both. Harder. No more jokes now. Harder."

He went back in and she arched to meet him.

Hard.

Damours hung in there, though.

Ten minutes later they lay on their backs, sharing a cigarrito. Breath coming evenly again.

"God, Auggy. You know if you kill me, I'll never get rich."

"But then I will. Twice as rich. And then I'll be the one with both all the money and all the memories."

She punched him with her elbow and he countered by reaching under her and grabbing her butt.

"Maybe I should quit while I'm ahead," she said. "I'd get away with my life then, and half the money."

He looked at her curiously.

"We cutting the others out now?"

"I meant to tell you earlier, we just found out that Carleton arrested Mowry last month. The game's changed."

"What does it mean?"

"We have no idea. Nobody seems to know. Maybe you can ask Carleton when he gets here."

"Nope, I don't think it'll be a good idea for me to hang around talking to Carleton, Lil. Not after today."

She puzzled over that for a second, then handed him the cigarrito and looked over at him.

He filled her in on his meeting with the Governor, and her eyes widened. "Auggy, you aren't thinking of taking that amount of money, too, are you? Not from the Governor?"

"You bet this ass I am."

He squeezed and she punched him again. Ashes fell on his chest and he just let it go.

"We're going to need Zapico to cash that kind of money," she said. "Unless you trust Cummings to do it."

"Neither one of us does. No point in discussing it. Do you think the Jew will do it?"

"If Zapico can do it without compromising himself, he will. If Zapico is suspected of anything and Mowry doesn't get out of jail, he'll always be able to blame the two of you. I think he'll find a way to do it. He'll wind up with a fortune and no tarnish."

"And you're okay with him blaming me."

"What do we care, Auggy? We'll both be long gone. Let Zapico take care of his reputation. And let Carleton and Canby worry about the Army's."

"And Cummings?"

"Who the hell knows, Auggy? We'll take care of Cummings when he forces us to. Until then, just keep taking the money."

"And you, Lil?"

"Just let me do the thinking from now on. I got nothin' else to do."

76

August 4, 1862

Chacon was enjoying a spectacular Santa Fe summer evening's walk. As he approached a guard house, he noticed one of his Corporals was being accosted by a regular Army Lieutenant.

"Lieutenant," Chacon said. "What's going on here?"

The officer either didn't speak Spanish or was too inebriated to understand, and Chacon's English wasn't sufficiently good to get through to the soldier.

"No understand," the Lieutenant said. "No hablo."

Chacon tried again. "Lieutenant. Stand back."

"You can't tell me what to do," he said, moving toward Chacon.

Chacon stepped forward and the Lieutenant took a wild swing at him, missing.

The Corporal clubbed the Lieutenant senseless with the butt of his rifle.

A half dozen men from both the Army and the Volunteers converged, shouting accusations at each other.

"You three take the Lieutenant to the jailhouse," Chacon said, restoring order. "All dismissed."

The American soldiers stood for a minute, then marched off to the Provost Marshal's office.

Chacon knew what was coming, so he made no attempt to continue his walk. He struck a match against the guardhouse and relit his cigar, waiting for Cummings.

Sure enough, presently a Captain came around the corner.

"You, sir, are ordered to the Provost Marshal's office," the Captain said.

Chacon proceeded to Cummings' office without bothering to reply to the Captain.

"Come in Captain Chacon," Cummings said. "I'm told that you and some of your men assaulted one of the Federal officers and several of his men. Is that true?"

"No, sir. It is not."

"Tell me what happened then, Captain."

Chacon told him his version of the story.

"So the Lieutenant is currently in the jailhouse, Chacon?"

"Yes, sir."

"I find it incredibly frustrating that you people get along fine with the regular soldiers and the Coloradans when you're fighting with them against Rebels and Navajos and Apaches, but afterwards, you take to fighting with your former comrades. Is there something about you people that requires you to be fighting with somebody all the time?"

Everybody knew the two each had a very low opinion of the other.

When Chacon didn't answer, Cummings tried again.

"What will it take to get you people to get along with your comrades in arms, Captain Chacon?"

"Should I call you 'Marshal' or 'Major,' sir?"

"Major Cummings is fine, Captain."

Chacon smirked at this. "Okay, then, Major. My account to you is entirely accurate. The Federal officers were in the wrong in this case. I do not represent, sir, as you do, that one side is entirely at fault every time. I think it takes two to fight. Sometimes it is the fault of the Americans. Sometimes the fault of the New Mexicans, sir. Sometimes, both sides are at fault."

When Cummings made no attempt to reply, Chacon continued.

"I, too, am frustrated by the fighting among our men and wish there were a simple solution. This is our home, sir. We will be here long after your kind and the Army have gone on to other battles."

"Certainly not, Captain. Someday this Godforsaken Territory will be a part of the United States, and you people should prepare yourselves for that inevitable outcome."

"We will see. The Confederates haven't surrendered that I've heard. Fifteen years ago we were Mexicans. Today, a Territory of yours. Tomorrow, quien sabe?"

"You gonna clean up the Indians all by yourselves?" Cummings said.

"Let us be open, as fellow officers," Chacon said. "We New Mexicans are not too impressed with soldiers who run from the enemy, or with an Army where gamblers can buy themselves a commission. We are not so sure that such an Army will ultimately be the victorious Army, Major."

77

August 24, 1862

Ickis and Damours stepped into Val Verde Hall together. Damours had promised his friend that he would show him a real Santa Fe fandango. Ickis had told him about the one in Albuquerque, where the gunfight had erupted and several of the Coloradans had been called in to keep the peace.

Ickis was eager to join the dancing, so they both headed past the food into the second room.

Damours gazed at the assembled people. They were different than the first time, but the crowd mood seemed the same. Different people, same feeling. It was a cultural event that took on a personality of its own. And Damours felt as if he had stepped right back into the same dance from a year and a half before. The major difference was that there were now more Americans, and more whiskey than champagne.

After several hours of dancing, they joined the line and danced a wild waltz with two giddy peasant women in moccasins.

Too many whiskeys and not enough dances later, sure enough a fight broke out between an American soldier, one of the Coloradans, and a young New Mexican rancher over one of the whores from Maria's. No doubt one too many 'greaser' epithets had finally been hurled.

A shot rang out, harmless fortunately. Ickis tackled his colleague from behind and the young rancher got in a couple of punches before he could be subdued.

Cummings and one of his deputies came in shortly to escort the two combatants to the safety of the Santa Fe jail.

Cummings and Damours made brief eye contact but gave no indication they knew each other.

This reminded Damours that he missed going to fandangos with Lily. Missed doing all manner of things with her, in fact. The four of them could no longer risk being seen together in public.

He and Cummings had the money and time was running short. With Mowry arrested and rumors rife that Canby was headed to Washington, Zapico was antsy to close up shop and split the proceeds.

Cummings and Damours insisted there was one more big take, this one from the Territory's Treasury, and a few more of Chacon's horses to sell and re-sell, just for fun, before breaking up the gang.

Besides, it was going to be delicate when Lily chose up sides, Damours thought. Might not be a clean break.

He watched his friend dance a waltz with Hattie, caught his eye, saluted him good night, and headed over to Lily's for the rest of the morning.

He suspected it had been his last fandango.

And he was right.

General Carleton sat at the table with Arnold and West at Fort Thorn, just south of Mesilla.

"It's just going to be about Indians now," Carleton said. "President Lincoln has replaced McClellan with John Pope. They have their hands full with Jackson and Lee for now."

"You're right, the Texans're gone and they ain't comin' back," Arnold said. "Cremony's a hundred miles east of Fort Bliss reestablishing that garrison. It's over out here."

"I heard that Sibley had the nerve to cable Jefferson Davis," West said. "Told him he'd beaten the Yankees, but that the New Mexico Territory had then beaten him."

"Yeah," Carleton said. "That's the same thing Napoleon said about Mother Russia. But he didn't have anybody to complain to. And the truth is that Henry is a whiner and a drunk. The New Mexico Territory didn't destroy all his supplies. The Coloradans did. And I'm sure somebody has told Jefferson Davis all that by now."

"Is Fort Bowie completed yet at Apache Pass?" Arnold said.

"Yes. Jeffords was right. We needed to rebuild the fort right there on that plateau above Apache Springs. We should be able to re-open the stage line now."

"Are we going to take on the Chiricahuas?" West said.

"Let's give Cochise some time to think about what Roberts did to him. We know he went to Mexico last month after he got his butt kicked at Apache Pass. My guess is that he's had his fill of taking on the U.S. Army for a while."

He lit a cigar while he thought.

"As I understand it, Canby has set Carson after the Mescalero and the Navajo, but, of course, he hasn't let him do anything about it for over three months. Ed always wants to sit and give somebody a chance to surrender. It isn't working on the Indians any better now than it did five years ago."

All of Carleton's officers had heard the stories of Carleton's New Mexico Indian days, his friendship with Kit Carson, how Canby and his Quaker instincts were always too cautious and always wrong, and he, Carleton, was always right.

In fact, nobody had ever heard Carleton admit to a mistake of any kind, no matter how trivial. If nobody cut him off, he'd sit there for hours with his mutton chops, bare chin, and flowing moustache, smoking cigar clenched in his teeth, and subject you to his Calvinist lectures in his curious Maine accent about such things as how he single handedly solved the '59 massacre of the pioneers by the Mormons in Utah, and how the Indians needed to be killed or moved off.

Carleton continued. "We missed out on our chance to throw the

Confederates out of here. I don't view Navajo slave-taking as any better than the southern plantation owners. A slave owner is a slave owner and should be dealt with at the working end of a rifle. Kit and I'd have them in Bosque Redondo in six months' time."

All of Carleton's officers had heard Carleton's endless stories about the beauty of the Pecos River to their east and relocating all the New Mexico Indians there, to his Bosque Redondo.

"You want us to take Roberts and go do the job?" Arnold said, trying to avoid the endless lecture.

"No. My orders are to await orders. And, in any case, killing Indians is one thing. Finding them when they don't want to be found another. And bringin' 'em in quite another. Nobody's better than Kit at that."

He lit another cigar. And then continued under a cloud of smoke.

"Pope and Lincoln'll give us our orders soon enough. When they've disposed of Lee. McClellan's as cautious as Ed. They deserve each other. Maybe George'll bring Ed home to him in Washington. By the way, have I ever told you two about the Bosque Redondo and the Pecos River......."

78

August 26, 1862

Cummings, Zapico, and Lily were in the back of Zapico's store.

"Now that Mowry's been arrested, I need to go to Tucson." Cummings said. "What's left of our deal before I go, Lily?"

She looked at Zapico. She had known that Cummings would eventually find out about Mowry, was actually surprised it had taken this long.

"There's no need for you to go to Tucson," she said. "You can't do anything for him there."

"If you decide to go later," Zapico said. "You can always take leave as Marshal. But there's no point in doing that right now."

"In the meantime," Lily said. "You and Auggy keep stealing what you can from the Army and the Governor until it gets too hot. Then we split it up five ways. Just like we always agreed."

"And then?"

"And then I'm out of here. Going to San Francisco," she lied. "Auggy better head for the hills. The Territory is going to be in an uproar when they find out what he's been up to. Auggy won't last a minute when people start finding out. You resign then, and take your and Mowry's share to Tucson."

"And him?" Cummings gestured toward Zapico.

"Don't worry about me, Joseph. You and Auggy bring in the money and I'll take my share. I'm good to stay here in Santa Fe. When you see Sylvester, he'll tell you the rest."

79

September 14, 1862

The Governor and Cummings looked up as Canby and Damours entered the Governor's office.

"Mornin' General," the Governor said.

"Mornin'."

The four men settled easily into their chairs, Canby's unlit cigar clenched in his teeth.

"The War's not going too well back East, gentlemen," Canby said. "John Pope got his butt kicked by Lee and Jackson at Manassas. Lincoln has now brought McClellan back to head up the Army, but Lee has actually crossed the Potomac into Maryland. The Confederates are now in the United States and threatening Washington itself."

"Maybe it'll all be over one way or the other in a few weeks," the Governor said. "Have you heard about your next assignment, General?"

"Yes," Canby said. "General Carleton should be here in four days, on the 18th. I expect that he will take command of the Department of New Mexico at that time and communicate the changes. We all agreed that Marshal Cummings should take charge of Fort Marcy and the District of Santa Fe during the transition."

"I took command five days ago, General."

Damours knew that Canby was going to be glad to never have to deal with Cummings again. He didn't trust him. He had refused to confirm the Governor's commissioning of Cummings as a Major. Damours had seen it as wise not to intervene.

"Yes, Marshal," Canby said. "I'm fully aware that you obeyed orders and took command on the 8th."

Canby then briefed everyone on his plans for the Indians. As it turned out, Carleton and the U.S. Congress would completely change Canby's intentions for the Mescalero and the Navajo.

And Canby was dead wrong about being rid of Cummings. Fate would bring the two of them back together again in roles neither could possibly foresee.

Two months and two thousand miles away.

80

September 16, 1862

Damours and Lily lay entwined in bed, Damours grinning as Lily tried to catch her breath.

"Damn, Auggy you *do* wear me out."

He reached his right hand back up under her skirt, while he rubbed her scalp with his left. Hard, just like she liked. She moaned under her breath, stretched into his right hand, and kissed him hard.

"You said you had something important," she said, pushing his hand away.

"*This* is important."

"To me too, Auggy. But why'd you want to meet? What's going on? I'm due at work in an hour and I can't look just-fucked."

He made a mock grimace and slid up the bed with his back to the headboard.

"The rumors that Canby's headed back East are true. He told me himself this morning. Carleton will be announced as his replacement tomorrow. Canby's going back to Washington in a few days. The decision had been waiting on where Lincoln wanted Carleton. The old Indian hater got his wish and he gets to stay out here and kill Indians. But our game is over now."

"What do we do now?" she asked.

"I've hidden all of Zapico's and my money, and..."

"Why don't we just meet with Cummings and Zapico tonight, split everything, and then head for the Washington Territory tomorrow?"

"I can't. Canby's ordered me to Washington with him. Lincoln and McClellan told him he could bring me."

"We should run with the money now, Auggy."

"We can't, Lil. If I go AWOL, they'll catch us with the money before we even get to the Colorado Territory. Then when Carleton's aide de camp discovers the missing money in a few days, you and I are dead."

"Then what's the plan?"

"I go with Canby to Washington. Then when things die down here after they discover the money's missing, I come back for you, we settle with the other three, and leave."

"How much do we have now, Auggy?"

"I don't know how much Cummings and Zapico each have, Lil."

"No, Auggy, how much do *you* have? And where is it?"

"What you don't know, Lil, nobody can get out of you."

Then Damours kissed her hard and ran his hand back up between her thighs and into her as she moaned and leaned back into him.

"Oh, Auggy. You're impossible."

81

September 22, 1862

Sensing somebody at the door, Carleton, in his new Fort Marcy office, looked up.

An uncharacteristically broad grin spread over his face, lifting each of his mutton chops up the side of his face and highlighting his bare chin.

There stood an old friend in a familiar beaver skin hat from New York City.

"Well hello, Colonel Carson," Carleton said. "The hat becomes you. Do you now wear it everywhere you go?"

"No, sir. Just on special occasions."

"And what is the special occasion today, Kit?"

"I'm retiring General. I'm here to wish you the best on your new assignment."

Carleton looked over at West and Arnold and winked. "Canby told us you'd say that. Said to just ignore you and give you your orders."

Carson just smiled his halfcocked smirk.

He entered the room and took off the hat, gesturing toward the New Mexican who accompanied him. "General, this is Captain Chacon of the New Mexico Volunteers. Rafael, General Carleton."

"Have a seat, gentlemen. We were just talking about our plans for the Apaches, and here you both are."

The five resettled on the other side of the desk, Chacon and Carson sitting next to each other on the couch.

"First things, first. How's Josefa?"

"Excited about my retirement. She asked me to congratulate you on chasing the Texans back to San Antonio without having to fire a shot. Victorious, she is confident you can protect the Territories without me."

Carleton looked at his old friend like he was humoring a child. "Say," he said to the three officers. "Do you know the story about that beaver skin hat? Kit, tell them."

"No," Carson said, hating Carleton's stories.

"Ah, the modest Indian killing, damsel saving frontiersman. A little over eight years ago, Kit and I were on the cold trail of some thievin' Jicarillas. They had stolen some horses northeast of here from us and the Cheyenne. Just a way of life for them. See somebody else's belongings. Take them. Run."

He looked to West for agreement and got the expected nod.

"As cold as the trail was, one day Kit saw something. So we kept going for a few more days. Then, this one morning Kit throws his coffee grounds into the fire and announces, 'Let's go. We'll be upon the Jicarillas at 2:00 o'clock today.' Mind you, the day before he wasn't even sure we were on the trail of the right Indians, and now he tells us what time we'll find them. This struck me as so farfetched, I bet him a small fortune he was wrong. Twenty hard miles later, we run the Jicarillas and the herd down in a small canyon off the Pecos. I look at my watch and damned if it isn't a few minutes past two. Most amazing tracking I've ever seen."

Carson just looked out the window, turning the hat over and over in his lap.

"I knew," Carleton said. "That Kit had trapped beaver for two decades and never kept any for himself. Pass that hat over to Major Arnold, Kit. Read the inscription inside the band."

Arnold looked at it and read out loud. "At 2:00 O'clock. Kit Carson, From Major Carleton."

Carson caught the look on West's face, knowing what he was thinking. This was the first evidence of General James Henry Carleton ever admitting he'd been wrong about anything.

"Okay, Kit," Carleton said. "You can retire after we're done with the Territories' Indians. I'll let others deal with Cochise. We've built Fort Bowie at Apache Pass and left a garrison in Tucson. Hopefully the Mexicans'll take it from there. And I'm sending West out to exterminate Mangas Coloradas and his Mimbres."

He leaned forward so that there would be no mistaking his orders. "And you know my feelings on this, Kit. Extermination is our only remaining recourse for the Apaches and the Navajo. Find them and kill them. Nothing else has worked."

"Because the whites keep breaking the Apache treaties," Carson said.

"Nobody broke any treaty with the damn Mescalero, Kit. They just took advantage of the Texans being here. Hell, they killed over forty-five New

Mexicans last month alone. And the Navajo? What treaty has any white man ever broken with the Navajo, Kit? Extermination. End of story. Soon this is all going to be a part of the United States and our job is to prepare for that day."

He turned to Carson. "You're in charge of New Mexico. The Mescalero and Navajo."

"And what do we do with them, sir?" Carson said.

"Kill them. Kill the men who resist and send all the rest to Bosque Redondo."

Carson was astonished. "Take ten thousand Navajo to Comanche country, General. How do you propose we do that?"

"I'm having Fort Sumner built at the Pecos, Kit. Kill the men who resist and then you and your men march the rest of them four hundred fifty miles to the Bosque Redondo."

The silence in the room became suffocating. And still nobody spoke.

"And then I retire," Kit Carson said, getting up to leave the room.

"Yes, Kit. Your work will be done. You can retire after you get them both to Bosque Redondo."

At the door, Carson turned.

"One more thing, General."

"Sure, Kit. What is it?"

"Where can I find Ed Canby? I'd like to wish him farewell."

"Too late, Kit. He left early this morning. Headed for the train to Washington. President Lincoln appears to want him and McClellan to try to defeat Lee by giving them a series of 'one more chances'."

"Damn," Carson said. "I would have liked to have wished Ed well. Dammit."

Carson looked thoughtful and then caught Arnold's eye. Arnold had shared his concerns about Damours with him. "Do you know where I can find his aide de camp, Lieutenant Damours?"

"Canby took Damours with him, Kit," Carleton said. "Lincoln and I both said that would be fine. Why do you ask?"

"Nothing. Well, maybe something. Captain Chacon has some serious concerns about some missing funds that Damours told Canby he had found last winter. We wanted to talk to him about it. Too late now, I guess."

"Is it something we should alert Canby to, Kit?" Arnold said.

"No, not for now. Let me and Chacon look into it for now. If we come up with something, we'll let you know."

That evening, Lily sat down across from Arnold at his favorite Santa Fe bar. He had her whiskey sitting there, waiting for her.

"Nice of you to drop by Santa Fe, John. I hear you're headed right back out again."

"You've got good sources, Lil." He sipped his whiskey. "When was the last time we saw each other?"

"You left to fight the Texans at Glorieta back in March, John. Six months." She took a sip of the whiskey.

"Been having fun, Major?" Teasing him.

He grimaced as he described his experiences since then, at Glorieta, following the Texans, chasing Navajos, meeting Carleton. "Now I'm headed out with Carson to round up the Mescalero."

"And then?"

"Then the Navajo. How about you?"

"Dealing cards. Saving money," she said. Now that I'm done stealing money with Auggy from the Governor, from the Army, from the Church, she thought to herself.

"Does it ever end, John?" Lily said. "Will they let you go home to Baltimore after you're done with the Navajo, or is that not until after the War?"

"After the War most likely. I talked to Carleton about getting sent back East and he said, 'Get these Indians off the New Mexicans' backs, and I'll ask McClellan to bring you back home'."

"I guess missing your family is just part of the deal?"

"It's what we all signed up for. Besides, going back East is no vacation. The Rebels are almost at Baltimore. I think the War back there is much worse than the fighting was out here. There are rumors that McClellan and some of the officers are so fed up with Lincoln that they're talking openly about a military takeover."

They finished their drinks in silence. Lily thinking about Damours and what he was heading into. She wanted to find out what Arnold thought now about Damours. He certainly knew he'd left for Washington. But it was too dangerous for her to show any curiosity about Auggy.

"Still planning for your ranch, kid?"

She smiled. "I live for it, John. Having my own ranch. Building something that'll last. Getting out of the saloons and away from the violence."

"Is it financially feasible for you, Lil, this ranch?"

She looked at him. What could she dare tell him? This father figure thing would end when she and Auggy took off. Arnold didn't like Damours. She suppressed a laugh. What father doesn't disapprove of his little girl's first man?

"John, I'm going to build a successful ranch in the Washington Territory. I'm saving money like you advised. You run off and round up your Indians. When you return, I'll be preparing to go."

"Okay Miss Smoot. You stay in touch. Maybe after the Indians and the Rebels I can come visit."

"See the results of all your advice?"

"Something like that. Maybe I won't like being back in Maryland after all this fun out West. You never know."

82

October 5, 1862

"Your forces ready to go, Kit?" Carleton said.

"Yes, sir. They've already set out for Cubero. Arnold and I head to Fort Union today on our way to Fort Stanton, arriving at the end of the month. Pfeiffer left Fort Union a couple of days ago to prepare for our arrival."

"Pfeiffer?" Carleton said.

"Captain Albert Pfeiffer, sir," Carson said. "Pfeiffer's been variously a mountain man, fur trapper, Indian fighter, and even a sub-agent for the Utes since he arrived from Germany in 1844. He's been an integral part of my forces for more than ten years."

"You'd get a kick out of Albert, General," Arnold said. "Despite being short, only about Kit's height, and almost completely bald, he wears these huge oversized coats that, along with his long grey beard, make him look like some kind of Chinese Emperor."

"We're clear then, gentlemen, you and your Chinese Emperor are to eradicate the Apaches?"

Arnold watched as Carson sighed his characteristic, frustrated sigh and Carleton smiled his standard patronizing smile. Old ground for two old warriors.

"Yes, General," Carson said and repeating his orders verbatim. "And then we will take the lot of them to Ft Sumner at Bosque Redondo."

"You good to go, Major Arnold?"

"Yes, sir. We report to Colonel Carson. Eliminate the Mescalero, sir."

Carleton looked out at the crisp Santa Fe Fall day, then turned back to his two officers.

"This is such a beautiful place. It's a damn shame that the Indians can't find a way to appreciate the opportunity we brought 'em. Both physically and spiritually. They've enjoyed this as their home for centuries and now insist on ruining it for us and their own people."

"With respect, sir," Carson said. "The real shame is that the whites, and the Mexicans and Spanish before them, I suppose, couldn't find a way to share it with them. As you point out, they were here first. It's their home after all."

Carson was the best in the business at understanding the Indians. He'd lived with them, been married to two of them, but above all, he was the best at conquering them and bringing them in.

Arnold had come to appreciate what everyone knew, that Carson was conflicted. Tortured actually. He knew that Carleton depended on his old friend, but they all knew deep down that Carson was terribly anguished.

"Hey," Carleton suddenly brightened. "Did you know that Herman Melville mentions you, Kit, in *Moby Dick* as the epitome of the true Wild West hero? Right there in the middle of a book about whaling and ships and the rolling ocean is the famous Kit Carson."

"No," Carson said. "Never heard of it."

"It's about this captain of a whaling ship who is obsessed with capturing and killing a great white whale. It's really a tale of man's obsessions."

When neither man seemed interested in discussing either Herman Melville or Carleton's obsessions, he moved on to a new topic.

"I assume you both have heard the latest from Washington? McClellan actually drove Lee out of Maryland. The Battle of Antietam at a place called Sharpsburg. There were twenty-three thousand casualties in one day. Think about that. Thirty-five hundred boys killed. It's hard to even conceive it. McClellan lost twelve thousand five hundred killed and wounded. And he won the battle."

He looked out the window as if he were still trying to understand it.

"All the damn politicians should be shot for not preventing this when they could have. Then, five days after that battle, Lincoln finally got around to freeing the slaves. Thirteen days ago. Slavery is finally dead and gone in America."

"So," Arnold said. "The war is over back East?"

"No. McClellan, with superior forces, just stood by and watched Lee march back to Virginia with his entire Army. Just like Canby and the Texans. Rather than crush them right then and there, he gave Lee one more chance to surrender honorably. More likely, though Lee'll continue the insurrection. He just let them go."

He shook his head in disbelief.

"Twenty three thousand," he said under his breath.

They never saw it coming.

There had been no incidents at Fort Bowie during its first two months in Apache Pass. The soldiers had come expecting to fight Chiricahuas, but there had been none to fight. Even the scouting expeditions never saw an Apache. Actually, not even a sign of one.

It was just an hour after dawn. A small party of soldiers had taken the horses down to the meadow between the stage coach station and the Springs. They had dismounted and were drinking coffee.

Everybody else was still up in the fort. The horses were grazing and drinking at the Spring.

And then a dozen mounted Apaches came out of nowhere.

In less than a minute, without firing a shot, they had killed all five soldiers. They shot them with arrows and stabbed them with lances. One Corporal pulled his sword just as he was hit by an arrow. Geronimo leaped off his horse and clubbed him to the ground, ripped the sword from his hand, and thrust it deep into his throat. Blood spurted all over Geronimo as he leaped back on his horse and led the men to the Army's horses.

As Cochise had instructed, he drove lances into the throats of each of the five dead White Eyes. Then, on his own, he cut off each of their right hands and threw them into the fire. Then poured the boiling coffee over their dead faces.

Sated, he led the Apaches and the herd of Army horses toward Cochise's Western Stronghold.

83

Cummings reported to Carleton as quickly as he could. He was requested urgently.

Like any scam artist, sometimes you have to beat yourself half to death looking for a scam. And then you have to work night and day for months just to keep it from falling apart, only to eventually come up empty.

And sometimes one just falls in your lap.

This was one of those times.

"Major, what is your opinion of Lieutenant Damours?" Carleton said.

Cummings shrugged to buy thinking time. "Fair poker player, sir. Not great, but it's been since before the war that I played against him. Nice enough kid, I suppose. People seem to like him. Trust him. General Canby thought the world of him. Although I heard he wasn't much of an aide."

Then he hadn't been able to help himself. "I hear he comes highly recommended by both the Governor and the Church."

"Where'd you hear that Marshal?" Captain Chacon said.

"Around."

Not even trying to hide his disdain for the little New Mexican.

Chacon looked at Carleton.

"Do you have any idea of his current whereabouts?" Carleton's adjutant said.

"I assume he's in Washington with Canby."

"Marshal," the General suddenly switching to Cummings' non-military title, "We were hoping that you knew the answer to that question."

An uneasy silence settled over the room as the three officers just stared at Cummings.

"I don't need to remind you that I'm the Marshal here, sir." His tone now steely. "Damours is a military officer. If he's not in Washington with Canby, then I have no idea where he might be. If any civilian had asked me officially where he was, I would be here as Marshal of Santa Fe asking you gentlemen these questions."

Cummings intention had been to anger the General, so he was surprised to see his amusement.

"Let me remind *you*, Major," Carleton said. "In the off chance you've lost sight of the fact, that you serve both as Major under Colonel Carson and me, and as Provost Marshal of Fort Marcy and Santa Fe at the pleasure of the Governor and me. And, truth be told, at the pleasure—although I think the term is inappropriate—of the good Captain here as well," gesturing toward Chacon.

Back to s room of silence.

Finally, Cummings couldn't stand it, characteristically rushing in with, "Is Lieutenant Damours AWOL?"

"Do you have any knowledge of his whereabouts?" Carleton said.

"I do not."

Silence.

"Does somebody say that I do?"

Carleton nodded toward Chacon.

"With all due respect, sir…."

"Marshal," Carleton said. "We all know the history between you and Chacon. There's no need for you to repeat it here."

"The Captain, sir, is misinformed. I have not seen or heard anything of the Lieutenant since he and Canby headed to Washington five weeks ago."

The three officers just looked at Cummings.

"Sir," Cummings said. "Will that be all, sir?"

"No," Carleton said. "Actually Marshal, your information is the same as ours. The Governor and I would like you to do something for us."

84

"You're making this up, right?" Lily said, disengaging from Cummings' kiss and rolling back over to her side of the bed.

"I'm not that good." He sat up in bed, bowed, and said, "U.S. Marshal Joseph Cummings has been ordered by General Carleton and both the Governor and head of the Church of the New Mexico Territory to apprehend Lieutenant Augustyn P. Damours and bring him back to the Territory along with any recovered monies."

"And they knew everything? They even knew about the money we stole from the Church?"

"Everything."

"They knew about the forged sales slips for the horses and the payroll scam with both the Army and the Territory?"

Cummings nodded with a smile.

"How do we know it's not a trap, designed to draw you to Damours and, well, anybody else he was working with?"

"We don't know for sure. But if they suspect us, it's hard to see what they get by giving me the job alone. If they'd sent Chacon to go with me, I'd be suspicious. But alone? No, it looks like they just want Damours. And then they want their money back."

"No mention of me or Zapico?"

"None. Has anybody questioned either of you?"

"No."

"We knew Damours was good," Cummings said. "But I had no idea he would be this good. He fooled everybody and left no tracks back to any of us."

"Or any tracks for any of us to follow," she lied. "The question for you is, where is he now, and has he double crossed us as well? Can I go with you to look for Auggy, Joseph?"

"Already arranged, babe. We leave for Kansas City, St, Louis, and then Washington first thing tomorrow morning. They think he's headed to the same place I do."

Lots of luck, cowboy, Lily thought as she hugged Cummings.

I, for one, am looking forward to our meeting with Auggy.

Should be fun.

"Tell me something, Lily," Zapico said.

He paused, looking uncomfortable.

"What?"

"I guess it's really none of my business." Zapico fumbled with something on his desk. "Hell, Lily. Are you sleeping with Cummings?"

She laughed.

"I didn't know you cared."

"Are you?"

"Yes I am," she said. "But only since Auggy left. Honest. I thought you and I were partners, not father, daughter. I had no idea you thought I needed a father, David. Or even that you wanted the job."

"There are five of us in this thing, Lily. Don't you think it might occur to me at some point that if you're sleeping with all the others, it might put my share at risk?"

She thought about that for a while. Then brightened. "I never slept with Mowry, David. Does that help?"

He just looked at her.

"And you forgot about Danson. I never fucked Danson, either."

She grinned up at him, safe in the knowledge she couldn't get caught in *that* lie.

She got up and went over and hugged him.

"I'm sorry, David. It didn't occur to me that you'd feel left out."

She caught the horrified look on his face. "Just kidding. C'mon. In all seriousness, it never occurred to me that it would bother you, or would affect your role."

"Has it ever occurred to you that by sleeping with these guys one of them might get the wrong impression? That one of them might decide the partnership goes beyond the money and try to both increase his share and eliminate a rival with one shot?"

"There's always that risk, Zapico. Even if I were a nun. Or worse, a guy."

"But sleeping with Cummings increases the risk dramatically, Lily."

That gave her pause. "Okay, Zapico, let's deal with this. Some of this is none of your business…" She caught his look and started over. "All right then, some of this *is* your business, but some of it isn't. I admit that. And I see where you…"

She stopped dead, realizing that she, not Zapico, might be the idiot here. She put her hands to her mouth.

"Ohmygod David. Is Sarah worried about this? Is she concerned about me and you?"

He didn't respond.

She stood back up.

"I'm so sorry. I've been an idiot. We should have had this talk a year ago. I'm so sorry."

She took both his hands in hers. Sat him down.

"Auggy and I fell in love a year and a half ago. Obviously we had to keep this from the Santa Fe public. You see that, right?" She waited until he looked at her. "Right?"

"Sure," he said. "It's obvious that we didn't want people in general knowing the two of you were that close. But your partners are different."

She thought about it. Could she still trust Zapico? Had she really screwed this up that badly? Wait a minute.

"'We'?"

"Of course, 'we'. Sarah and I knew from day one. Danson certainly knew too. Think about it. Did he ever come on to you?"

She thought about it. He hadn't. Not really, anyway. She'd been the aggressor there. What about Cummings? Constantly. Just another dimension of his being a jerk.

"The question is, does Cummings know?" they both said together.

"And does it matter?" Lily said.

"It might matter," he said. "Might not. The important thing is what Cummings is going to do. You know you can't trust him, right?"

She made a face at him that said 'of course'. "Let's get one thing behind us, okay Zapico? Are you upset that I never slept with you? Is this an issue between you and me?"

"No. That's not it at all."

"Because I never could have even considered it. You've got Sarah and the kids, so it was out of the question. Completely."

"Good to know."

Making no effort to cover his sarcasm.

Lily frowned. Neither had anything more to say on the subject. It was now behind them. Like it or not.

And now Zapico had raised yet a new issue in the event things went badly with Cummings. Sex. At least until Auggy came back.

She knew that whores generally fell into two categories. Some were just too dumb to make more than a subsistence living any other way. The others were girls who just loved sex. Really loved it. For them, prostitution was a godsend. Especially for those who also had the gift of being able to manipulate men.

Lily knew she was definitely the sex-loving type. She had actually loved being in the brothels. She didn't miss being paid for sex, but she *did* miss the sex.

Zapico had just made her realize that she might have a problem waiting for Auggy. Nunneries had never appealed to her.

"Did Cummings say whether or not he has orders to kill Damours, Lily?"

"He said his orders are to capture him and recover the money he stole. I asked him if it meant alive, or dead or alive? And he said…" She looked out the window while she thought. She needed to remember it right. "He said 'Carleton told me my first priority was the money and my second priority was Damours. When I asked him if he wanted Damours alive or dead, he said it'll be Auggy's choice'."

"You see," Zapico said. "If Cummings is planning to kill Auggy, does his sleeping with you and knowing or not knowing you had been sleeping with Auggy, decrease or increase the chance he's going to try to kill you, too?"

Uncharacteristically, she hadn't thought about that. She had just been assuming all along that it decreased it. That she and Auggy could just handle it on the spot.

"When do you and Cummings leave?"

"In the morning."

"Are you sure you know where Auggy is?"

"Yes."

"And he knows you'll be with Cummings?"

She nodded. Said, "He will by then."

"Okay, here's the tough part, Lil. And you knew it was coming."

She just gave him her best business look and waited.

"Are you sure you can trust me?"

She hadn't actually been expecting that. "Absolutely."

"How sure are you that you can trust Auggy, Lil?"

Just like that. Out of the blue.

She pretended to think about it. No sense giving Zapico the impression she was naive. She worked her hands together in her lap. Hamming it up a little.

"Well, David. I've never been surer of anything in my life. He has the money. He has the plan to bring it all together for us. And even if it sounds corny, he has my heart."

"Then," he said, "Be very, very careful around Cummings, Lil. Watch your back and always be armed. You're going to have to be careful and good to pull this off. Very good. This won't be like calling for the guard to pull you out of a mess in a brothel, kid. Among all his other obvious advantages, Cummings has the law on his side."

"Okay, Dad."

"Oh, yes," he said. "One more thing."

She turned and looked up at him.

"Can I trust you?" Zapico said.

She walked out the door without a word.

I do love this old Jew, she thought to herself as she headed out into the Plaza.

85

November 5, 1862

Damours had just intercepted the October 27[h] cable from General Carleton to Canby that laid out Damours' thefts in painstaking detail. He had been tempted to simply destroy it, but knew that this was a waste of time. Cummings was on his way to Canby and would be bringing all the evidence and details with him.

He walked unannounced into Canby's War Department office.

"General?"

"Yes, Auggy?"

Canby didn't even look up from his work.

Damours had known it would eventually come to this. He had become quite close to Canby and actually liked him. Stealing from the Army and the Church and the New Mexico Territory was just the business he had fallen into.

And he knew the General was fond of him as well. But things had just turned out this way. Canby ordered men to kill other men without any personal animosity toward them at all. And Damours just stole money from those men rather than killing them. Nothing personal there either.

He had been tempted to discuss all this with Canby when the end came. But Lily had told him that it was ridiculous. Just run when it was all over. As fast and as far as he could.

Everybody loved and trusted Damours. But he wasn't going to be able to talk his way out of this. Canby would see it as a betrayal. He'd have him hunted down very professionally. Even though it might actually be personal to Canby when he saw the extent of the thefts.

Canby finally looked up. "Yes, Auggy. What is it?"

"It's my bronchitis, sir. Ever since I got to this fly-infested swamp, my breathing has just been getting worse and worse. And now my coughing appears to be completely debilitating. I've lost my appetite, weight, and am exhausted, sir."

"Have you been to a doctor?"

Damours had to look away from the concern on his friend and boss's face. "Yes. He has urged me to see a specialist in New York."

"Then go to New York, Auggy. Write yourself a requisition and draw the funds. Go immediately, son."

"Thank you, sir."

"Do you need anything else?"

"No, sir. Don't worry, I'll be fine. I should be back in a day or two."

It was the last lie he would ever tell Canby.

He walked into his outlying office and slipped Carleton's cable into the middle of the pile of papers on his desk.

As he stepped out of the War Department onto 17th Street, Lieutenant Augustyn P. Damours was officially, and permanently, AWOL.

86

The train from Kansas City pulled into the St. Louis train station on time at precisely 2:00. Nobody noticed the Major and a lady get off and head straight into town.

Lily had made sure during the dreary train ride that the sex was as personally uninformative as the conversation. As far as Cummings knew, she was madly in love with him and hell bent on finding and mutilating Damours. He'd commented that he finally understood why the Indians turned their prisoners over to the squaws.

The only truthful thing she had told him during the entire, dreadfully boring eleven day trek by coach and then train, was that Zapico would let them know from Santa Fe if he heard where Auggy was. For information, they knew they could trust Canby once they got to Washington, and maybe Carleton if he got any, but certainly not Chacon.

As he was walking out the door of their room, Lily said, "One things been bothering me, Joseph."

He stopped and looked at her.

"Won't the Army find it odd that I'm accompanying you?"

She was worried that Arnold would finally put her with Damours.

"I told them you could be helpful back East. Either as cover for me when I'm out of uniform or as a second pair of eyes."

"And they're too dumb to know that he and I knew each other in Santa Fe before the War?"

"No. I told them that too."

He closed the door behind him.

She stared at the door. Can he be that stupid? Or is he that good after all?

Good question, Lily.

A little late, but a good question.

Carson was still trying to get over his fury at the cold blooded murder of the Mescalero chief, Manuelito by one of his Captains. And then the killing of the Captain himself in a duel here at Fort Stanton.

More than a hundred Mescalero had already turned themselves in. And Pfeiffer had brought in three of the Mescalero chiefs just today. Carson needed his concentration for this meeting with the chiefs.

The three chiefs were escorted into Carson's office.

"Good afternoon Chief Cadete," Carson said to the senior of the three, who represented the largest clan that had come in and deserved the most respect.

"Good day, Chief Carson."

"Thank you for your decision to come in honorably."

All three nodded.

"Do all of your people agree to stop stealing forever? To stop killing the New Mexicans?"

They nodded yes.

"And do you agree to move all your people to the new Fort Sumner? To the east, at the Pecos River?"

"Forever?" Cadete said.

"Yes, forever," Carson said.

"That is very far from our home, Chief Carson," Cadete said.

Carson decided to let them save face and let the lie stand. The Mescalero were known to roam that far.

"Will your Great Chief take care of the Apache people at this Fort Sumner? Forever?"

"Yes. Chief Cremony, your old friend, has been put in charge of your new home, and is insisting that you be treated fairly."

"What is our other choice, Chief Carson?"

Carson cocked his head. He might as well make the best use of the unfortunate murders.

"There is always Chief Manuelito's way, Chief Cadete."

Predictably, at this the Apaches grew visibly angry.

"Chief Cadete, you need to know that my chief, Chief General Carleton, wants to kill you. Kill you and all your men."

"Then, Chief Carson, do you plan to kill us, just as your men killed Manuelito?"

"No, I am sending the three of you to Santa Fe to meet Chief Carleton."

"We would rather die here among our people, Chief Carson. We do not want to die in Santa Fe to satisfy Chief Carleton."

"Please sit down. I will explain."

They did.

"You and I trust each other, Chief Cadete. But Chief Carleton believes the Apaches will not stop stealing and killing the New Mexicans just because I say so. Many Mescalero still have not come in. If you go to Santa Fe and tell him that you will take your people to his Bosque Redondo, he will believe you. And you will then believe his word that Chief Cremony will take care of your people. Forever."

They were impassive.

"When you return with this agreement, the rest of the Mescalero clans will hear of this. They, too, can then come here, and then I, personally, will escort all of the Mescalero people to their beautiful new home. And the cycle of killing and being killed will finally stop for your people. Forever."

He looked directly at Cadete.

"Chief Cadete will be known as a great Apache chief. Forever."

And that is precisely what came to pass. The Mescalero Wars were over and officially ended when Cadete returned to Fort Stanton from his meeting with Carleton in Santa Fe. And Carson then led the Mescalero Apaches to Bosque Redondo.

87

November 17, 1862

Lily looked out at the Maryland countryside, two hours north of Washington.

Thinking she was pretty sure that Cummings didn't suspect her of knowing anything. And knowing that Auggy was in Baltimore as both the Kansas City and St. Louis doctors had confirmed. No confirmation from Zapico yet, but they were now actually travelling away from Auggy. She had to let Cummings find Auggy on his own and then she could control it from there.

Until this trip, the Civil War for her had been solely about Valverde and Glorieta. The rest had been talk by the soldiers and stories in the papers about the horrors of the War back East.

She had known before they left Santa Fe that the Union forces had started pushing Lee's Army of the Potomac back south. In fact, only two months had passed since the horror of Antietam, near where they were currently travelling.

The Union appeared to be winning the War, and Washington should be safe again. Looking out the windows, she saw Union soldiers on foot and on horseback heading south. Some healthy, but most wounded one way or another. Many wounded young soldiers with them on the train. Lily was used to seeing soldiers. But never so many. And so many wounded, vacant eyed boys.

She'd never gone this long as an adult without seeing Mexicans and Indians and cactus and mountains. Back East was like a strange new land. A foreign country, in the grips of a terrible conflict.

They disembarked as the train arrived in Washington, and took a carriage directly to the Willard's Hotel. They were both stunned by the city scene, the number of soldiers and the frenetic bustling everywhere along Pennsylvania Avenue. And the swarms of flies. The flies were everywhere.

Cummings was ushered in to their small hotel room looking out over the Treasury Department, with Lily following with their bags.

As they had agreed, first thing, Lily walked over to the bronchitis doctor they had been referred to. Cummings, despite being assured it was a short walk, caught a carriage over to the War Department on the other side of the White House at 17ᵗʰ and Pennsylvania.

It was hard to imagine that General Canby had time for him, but those had been the orders at the Willard's.

He was immediately ushered into a small office by Canby's new aide.

"General Canby's over at McClellan's headquarters across the street in the Winder Annex," the Lieutenant said. "He's been expecting you, sir. Things have been a bit hectic since President Lincoln asked General Burnside to take command of the Army of the Potomac from McClellan ten days ago."

"Thank you Lieutenant."

There was nothing to see in the sparse office, so Cummings busied himself looking out the window. This was his first time back East since he'd left Boston seventeen years ago. He looked out at Washington and then at the traffic on 17ᵗʰ Street below him.

Not surprisingly, it was mostly soldiers walking and riding up and down the street. A few civilians, a few women, but mostly the busy, behind the lines business, of running a War.

He watched as two Confederate prisoners were escorted by four guards out of a wagon and into the entrance just below him.

And then he saw Canby walk down the stairs of the Winder Annex and look up at the window where he was standing.

And then he saw Damours.

Damours, in civilian clothes, walked right up to Canby and said something. The two exchanged a few words and then Damours headed east on 17ᵗʰ and Canby proceeded to cross the street toward the War Department. Canby had just let Damours walk away.

"Lieutenant," Cummings said as he turned and ran out of the office and headed for the stairs. "Lieutenant. We've got him."

The aide raced behind him and the two took the stairs two at a time.

"Damours is headed up 17ᵗʰ Street. Towards Pennsylvania Avenue."

They raced out the door and down the steps to the street. In their haste, they completely missed Canby entering the War Department.

The two raced up 17ᵗʰ Street, with the Lieutenant saying inanely, "Where is he? Which one is he Major?"

They reached Pennsylvania Avenue. Cummings looked left. No Damours.

He looked right, toward the White House, and saw him mount a horse and head east and across the wide avenue.

"Auggy," he shouted. "Auggy."

Damours looked back and kicked his horse into a gallop.

Cummings took careful aim and got off two shots before Damours disappeared up the street.

He turned to the aide.

"Lieutenant, can we get a horse? Dammit Lieutenant, how do I get a horse? He'll be gone in a minute."

The Lieutenant looked frantically around. Saw two mounted soldiers idly watching them in front of the Blair House. "Sergeant, give us those horses."

He and Cummings raced across Pennsylvania Avenue.

"Can't do that and you know it Lieutenant. I'm responsible for these cavalry mounts."

"Dammit Sergeant, I order you to lend us those horses," Cummings said. He was frantic. He pointed toward Damours, trotting away from them. "I've travelled two thousand miles to arrest that man. He's wanted for any number of crimes. I order you directly from General Carleton to give us those horses."

He pulled his gun and drew down on the two soldiers. Nearby spectators now took an interest in the growing drama.

The Sergeant looked more amused than anything else. He arrogantly didn't even reach for his pistol.

"Show me your orders, sir. You're a civilian, I take no orders from civilians, sir."

"I'm a U.S. Marshal on official U.S. Army business, Sergeant."

Thrusting his papers up into the hands of the soldier and reaching for the horse's reins. "Lieutenant, sign for the horses. We may already be too late."

He looked down the street, but no longer could see any sign of Damours.

When the two of them finally got the horses, they took off up Pennsylvania Avenue.

The Sergeant yelled after them, "Return those horses to the Armory. To Captain Anderson." He scowled, looked down at the papers, and spat into the street. "Those two better be after some weakling or coward or we're never gonna see our horses again."

The small crowd, having been spared any real drama, now looked up the street at the receding horses.

Cummings no longer saw any sign of Damours. He turned his horse left into Lafayette Square on a dead run in the hopes of getting a bead on him.

No Damours.

"Lieutenant, did you get a look at Damours? If we split up, will you be able to recognize him?"

"Certainly, sir. Are you sure that's Damours? That man is a civilian, sir."

"It definitely was Damours. No doubt about it. I saw him speak to Canby as the General came out of McClellan's headquarters. Lieutenant, you continue up Pennsylvania Avenue in case he continued in that direction. I'll go this way and then backtrack toward you. If you catch him, arrest him. If we both come up empty, we'll meet at 10th Street. Let's go. Now."

He continued through the Park until he came to K Street. He looked both ways. Nothing.

He turned his horse around full circle, desperately trying to see any sign of Damours.

And then he heard shots.

There were clear sounds of a fire fight coming from the direction the aide had headed. He spurred his horse down K Street and followed the sounds to 14th Street, just three blocks north of the Willard's.

There were about a half dozen soldiers and police, dismounted and facing a small office building. The shooting had stopped, but many of the windows were shot out, and somebody was waving a shirt in surrender. It was hard to tell what had happened, but when the beleaguered and wounded men came out of the building with their hands out, it was clear none of them were Damours.

"Is that all of them? Any killed or still in the building," he said to a Major who appeared to be in charge

The Major looked curiously at Cummings.

"No, that's it."

He turned back to the job of securing whoever they now had in custody.

Cummings looked carefully at all the spectators, but there was no sign of Damours. And, thankfully, the aide hadn't rushed to the scene.

He had little hope of finding Damours now. He was going to have to rely on the Lieutenant. Still looking carefully at everyone, but now without hope, he pushed his horse toward 10th and down toward Pennsylvania Avenue.

Shortly, he saw the Lieutenant heading toward him up 10th. They met at E Street.

No Damours.

Cummings shook Canby's hand back at his War Department office.

"Good to see you again, General."

"I hear you and my aide had a merry goose chase around Washington, Major."

From his look, Canby was joking.

"Sir," Cummings said. "You know that I've travelled here from Santa Fe to find and arrest Lieutenant Damours, right?"

"I do."

"Then why did you let him walk away this afternoon?"

"What are you talking about? I haven't seen Damours in over ten days since he went to New York to see a doctor. He never came back."

"But sir," and he pointed out the window down at 17th Street. "I saw you talking to him right there as you started to cross the street no more than two hours ago. That's why the Lieutenant and I took off. We saw Damours leave you and we chased him."

Canby looked genuinely confused. He stood up and walked over to the window and looked over at the Annex and down at the street. His frown suddenly turned into a chuckle as he turned back to Cummings.

"Major. That wasn't Lieutenant Damours. That was John Wilkes Booth. I'd forgotten how much they look alike."

"That was really Booth?" Cummings said. "I thought he was a southern sympathizer."

"He is. We're at war with the Confederacy and General Lee, Major. If we had to round up every civilian who sympathized with the Rebels in and around Washington, we wouldn't have the manpower left to wage a war."

"Are you sure? I thought for sure that was Lieutenant Damours."

He saw the General's reaction.

"What a waste of time and energy," Cummings said. "I'm sorry, General."

"I'm still shocked by the charges against Auggy," Canby said. "I had no idea. I never suspected him of anything."

"Carleton's furious. He's responsible for retrieving the funds for all three jurisdictions. That's why I'm here in my capacity as Marshal, sir."

"But Marshal, if I'm not mistaken, Lieutenant Damours told me that the two of you were friends."

"Exaggeration is one of Lieutenant Damours talents, sir. He and I had played poker against each other now and then before the War."

"Does Carleton know that?"

"Yes, sir. He does."

"And he wasn't concerned about any conflict?"

"I assure you General, as I did General Carleton, when it comes to the law there is no conflict. I will have Damours under arms when I return to Santa Fe. Acquaintance or not, it's my job to find him and bring him back."

He stood to leave.

"One more thing, Marshal." Canby looked up from behind his desk. "It's a damn good thing you didn't kill Booth. That would have created a hell of a mess for us here in Washington."

88

November 18, 1862

When he told her, Lily couldn't help but laugh.

"You raced around Washington on horseback chasing an actor?"

Cummings let her have her needed laugh. He was looking out at the Treasury building through what now was a gloomy, rainy Washington Winter's dusk.

"What if you'd killed him, Joseph? What if you'd killed Auggy?" She shuddered at the thought, realizing she needed to stay closer to Cummings.

"It wasn't even Auggy, Lily. Relax. And I was only trying to wound him anyway."

"Well, if you'd killed Auggy, that'd be the end of the money for us. And if you'd killed John Wilkes Booth, who knows how long you'da had to hang around here answering questions."

Cummings really was an idiot, she thought.

"Well I missed. I missed him. Now Canby has given me the papers authorizing me to chase Damours all the way to Canada if I have to."

He turned from the window and stared at her. "Do you think Damours somehow knows we're coming and it's us he's now running from?"

"There's no way he would know Carleton would send you after him," she lied. "As far as he knows, we're still waiting for his return and an eventual split."

"Any idea where he hid his take?"

"No."

"Okay. Did you learn anything from the doctor today?"

"His bronchitis wasn't getting any better," she said. "This doctor claims he's now headed to a New York City specialist he referred him to."

"Canby's aide did some work and traced him to a train to Baltimore on the 5th. He then headed north from Baltimore on the 6th. I'm beginning to wonder, why Baltimore?"

"Maybe he was looking for Booth, too."

Cummings just looked back from the window and stared at her. Letting her joke fall flat.

"Did I ever tell you I was born in Baltimore," she said.

"No. Is that your home?"

"No. I was just born there. My parents died when I was a baby. A Mormon family took me to Utah and raised me there. This is really my first time back East. I made up my last name in Virginia City. I never wanted anybody knowing I was a Mormon."

Cummings showed no interest in her family history.

Embarrassed, she said, "So Damours is headed to the New York specialist then."

"Could there be something else other than bronchitis? Could there be some other reason for him going from doctor to doctor?"

She couldn't let Cummings go there. He had no reason to suspect the doctors' communication role. And he'd never need to. Just like he didn't need to know yet that Auggy was headed to Buffalo.

"Like what, Joseph? Some secret underground railroad that Damours is using to hide our money from us?"

"No, it's just odd is all."

"Hell, I don't know. I suspect he's headed to Canada. Makes sense."

"And he has twelve days on us."

"But doesn't know he's being chased," she lied.

"We hope," he said.

89

November 20, 1862

Canby's letter worked its logistical magic as they headed north in intermittent snow and rain and sleet through the dreary November days. Mostly empty cars on the overnight train heading away from the War. A few wounded soldiers. Some obvious businessmen heading north.

Lily was usually the only woman in any given car. She got curious looks from the businessmen but indifference from the glum soldiers.

The two of them pretty much kept to themselves, looking out the window at the grey brown countryside, anxious about the uncertainty of their destination, the timing, and what might await them there.

Lily unsure how she was going to play it when they got together with Damours. Hell, unsure of what Damours was going to do. Or be thinking.

The trains worked their way inexorably northward, like snakes fleeing a prairie fire. The southbound trains could be seen briefly flying past, filled, and sometimes overfilled, with young soldiers in blue.

They went by too fast to gauge the soldiers' mood. But at the stops and in the stations, they seemed enthusiastic. Hell bent on preserving the country.

And young. All of them seemed so very, very young.

In New York City another message from Canby was waiting at the station. Turns out that Damours hadn't met with the New York doctor after all. He was now headed to Buffalo, and there was no confirmation that he had yet arrived. He hadn't surfaced anywhere that the Army could determine.

Thrusting the telegram into Lily's hands, Cummings headed to the ticket master to find the next train to Buffalo. He came back minutes later grinning.

"Finally a turn in our favor. We're out of here in less than an hour. We'll be in Buffalo in the morning. No matter how much time he spent in New York, we're gaining on him."

"Joseph, I'm exhausted. Can't we leave in the morning?"

"Sorry, Lil. We have to go now. It's a damn good thing Auggy's not running us through the Rockies on horseback. So far, this chase has been luxurious compared to what I'd expected."

She unhappily gathered up her things.

"Save your emotional energy for finding Damours, honey," he said.

He grabbed his bag and plunged after her.

"By the way," he said. "Did the Washington doctor happen to mention another doctor for him in Buffalo?"

"No," she lied, and signaled a porter to help her get her things off to Buffalo for the final leg of the confrontation they each were separately planning.

90

November 22, 1862

As Lily came out of the Buffalo train station into the bitter cold, the snow piled up several feet deep, and oceans of slush everywhere, she thought why would anybody ever live in Buffalo after they grew up or, especially, when they stopped working?

"Lil," Cummings said. "If Damours had been going on to Canada, logically he didn't even need to have come to Buffalo. Or stop here. Or stay long enough to still be here."

Lily ignored his useless comments. Although, in fairness, she knew the answers and he didn't need to. For her part, she looked around the frigid surroundings of the Buffalo train station. There were no soldiers here. More women walking the sidewalks than there had been in Washington, presumably shopping for whatever they could get, given the war shortages. All the men either old or very young. Boys, really. There weren't going to be a lot of men Damours' age out of uniform, that was for sure. Probably he was wearing his uniform to solve that problem. But he would be uncomfortable here. In a hurry to leave. She was going to have to be quick and determined for the next day if this was going to work.

As they climbed into a carriage, they saw charred buildings and piles of destroyed materials over to the right.

"What happened here, sir," Cummings said, pointing to the charred remains of a row of houses.

"We had a great fire two months ago. Though we were going to lose the whole city at one point there."

"We're headed to the Canal Hotel if it's still standing. Over off Norton?"

The driver set out as Cummings directed.

Damours watched them leave the station and caught a carriage a safe distance behind.

Spotting them was a relief, actually. Lily had changed the original Baltimore meeting and then telegraphed him they were coming.

Dealing with Cummings was all there was left at this point. If he listened to reason, they could all rest easy. If not, then they'd have to kill him. Either way, they could then move to the end game. God knows what Cummings himself wants out of this. Why hadn't he just gone back empty handed? Lily's view of him as an idiot was the easiest way to figure it.

It would all be over soon. Better to be the one hunting than the one being hunted. It had never been likely to end well between him and Cummings. He had told Jim that any number of times, and now the time was near.

He saw them get out a block ahead at The Canal. Damours ordered his driver to stop.

91

Lily, Cummings, and Damours sat facing each other in a freezing cold clearing northeast of the edge of Buffalo's outskirts. Lily had invented some information that got Cummings close enough that he had, single handedly, he bragged, spotted Damours riding away. They had then run down the "fleeing" fugitive.

"Okay, kid let's get this over with," Cummings said.

Damours looked genuinely confused. "Get what over with, Cummings? I've been freezing my ass off here waiting for you two since Lily telegraphed me you were coming."

Lily suppressed a smile. God, Auggy was good at this.

Now it was Cummings' turn to look confused. "He was telling you where he was all this time, Lil?"

"I told you where he was when we got to Kansas City, but you wouldn't believe me. You wouldn't listen, so I just gave the information to officers along the way who you'd listen to."

He stared at her as if she'd just said she was a Confederate spy.

"Look Cummings," she said. "You two couldn't pull off a scam if somebody handed you a script. You don't work well together and you don't trust each other. Somebody had to hold this whole thing together while you two stumbled around." She looked at the now furious Cummings. "For example, how could you have agreed to chase down your own partner?"

"Carleton didn't ask what I wanted to do, Lil. He ordered me to bring back Damours. Are you crazy?"

"Jesus, Joseph you can't be this dumb. You shoulda been running around pretending you were looking for Damours in Washington for a few weeks, and then gone back and told Carleton and Chacon you couldn't find him. You don't go looking for him for real, you idiot."

"Wait a minute," Damours said, as if hearing all this for the first time. "It's crazy for Carleton to order you to come find me. They knew we were friends.

Maybe they expect you to find me, kill me, and come back with the money so they can arrest you?"

"Carleton isn't that dumb," Lily said. "Carleton knew that Joseph wouldn't come back with the money, whether he found you or not."

"Then why did Carleton send him?" Damours said.

"I've been wondering about that. They had to do something for show for the Governor and the Church? Cummings was in their way? They could fire him if he failed? They have something else in mind for him when he returns? They figure he's easier to find than you if he's dumb enough to find you and not return?" She looked at Cummings for a reaction. Getting none, she continued. "Probably they had to make a show of it and they figured that Cummings would somehow screw it up and they could kill two birds with one stone."

Cummings' expression turned to anger. "So you two have been playing me all this time? I came to Damours and Danson from Mowry and you started playing me?"

He pulled his Colt and pointed it at Damours. Damours didn't move from where he was sitting. "Okay, Auggy. Where's the money?"

"Some's in my saddlebags over there. But most is in Santa Fe, where I intend to give you your share when the dust settles."

"How much we talking about?"

"Around forty thousand for you, Zapico, and Mowry to split up. Plus your share of whatever you're holding."

Cummings whistled softly as if he were stunned. "You're leveling with me on this?"

"Yes," Lily said. "But Cummings, you don't have a choice. You go back empty handed and you get your money from me and Auggy and Zapico next year. But if you try to bring Damours in, you either die tryin' or get part of what's on Auggy's horse there."

"So that makes it my call, right?" Cummings said, indicating that Auggy was to stand. "Tell me where the rest of the money is Auggy or I'll shoot you down, take your body back to Carleton, and tell Zapico you stole his money, too."

"No you won't Joseph," Lily said.

Damours looked back and forth between the two, trying not to laugh.

"And you wonder why I play you Joseph," Lily said. "You're an idiot. Zapico has hidden his share and given Auggy the rest for safekeeping. He'll think you're a lunatic if you show up with that story. If you shoot Auggy, the best you get is part of what's in that saddlebag over there. Less my share. Unless you're planning to kill me too?" She cocked her head questionably at Cummings. "And the worst you get is dead."

She lifted the bag in her lap to reveal the pistol that had been continuously leveled at Cummings' chest.

"You'd shoot me?"

"In a heartbeat. I'm betting you can't hit Damours at that distance and I can shoot you from right here before you smell the smoke from your own gun. Then Damours and I end up getting half instead of forty percent."

She cocked her pistol. "And Carleton and Chacon pretend to be sad to hear that you died."

Cummings looked at Damours, then back at Lily. "What if all the money is right there in those saddlebags and you and I just split it fifty, fifty right now?"

"That would be a typical Joseph Cummings move. Gamble your one fifth share of a fortune, for part of a saddlebag full of who knows what. You'd have to then double cross Mowry and Zapico to get all of it. Not to mention, again, that you get killed trying."

"You'd really shoot me?"

She pointed the revolver at his chest. "I already answered that, Cummings."

Damours settled in, watching the two of them as if confident in the outcome.

"I've more or less enjoyed working with you, Cummings," she said. "I have half a mind to shoot you in cold blood. But you haven't earned that. Not yet anyway. Put the gun down. Now."

He did so.

Cummings turned to Damours. "How do I know you'll come back with my money back home in Santa Fe?"

"You don't trust the rest of us, Joseph," Damours said. "But the rest of us trust each other. As long as you're alive, you're still Zapico and Mowry's partner. And we'd never cut them out. There's plenty of money for all five of us."

"Who knows where the money is?" Cummings said.

"I do," Damours said. "And Lily and Zapico each know enough so they can find it if something happens to me. But neither can find it without the other. It's buried outside a building in Santa Fe. And Zapico has hidden his money separately."

Cummings digested that. "So I never found you. Simple as that?"

"You finally figured it out," Lily said. "Damours escaped to Canada."

They could see him thinking about it. Looking off into the distance.

"I've never been to Niagara Falls," Cummings said. "My Mom promised me but never took me."

He looked off to the northwest into the clouds and the snow.

"Tell me something, Joseph," Damours said. "A minute ago you surprised me. You questioned if I would ever bring your money back home to you in Santa Fe. You actually used the word 'home'. Where's home for you, Joseph?"

Damours looked over at Lily and something intimate passed between the two of them for an instant.

The Washington Territory.

"I don't know," Cummings said. "I haven't thought about it much. All this tramping and fighting 'round the Western mountains and deserts. All this wandering. No wife. No kids. Not many friends. Thinkin' about it now, for the first time, I guess in the life you and I are livin', Auggy, our graves are going to be the place home turns out to be."

He looked at Damours.

"Home'll be where they bury you, kid."

92

November 25, 1862

"Lily?"

She looked up wearily at Cummings from her bench in the Buffalo train station.

"There's something I need to do before I go back to Washington," he said.

"What is it now Cummings?"

"It's personal. It's got nothin' to do with Damours or my orders. Something I need to do in Boston."

"Just leaving me here to find my own way to Santa Fe? Or do I go to Washington to wait for you now?"

"You'll be okay either way. It'll be easier if you go on to our hotel in Washington, though. I'll be there in a day or so. There's no danger for me in Boston."

There's danger everywhere for idiots like you.

Working hard not to say it out loud.

93

November 26, 1862

He didn't feel bad about leaving Lily like that. Not the way she'd been playing him. She'd have no trouble getting to Washington and into the hotel on his orders and tickets.

He had no idea how this was going to go in Boston, and the last thing he needed was the distraction of dealing with Lily. Would she really have killed me? Choosing Damours and the money over me?

He stood in the dirty Boston snow along Commonwealth Avenue, getting up the nerve to do this thing. Not sure why he was doing it, but it felt like the right thing to do, and it certainly would be his only chance.

He knocked on the familiar door. Stepped back. He had no idea what to expect. After an interminable wait, there was a noise on the other side of the door. And it opened very slowly.

Cummings was shocked. A little old lady, left hand on a cane to support her frail body, short white hair, rheumy blue eyes looked up at him from under a pale yellow bonnet. A shapeless blue checkered house dress. A white shawl.

It was definitely her, but now so old. How had this happened?

She looked carefully at his badge and then up at the black hat. And only then at his face.

"Yes, Marshal. Is there a problem?"

He tried to look at the confrontation from her viewpoint. Cowboy boots, large black overcoat with the badge prominently displayed, eyes hooded between the bushy moustache and the black hat. He'd probably put on what, fifty, sixty pounds since she'd last seen him. Grown from a scraggly teenager to an oversized U.S. Marshal, while she'd turned from a beautiful, healthy brunette into a…well, into a little old lady.

He towered over her at her doorstep while she towered over him in his memory. At this very doorstep.

"Sir? Is something wrong? What's wrong?"

She stepped back and looked up at him. Now appearing to be on guard. Maybe even scared.

Maybe he should turn and leave. Just let it go. Leave her with her memories. Leave him with his.

But it was too late for him. His memories would now always include her as this little old shrunken lady.

"Hi Mom. How are you?"

She almost stumbled back, but caught herself just as he reached out to help. Then she stared. Just stared.

"Joseph?"

He realized that she hadn't had the benefit of any rehearsals for such a moment. It had been seventeen years since this woman had seen or heard from her only son. She'd gone from a vibrant newly remarried woman to an old lady. And he'd, inexplicably, gone from her little boy to a huge U.S. Marshal standing suddenly before her, as if dropped from another planet onto her doorstep.

"Yes, Mom." He stepped back even further, as if to respect whatever feelings she was having. "It's me. Joseph."

He didn't know what he'd been expecting, but silence wasn't it.

"Mom? May I please come in?"

"Well, certainly. Certainly, Joseph. How…how have you been?" Then said, "*Where* have you been?"

Starting to show a little life now. Her cheeks starting to color.

Cummings stepped into her parlor. The smells precisely as he remembered them. The memories of his boyhood flooding back. Smells and memories he hadn't had occasion to think about for well over a decade. A decade of roaming and scrounging. Of gambling and cheating and Marshaling. It had come full circle, now plunged back into his boyhood and to the boy's home, unchanged.

"Well, Joseph, you've grown a foot and a badge since the last time you stood on this doorstep and said 'goodbye'. If you give me a chance to catch my breath, I'd certainly like to hear what I've missed these past twenty or so years. My word son. How'd you know I was even still alive?"

"I didn't, Mom." He looked down at her with regret and affection all mixed together. "I didn't."

94

December 19, 1862

"Chief Carleton," the oldest of the Navajo chiefs said. "We are here in Santa Fe today representing all the clans of the Dine."

"I would like to thank all eighteen of you for coming here in peace today."

"We have stayed west as we promised Chief Canby. But now the soldiers are returning and have built the new Fort Defiance on our sacred lands. We have come to learn why, Chief Carleton."

"You chiefs," Carleton swept his arm across the room. "Have honored your word, but many young Dine have not."

"It is possible," the spokesman said, "That some of our young men have left our lands without our knowledge and taken a few sheep. If what you say is true, it was not enough for us to have noticed."

"The soldiers and the forts," Carleton said, "As always, are there to protect the peaceful Dine from the other Indians and the angry New Mexicans, and to protect our people from your Navajo braves who will not stop stealing and killing."

He gestured toward the newly promoted General Joseph West.

"Next month General West will track down and destroy Mangas Coloradas and the Mimbres people near your lands. Do not be alarmed when this happens. The Apaches have been attacking and killing the white ranchers and soldiers. We know the Dine are not like the Apaches."

When the room became completely quiet again, he resumed.

"I have been patient with the Dine people. We are not murderers. I, personally, am a devout Christian and have been sobered by my experiences with Manuelito and the Mormons and other unjustified murders in these lands. Instead of war, we will grant you six months to decide the fate of all the clans of the Dine. Since your promises to control your people are no longer credible, we will control them for you."

He again waited for the silence to return.

"Within six months, you must deliver all the Dine to Fort Defiance to be deported to the Pecos River southeast of here. The U S. Congress last month granted this place as the new home of the Dine people."

"We do not know this place," the eldest chief said. "A River of Pecos. Where is this place?"

West showed them his map. Showed them where their homeland was, their four sacred mountains, Santa Fe, and Bosque Redondo.

"Chief Carleton, we do not know of this round forest. It is not near our home. How do we know we will be safe from the whites and the Cheyenne and the Comanches there?"

"Kit Carson and I give you our personal assurances."

"Chief Carson?"

"Yes. He is there now. Preparing it for your arrival."

"And if we choose not to leave our homes? To not go so far from our home? What will become of those Dine who choose not to go?"

"Then they will have chosen war with the United States and Colonel Carson. It is your choice. Relocate to Bosque Redondo or be at war. It is up to the Dine."

"And how do we get to this place if that is what we choose?"

"You will walk."

The chiefs were astonished, all talking at once.

"All of us? Women, children, old men? All our belongings? How far is it?"

"Kit Carson will take you there. It is four hundred miles. Only a month's walk. The Dine will then be safe forever in their new home."

95

The first thing that happened when he returned, Cummings ran into Chacon as the two walked into headquarters together.

Cummings saluted.

"Afternoon, Captain."

"Marshal. Afternoon. When did you get back?"

"Just now. I haven't even had a chance to go to my room."

"Any luck finding Damours?"

He thought about it. Decided to have a little fun with Chacon.

"Yes, as a matter of fact I did."

"And the money?"

"No luck there, I'm afraid."

"What happened?"

Chacon looked to be on the verge of one of his famous eruptions.

"C'mon into the office, Captain. It's a good story."

Cummings spent the next twenty minutes spinning out a fictitious tale of a roundtrip between Santa Fe and Cuba, via Washington and New York.

"You mean to tell me," Chacon said, "You tracked Damours all the way across the country, then to Cuba, and then when you said 'Hey Lieutenant,' or 'Hey Auggy' or whatever the hell you call him, he just snatched your pistol out of your hand and blew his brains out? Used your pistol?"

"Yes. Precisely."

"Any witnesses?"

"A coupla Cuban fellows. They didn't appear to speak much English. They took one look and ran into the cane fields or whatever."

"And where's the hundred thousand dollars or so he stole from us and the Bishop and the Governor?"

"No sign of it."

"Not any of it?"

"He had five bucks and some change on him. I brought it back and will include it with my report to General Carleton tomorrow."

"Did you bring Damours' body back, Marshal?"

"Nope. The Captain of the charter boat wouldn't let me. Said he didn't want any 'dead greasers' on his boat."

Glaring, Chacon said, "Damours was white."

"Correct. But the Captain didn't know that. He thought I was trying to bring a dead Cuban onto his boat."

"How about his identification badge?"

"Unfortunately, Damours wasn't wearing his uniform or any other form of identification. So, no, I have no proof of his death. And I didn't think to scalp him."

With that, a very angry Captain Chacon stood up. "Thank you, Marshal. Good evening." And he walked out.

It was the most fun Cummings had had all year.

96

December 31, 1862

Cummings reported to Carleton first thing in the morning. Carleton was already well into his first cigar of the day. The room was already smoke filled.

"Morning, General. Morning, Colonel Carson."

Carleton gestured to the chair in front of Cummings. "Be seated Marshal."

"Kit just arrived from Fort Stanton this morning. We know you have returned without Lieutenant Damours, Marshal, and we are eager to hear what happened. But I think you will want to hear where we stand with the Indians first. This will concern you."

"The Mescalero are Cremony's problem now," Carson said.

"And you're comfortable enough with this Kit, that I can report the end of the Mescalero War to Washington?"

"Yes, sir."

"Did you receive my report on the meeting with the Navajo chiefs, Kit?"

"No, sir. I did not."

Carleton briefed them both on his meeting the previous week with the Navajo and their noncommittal response.

"So what do you make of it, Kit?" Carleton said.

"Nobody likes to be told to move from their homeland at the point of a gun, sir. The Navajo deeply believe they have been wronged by first the Spaniards, and then all white men. And like all elders everywhere, the Navajo chiefs do actually have trouble controlling their younger generation. They are as unhappy with the Apaches and Utes and Cheyenne as you are with them, sir."

"Dammit, Kit, let's not go through this tiresome discussion again."

"Yes, sir. I'm not arguing with you, I'm merely stating the obvious. This is going to be a hard sell for the chiefs. Walk four hundred and fifty miles or fight? Ten thousand Navajo aren't going to just abandon their home and report to Fort Wingate for a one month march." Carson looked distressed. "I understand my orders, sir. That's that, next June we go to war with the Navajo."

Carleton turned to Cummings.

"Marshal? Your turn."

Cummings started to brief them, but was immediately cut off by Carleton.

"Oh, sorry Marshal. One more thing. Joe West will re-occupy Fort McLane near Pinos Altos in the next few days on his way to kill Mangas and his Apaches. Hopefully that'll remove the need to go after Cochise."

"We'll see," Carson said.

Cummings then briefed the two of them on his pursuit of Damours. The truthful version. Leaving out the meeting in Buffalo.

"And then the Department of the Army ordered you back here instead of continuing on to Canada?" Carleton said.

"Yes, sir."

"Chacon says you told him you chased Damours to Cuba and he shot himself dead with your pistol rather than be captured."

"I've found that the Captain and I have serious communication problems, sir."

Carson frowned.

"Do you think he has the money with him, Marshal," Carleton said.

They were both eyeing him carefully now.

"I have no way of knowing, sir."

"You knew him, right," Carleton said.

"Not well, sir. But yes, I knew him."

"What was Canby's reaction to the thefts, Marshal?"

"He was horrified, sir. He kept saying he couldn't see how it could be true."

"A very curious case, don't you think, Kit," Carleton said. "One of the Army's most trusted officers embezzles money from everyone in the Territory. Even the Franciscans. Right under everyone's noses. Even the Marshal's here."

"Maybe he was a secret weapon for the Confederacy, General," Carson said. "Maybe Jefferson Davis has a Lieutenant Damours in each State and Territory."

Carleton puffed furiously on his cigar in silent response. "Well I'll be damned if I understand how such a thing can happen. Rumors have it near a hundred thousand dollars. It's incomprehensible."

Cummings sensibly did not challenge the high estimate.

"Will that be all, then?" Cummings said. "I have my written report here, sir."

"What's Washington like?" Carson said. "I was last there fourteen years ago. What's the mood? How's morale about the War?"

"Mostly Washington is all about the War, sir. People are still reeling from Manassas last summer. They're openly calling it the second Bull Run. McClellan's failure to follow up his defeat of Lee at Antietam has people concerned that Washington might still not be safe from attack. It's like the small southern town it's always been, 'cept now it's been completely overrun by U.S. troops."

Carleton signaled him to continue.

"Nobody seems to have much confidence in 'Lincoln's Army,' as they call it now. I got there just as Lincoln replaced McClellan with Burnside. When I got back from chasing Damours up and down the East Coast, everybody was panicked that Burnside had let Lee out of his grasp at Fredericksburg, yet another disaster. Canby told me that Lincoln is desperate to find a General he can count on. There are rumors all over the city about practically every General in the Army. Lee's making the U.S Army look like amateurs."

"Who was the lady you were with, Marshal?" Carleton said.

He put his feet on his desk, almost completely shrouded in cigar smoke in the gloomy room.

"Lily Smoot. She worked at the Princess here in town. Dealt some poker games I was in. Did some bartending."

"Is there any truth to her also being a friend of Damours?"

Carleton was asking the questions, but it was starting to feel like Chacon had been feeding them to him.

"Bartending and card dealing here in town, she was bound to know him. I thought she knew him better than she did, though. I was disappointed that she was no help looking for him. When we got to Washington she admitted that she doubted she could even pick him out on the street."

Carson now looked skeptical.

"General," Cummings said. "You ordered me to go get Damours. Arrest him and get him to reveal where he had what was left of the Army's money. Then bring him back. He wasn't a friend of mine. We played cards against each other and hung out at some of the same Santa Fe spots. I knew him some. Won some of his money long before we all knew it wasn't his. He tried to cheat me same as everybody else. The fact I knew him didn't matter."

He paused.

"It was my job. You ordered me. With all due respect, sir, if I didn't like the order, I coulda always resigned as Marshal instead of running all over the country, and beyond, for two months. I did the job. But I couldn't find him. That's all there is to it. He's most likely in Canada somewhere. Probably with some of the money, but maybe not."

Carson looked thoughtfully at the two men. He already knew Cummings to be reckless and impatient. Knew him to be a gambler and a lady's man. But so were many that he led or worked with.

Mostly what mattered was underlying trust. And results. Could you trust them to do what you needed done?

The Army, and New Mexico for that matter, were well rid of Damours.

The Marshal's story didn't completely hold up. But no matter how you looked at it, Cummings had completed at least half the job. Damours was gone for good. The money? Carson wouldn'ta given a buffalo chip for the money.

He'd got what he come for today.

Kit Carson looked directly at Cummings. "Cummings," Carson said. "As you just heard, General Carleton has ordered us to round up the Navajo. Move 'em out to Bosque Redondo with the Mescalero. I'd like you to come back solely as a Major in the Volunteers. Resign as Marshal. Help us rid New Mexico of the Navajo problem forever. Just like you did with Damours."

"How long do I have to think about it?"

"The same as you had with Damours, Marshal. It's an order."

97

January 1, 1863

Carson and Arnold entered Carleton's mess the next morning for breakfast.

"This Cummings fellow, are you sure you can use him against the Navajo?" Carleton said. "He seems undisciplined and unreliable."

"He's reckless," Carson said. "But we may need some of that. And he's useless to you here in Santa Fe. We may as well put him to good use somewhere, and the California officers have developed good relations with him here over the past six months."

"Well, his results are damn queer, that's all I can say. Chacon is furious with him about what he told him about the Damours saga."

"Let's stick with the plan," Carson said. "Let's get him out of Santa Fe. There are rumored to be more gamblers and whores preparing to accompany me against the Navajo than ever. I'm gonna need peacekeepers at the forts and the camps along the way. Cummings will be more useful to me than he will be to you back here."

"Do you think he's lying about Damours?" Carleton said.

"If he found Damours, why would he come back and lie to us about it?"

"Maybe he killed Damours, like he told Chacon, and just kept the money for himself?"

"Then why come back?" Carson said. "And why come back and tell Chacon anything? He just hates Chacon is all, and he couldn't resist annoying him. Cummings couldn't find Damours. Otherwise why ask Washington for permission to go to Canada after him?"

"I don't know. It doesn't smell right. And what about the girl?"

"The Smoot girl," Carson said. "A common whore. Chacon says she deals poker at one of the saloons on the side. The fact that she knew Damours and accompanied Cummings after him means nothing. She probably knows 90% of the white men in town. Cummings wanted the company or thought she could help him catch Damours."

Arnold overheard this exchange and interrupted. "I couldn't help but overhear, Colonel. Did you say 'the Smoot girl'?'"

"Yes, Arnold. Why?" Carson said.

"You say Lily Smoot accompanied Cummings in his search for Damours?"

"Yes."

"Did you get her version?"

"No point, Major. I wouldn't believe a word she said."

"With all due respect, Kit, I know her very well. I don't agree with you that she's a 'common whore,' and I think she would tell me what really happened out there."

Carleton appeared amused by this unexpected disagreement between two of his best officers.

"Major Arnold," Carleton said. "If you know this woman that well, why don't you see what she can add to Cummings' story? I'm sure Kit's character assessment is based on hearsay and not personal experience, right Kit?"

Carleton chuckled at his assessment, but Carson was not amused.

"You're right, I don't know firsthand, General," Carson said. "But several of my men knew her in Nevada. I'll grant she could have reformed. I didn't mean to offend, Major."

"I'll talk to her," Arnold said. "I'll report back."

Carleton sat back down, then looked up at Carson. "How do you think this Damours fellow embezzled all this money right in front of everybody? Didn't anybody suspect anything?"

"If you'd ever met Auggy," Carson said. "You wouldn't have suspected anything either, General. Damnedest kid I ever knew."

John Arnold and Lily Smoot sat on a bench in the Plaza early that evening. Arnold told her of the conversation with Carson and Carleton and his surprise and concerns that she had gone back East with Cummings.

She gave Arnold an accounting that was precisely what Cummings had included in his report, neglecting, of course, to mention her side trip to Baltimore between Buffalo and Washington.

Baltimore had been a mistake. There had been nothing there for her. She didn't even know an address where her parents had lived. On a whim, she had even gone by Arnold's house and had seen his wife and one of his sons. As she had no message or news from John, she just watched them unseen. Nothing good could have come from introducing herself to them.

"The whole trip, was a mistake, John," she said. Especially Baltimore, she added to herself.

"Well, Lily, you confirm Cummings' report. That, at least, is a relief."

"Are you finished with your questions?" she said.

"Yes."

"From what you say, Cummings lied to me. For what it's worth he told me he'd briefed Carleton on who I was before we left."

"Why would he make that up?"

"I have no idea, John. Cummings is an idiot."

He looked at her in the dim light. "What are you doing running around with guys like Cummings and Damours, Lily?"

"Cummings is a U.S. Marshal, John. And I wasn't running around with Damours. We were chasing him. What's your point?"

"Cummings is not much of a Marshal and you know it, Lil. Is it true you worked in the Nevada brothels?"

She looked up at his face. Clearly his feelings had been hurt.

"Yes, John. When I left Utah, I looked into all the political and military and business management jobs open to teenage girls, but they were all filled. I didn't meet any guys like you who were single and sitting around that I could safely live off, so I got a job where I could save some money."

She looked closely and caught his scowl. "John, unless you're offering to adopt me or to start taking care of me, I have to look out for myself. And for my ranch."

He looked down at her. For the first time ever, he hugged her. "I'm sorry, Lil. You're right. It might not be appropriate, but I care about you and want to see you succeed."

She stood up. Bent down to him and kissed him gently.

"Appropriate," she said, "Is overrated."

And she walked out of the Plaza, leaving him sitting alone on the bench.

98

Chacon was briefing Carleton. "We've chased four different bands of Navajo back toward Fort Wingate, sir in the past three weeks. Each had made off with a small herd of livestock. It feels like a different band tries their hand at this every four or five days, sir. We retrieved three of the herds and arrested two Navajo."

"Are their chiefs planning to move out in five months?" Carleton said.

"They had no idea what we were talking about, sir."

"You and Carson are by God going to put an end to this in five months' time."

"Yes, sir."

West had set up his Fort McLane headquarters. Scouts had identified the location of Mangas Coloradas' main camp, some twenty miles to the northwest of the fort.

"Can we just end this with a frontal assault," West said to his most senior Lieutenant.

"You're not going to get that opportunity, General," the Lieutenant said. "They've been fighting whites in these parts for years. They'll be gone the minute you head out."

"What do you suggest then?"

The two had been together since before Los Angeles. They were at the point where they could practically read each other's minds.

"What's your goal here, General?" the Lieutenant said over the lip of his coffee cup.

"Carleton wants them dead. Thinks that'll break the Chiricahuas for good. Even if Mangas surrenders, he's one request from Cochise away from going right back." He turned to Swilling. "The Guards feel any different, Jack?"

"As long as Mangas is alive, nobody's life up here is worth a damn. But I don't agree Cochise will give up if you dispose of Mangas."

"First things first," West said. "We take out the Mimbres. Cochise'll be tougher. We have Fort Bowie to keep the stage line going. And Cochise will eventually lose a war of attrition."

"So how do you want us to do this, General?" the Lieutenant said.

The platoon set out under a white flag. They headed straight for Mangas's camp. West's full force at Fort McLane was too large for the Indians to even think about a full assault. But one platoon wouldn't threaten them.

Several miles back, an entire Company of cavalry followed the Lieutenant's platoon. Unbeknownst to Mangas, if he wanted peace he was a dead man. Actually, either way, the great Mimbres chief's days were numbered.

The platoon set up camp a hundred yards from an arroyo a half hour short of the Mimbres main encampment to wait.

At dawn the next morning, three Apaches in red bandanas and ammunition belts across their chests were just standing silently at the edge of the arroyo.

One of them had a white flag tied to his rifle stock.

"You come in peace," a very short and ugly Apache said. It was a statement.

The Lieutenant held up the white flag. "Yes. We would like to talk to Mangas Coloradas."

"Mangas says to tell you that he wants to talk with your Chief West. He is tired of fighting. But he is now an old man, and likes to sleep late. So, maybe you would talk to me instead."

"You say Mangas wants peace. You also? Or is it only your old chief who is tired of fighting?"

"No. I am not tired. I like my life. Con mucho gusto. Perhaps you and your men would like to come to our camp and see our mood for yourselves."

"No," the Lieutenant said. "You can see we are few in number. If you came to bring us back, you have your answer."

"We know of the forces behind you."

He actually sneered.

"We want to talk to Mangas," the Lieutenant said. "We will wait for him to wake up."

"If we wanted to kill you White Eye, you would already be dead."

The two stood facing each other. Two seasoned warriors.

"My name is Geronimo. I will come back with your answer before nightfall."

And the three vanished back into the arroyo.

At midafternoon, a dozen Apaches rose out of the arroyo to face the platoon.

The two sides faced each other. No weapons were drawn. White flags flew on both sides.

There was no sign of Geronimo.

At a signal from one of the Apaches, an immense Indian with a huge head walked slowly out of the arroyo and approached the Lieutenant.

"I am Mangas Coloradas, chief of the Mimbres clan of the Chiricahuas." Mangas was a shadow of his former self. Now very old and in very poor health. He had survived his chest wound but had aged considerably in a short time.

"I represent Chief West. We come to meet the great Chief Mangas in peace."

"My people are tired of war, Lieutenant. The white soldiers leave us no peace here in our homeland. They kill our women and children and old men. You do not allow us to hunt, so we no longer can feed ourselves. We are prepared to stop fighting."

He dropped his bow to the ground and looked down on the Lieutenant.

The Lieutenant knew that this man had killed and tortured hundreds of innocent settlers for decades. Carleton and West had no doubts that he was incapable of stopping. And even if he stopped, many Mimbres would not.

"This is our hope too, Chief Mangas."

"May I meet with your Chief West to let him know of my hopes and plans for my people?"

"Yes you may." And, in a pre-arranged move, he pointed his finger at the old man's chest.

In a move that even the Apaches admired , the entire following Company of cavalry appeared in a semi-circle around the impassive Indians.

Rifles were pointed at every Indian.

The platoon had every revolver pointed at Mangas Coloradas' massive chest and head.

"Please come with me now, Mangas."

The Lieutenant no longer using his respected title.

"I come in peace, Lieutenant."

"So do we, Mangas. But we do not intend to die out of carelessness."

"And my men," he said as he turned and swept his arm outward toward the arroyo.

It sounded as if a thousand guns were cocked at once in the otherwise silent desert.

"Your men should return to your people and tell them that you have gone to visit Chief West at Fort McLane."

At a signal from Mangas Coloradas, the twelve Apaches vanished soundlessly into the arroyo.

The soldiers knew they would be back in force in less than ten minutes. That was all they needed.

They shackled the old chief and raced back to the fort.

It was now near midnight.

Mangas Coloradas, hands and feet in chains, lay on a blanket by the fire. Two guards, nearing the end of their one hour shift, stood over him.

West walked over to the old Indian and squatted down over him. His men were right, the size of his head was not believable.

"I'm told you wanted to see me."

"Are you Chief General West?"

"I am."

"Why am I under arrest, Chief West? My people and I came to you under a white flag of truce. We desire an end to all the killing of our people."

"You have killed many people, including many innocent people."

"Such is the nature of war. You are a great General, Chief West. You certainly know this. I come to you so that we can, together, stop this war."

"Do you speak for all the Chiricahuas?"

"No. In truth, Chief West, I speak only for the Mimbres clan. The Gila Apaches."

"And do you speak, then, for all the Mimbres?"

"They are my people. I am their Chief," he said, not answering the question.

"Many innocent people have been killed, and are still being killed and tortured, by the Apaches, Mangas. Justice requires that somebody pays for this," West said.

The guard was changing as he stood up. He walked over to the two men just coming on duty.

"Kill him," he said under his breath so that no one else could hear.

He got on his horse and rode back to the fort as Mangas Coloradas curled up to sleep as best he could by the fire.

The two soldiers didn't need any further prompting or direction. They had an hour before there would be any witnesses. As soon as they were alone, they placed their bayonets in the fire.

They then each took turns laying them against the bottoms of the old man's feet. He appeared to sleep through the pain without wincing.

So, laughing as they worked, they moved to his toes and his calves.

Finally, Mangas looked at them. His pain tolerance appeared to be inhuman.

One of the soldiers pierced his calf with a red hot bayonet.

"Why do you do this," Mangas said, over the sound of his sizzling flesh.

The soldier placed the blade in his running blood, which immediately hissed and boiled up a curious pink smoke.

"Chief West knows that I come in peace. Why do you torture me?"

The soldiers just laughed and continued burning the stoic old man. Frustrated, one of them lay his red hot blade across the Indian's stomach, causing the blanket to catch fire and the soft flesh to ignite.

Mangas Coloradas leaped to his feet.

The other soldier shot him in the stomach. Then in the chest. The first soldier then stabbed him in the stomach and shot him one more time for good measure.

The Sergeant of the guard and two Privates rushed in.

"He tried to escape. We had to shoot him."

"General West will be very disappointed."

They all laughed.

The next day, a few of the soldiers dug Mangas Coloradas' body out of his shallow grave, cut off his head, and boiled off all the skin.

It was the largest human skull any of them had ever seen.

When West attacked the Mimbres camp, he was able to scatter, but not defeat them. The soldiers left Mangas Coloradas' headless body behind for his people to see.

Contrary to Carleton and West's expectations, the cold blooded torture, murder, and mutilation of the great Apache chief did not end the Chiricahua wars.

They were, in fact, to last another twenty-three years.

99

February 3, 1863

Lily entered Zapico's store. The news had broken this morning. Damours was headline news in every paper in the Territory.

"You see the paper today, Zapico?" Lily said.

"Yes. Guess we couldn't have expected much different. Damours is now a public villain. He'll be big news."

"It says here his court martial is retroactive to last November 5th," she said. "That's the day he went AWOL. They know he was stealing well before then."

"The Army doesn't know when he started stealing, and they need a specific date, I guess. No need to set them straight that I see."

Lily laughed.

"Have you heard anything from Damours?" Zapico said.

"No. I don't expect to for at least a few months now. This article will slow him up. The entire Territory is in an uproar over this. Everybody has their own private little Damours story. Everybody wants to sound important enough to have been swindled by him. It'll be risky for him to come anywhere near here now, no matter how well he's disguised. You still okay waiting?"

"Yes," Zapico said. "I'm worried about Cummings, though. They're sending him out to Navajo country, and he's been nosing around."

"Well he knows to stay clear of me. You be careful, Zapico."

"Carson resigned again today," Arnold said, his amusement evident.

Carleton sighed. "Just ignore him. I don't have time for this. He'll be there at the head of his troops in June to go after the Navajo. He'll do his duty. Just leave him be."

He looked back down at his desk.

"It's now become a full time job just answering all these questions about Damours. Can't we get Lincoln to send Canby back for this?"

Arnold knew enough to be silent.

100

April 25, 1863

Carleton looked at the two Navajo chiefs he had travelled to Cubero to meet. He looked at the one on his left. "Chief Delgadito, you met with me in Santa Fe four months ago. I have come in peace to the edge of your lands to see if I can have my answer."

"No, we have no answer for you yet Chief Carleton. We are not like you white people. My people don't just do as I tell them. They are still thinking about the difficult choice you have given them."

"And the continued raiding by your young men?"

"My clan has stopped raiding."

He turned to the second Navajo chief. "And you, Chief Barboncito?"

"My Dine also no longer raid the New Mexicans. We want to live in peace with all people. My clan will not move to this round forest you speak of. It is too far for the women, children, and old men to walk. We would only die there, away from the homes of our kin and our ancestors."

The old chief looked over at Delgadito before continuing.

"We choose instead to live in peace near Fort Wingate. Even if this means that your soldiers will come and kill us there. Better to die at home than to wander in the desert and die in a strange land."

Carleton drummed his fingers on the desk. "Very well then, in two months we will attack and destroy those who fail to surrender themselves."

That afternoon, Carleton waited for his assembled officers to settle in. Many had come in from Fort Wingate and others from Los Pinos to join those who had accompanied him on the week's ride from Santa Fe.

"Gentlemen. I want to thank each of you for meeting here today. We will be at war with the Navajo on June 20. Carson is in Taos, organizing his best Utes and Jicarillas to take them and his Companies to Los Pinos to prepare for war."

He lit a new cigar.

"Carson's force will be a thousand strong and will proceed to Fort Defiance and Navajo country. You will use every means possible to kill every resisting Navajo, and cause those who eventually choose surrender over death to be removed to Bosque Redondo. Are there any questions?"

There were none.

"Other matters of general interest to all of you are as follows. 'Fighting Joe' Hooker has replaced Burnside as Commander of the Army of the Potomac. More importantly, General U.S. Grant has been placed in command of the Army of the West."

"Ol' Abe may have finally found himself a winning General, Jim," Arnold said.

"Which one?" Carleton said.

"Grant."

"I agree with you on that, Major. As long as he stays sober."

Nobody laughed.

"And last month," Carleton said. "Cochise and Geronimo stole all sixty of the horses from Fort West in an uncharacteristically bold frontal attack. We pursued them and killed twenty-five Apaches at a rancheria seventy miles from the fort."

"Did your soldiers recover the horses?" Arnold said. "And were they the right Apaches?"

"No to the first question. And we don't know the answer to the second."

A weary Joseph Cummings joined Zapico and Lily in the back of Zapico's store.

"How was Tucson?" Lily said, looking up from some papers she was reading.

"A waste of time," he said. "No sooner had I arrived than they announced Tucson was too peaceful to need another Marshal."

"And Mowry? Is he still in jail," Zapico said.

"No. He was released five months ago. In November after his trial. The charge of selling lead to the Confederates was dropped for lack of evidence. I couldn't find him, but I left word. He's presumably working to get his properties back. The mines are a mess."

He lit a cigar. Tired, but coming around.

"I did see Angela while I was there. It seems she ran off to Tucson with those bank robbers."

"How are they?" Lily said.

"The three men went to California long ago. Angela's dead, actually. She asked how you two and I were doing. She knew too much. So I shot her."

Lily couldn't mask her horror.

"Nice to know our Marshal has such respect for the law," Zapico said.

Cummings let it go.

"When'd you get back," Lily said.

"An hour ago. I got your message and rode over immediately. Any word from Damours?"

"Nothing," Lily said.

"So what do we do about the money? I'm scheduled to turn right around and head to Los Pinos with Carson. And then go after the Navajo in two months."

"We wait for Damours," Zapico said.

"And if we never hear from the little bastard?"

"We'll hear, Joseph," Lily said. "The money's here and we all know it. Auggy will contact us."

She looked at Zapico, then back at Cummings. "How's this, Joseph? If we haven't heard from Auggy by the time you get back from chasing Indians, we'll all look for the money together and split it then."

"Do you two know where it is?"

"I know where I've put mine," Zapico said. "But I'll be damned if I remember you telling me where you put yours."

"And you two know where Damours buried his, right? And it's by the far the most, right?"

"Yes," Lily said. "Auggy buried the most, Zapico has the second most, and you've held out on us from the beginning. When we split it up, you've got a lot more coming to you. David and I, between us, know how to find Auggy's buried money. You know that. But neither of us on our own knows enough to find it."

Cummings looked thoughtful. He pulled out his Colt. Looked in the chambers.

"Any way I can convince you two to end this nonsense before I head out to kill Navajos?"

"I'll tell you this much," Zapico said. "Auggy buried his outside a building here in Santa Fe."

"And yours, David? Where's yours buried?"

"It's not buried, Joseph. It's just in a safe place. A very safe place."

Lily looked hard at Zapico, wondering why he'd told Cummings anything at all. Then she remembered, Auggy had already told Cummings that much in Buffalo.

"We're partners. It'll all work out fine," she said.

101

June 17, 1863

Carleton and his smoking cigar entered the Governor's office in the Palace for the weekly briefing.

First, Carleton caught the Governor up on Carson's impending departure westward and the plans to build Fort Canby at Pueblo Colorado.

"Second," he said, "Lee lost Stonewall Jackson but still destroyed Hooker at Chancellorsville. Lee has now led seventy-five thousand Rebel troops into Pennsylvania. If Lincoln can't find someone to defeat Lee in Pennsylvania, the Union is in mortal danger."

"And the implications for us, General?"

"There's no way to tell. The Union in the end will probably be preserved. All we can do is our jobs here. We need to make New Mexico safe from the Navajo and, God willing, let President Lincoln and General Hooker do their jobs back East."

There was a knock at Lily's door. She opened it to discover Sarah Zapico standing there.

She knew immediately that something was terribly wrong. Zapico *himself* had never come to her room.

"What is it, Sarah?"

"David needs to see you, Lily."

"Why didn't he come himself?"

"He would never violate your privacy, Lily. Please come quickly. Something is terribly wrong."

Damours? What else could it be? Lily locked the door, took Sarah's arm, and hurried out into the street.

When they arrived at the store, Sarah unlocked the back door, let Lily in, and left for her home.

A very distressed Zapico sat on his desk. The room was a mess.

"What is it, David? What's happened?"

"The money's gone."

"Are you sure?"

It was inane, but what else was there to say?

Zapico pointed to the cabinet that he had pulled from the wall. It revealed broken plaster and a large hole. She peered into the emptiness.

"That was your very safe place."

It wasn't a question.

She felt as if she were about to faint, and sat on the floor.

"Who else knew about it?"

"Nobody. I created the space myself and plastered it over myself. I didn't even tell Sarah. She doesn't know about any of this."

"Who else knew you even had money?"

"Mowry, Damours, you, and Cummings. Lily, I have to ask you, have you heard anything from Damours?"

"Yes, he's working in a saloon outside of Denver. Waiting for things to blow over here. There's no way Damours would steal from you and me, David, and there's no way he's been to Santa Fe."

"Mowry would ask us first and there would be no point in his coming here. Not with the Union still suspecting him."

"That only leaves Cummings, Zapico. When is the last time you checked behind the cabinet?"

"Late April. Just after our last meeting with Cummings."

"But before he headed out with Carson?"

"Yes. Before that."

They both thought the unthinkable. Damours' burial spot. Was it possible that all was lost?

"David, Auggy told me that he buried our money against a Santa Fe building. The northwest corner. Outside."

"And he told me it was on the block off of San Francisco Street past the jeweler where you got his cufflinks."

They both thought about that.

"Let's go, David. I know where it has to be."

The two of them left together, Zapico grabbing a shovel, each hoping that she was right and that it was still there.

Val Verde Hall.

Of course, that's where Auggy would've buried it.

There was no fandango tonight and the streets were still.

They looked down at the northwest corner of Val Verde Hall.

Zapico took one look and knew. The ground was not uniform. The earth was darker at the corner.

Sick at heart, he began to dig. Two feet down he hit hard earth. Undisturbed for years. Something had been buried here. And now it was gone.

The two of them leaned against the building.

"Did that fool Cummings head out to the Navajo wars with more than seventy thousand dollars in cash?" Lily said, more to herself than to Zapico.

"I seriously doubt he reburied it, Lil. He almost certainly plans to go AWOL in the Arizona Territory. He has the money on him. You can count on it."

"Time for Auggy to come home, Zapico. We're in need of a new plan."

PART IV
GOING HOME

102

Carson sat on his horse in front of what he intended to be his last Army. A thousand men. Against ten thousand Navajo.

He looked over at Major John Arnold and Major Joseph Cummings, talking easily to each other in front of the waiting men.

"You ready, gentlemen?"

"Yes, sir," Arnold said.

"Then you lead."

"And you, Colonel?"

"I'll be in the back with my Indians."

And he turned his horse and trotted toward the rear.

Arnold turned and whistled shrilly. "Forward, march."

The two hundred eighty mile march was underway.

Carson's aide rode toward him as he headed to the back. "Colonel."

"Yes, Captain."

"I see Cummings is leading the men, sir?"

"Yes. It's not that I don't appreciate your coming forward yesterday, informing me that Cummings had never been properly mustered in last year as a Major by the Governor or Canby, but, yes he is."

"What did you do about Cummings' status, sir?"

"I mustered him in, Captain."

The aide didn't argue the technical point any further. He'd done his job. "Yes, sir. How are Captain Pfeiffer and his family doing, Colonel?"

Two weeks earlier, Pfeiffer had been preparing his Companies for this march. He and his family had been bathing in a hot springs when they were attacked by Chiricahuas.

"Not good, Captain. Tragically, his wife and daughter died. He will recover from his wounds, but his two Companies will now be about ten days behind us. We'll need both Pfeiffer and Cummings if we are to succeed, Captain."

Carson saw his Indians just up ahead. "Anything else, Captain?"

"No, sir." The aide turned his horse around and trotted forward.

Carson saluted Kaniache, Yellow Horse, and Red Cloud as they approached with their warriors at the rear of the column.

"Greetings Father Kit," Kaniache said. "Some Dine just murdered our great Chief Benito, and we are grateful to you for keeping your promise to include us on this great day."

Carson had known about the Navajo treachery. "Not happily, old friend. These are very sad times."

"Not for us," Red Cloud said. "We will help you kill the Dine. We will avenge our people."

"I remain hopeful," Carson said, "That the Dine will come to see the wisdom of moving to the Bosque Redondo without a fight."

"We thought Chief Carleton had ordered you to kill the Dine," Yellow Horse said.

"Yes, my orders authorize me to kill resisting Dine, Yellow Horse. But my respect and friendship with the Jicarillas and Utes and now with the Mescalero, does not come from my killing them. You know I do not seek to kill Indians, my friend. I will try to bring the Dine willingly to a decision to move."

"You will fail, Father Kit," Kaniache said. "We will help you kill many Dine. We will take their women and their children and their sheep home to our deserving people."

Carson grunted an ambiguous reply.

"This will be a long ride," Yellow Horse said. "Would you all like to hear the story of 'Coyote Visits the Navajo'?"

"Oh no." Carson threw his hands up in mock exasperation. "We all know that Coyote scatters the wool when he kills sheep and can't understand of what use the wool could be to the Navajo, and then he burns his own moccasins in the fire."

"How about 'Coyote and the Talking Tree'?" Red Cloud said, wanting to hear the story of the talking tree in the Chiricahua Mountains again.

"No Chiricahuas today," Carson said. "Let's focus on the Dine."

Kaniache and a disappointed Red Cloud both slapped Yellow Horse on the back.

"Your philosophy is lost on Father Kit," Kaniache said. "White men are hopeless."

The four friends rode on in silence for a mile.

"I see you have the horse killer leading your soldiers," Red Cloud said.

Carson was genuinely perplexed. He looked at Red Cloud questioningly.

And then he remembered. Cummings had told them that day in the Plaza that he had killed Cochise's horse.

He wondered if Cummings still had Cochise's quiver and bow case attached to his saddle.

He made a mental note to check that.

103

July 10, 1863

Three days later, Carleton arrived in Los Pinos to give final instructions to the recovering Captain Pfeiffer as he prepared his Companies to depart and join Carson.

"I was terribly sorry to hear about your family, Captain," Carleton said.

"Thank you, General. I don't think I will ever be able to forgive myself, sir."

Carleton stared at him oddly, making Pfeiffer uncomfortable.

"I guess I can see, at least a little, what Arnold and Carson were saying about you."

"What's that sir?"

"They said you look a little like a Chinese Emperor. It's the beard, I guess."

Pfeiffer didn't say anything to that.

Upon his arrival, Carleton had learned of both the surrender of Vicksburg to Grant and the victory over Lee at Gettysburg the week before.

"Lincoln has finally found his Generals, Captain," he said. "When you get to Pueblo Colorado, make sure Carson carries out the celebration that I'm ordering at all our western forts. And then finish off the Navajo to complete the celebration."

"Yes, sir."

Carleton, personally, then went out in front of his troops at Los Pinos and led the rifle volleys saluting the twin Union victories back East.

104

July 24, 1863

Kaniache bent down close to the ground, looking over the entire abandoned campsite. The Navajo woman yesterday had been right. There had been a large encampment of Navajo here recently.

Pfeiffer and the Utes had routed a small group of Navajo yesterday, easily killing the three men and capturing the women and children who had told them of this camp.

"Is there any point in chasing them down?" Carson said.

In answer Kaniache and Red Cloud mounted their horses and followed the trail. They rode briskly for two hours before the three men dismounted and walked around the parched desert floor. Looking for any hopeful signs.

"Their horses are in better shape than ours," Carson said.

"It will take us many hours and at least ninety miles before we can catch them, Father Kit," Kaniache said.

"And we do not have enough water," Red Cloud said.

The three quickly concluded that their best course was to head back to Pueblo Colorado and join up with the rest of the soldiers arriving from Fort Defiance.

Carson was beginning to despair of finding enough Navajos to make any progress. The Navajo were staying out of sight and proving difficult to find.

105

The next day, Carson sat with the three chiefs and his executive officers in his tent at the Pueblo Colorado headquarters.

"New orders," Carson said. "We are not going to build Fort Canby here. Carleton and I have decided that Fort Defiance, to be rebuilt and named Fort Canby, is a superior location. Pueblo Colorado will remain as our southwestern scouting base."

He then realized that many of these men had served under Canby. "Incidentally, Lincoln has assigned General Canby to be the Commanding General of the City and Harbor of New York. Irish immigrants responded to the newly instituted draft law by lynching eleven Negroes there and rioting for four days. One hundred and twenty citizens were killed during the riots."

This was met with shocked silence. This was difficult news to hear, even for hardened soldiers. That they represented the rioters was inescapable.

"For our part, I have grown tired of daily, failed attempts to find the Navajo. In two days, we move out for the next two weeks. I want you each to prepare your Companies for two weeks of hard riding. General Carleton has also ordered us to stop the practice of enslaving Navajo women and children. They are to be sent to Bosque Redondo."

He did not translate this for his three Indians. He would hoped Red Cloud would remain silent so that he could manage them through this change later. He knew he would probably lose them in a matter of weeks once they knew.

"I have decided that our focus will no longer be to chase after the Navajo. It simply isn't working. We will now start to burn their crops and homes and take all their livestock."

He waited until he had everyone's attention again.

"Gentlemen, we will destroy the Navajo's ability to house, clothe, and feed themselves. I want every orchard, every wheat field, all grasslands that we don't need for ourselves destroyed. Burned. I want the entire Navajo nation to be able to see the smoke in the air. From each of their four sacred mountains."

He looked directly at Cummings. "Major Cummings. I want you to head up this scorched land policy. I want you to have men assigned to every Company whose specific job it will be to destroy the homes and burn the crops. Let the Utes and Jicarillas and other companies run down the Navajo. Your job is to destroy their ability to live here. The Dine will then come to us. There will be no fight left in them."

"Yes, sir."

He surveyed his officers' faces.

This was going to be very painful work. Not what these soldiers were trained for.

But Carson did not want to kill Navajos. He wanted them to surrender without a fight and agree to be relocated.

And then he wanted to go home to Josefa in Taos.

"Major Cummings, may I please see you in private?" Carson said as everybody was leaving the tent. "Let's step outside, Major."

The two walked toward the river. They both could see the Indians and the officers now meeting with their men. They could see the supply wagons being prepared.

And the camp followers looked on from the Cottonwood trees at the river.

Carson pretended not to notice, and turned away from the scene.

"Are you okay with this responsibility, Major?"

"Yes, sir. Of course."

"It's going to be dehumanizing, Major. In a different way than just killing them is. Soldiers kill each other in war. That's what they do. Both sides know what they are getting into and both sides are trained for the battle. But this will be different. You will be depriving them of their ability to live their lives. Not only the fighting warriors, but also the old men, the women, and the children. You will be rendering them defenseless. And many could die of starvation, Major."

"I see that, Colonel. But many fewer on both sides will die as a result, right?"

"That is my hope, Major. That is why I am asking you to do this. The Navajo prize their peach orchards so. This will be a very terrible thing."

They walked on in silence.

Finally, Carson turned around and headed back to camp.

"Colonel," Cummings said.

"Yes, Major."

"I have decided to accept your and General Carleton's offer of membership in the Masons."

"Very good, Major. I'm pleased. We will see to it when we return to Santa Fe. After the Navajo campaign."

"Thank you, sir."

"Major," Carson said. "Something else is bothering me. Many of my men behave shamefully. It is wearing on me to command such men."

"Who do you mean, sir?"

"There is much drunkenness. I fear the officers' drinking could bring us all to harm. And the two Lieutenants last week, drunk and fighting like women in front of their men. Why does no one stop these things when they start?"

Cummings looked idly over at the whores' wagons in the Cottonwoods.

"This war is wearing for the men, Colonel. I guess things like that break the boredom."

"Like when the two whores had their knife fight last week right in front of the cheering soldiers? And no one stepped in to stop it until one had been killed and the other one bloodied. Were the men actually wagering on the two of them, Major?"

But Cummings was no longer listening. He was staring over at the Cottonwoods.

"Major?"

"Sorry, sir. Yes, they were betting on the whores, sir. This whole sorry mess is debilitating for the men, sir. The men are bored."

He stared silently into the trees as they walked.

Carson sensed it was time to move on.

"So, Major. You are fine with your assignment, then?"

"Yes, sir," Cummings said. Trying to end the conversation.

His head was spinning. Trying to figure out if that had really been Lily Smoot he had just glimpsed in the trees among the whores. It had certainly looked like her. Talking to John Arnold.

"Yes, sir," Cummings said. "I will do my duty. Just as you will."

106

Three weeks later, Red Cloud sat next to Carson in front of his fire at Pueblo Colorado. The two friends sat in silence for a long while, neither wanting to interrupt the thoughts of the other. Sharing the immensity of the summer sky and the uncountable stars above.

"Are you content with how it's going, Father Kit?" Red Cloud said.

"With some things, yes. We destroyed hundreds and hundreds of acres of Navajo farmland and we captured thousands of their sheep and horses. And we captured and relocated fourteen of their women and children."

"And you killed three Dine, right?"

"That does not make me happy, Red Cloud."

"I know, Father Kit. The fourteen do not count those taken by my people, right?"

"No, the numbers taken by the Utes and Jicarilla are unknown to me."

They sat in silence for a while.

"Are the Utes and Jicarillas really leaving now to go back to Taos?" Carson said.

"Yes."

"I envy them. But why do you leave?"

"They leave," he said, "because they say they are not being allowed to keep the Navajo captives and the Navajo herds like they were promised."

"Red Cloud, we have fought against each other and with each other for many years. We have lived together in peace for a very long time. You and I both know that they are not being truthful about this. They are actually leaving because they already have the sheep and goats and horses that they need. And they already have the number of Navajo women and children they came for."

He looked over at Red Cloud. "So there is more, right?"

"Yes, there is more Father Kit."

After a lengthy silence Red Cloud said, "Their way of life is going away. Killing and stealing by and from the Dine have always been a part of their lives. They know this kind of life. They are comfortable when they win and accept when they lose. According to their way. But destroying Dine farms and homes and crops and livestock and their ability to live is the white man's way. It is not the Ute or Jicarilla way."

He looked at Carson in the flickering fire light.

"They are uncomfortable with what you are doing, Father Kit. They now just want to go home and live the best they can to accommodate the white man."

"'They', Red Cloud? You keep saying 'they'. What about Red Cloud? What is Red Cloud going to do?" He looked at his old friend.

"I am going home."

"So you are going to Taos with the rest? I am confused, Red Cloud."

"No, Father Kit, I am going to Red Cloud's home, the land of the Talking Tree."

The Chiricahuas, Carson realized. Surprised. Carson envied Red Cloud's chance to go home on his own terms.

And Red Cloud stood, gestured with his arms held out toward his friend, Father Kit, turned, and walked out into the darkness.

107

August 18, 1863

"Major Cummings," the Sergeant said. "There's a man asking to see you."

"Who is he?"

"I have no idea. A New Mexican I've never seen before."

"Why didn't he come to me himself?"

"He says he doesn't know you. Says he rode in from Santa Fe through Fort Defiance with orders directly from General Carleton."

"Curious. Send him over I suppose."

A nondescript New Mexican on a worn out old mule rode up to Cummings about ten minutes later. "Are you Major Joseph Cummings?"

"I am."

"I have orders from General Carleton to take you to a meeting at noon today."

"To meet who? About what?"

"I don't know, sir. He told me nothing."

"Does Colonel Carson know about this meeting?"

"I have no idea. He may be at the meeting for all I know."

Cummings thought about this. "How far from here?"

"A half hour, maybe less."

"Let me see the orders."

The man reached into his pocket and produced a sealed envelope. Handed it down to Cummings.

It looked genuine enough. It said this man would take Cummings to an urgent and important meeting at noon on the 18th. It was dated August 1st and was cosigned by both Carleton's adjutant and his aide de camp.

Good thing he had returned in time from burning Navajo crops, or he would have missed it.

"Okay. Let me get my things."

He returned shortly on his horse, leading a mule loaded with several bags.

The bags were a constant source of merriment among the men. They claimed he travelled like a rich woman. Cummings would tell the men he didn't care what they thought. He wasn't leaving his things just lying around. He wasn't a rich old woman, but he was, after all, Boston-bred.

"Let's go," Cummings said. "Leave your weapons here by my tent," indicating the pistol and the knife in the New Mexican's belt. "If we need those things, I'm not following you."

The New Mexican tossed the knife and gun to Cummings.

They travelled south and west in silence for nearly half an hour, until they came to a large arroyo on their right that had been created by the flood waters from the monsoon rains. It was wide, choked with Willows, Cottonwoods, and Mesquite. You could not see to the end of it. If it meandered all the way back toward the river, then it was at least another ten minute ride.

They rode into the arroyo. The ground was slightly muddy from the recent rains. Both the Cottonwoods and the underlying brush were green. The horse and the two mules grabbed clumps of growth and chewed as they plodded along.

"How did you know of this particular arroyo if you just rode in from Fort Defiance?"

"My directions were very specific, Major."

They rode on.

As the arroyo wound its way to their left, they had to duck under the low hanging branches.

Cummings had a sudden flash that he had forgotten to check and see if that had been Lily back at Pueblo Colorado with the whores.

And then he pulled up short.

For there she was. Sitting on a rock. A rifle pointed at his chest.

"Hi, Joseph. Thanks for dropping by."

Cummings was too astonished to reply.

The New Mexican just continued riding on. Past Lily, deeper into the arroyo.

"Are you going to shoot me, Lil? A U.S. Marshal? In cold blood?"

"Don't know yet."

"Hi Joseph."

A familiar voice above him to his right. He looked up. Right into the barrel of two Colts in the hands of David Zapico. "Where's the money you stole from us, Marshal?"

Cummings looked back and forth between them.

"No idea what you're talking about. I've got my part of the money with me. I'm still waiting for you and Damours to signal me that we can get back together and split the money five ways."

"Damours' and our money mysteriously disappeared about the time you left Santa Fe, Joseph," she said.

"And you think I took it?" His face took on a look of unconvincing puzzlement. "How do you know it's missing, anyway? I thought you two didn't know where it was. My money's on Damours sneaking back in and making off with it. That sorry sunovabitch probably came back and took it right out from under your noses."

"Nope. Wasn't me," Damours said.

Cummings whirled, startled, to his left.

Damours, sitting on a rock above and to Cummings' left, with a rifle pointed at him.

"All three of you? I'm impressed. However, as U.S. Marshal for the Santa Fe region, I must inform you, Mr. Damours, that you are under arrest for grand theft and being AWOL in a time of war. That's a capital offense, Auggy."

"Well," Damours said. "When we're done talking here, we'll sort out whose capital offense trumps whose. Okay, Joseph?"

"You know," Cummings said. "It's always a pleasure when the gang gets together. I'm sure Danson would have been sorry he didn't make it to be here today. But I'll bet that not one of you has the grit to pull those triggers. And even if you did, the cavalry would be here in two minutes. There's no way out of this arroyo, so you'd be trapped."

He smiled at Damours. "So, whereas it was great seeing you all again, I'll be on my way now."

He turned his horse to head back to camp.

And he stopped cold.

There, not four feet behind him, sitting on a beautiful Apache pony, was Red Cloud. Just staring at him.

Rifle pointed at the small of his back.

"Easy, Joseph," Lily said. "I can maybe control a pissed off Damours, and maybe even Zapico, but Red Cloud's on his own mission here."

"What the hell does he have to do with any of this? What does he think he's doing here?"

"I think he just doesn't like you, Joseph," she said. "He just asked us if he could stop by and join the fun."

"Where's our money, Joseph?" Damours said.

"Would it help any if I pointed out that it's not your money? It's actually the Army's money. The Territory's money. And the Church's money."

"Nope," Damours said. "If I remember correctly, it was you recruited me to this job, Joseph. And if I'm not mistaken, that makes it our money."

He swept his rifle around the arroyo, aiming to include everyone present.

Suddenly a group of eight New Mexicans with a dozen horses and mules emerged from deep within the arroyo, behind Damours and Lily.

And Red Cloud moved over to Damours' right. The two of them training their rifles at Cummings' stomach.

"You see Joseph," Lily said. "I took the precaution of peeking into your baggage. So we know the money is with you now, right there on that mule. You were kind enough to deliver it to us here today."

She pointed her rifle at Cummings' mule behind him.

"How'd you know in Santa Fe where it was, Joseph?"

He looked at Damours and Red Cloud and the two rifles. "Zapico's not much of a criminal mind, Lil."

"Good point, Joseph," Zapico said. "But that was never really one of my lifetime goals."

His hands shook in anger. The two pistols wavering in the air.

"That day we were together in the back of the store, Zapico looked twice at his hiding place. And, when I got to thinking where Damours might have buried his share, only a few buildings came to mind. Santa Fe's not such a big town. Val Verde Hall was my third guess. I knew he liked to go there."

"Good job," she said. "And, again, thanks so much for bringing it all to us. We had figured on more than fifteen thousand for each of the five of us, Joseph. But the way you've handled it, the remaining four members of the gang will now each get about nineteen thousand."

She smiled and tipped her hat, the signal they'd all agreed on, and said, "I'd like to be the first to thank you so very much, Joseph, for my raise."

Damours and Red Cloud fired as one.

Cummings catapulted backwards off his horse, one bullet through his stomach and into his spine.

Zapico scrambled down and checked his pulse.

"Dead. Want to count it out, Lily?" Zapico said.

"No. You take what looks like half off the mule and we'll take the rest."

"Half of mine goes to Mowry, Lil. Like we agreed."

"Up to you," she shrugged. "It's up to you, David."

"What about Cummings' saddlebags, Lil?"

She looked at Cummings' horse. "Nope. I checked them the other day. He carries all of the money in the bags on the mule. His saddlebags only have clothes and food. Leave them here on his horse. Let the Army have his personal belongings."

Red Cloud walked over and took Cochise's quiver off Cummings' saddle, patting the horse's neck to calm it.

He nodded to Zapico and Lily, jumped on his horse, and started to head back out of the arroyo.

"Hey, Red Cloud" Lily said. "Wait a minute." She reached into her saddlebag and pulled something out. "Here. Please give this to Cochise's little boy, Naiche, when you meet him."

She tossed Red Cloud a small wooden dog. He caught it. Looked at it, then smiled. "We are now even Miss Smoot." He saluted her and turned his horse out of the arroyo.

Zapico hugged Damours and Lily. They each said their good-byes.

Zapico headed with his New Mexicans and their horses and mules up the eastern embankment of the arroyo.

Santa Fe was a two week ride away.

Damours and Lily were alone in the arroyo with Cummings' body.

Damours turned to her. "It's going to take us more than a month to get to where I think you'll want our ranch to be, Lil. On the way I want to show you a group of natural hot springs the Utes showed me northeast of here on the San Juan River. On my way down from Denver. An Indian place. The Utes call it 'Pah Gosah'. From there, we'll head home."

She kissed him hard on the mouth, and he ran his right hand up all the way inside her dress. She moaned. Pushed him away. She kissed him again. Thought of Arnold warning her back at the camp that she had no business here. Thought about how disappointed he would be if he knew. Wondered how he was going to react to the news that Cummings had been killed and that she was no longer in camp.

Once on their horses, they and their mules headed north out of the back of the arroyo and across the river. Damours thinking of the hot springs, Washington Territory, and Lily's thighs. Lily thinking of all that was going to be, and that, once she and Auggy got to their new home, there was nothing she was going to miss about the New Mexico Territory. Well, except for the old Jew and John Arnold, of course.

A half hour later, Kit Carson looked up and saw Red Cloud sitting on his pony, looking down on him from a hilltop a few hundred yards away.

His old friend held his arm up to him, holding something in his hand. Carson couldn't make out what it was. He waved back.

And Red Cloud kicked his pony down the hill. Heading due south. Disappeared.

Red Cloud was heading home.

AUTHOR'S HISTORICAL NOTE

Bernard Cornwell, the master of current historical fiction, points out that in any such work there is a " big story" and a "little story." I think he forgot to warn me that, obviously, when the little story ends, the "big story" continues rolling on.

We leave this story with the Civil War still unresolved. Similarly, we leave Cochise in an unresolved quandary, partly of his own making, partly not. The Navajo as yet unfound, but also with their infamous "Long Walk" and its ultimate reversal still to come. Kit Carson yet to be, finally, retired.

And, of course, we leave the soon to be "lamented" Major Joseph Cummings undiscovered. Dead in an arroyo near what is today the Hubbell Trading Post in Ganado, Arizona.

Only the participants in the "little story" get the sort of satisfaction that can come through resolution. Lily Smoot and John Arnold and Red Cloud and David Zapico never existed at all, so their collective endings are known only to us. Auggy Damours actually did exist and actually did get away with it all. There is no record that can be found of how much he took with him or where he actually got to enjoy the fruits of his labors. Historians lose sight of him when he goes AWOL on his November 5, 1862 trip to his bogus New York doctor. Cummings did report that he thought he'd gone to Canada and requested permission to follow him, but was denied.

Cummings body was discovered the day of his death. Kit Carson reported in official letters that his "rash bravery" led to his death and that he was killed by a concealed Indian who made his escape. Curiously, Carson also reported that he was accompanied by an unidentified, unarmed citizen and his belongings included $5,031.78 in cash and valuables in his saddlebags.

That's between $700,000 and $1,000,000 today, depending on how you calculate it.

Carson had him buried in Santa Fe. Later, at his mother's request, the Army had his remains shipped to Boston where he was, presumably permanently, reburied. Home at last.

Bizarrely, General Carleton had the Army build a fort in the Arizona Territory directed at the Chiricahua Apaches and named it Fort Cummings for the "brave and lamented" Major.

Kit Carson did eventually find the Navajo. Or, more to the point, after he chased them and he, and Major Cummings before his death, had burned their homes and their crops, they came to him by the thousands and surrendered beginning in February 1864. And thus, for the next nine months, approximately 9,000 Navajo undertook the heinous forced "Long Walk" to Bosque Redondo under the unforgiving Arizona and New Mexico sun. Hundreds died on the walk and were just left where they dropped. Estimates vary from two hundred to twenty-five hundred deaths. Additionally, an unknown number of women and children were stolen by the New Mexicans and neighboring Pueblans along the way.

Carleton's Bosque Redondo turned out to be a total failure. The Indians didn't take to farming in a strange land and a strange climate, and they continued to be raided by neighboring Indians, primarily the Comanches. On November 3, 1865, under cover of darkness, the Mescalero just walked out and returned to their ancestral home near Fort Stanton, where they are to this day. The Navajo, due to sheer numbers, took longer. They gave up and negotiated the ability to make the long, four hundred mile walk back home in June of 1868.

Carson took two months off during the "Long Walk" and was with Josefa for the birth of their sixth child. He insisted on becoming superintendent of Bosque Redondo in the Spring of 1864 to try to help the Navajo. That lasted for three months until Carleton sent him to Texas to subdue the Comanche. In the Spring of 1868, he returned to Santa Fe from a New York and Boston trip for the birth of his and Josefa's seventh child. Josefa died shortly after the birth, on April 27. And shortly after that, on May 23, 1868, Kit Carson died at his Taos home at the age of 58.

History can be unforgiving. To this day many of the Navajo people hold Kit Carson rather than General Carleton personally responsible for the depravations they were subjected to as a result of Carleton's Indian policy. In fairness, some modern Navajo also point to Navajo behavior toward the other tribes and the New Mexicans in the 1850's and 1860's as partly to blame. Historians feel certain that the Navajo would have fared much better if Carleton had not succeeded the more even handed Canby.

Edward R.S. Canby went on during the Civil War to oversee a New York City prisoner of war camp and then become commander of the Military Division of Western Mississippi, where he defeated the Confederate forces both in Alabama and west of the Mississippi. After the war he had several commands overseeing Reconstruction in North Carolina, South Carolina, Texas, and Virginia. In 1872 he became commander of the Pacific Northwest. He was shot twice in the head and had his throat slit during a peace parlay with the Modoc Indians on April 11, 1873, thus earning the distinction of being the only General killed in the American Indian Wars. He was 55 years old.

James. H. Carleton, after the spectacular failure of his Bosque Redondo, was reassigned in 1867 as a Lieutenant Colonel in the Texas Cavalry. He died in San Antonio, Texas of pneumonia on January 3, 1873 at age 58. He was the author of several military books.

Rafael Chacon, colleague and combatant of both Damours and Cummings, resigned on October 1, 1863 from the Volunteers because Carleton passed him over for Cummings' job. He was as successful at retiring as his superior and mentor Kit Carson. Carleton talked him out of it. Due to his rheumatism, he was honorably discharged on September 2, 1864. In November of 1870 he moved his family to Trinidad, in the Territory of Colorado. There, he was a successful businessman, and, ultimately, an important patriarch of the community until his death at age 92 on July 23, 1925. His memoirs, reproduced with extremely useful historical context in Jacqueline Dorgan Meketa's *Legacy of Honor*, provide a very entertaining story of his life. While not a flattering portrait of Damours and Cummings, it reveals much of what we actually know about the lives of those two men.

President Lincoln, famously, finally did find his General, appointing U.S. Grant to be the head of all the armies of the United States on March 9, 1864. Thirteen months later, Grant accepted General Robert E. Lee's unconditional surrender at Appomattox Court House on April 9, 1865.

Five days later, President Lincoln was assassinated by the actor John Wilkes Booth at Ford's Theatre on 10th Street, near E Street in Washington, D.C. Precisely where Cummings gave up looking for him two and a half years earlier.

John Cremony served out a successful tour in charge of the Bosque Redondo Reservation. He describes this experience, the beauty of Fort Sumner, the hardships of Bosque Redondo, and many of his other experiences with the Apaches in his book, *Life Among the Apaches*. He left the American Southwest and retired in San Francisco, where he was a founding member of the Bohemian Club in 1872. He died of tuberculosis on April 24, 1879 at age 64.

John M. Chivington, the Indian hater and hero of Glorieta, was best known for a singular act of barbarity. It was a deplorable massacre of the Cheyenne Indians. Arguably, the worst atrocity committed against the American Indian peoples. On November 29th, 1864 Chivington led his Colorado Volunteers into a Cheyenne village at Sand Creek, and, despite the fact the village was at peace, was flying the American flag, and sported white flags all throughout the massacre, Chivington slaughtered over a hundred and fifty Cheyenne. Two-thirds were women and children. He died thirty years later of cancer at age 73 on October 4, 1894 in Denver, Colorado, still defending his decision to order the massacre.

Henry H. Sibley. Historians are split as to how much poor strategy, alcohol, and insufficient resources each contributed to the failure of General Sibley's plans to capture the western Territories for Jefferson Davis and the Confederacy. But they are united in the view that the rest of his career was destroyed by the bottle. Upon his return to Texas, he was given only minor commands. He was court martialed in Louisiana in 1863, and was censured rather than convicted of cowardice. He went on to be a military adviser to the Khedive of Egypt and died, broke, at age 70 in Fredericksburg, Virginia on August 23, 1886.

John Robert Baylor, not one to easily give up, was elected to the Second Confederate Congress after his return to Texas, reenlisted as a Private, later mounted a failed attempt to organize another Confederate Army to go after Carleton, lost election for Governor of Texas in 1873, and even tried to enlist in the U.S. Army to go after the Sioux in 1876. He then became a rancher in Uvalde, Texas in 1878, where he continued being John Baylor, reportedly brawling with neighbors and even killing a fellow rancher over some cattle. He died at age 71 on February 8, 1894 near Uvalde.

After murdering Mangas Coloradas, Joseph West was reassigned to fight Confederates in Arkansas and points East. After the War he returned to New Orleans and was elected to the U.S. Senate. He died in Washington, D.C. at age 76 on October 31, 1898.

Alonzo Ferdinand Ickis' wonderful daily journal, full of the personalities of the soldiers and the up close and personal hardships and tragedies of the war, is available in Nolie Mumey's *Bloody Trails Along the Rio Grande*. Ickis later served as Carson's secretary in his pursuit of the Comanches. He married and had six sons in Iowa, before returning to Colorado in the early 1890's. He died at his Denver, Colorado home at age 80 on June 5, 1917.

Albert H. Pfeiffer, the German, or some say Dutch, immigrant who tragically lost his wife and daughter to the Chiricahuas in 1863, was instrumental in ultimately bringing in the Navajo from Canyon de Chelly. He became close to the Utes, even serving as Indian Agent and marrying a Ute. In 1866 he famously agreed to represent the Utes in a one-on-one knife fight against a Navajo warrior when the Navajo disputed the Utes' claim to the very Pah Gosah hot springs that Damours mentions to Lily. Pfeiffer killed the Navajo warrior but was unable to save Pah Gosah for the Utes for long, as a more formidable foe, the U.S. Government, took it from them in 1873. The hot springs are still a major tourist attraction in Pagosa Springs, Colorado. Pfeiffer eventually turned to homesteading about 50 miles east of his knife fight, where he died in his bed at age 58 in 1881.

Jack Swilling added to his already full resume after the war. He, variously, became a gold miner, farmer, flour miller, and postal contractor before stumbling into his biggest contribution to American history. Intrigued by the ancient Hohokam canals in the middle of Arizona's forbidding desert, on November 16, 1867, he formed the Swilling Irrigating and Canal Company. The company constructed irrigation canals in the valley and the first crops from the farms there were harvested in 1868. He claimed a section for himself, where he farmed and built a forty-seven hundred square foot house, Swilling's Castle, south of what was to become Van Buren Street between 32nd and 36th Streets in Phoenix, Arizona. Swilling was, in fact, the founder of Phoenix, Arizona. On August 12, 1878, at age 48, he died in the Yuma jail facing false charges that he had robbed a stagecoach. Cause of death was essentially the use of pain killers and alcohol to treat major injuries sustained in 1854. Busy as he was, he finds himself in action in some scenes in this book when, in actuality, he may have been miles away at the time.

Sylvester Mowry spent years getting his properties back. By then his mines were ruined and he was not able to get them into productive shape. He was elected to Congress after the Civil War and died at age 40 on October 15, 1871 while travelling in London, England. There is no evidence whatsoever that he knew either Damours or Cummings.

Cochise met Tom Jeffords, verifiably, in the Fall of 1870, although Jeffords always claimed it was earlier. The Chiricahua were then still at war with the

Mexicans and the White Eyes. The two became close personal friends through and beyond Cochise's negotiated surrender to General Oliver O. Howard on October 12, 1872. The resulting Chiricahua Apache Reservation, with Jeffords as agent, included the Western Stronghold in the Dragoon Mountains and the Chiricahua Mountains. Cochise died at age 69 on June 8, 1874, and was buried along with his favorite horse secretly by the Apaches and Jeffords in his Stronghold.

Tom Jeffords became a stage coach driver, a deputy sheriff of Tombstone, Arizona, and a gold miner after the U.S. Government broke the treaty with the Chiricahuas and sent them to the San Carlos Reservation in 1875. He died at age 82 at his home near Tucson, Arizona on February 21, 1914.

Cochise and Jeffords' friendship has been dramatically portrayed in the novel, *Blood Brother* by Elliott Arnold, a television series, and a movie of the same name, "Broken Arrow." Jeff Chandler played Cochise and James Stewart played Jeffords in the movie. An engrossing non-fiction work has been written by Edwin R. Sweeney, *Cochise: Chiricahua Apache Chief*.

John Ward's stepson was in fact kidnapped by the Arivaipa Apaches. As Cochise said, he never had anything to do with that thirteen year-old boy Felix, called Mickey Free. Free spent the rest of his life with the Western Apaches and went on to be a Sergeant and a scout for the Army in their wars against the Chiricahuas in the 1870's and 1880's. Whereas Cochise never had anything to do with Free, ironically he had twelve years earlier, in April 1849, fought a pitched battle in Mexico against Free's grandfather. Mickey Free died of old age on the Western Apache Reservation with his Apache family in 1915.

Kaniache was instrumental in leading the Utes toward more acceptable permanent Reservations. He was famously struck by lightning during one set of negotiations. He lived, and the Utes took it as a sign that they should agree to the terms. There is no record of the great Ute Chief after 1881. The Southern Ute reservation is in southwestern Colorado.

The Jicarilla Apaches currently reside on their million acre reservation in northern New Mexico and southern Colorado, and, to this day, the llaneros and olleros clans still hold their annual relay race and festival every Fall south of Dulce, New Mexico.

Mangas Coloradas' skull was sold to a collector back East. Apache folklore has it that it was put on display at the Smithsonian, but there is no evidence that this is true, and it's whereabouts today are unknown. The cold blooded murder of Mangas Coloradas stands as one of the most heinous in a long list of heinous acts in the sad annals of the white man's relationship with the American Indians.

Geronimo escaped with his people to Mexico when the Chiricahuas were ordered to the San Carlos Reservation in 1875, but returned after his capture in May of 1882. He escaped with his followers again three years later. He surrendered, only to escape again in early 1886, and was finally permanently defeated on September 4, 1886. The U.S. Government broke its agreement with him and shipped him and four hundred fifty Apaches to prison in Florida until 1894. They were later relocated to Fort Sill, Oklahoma. Geronimo became an American icon and tourist attraction, even riding in Teddy Roosevelt's 1905 Inaugural Day parade. He died at age 79 on February 17, 1909 at Fort Sill. He went to his grave believing his oft-repeated claim that bullets could not kill him. The fifty bullet hole scars on his body were testament to his belief, and, in the end, the truth of the statement. He, like Jack Swilling, finds himself in action in some scenes in this book when, in actuality, he was probably miles away at the time.

Geronimo, the last of America's fighting Indians, lies buried at Fort Sill. A rock monument topped by a stone eagle towers over his grave. Buried by him are the most famous of the Apaches: Loco, Nana, and the sons and grandsons of Cochise, Mangas Coloradas, Victorio, Naiche, and Juh. After his death, many of his clan walked five hundred miles to the Mescalero Reservation near Fort Stanton where their descendants still live today.

Sadly, it is impossible to find a good fandango today in Santa Fe, New Mexico.

Triumphantly, the flag that Kit Carson and his colleagues raised in the Taos Square in April, 1861 continues to fly 24/7 to this day.

Readers Guides to *Where They Bury You*

*W*here They Bury You is a historical fiction novel. Besides the generally known historical facts about the Indian wars and the Civil War, the following all actually *did* factually happen: Damours and Cummings gambling at the same time and places in Santa Fe, Val Verde Hall hosted many fandangos, the embezzlements by Damours as Canby's aide de camp, the search from Washington, D.C. to New York State for Damours by Marshal Cummings under Carleton's orders, Cummings' bizarre conflicting reports of that chase to Chacon and Carleton, the run-ins between Chacon and each of Damours and Cummings, and, of course, the murder (and the discovery of the $5,000) of Cummings under Carson's command.

Since the mystery of Cummings' murder and his interaction with all the fictional (and non-fictional) characters is one thread, and the factual issues raised by the history of the Indian wars and the Civil War are another, I have separated this Guide into two sections: one fictional, and the other historical.

Guide to Fictional Story:

1. Was Lily motivated more by her desire to own her own ranch or by her feelings toward Auggy? Or *only* by her desire for the ranch? Or something else?

2. In what ways can we tell that Auggy believes that Lily really loves him? How can a con man be so trusting of someone? Is he? Similarly, how do we know if Lily is as trusting and in love with Auggy as she seems to represent? Where's the weak link in the likelihood of a long-term relationship between them?

3. Does Lily's platonic attraction to father figures, both John Arnold and David Zapico, reveal anything about the genuineness of her feelings toward Auggy?

4. In the coming sequel, which outcome is more likely: Lily kills Auggy on their way to Washington Territory and takes all the money? Lily and Auggy build a ranch in the Washington Territory, have ten children, and live happily ever after? Lily and Auggy decide to open a bordello saloon in Colorado instead of their ranch? John Arnold arrives to test Lily's notion of "appropriateness"? Arnold arrives and arrests Damours? If this last happens, what would Lily do in response?

5. Does Lily view sex as recreation, a means to an end, a tool of manipulation, a way to degrade men, a validation of herself?

6. What does Joseph Cummings' indecisiveness reveal about the origins of his reputation for being brash and reckless?

7. What should David Zapico's concerns be when he realizes Lily is sleeping with Cummings? Or should honor among thieves include accepting each other's warts as is?

8. In what ways is Pepper's response to Danson and Lily's "infidelity" reasonable? Is the answer worth re-thinking in light of a young woman's opportunities in that time and place? See, for example, Lily's sarcastic comment to John Arnold about her career search.

9. If Lily had chosen to answer Zapico's question from Mowry about her role in "the gang," what might she have told him? How did she view herself in relation to the con men?

10. What could Lily Smoot and John Arnold have been discussing by the camp followers' wagons when seen there by Cummings? If she is denying being back into prostitution, what can she tell Arnold about why she's there?

11. What would the proverbial fly on the wickiup wall have heard when Red Cloud gave the toy dog from Lily to Naiche and Cochise? What would Cochise and Red Cloud make of this white woman who had coincidentally befriended each of them?

12. Kit Carson was illiterate. How reliable then is his letter, actually still in today's U.S. Army Archives, claiming a concealed Indian had killed Cummings? Who actually wrote that report, and did Carson really know what was written in it? And did the author possibly have an ulterior motive? Who was the "unarmed civilian" with Cummings' body? Who *did* kill Major Cummings and why was there in excess of $5,000 on his horse? How many possibilities are there?

13. Screenwriters are urged to be able to answer the question, "What's your story about? We know your plot, but what's it *really* about"? What is *Where They Bury You* really about? Hint: the title gives the answer away when it is spoken by Cummings to Damours. How does this concept resonate for Red Cloud? Lily? Carson? Cochise? The Navajo? The New Mexicans?

14. Fandangos impressed and delighted the Colorado Volunteers and Union soldiers new to the New Mexico Territory. What are the likely origins of this uniquely Southwestern activity? What social gatherings today feel like they are descended from Santa Fe's fandangos?

15. Where on earth *did* the oysters come from?

16. Cochise was arguably one of the great leaders of 19th Century Western America. Was there a practical way for him to solve the dilemma presented to him by Bascom's incompetence? If he could offer to go with the Army to find the Ward boy, why couldn't he have seen that going alone, finding him, and bringing him back might have worked as well?

17. More importantly, why couldn't the white settlers find a way to remain at peace with twelve hundred Chiricahaus?

18. Kit Carson was one of the most fascinating characters in American history. Are those modern day Navajos who vilify his memory justified? Does his agreement to command Carleton's plan, no matter how reluctantly executed, justify his receiving such a large share of the blame for the tragedy of the Long Walk and the Bosque Redondo experiment? Why did Carleton's Ahab-like obsession with getting the Navajo into Bosque Redondo not leave him with the bulk of the blame for this fiasco by current history buffs?

19. Why were the Navajo universally held in disfavor among everyone on the mid-19th Century Southwestern stage, and yet they are viewed positively today?

20. In the context of the times and the problem he faced, how reprehensible was Carson's decision to use Cummings to execute a scorched earth policy?

21. Can we reconcile the Utes' and Jicarilla Apaches' "Father Kit" with the man many Navajo revile today?

22. Looking back from the 21ˢ Century it is hard to claim that the Founding Fathers and a century of subsequent leaders got the Native American problem right. Even allowing for being a "product of their times," can we justify the behavior of the Baylors, Wests, Carletons, Chivingtons and others who finally concluded to just "kill them all?"

23. If the Founding Fathers *had* demanded that the Army forcibly remove whites encroaching on treaties from the very beginning in the 18th Century, would that have worked? How would the history of the U.S. have been changed? Or, if not, why was the ultimate outcome inevitable?

24. Was a successful strategy available to Jefferson Davis and General Sibley that could have enabled the Confederacy to conquer and hold the Western Territories? And from there, take the entire West for the Confederacy? Was Canby's strategy clever beyond the credit he received at the time? Or was the outcome doomed from the start and neither man could have changed it?

25. Is there any merit to Carson's perception that the Civil War was a competitive "game" for former West Point classmates and comrades from the Mexican War and the Indian Wars?

26. Is there any value in considering Carson's suggestion that Lincoln might have prevented the War by paying the southern plantation owners the revenues they would have earned anyway if they would only free their slaves? Or if the government had just bought all the slaves? Would this have been a less costly path for the U.S.? Would it have worked?

27. Alonzo Ickis observes that war is degrading. Was it degrading to Col. Joseph West? How can one reconcile the truthful torture/murder of Mangas Coloradas with the truthful election to the U.S. Senate of his murderer? How do the Grants and Lees and Lincolns live with the close up and personal deaths of 700,000 of Carson's "twenty year old kids"? Or in the end, is it as simple as that people just "don't get along" and those among us who are tough enough to deal with slaughter are left to sort it out on our behalf?

28. What manner of military leader was Rafael Chacon? Right hand man to Carson, yet openly hostile to other non-New Mexican officers? If Cummings and Damours were really so impossible to deal with why did Carson and Canby ultimately entrust them with so much? Alone among the cast of characters. Chacon went on to become a respected community leader.

29. Why did Cummings invent and tell Chacon of his ridiculous adventure in Cuba? And if he didn't, why did Chacon say he did?

30. Carleton's October 27, 1862 letter to General Canby details more than five specific Auggy Damours embezzlements in excess of $22,000, and even more are included as attachments. What on earth *did* happen to Auggy Damours after he fled Canby's office on November 5th? How many possible explanations are there? Where'd the money go?

CPSIA information can be obtained at www.ICGtesting.com
Printed in the USA
LVOW11*1753071014

407666LV00004B/32/P